Dear Reader,

Firstly may I than[k] ... ...naires
you have returned ... ...naire,
we'd be delighted ... ...back of this
book and let us have it back. It is only by hearing from you that we
can continue to provide the type of *Scarlet* books you want to
read.

Perhaps you'd like to know how we go about finding four new
books for you each month? Well, when we decided to launch
Scarlet we 'advertised' for authors through writers' organiza-
tions, magazines, literary agents and so on. As a result, we are
delighted to have been inundated with manuscripts – particularly
from the UK and North America. Now, of course, some of these
books have to be returned to their authors because they just aren't
right for *your* list. But others, submitted either by authors who've
already had books published or by brand new writers, are exactly
what we know readers are looking for. Sometimes, the book is
almost perfect when it arrives on my desk, but usually we enjoy
working closely with the author to give their book that essential,
final polish.

What you'll notice over the coming months are more books from
authors who've already appeared in *Scarlet*. Do let me know,
won't you, if there's a particular author we've featured who *you'd*
like to see again? See you next month and, in the meantime, thank
you for continuing to be a *Scarlet* woman.

Best wishes,

Sally Cooper

SALLY COOPER,
Editor-in-Chief – *Scarlet*

About the Author

Maxine Barry lives in a small Oxfordshire village on the edge of the Cotswolds, with her disabled parents and a grey cat called Keats.

She worked for five years as the Assistant College Secretary at Somerville College, Oxford, where she spent most of her free time in the extensive and famous college library, before turning to full-time writing.

Maxine's a skilled calligrapher, and numbers her other hobbies as reading, walking, nature-watching and avoiding shopping! Her first novel, *Stolen Fire*, was successful as far afield as Russia. *Caribbean Flame* is Maxine's second book for **Scarlet** and we look forward to publishing more novels by this extremely talented author.

Caribbean Flame

MAXINE BARRY

CARIBBEAN FLAME

SCARLET

Enquiries to:
Robinson Publishing Ltd
7 Kensington Church Court
London W8 4SP

First published in the UK by Scarlet, 1996

A copy of the British Library Cataloguing in
Publication data is available from the British Library

ISBN 1-85487-497-7

Printed and bound in the EC

10 9 8 7 6 5 4 3 2 1

PROLOGUE

England

Keith Treadstone's hand shook as he reached for his third glass of brandy of the evening. He was in the study of his just-sold weekend cottage near Oxford, facing up to a bleak, uncertain future. Working in the madhouse that was the London Stock Exchange played havoc with a man's soul and a quiet retreat had always seemed a necessity, not a luxury. But the cottage would soon be a memory, along with just about every other asset he had once owned. He'd wagered it all on one gigantic gamble that would now never pay off. A gamble called the *Alexandria*.

Keith hiccoughed, and took another swallow of his brandy. 'Oh God,' he said bleakly, and reached across his desk to pick up a photograph. For a long moment he gazed down at the beautiful face it portrayed. 'Oh Ramona . . .' He bowed his sandy-haired head over the picture of the woman dressed in the flowing robes of an Oxford Don and sighed. 'You've always been so clever. How will you feel, knowing I've been so . . . stupid, stupid, *stupid!*'

He should have known he was only being used. Should have easily seen the machinations behind the smiling face and cajoling voice. He, who regularly juggled millions on the stock-market for clients as diverse as foreign royalty to British bookmakers, thought that he had seen it all. Knew it all. What a joke! That he, a fully-fledged member of 'the City' could be so taken in . . . And now he would need all his courage, and more, to do what must be done.

He looked again at the picture of the woman that he knew in his heart that he needed, more than actually loved, and sighed. Time to confess. He reached for a piece of headed paper and dated it. He got as far as, 'Dear Ramona,' and stopped. What could he say? That they had no future together now, only shares in that cursed, bloody ship? No. No good thinking that way now. He had to think of Ramona. Ramona, who was so much more than just a beautiful face. Ramona, who possessed a sharp, brilliant brain and a huge, loving, forgiving heart. He had to remember that now. It was his only hope. Her kind, understanding heart . . .

With a shaking hand he forced himself to write. 'I know you'll forgive me, my darling, for all the mistakes I've made. You know that I love you.' Then he paused, breathing hard. He still couldn't bring himself to actually write it, to put it all down in harsh, stark print. He couldn't do it to her and yet . . . She had to know. But how could he explain to someone of Ramona's honest personality the nature of the beast that was his own greed, or the sheer ruthless ambition of the shark who called himself an honest business-

4

man? A man who'd stop at nothing to get what he wanted? A man so dangerous, Keith shook just to think of him.

Just write it, a small voice insisted urgently. Get it over with. Suddenly, a creak outside the study door made him lift his head, his heart hammering in fear. His bleary eyes narrowed for a moment, but there was no other sound. It was probably just the cat. He turned his thoughts to his troubles once more. Could he salvage anything? Keith wondered. Ramona had put up with so much from him; would she, *could* she, cope with his inevitable bankruptcy as well? Recently, he'd begun to sense a restlessness in her she'd never shown before. Once or twice she'd tried to have one of her famous 'serious talks' about their relationship and where it was heading. Before, he'd always been able to put her off. Appeal to her sympathy. Reassure her of his love, his need, his loyalty.

But not his desire. Keith had no desire to give.

Outside, a large black and white tomcat leapt lithely onto the garden wall and began to wash his face, his green eyes swinging towards his master's house as a sharp crack echoed from within. Bartholomew's ears flattened, and a low, frightened growl rumbled in his throat. A minute later, the cat watched a man walk calmly across the garden lawn, look left and right down the deserted village street, then get into a car. By the time the car had driven away, Bartholomew had begun to wash his face again. In a few minutes he would go to the back door and cry to be let in. He'd purr happily as he was stroked and chucked under his white chin, and then he'd have his tasty cat-treats for supper.

But there would be no cat-treats from his master that night. There would be no cat-treats from his master ever again.

CHAPTER 1

Ramona King stepped into the quiet dim church, her mother close behind her. Barbara King glanced anxiously at the tense back and set shoulders of her daughter's tall, lean frame and sighed deeply. Ramona's silvery gold hair instantly attracted what light there was, and many heads turned in her direction. Although Keith was being buried in the small village of Foyle, many of his colleagues from London had attended.

The service, however, was mercifully quick, and Ramona sat through it in numbed silence. In the churchyard, a blackbird sang beautifully in the boughs of a silver birch, and not for the first time, Ramona felt tears fill her eyes. She felt a small nudge in her ribs and looked blankly at her mother, who pointedly scooped and threw a handful of earth onto the teak coffin. She'd barely heard a word the parson had said, she felt so numb. Grimly, she followed her mother's example, the futility of it making her want to scream out loud.

Keith was gone, and he'd planned it that way. That was what she just couldn't accept. Keith was not the suicidal type, no matter what the police and press said.

7

She just couldn't understand it. And she was so used to making herself understand things. Her academic brilliance had stemmed from her very earliest days, when even as a small child, she had hated not to understand. Her thirst for knowledge had only grown over the years, finally earning her a Fellowship at Somerville College in the competitive arena of Economics.

But now, suddenly, she was in the dark . . .

The police had told her that her fiancé had died from a single gunshot wound to the head, and asked her to confirm that Keith Treadstone had a German-made gun from the Second World War. No mystery there, of course. It had belonged to his father, who'd brought it home as a war memento. But why would he turn it on himself? Why, at the very least, did he leave no note, explaining it all?

Ramona stirred, surprised to find herself once more in the long sleek black car, heading towards the outskirts of the village and Keith's cottage. She couldn't remember anything of leaving the churchyard and shivered. Get a grip, girl, she told herself grimly. This simply wouldn't do.

'Are you alright, darling?' Barbara asked her softly, and she nodded automatically. But she was not alright, and they both knew it. The next moment, the car pulled up behind a dark blue Rover it had been following, and the chauffeur quickly opened the door for them, trying not to look at the beautiful blonde's generous breasts, demurely hidden behind the black silk lapels of her jacket, or the long, shapely calves beneath the pencil-slim skirt.

Martin Turner, Keith's solicitor, watched the two women emerge from the discreet black car, his eyes running appreciatively over his client's fiancée. The long, ruler-straight curtain of silver-blonde hair was striking at any time, but set against the sombre black of her clothes, it was especially so. As he approached, holding out his hand and finding it being shaken in a surprisingly firm grip, he suddenly remembered that this girl was a Don from Oxford. Large, silvery blue eyes watched him, cool and yet oddly vulnerable. She was not as calm as she pretended, he thought wisely and wondered, sadly, how Ramona King would take what was to soon to come. The will, such as it was, was simple enough but the circumstances surrounding it . . . Martin opened the gate and then nearly jumped out of his skin as a black and white cat leapt onto the wall beside him and miaowed loudly.

'Hello, Bartholomew,' Ramona said, holding out her hand and watching the cat push his head into it, his long white whiskers tickling her wrist. 'I'd forgotten about you. Sorry old fella.'

'Er, I think Mrs Wibbiscombe has been feeding him,' Martin said, giving the animal a wide berth. The last thing he wanted was cat hairs on his new suit. Scooping the hefty tomcat into her arms and rubbing her cheek against his silky head, Ramona King walked into the cottage she had visited so many times before. Everything was still the same, and yet different. It puzzled her for a while, until she realized things were missing. Wasn't a picture usually hanging next to the stair-rail? And what had happened to that beautiful Meissen figurine she had always loved?

They settled themselves into the study, Ramona cuddling the cat on her lap. Keith had loved Bartholomew so much.

'Well, with your permission, I'll skip the legal chitchat, and just explain the basics,' Martin began briskly. 'Keith left everything to you, Ramona,' he assured her, getting the easy bit over with first.

Ramona nodded. She hadn't expected anything else. Keith had no immediate family, just a few cousins he had never met before.

'However . . .' Martin Turner coughed, beginning to look nervous. 'Er, Miss King, were you aware of the share purchases that Keith had made over the last four months or so? For his private portfolio, I mean?'

Ramona's silvery eyes fixed on him like blue shards of electricity. Suddenly they seemed to blaze with sharp, acute intelligence, and Martin found the breath catching in his throat.

'Shares? No. Keith rarely talked about the stockmarket. As an economist myself, we tried not to talk shop too much,' she explained quietly. That had been her idea, of course. She wanted to talk of other things. Family. Children. Their future together. It had been just another, abortive attempt on her part to pull them closer together. She swallowed hard, a tight ache in the back of her throat. But she mustn't break down now. Not now.

'Hmm. Well. Have you heard of the Alexander Line?'

'Of course,' Ramona said. 'As an economist, and tutor, I like to keep abreast on the big British companies. The Alexander Line operates a fleet of cruise ships, and is currently the biggest in Britain. It was once privately owned, having been founded in the fifties by Michael Alexander. But on his death nearly twenty years ago, it went public and was run by his right-hand man. It went downhill somewhat during those years, but now his son, Damon, has taken over, and seems to be bringing it around again.' She recited the information from her huge memory simply and without vanity, unaware that her obvious intelligence made her intimidating.

'I see,' Martin said, unaware of the reserve that had crept into his voice. 'Then you probably know that Damon Alexander was just eighteen when he first joined the company, but only managed to become the majority shareholder and chairman a few years ago. Now, although the Alexander Line is still, technically, the biggest of the British cruise companies, it faces increasingly growing competition. It's been steadily losing customers and ground since Michael Alexander died, although his son wants to get the company moving again. Since his boardroom coup, he went against all their advice, and comissioned the building of the *Alexandria*.'

He paused, aware that Ramona King was not only following him, but was probably way ahead of him. It stung his male ego a little but nevertheless he ploughed on. 'Up until now, Alexander has never been in the real super-class of sea travel, so to speak. But the *Alexandria* is definitely up there with the best. Bigger and better than the *Queen Elizabeth II*, in fact. I understand it's

11

about to undergo sea trials, and its maiden voyage is scheduled for January. That's one of the best times to cruise the Caribbean, I'm told.'

'And Keith has shares in this ship?' she asked bluntly.

'Yes. Rather a lot of shares.'

'I see. As I understand it, the *Alexandria* is something of an experiment in that it's the first liner ever built to cater to the 1990s' super-rich brigade,' she mused, marshalling her thoughts. 'I've not made an in-depth study of it, of course, but basically most liners cram as many cabins as possible into every ship, in order to get as many passengers, and so make as much money as possible. But the *Alexandria* has fewer but much more spacious cabins. From all accounts, it's like a floating Buckingham Palace. The profits are expected to come from the exorbitant fares charged, and not from the number of passengers.' As an economist, she thought the idea was brilliant. But that was not what concerned her now. 'How much did Keith spend on these shares of his?' she asked, unaware that she was holding her breath.

Martin coughed. 'Everything he had, Miss King,' he said fatalistically. 'All his savings, even this cottage which, incidentally, he sold to a colleague of his. Everything. And as you inherit it all, you now own just over 5 per cent of the *Alexandria*.'

Ramona shook her head, bewildered. 'I just don't understand it,' she finally said. 'Keith never believed in putting all your eggs into one basket. Economically, it makes sense to keep your assets as diversified as possible. Unless you've millions to play around with,

12

of course.' And why, she thought miserably, hadn't he told her what he was doing? This wasn't just another part of his job. This was their future he was playing with. 'What if the *Alexandria* is a failure?' she asked, but it was a rhetorical question. She already knew the answer to that.

'I don't think it will be,' Martin said quickly. 'Damon Alexander is considered a financial and business genius in the City. But then, I hardly need to tell *you* that,' he said wryly. 'Alexander himself is the major stock- *and* shareholder of the ship, of course, owning something like 40 per cent, but the list of businessmen who have invested in her reads like a *Who's Who* listing. Chairmen of banks have invested millions. Oil sheiks, foreign royalty, playboys, Texas oilmen . . . everyone who's anyone has invested in the *Alexandria*.'

Ramona didn't feel reassured. She felt, in fact, even more confused than ever. 'Wait a minute,' she said, a sudden thought breaking through her miasma of misery and confusion. 'Even if Keith had sold everything he owns, surely it wouldn't have brought him 5 per cent of such a mammoth project?'

Martin coughed. He had hoped she wouldn't pick up on that. A vain hope, he now realized. She might look like an angel, but Ramona King had a mind like a steel trap. 'No. I wouldn't have thought so either,' he admitted glumly. 'But I have the shares right here . . .' He held up an impressive, sealed envelope. 'I've checked it out thoroughly. As of six days ago, Keith Treadstone owned 5 per cent of the *Alexandria*. Now you own it, which automatically entitles you,

13

amongst other things, to a cabin on her maiden voyage, voting privileges, of course, and any other number of financial options. If you wanted to, I'm sure you could sell the shares tomorrow and make a huge profit.'

She shook her head, not wanting to think about sorting out Keith's affairs just yet. She'd cried herself to sleep last night and now she felt so tired and emotionally drained she just wanted to curl up and sleep for a year. Oh Keith, she thought sadly, What on earth did you got yourself into?

'Well, that's the will, as it stands,' Martin said, anxious to get away from the place and wash his hands of Keith Treadstone as quickly as possible. 'If there's nothing else?'

Ramona nodded. 'I want Bartholomew,' she said, and gave the cat, who had curled up into a ball and gone to sleep on her lap, a gentle stroke. Then she glanced across at her mother. 'If that's alright . . .'

'Of course it is,' Barbara King said gently, her own voice husky. To see her daughter in such pain, and to be unable to do anything to help her was almost more than she could bear.

Without a word Ramona stood up, cradling the cat in her arms and following her mother outside. Like Martin, she was not anxious to stay either.

Once back in their spacious home in the Woodstock Road, Ramona set Bartholomew down to explore his new address and followed her mother into the cheerful peach and green kitchen. There was something comforting in watching her mother go about making the tea.

14

Something so normal. So usual. It felt like returning home after visiting Oz, that crazy land where nothing seemed real.

'Well, sip that and tell me what you're thinking,' Barbara King said firmly, setting the cup and saucer in front of her daughter and sinking down at the kitchen table with a heartfelt sigh. With a weary smile she slipped her shoes off and reached for her own cup. What a day.

'I don't know what to think. Yet,' Ramona said. 'But I have a feeling that those shares he bought had something to do with Keith's . . . suicide.'

'Suicide. Yes,' Barbara said, an odd inflection in her tone making her daughter's silver-gold head snap up. Two pairs of blue eyes met one another candidly. 'You too?' Ramona said softly. 'You feel it too? I can't help but think that suicide . . . it just doesn't seem like something that Keith would *do*.'

Barbara nodded. 'I always thought Keith was too . . . self-contained . . . to despair easily.' She chose her words with care, but even so, Ramona shot her a quick, worried look. How much did her mother know?

Barbara, who'd always been so close to her only child, read the question easily, and sighed deeply, putting down her cup. 'I'll admit, darling, that Keith worried me a little. You two were together so long and yet . . .' She trailed off, wondering if there were some things, even between mother and daughter, that were best left unsaid.

'And yet?' Ramona prompted, knowing it was dangerous, but suddenly needing, desperately, to confide in someone.

15

'You seemed more like brother and sister than lovers, darling,' Barbara said, and looked at her anxiously. 'I don't want to hurt you but – I never really thought Keith was the man for you.'

Ramona looked down for a long moment into her teacup, then said, quite deliberately, 'Mother, Keith and I were never lovers.' There, it was said. Out in the open. Slowly, fearfully, she looked up, but her mother only reached for her hand and smiled sadly. Her eyes were so kind, so incredibly kind, that Ramona felt two hot tears run down her cheeks.

'I thought so,' Barbara said softly. 'Some men . . . well, some men just don't need . . . that kind of love. But you do. That's what scared me, Ramona,' she said softly. 'Underneath that shyness of yours, you're a woman, Ramona. With all a woman's needs and desires.'

Ramona nodded and heaved a shuddering sigh. She wiped the tears from her face and sniffed. 'I know. Sometimes our relationship seemed so barren, it scared me too. But men have never really featured much in my life, you know that. At school I was always working too hard on my exams to have time for a boyfriend.'

'And you were so bashful,' her mother said, a fond smile creasing her face. 'You used to blush beetroot if a boy so much as looked at you. And many of them did, Ramona.'

Ramona nodded. 'And then, at Oxford, I knew I had to get a First if I wanted to stay on to do a D.Phil. So I was studying even harder than ever.'

'You remember, I was always urging you to go out

16

more?' Barbara laughed softly. 'Whilst most mothers were warning their daughters not to go to too many parties, I was always scouring the city for social events for you to go to!'

Ramona laughed. 'And then I met Keith,' she said, and the laughter fled. She picked at the tissue her mother had given her, her fair brows creased in thought. 'At first, you know, I didn't really notice . . . well, how odd we were together. When he left me on my doorstep with a kiss and a smile, I thought he was being sweet. That he knew how nervous I was. How shy, still. And then, later, I got distracted with my career again. I got my D.Phil. and then a Research Fellowship and all the time, Keith and I just . . . well . . . drifted, I suppose,' she admitted painfully. 'It was only recently that I began to take a good hard look at my life. I had my full Fellowship at Oxford, but somehow it wasn't enough any more. I could see the years slipping by, and still there was no husband, no family. No love.'

'Did you tell Keith how you felt?' Barbara urged gently, being very careful now. She didn't want to make her daughter's grief any harder to bear than it already was.

Ramona sighed. 'Oh, I tried. But he always evaded the issue. Finally, he told me he was impotent.'

Barbara King sighed. 'And that, of course, meant leaving him was almost impossible,' she said wearily.

Ramona nodded, gripping her mother's hand tightly. 'Yes! You do see, don't you? How could I just abandon him? We'd been together for years. It would have been too cruel . . . like saying he wasn't man enough for me.

Wasn't good enough. That all that mattered was sex, or the lack of it. I tried to help him. I arranged for him to go to doctors, therapists, but I wonder now if he actually kept the appointments. It was all getting to be too much and then . . .'

Barbara sighed tremulously. 'And then . . . this.'

Ramona nodded. 'Yes. Suicide,' she said bleakly, the pain pressing in all around her again. 'This *Alexandria* business. Whatever went wrong, it had to have something to do with that,' she said determinedly. She didn't want to even consider the possibility that perhaps she might be responsible. That the pressure she herself had been putting on him was the straw that broke the camel's back.

'I agree,' Barbara said. 'So what are you going to do?'

Ramona ran a weary hand through her long, silver hair. 'I don't know. Investigate, I suppose. Try and find out *why* Keith bought all those shares. Where he got the money from. And do something about it.'

Barbara nodded. She knew her daughter well enough to know that she'd see it through, no matter what it took. But then, she herself had had to face up to some hard facts in her life, learning the difficult way that the only way to cope was to meet life head on. Look it straight in the eye and deal with it. In Barbara's case, a husband who was no husband at all. A marriage that was no marriage. Betrayal. Fear. Whatever rock life threw at you, the only way to avoid being hit was to keep your head up and your eyes open. And she'd been careful to pass her wisdom along to her daughter. Now, she wondered if it wasn't time to give her

18

daughter some more tough but vital advice.

'I know what you're going through, darling, and I'm behind you all the way. But once . . . well, once you've put Keith behind you, perhaps you ought to think about leaving Oxford for a while. Get out, see the world. Find yourself a man – a *passionate* man. You can't hide forever, darling. Nobody can.'

'Hide? Hide from what?' Ramona asked, bewildered.

'From life, my darling,' Barbara King said firmly, meeting her daughter's eyes, her gaze unwavering. 'From *life*, Ramona.'

CHAPTER 2

The man facing the hordes of press was a godsend to the photographers. Southampton Docks were not the sightliest of subjects, and although the truly magnificent liner had been bathed in solid flashlight for at least half an hour, there was nothing like a handsome face to set off the perfect story.

Cameras from the BBC and rival networks were jammed next to seasoned reporters from London's top-drawer papers and the younger, hungrier hopefuls from the tabloids. The room set aside for the press conference was chaos, the noise level indescribable.

The man who sat at the table crammed with microphones looked over them all, a slight smile coming to his lips, and instantly the flashbulbs exploded. Ralph Ornsgood, a tall blond Swede and Damon's right-hand man, leaned closer. 'Everything's set, Damon,' he shouted. And crossed his fingers.

Damon looked out over the sea of avid faces, so hyped up by the launching of a new super-liner, and smiled. Most of them had no idea of the sheer work that had gone into the *Alexandria*. From the first tentative blueprints to the final fitting of doorknobs, he'd sweated blood over the project, knowing it was the future. The Alexander Line needed a star, and if this ship wasn't it, then he was finished. The board would have a field day.

'Ladies and gentlemen,' he said, and in an instant there was silence. The more seasoned camera crews looked at one another, and nodded knowingly. They'd seen good media men before, men who had that 'something' on camera that denoted the best, but this Damon Alexander was something else. Not only did he have looks but he had an aura of power that was unmistakable. Instantly, every female heart in the room skipped a beat.

'I would like to start this press conference by apologizing for the lack of romance in the launching of the *Alexandria*,' Damon began. 'I know that most of you envisioned a huge ship sliding gracefully and majestically down the slips and into the open sea. Unfortunately, ships aren't launched like that nowadays. Instead, the dock that holds the *Alexandria* will have its locks opened, and will be slowly flooded. This can take anything up to fifteen hours, which isn't nearly as dramatic, I know. However, we do have a very beautiful lady who will shortly be arriving to scatter champagne over the *Alexandria*'s bows, as I'm sure you all know.' There was a immediate buzz. Of course everybody knew. A lady of very high royal rank had given her consent to launch the great British ship, and her beauty was world-renowned. 'Later, the *Alexandria* will be towed by tugboat to the harbour, where the harbour pilot will take her out into open sea, and the ship will then undergo the first of her three planned sea trials. As you will see from the brochures you should all have been given at the door, the engines on the *Alexandria* are twin-screw Pielstick Diesels, which are the best in the world. The *Alexandria* has a crew complement of eight hundred . . . yes, as many as that,' he added as there was a surprised murmur. 'As you can see from the ship's list of statistics, there is a passenger capacity of 1,600 which is a lot less than on most liners, but then the *Alexandria* wasn't built with quantity, but quality, in mind. Each passenger on the *Alexandria* is assured instant service of the highest quality.'

'Are you confident the *Alexandria* will be ready for her maiden voyage next January?' a voice piped up from the back.

Damon nodded. 'Yes.'

The shortness and the certainty of the answer took them momentarily by surprise, but now that question-and-answer time had begun, the mob began to do its mobbing.

'Why did you choose the Caribbean for its maiden voyage, Mr Alexander?'

'Because that time of year is perfect for a winter break, and the Caribbean has everything to offer.'

'Isn't it true to say that the Caribbean is already heavily serviced by other cruise lines? And that the success, or otherwise, of the *Alexandria* has to be proved straightaway by going in, as it were, at the deep end?'

Damon Alexander smiled, and again the flashlights

popped. It was not hard to see why. At thirty-three, he was one of Britain's richest magnates, certainly the most controversial, and was a very private and therefore mysterious and romantic figure. Add to that a six-foot-one-inch body of perfectly fit, lean muscle, a head of rich, thick, almost black hair, and wide, steel-grey eyes, and you had a phenomenon. Add to that the fact that he was also a bachelor, and you had near-hysteria. The pictures taken that day would adorn every newspaper in the country.

'The *Alexandria* is a unique ship,' Damon Alexander said, a quiet but awesome pride in his voice. 'No other has ever been built like her.'

'Some would say it was snobbery gone wild,' an envious, spiteful voice came from one of the more seedy tabloids. 'In an age when more and more of the common people can afford to take cruises, is it really right that you should build a ship that caters only to the super-rich?'

There was a general stirring as the mob scented blood. As one animal, they turned to look at the prey.

'I don't regard people as either common, or super-rich, though you seem to,' Damon said, his voice pure ice. 'If you want an example of affordable, comfortable cruising for those who have to live on a budget, I suggest you take a one-week cruise on the *Athens*, just one of many Alexander Line ships that regularly sail the Mediterranean. As you know, or would do if you'd bothered to do your homework, the Alexander Line offers the most competitive and affordable prices of any cruise line worldwide.'

The eyes, steel in colour, steel in looks, bore into the now red-faced reporter. 'The *Alexandria* is simply a natural extension to our line. We're into the nineties, ladies and gentlemen, and there are more millionaires in the world now than at any other time in history. The *Alexandria*, simply put, is a millionaire's ship. Don't expect an apology for that, because you'll have a very long wait.' His words had now turned defiant, and the mob began to sense a shift in the balance of power. Damon Alexander was no longer the prey, but the hunter, and how he had brought that about was fascinating. There were not many men that could take on the might of the press and win. 'As you will see from the specifications – ' he turned once more to the room as a whole, and watched as brochures were quickly opened and perused – 'the cabins on board are all first-class. There are no cabins for passengers that look out over the lifeboats, for example, for those are occupied by crew quarters. Likewise, there are no cabins for passengers that are windowless. There are one hundred single cabins. The Alexander Line, unlike others, doesn't penalize the growing number of people who want to travel alone. There are also ten cabins fitted specifically for the handicapped, but the whole ship is wheelchair friendly. But above all, the name of the game, gentlemen – ' he spared the now cowering reporter a brief glower, – 'is luxury. LUXURY,' he all but thundered. 'The *Alexandria* is a floating palace, because that's what I made her. She's perfect, and she's British, and she's going to take over the crown of the *Queen Elizabeth II* as the finest ship afloat!' His voice rose just an octave and he thumped once on the podium. The crowd errupted into spontaneous applause. But as Damon rose to lead the crowd towards the opening ceremony he was thinking not of his success but of the bad news he'd received that morning. About the shares. About that *damned* man. Joe King.

In a small room at the John Radcliffe Hospital in Oxford, Dr Verity Fox sat nervously on a chair and pushed one of her white coat-sleeves up her bare arm. She'd just finished performing a routine triple-heart bypass, and her patient's chances of recovery were good. But right now she had other things on her mind. Her heart thumped sickeningly. She had waited three days for the results of her tests, but it had felt like three years. And now the waiting was over.

Dr Gordon Dryer, a friend of many years, entered the room and sat behind a desk. He looked haggard, and for a long, long moment, the two doctors sat looking at one another in complete silence. Verity was the first to break it. 'Is it what you thought it was?' she asked simply.

Gordon nodded. 'Yes. Yes it is. I'm sorry, Verity. Oh God,' he said wearily, real despair creeping into his voice. 'How often have I had to say that to people?'

Verity nodded and took a deep, shaky breath, hardly able to believe it, even now the final proof was in. It had all happened so fast. Just three months ago, she'd noticed a creeping fatigue followed by a few minor

25

aches, and had gone to Gordon for tests. Anaemia, they had both originally thought. Until the other symptoms. Until the results of the initial blood tests . . . The hurried scrambling for more blood, just to make sure . . .

'I feel so damned useless,' Gordon groaned. 'I'm supposed to be the blood specialist around here . . .'

Verity shook her head. 'Don't, Gordon,' she said sharply. She knew she should be offering him words of comfort, but, for the moment, she couldn't manage it. Outside, a rare sunny September day waited, with blue skies and singing birds, and gardens full of flowers. And she was going to die.

'So,' Verity said after a while, and swallowed hard. There was the copper taste of fear in her mouth, and she swallowed it back like bile. 'I'm just a surgeon, you're the authority on this kind of thing. Tell me, Gordon. Straight and simple. What can I expect?' Gordon looked at her, at the cap of raven-black hair framing a pale, pretty, heart-shaped face, and found he couldn't look into her wide, ebony eyes. Instead he stared down at the results in front of him and quickly, crisply, began to give her the facts. The leukaemia was rare. Very rare. Blood transfusions would help, and would allow her to continue working safely for another month, maybe two if she responded well. But no more surgery. Inevitably, even with a hoped-for period of remission, she would soon become too tired even for paperwork and consultations. She would need to sleep longer hours. After a while she would lose up to 20 per cent of her co-ordination skills. But there would be hardly any pain.

Cancer of the blood was not the same as cancer of organs. There was always that.

Verity listened and nodded. As a doctor who dealt regularly with pain, she knew she should be grateful for that blessing at least. But she wasn't. She was angry. She was . . . terrified. She was thirty years old, and in a few years time she'd always envisioned a marriage and children, even though she had no permanent boyfriend at the moment. Now there would be nothing. 'I haven't got a clue what to do,' she said at last. 'Isn't that stupid? Me, a doctor.'

'What difference does that make?' Gordon asked gently. 'It'll take time for you to come to terms with it, just like anyone else.'

Verity nodded. Time. Suddenly, her whole life, what was left of it . . . now revolved around time. She could feel panic, like a tidal wave, coming towards her from a great distance and stood up abruptly. 'I'm going home,' she said just as abruptly, and headed for the door before Gordon could react.

She took a taxi home, which was a large detached house on Five Mile Drive. In the spring, flowering cherry trees made it an avenue of blossom. She'd be able to see that one more time at least, she thought, paying off the driver.

Oh God, she moaned silently, it was ridiculous. Was she going to go around looking at everything because it might be the last time she'd ever see it? Perhaps. She just didn't know. She ran up the garden path, slamming the front door shut behind her and leaning against it as if she'd just reached a safe haven. She began to laugh.

And then to cry. For a long, long time, she just stood there, leaning against the door, laughing and crying . . .

Ramona King walked into Raymond Young's hectic office, and glanced around. She didn't come to London often but when she did she appreciated the frantic, manic hubbub that surrounded the Stock Exchange. Abercrombie and Guildhall was a much respected name in stock brokerage, and she'd met many of its wheelers and dealers through Keith and his company.

'Ramona. It's so good to see you. I'm really glad you called me, I've been wanting to talk to you,' Ray said, talking in that quick rapid-fire way that was typical of people who worked on the stock-market. 'I was really cut up about Keith, you know,' he added, winding down a bit, and ushering her into a chair.

'I'm glad you could see me on such short notice,' she said, and hesitated as Ray gave her a quick, searching look. Was it her imagination, or did he look rather sceptical? 'I want to talk to you about the Alexander shares Keith bought. You do know about that?'

Raymond nodded, his face going curiously, and ominously, blank. 'Yes, I do. In fact, I think I know a little too much about it.' Again, he gave her an odd look.

'Oh?' Ramona found her throat going dry and took a quick breath. 'Something's wrong, isn't it?' she said bluntly.

Ray nodded. He too, had no wish to beat about the bush. 'Yes. Very wrong. Quite simply, Ramona, I think that Keith embezzled millions from the firm. Or rather, from a certain client of this firm.' He hesitated, as if

28

waiting for something. His eyes remained fixed on her, a speculative gleam deep in their depths.

Ramona blinked once, then took a deep breath. 'I thought it might be something like that,' she said shakily. 'Keith left me over 5 per cent of the *Alexandria*, the billion-pound ship, as they're calling it in the press.'

'Five percent?' Raymond almost blanched. Sitting before him now was a very, very rich and powerful woman. 'As much as that?'

'Of course, that's all changed now,' Ramona said, forcing herself to think practically. 'As Keith's heir, this client of yours must surely have plans to sue me for the embezzled money?'

Ray said nothing, but he was beginning to look distinctly puzzled.

'And the only way to raise it is to sell the *Alexandria* stock. Tell me . . .' she cleared her throat nervously 'exactly how much did Keith . . . borrow?'

'Two million, two hundred and fifty-five thousand.'

Ramona licked bone-dry lips. 'I see. And the name of the client?'

Ray shifted in his chair. 'You really don't know, do you?' he said, as if unwilling to believe her, but recognizing that he had no other choice.

Ramona looked at him, puzzled. 'Should I?'

'I thought . . .' Ray began, then shook his head. He'd thought she was in on it, but obviously not. 'I'm sorry. I can't disclose the name of our client. He has no wish for the bad publicity, and since Keith is dead . . .' He shrugged.

'But I can expect to hear from this client of yours about the handing over of the shares. Yes?' she added, as Ray continued to look at her, a puzzled frown playing with his eyebrows. He spread his hands. 'I assume so. Yes. I really don't know.' Which was true enough, he thought wryly. He had no idea what was going on. Not now. Not if Ramona King really *wasn't* in on it.

'It doesn't make sense. Any of it,' Ramona murmured. She'd have to consult a lawyer. Make sure there were no legal ramifications for her. But it was so bizzare! *If* Keith had embezzled the money . . . But what if he hadn't?

'I need to know, Ray,' she said. 'Who's the client?'

Ray shook his head. 'Sorry.' He was sympathetic, but it was his head on the chopping block. Nobody messed with Joe King. Not even his own daughter, if she had any sense.

'Keith had to have been acting privately,' Ramona thought out loud. 'Someone was paying him, or had persuaded him, to buy those shares under his own name. But why go to all that trouble? Unless . . . Could it be Damon Alexander himself?' she asked, trying to judge by Ray's expression if she'd hit pay dirt, but the other man didn't so much as flicker an eyelash. 'Some people might cry "foul" if Damon Alexander was seen to be accruing too much stock. And the *Alexandria* doesn't need bad publicity at this stage. But if there is a takeover bid for the *Alexandria* in the offing, then Alexander will need to acquire as many shares on the Q.T. as he can get,' she carried on, warming up on her theme.

Ray continued to stare at her, growing more and more uneasy. She really *was* in the dark. What was Joe King playing at?

'But then . . . Keith killed himself,' she continued, both her voice and her logic stumbling. But why would Keith, if he was in on a good thing, do such a thing? Unless . . .

'I think that's where things must have gone wrong somehow,' she murmured, sighing deeply. 'Keith was probably meant to hand those shares over to somebody. And if not Alexander himself, then who? And why aren't they coming out of the woodwork to claim those shares?' Ramona asked, her voice rising in her frustration. It was madness! Unless Alexander was just biding his time. Waiting for the ship to be a success, waiting for the share situation to settle. After all, he couldn't just show up on her doorstep, demanding his ill-gotten shares. She might threaten to give the story of his dirty trading and secret deals to the press. If all her suppositions were true, then Mr Damon Alexander had got himself into a right old mess.

One thing was for certain. Ray wasn't going to give her any answers. 'I intend to get to the bottom of this,' she said, her voice grim. And it looked as if the answers lay in *Alexandria*.

A few miles away, Verity Fox had stumbled from her door to the sofa, and now lay staring numbly at her television set. She'd put it on to have some noise in the room – something else to concentrate on. And in Southampton, a royal princess was cracking a bottle of champagne over the gleaming white hull of the most beautiful ship she'd ever seen. A handsome man stood beside her, the glow of pride and sheer joy in his eyes, and Verity abruptly sat up straighter, recognizing her old friend instantly. 'Damon,' she said softly. And managed a weak but genuine smile. Life was going on all around her, regardless of her own plight, and she had to face it sooner or later, and she had to plan. She had between nine and twelve months to live. And something about the beautiful ship that belonged to her old friend made her decide there and then that she was going to live those remaining months to the full.

Damon Alexander, she thought, and smiled again. She could remember him as a gangly teenager giving her piggyback rides. The old Alexander house, where they'd had so much fun, riding the ponies and climbing the big beech trees.

And then she remembered his mother. Joceline Alexander.

And she shuddered.

CHAPTER 3

In a storm-tossed English Channel, a small fishing trawler tossed and bucked on a huge swell. Many anxious eyes were squinting out of the windows for the first sight of land when, suddenly, out of the rain-misted gloom, a huge, beautiful white apparition appeared on their port bow.

The crew fell silent as they watched the huge, gleaming white liner slide by them, as graceful as a swan. None of them had seen anything so majestic. So regal.

'She's going a fair clip,' the captain said, his voice awestruck, 'and barely a roll on her.' He gave the trawler's old steam whistle a couple of excited tugs in tribute to a queen of the sea, but none of them expected an answer. In winds that howled like banshees, who would hear it?

On the Nasa-like bridge of the *Alexandria*, Captain Gregory Paris Harding, binoculars fixed on the small trawler, saw the small steam stack spout a white plume and smiled. 'Sound the horn,' he said to Jim Goldsmith, staff captain and second in seniority. A moment later a thundering, echoing blast cut into the air, clearly reaching the men in the trawler who broke into spontaneous cheering.

The two vessels, so different in every way, passed by and continued on their separate courses, and Greg left the bridge to begin his inspection. It was one of the captain's duties to do an inspection of the entire ship every day. No mean feat, when the ship was the size of the *Alexandria*.

In the galley, it was a scene of organized chaos, in which the executive chef reigned supreme. Greg watched them working for a moment, his eagle eye taking in everything. After all, these were the people responsible for that most talked-about aspect of modern-day cruising – the cuisine. Food of outstanding quality and unstinting variety had to be constantly available; breakfast, lunch, high tea, dinner, and, of course, the famous Midnight Buffet.

Taking a deep breath, Greg strode into the war-zone. 'Monsieur De La Tour, may I take a look at the menu please?' He'd ordered a full menu to be prepared, even though they had no passengers. They needed the practice. The chef, all four feet ten inches of him, spun around, eyes blazing, ready to do battle. But nobody was more superior on a ship than its captain. Especially if that captain was Gregory Paris Harding.

At thirty-seven, he was the youngest ever captain of a ship this size and he was well aware that his appointment as captain of *the* ship, had caused shock waves throughout the board. Granted, he'd been, at the time, captain of the *Athens* for over four years, and had worked for the Line itself for over fifteen years. But still, the more senior captains had huffed and puffed and threatened to resign. Damon Alexander had responded by telling them simply that if they wanted to go, they could. Yet nobody could cry favouritism, for the two men were hardly friends. They'd met, of course, and dined together at company functions, but that was all. Damon had put him in charge of this, his biggest gamble, for no other reason than that he trusted the man. He liked his no-nonsense approach and his cool head, and recognized, when he saw it, the unmistakable aura of a man of command.

The son of a landlocked postman, Greg had always wanted to go to sea. At first, of course, his parents had been amused by their five-year-old son's avowal to be a captain of a big ship some day. His lack of proper old-school ties, and upper-class deportment had not mattered one whit to the new chairman of the Alexander Line when it had been pointed out to him by a jealous rival.

Greg wasn't stupid. He knew the older captains regarded him as a threat and an upstart. So everything had to be just right. He was determined neither Damon Alexander nor any of his first passengers should find anything to criticize on the maiden voyage. He'd insisted on Jim as his staff captain, and had picked the best of the more junior officers with extreme care. Greg couldn't afford to fail. He'd worked too long and too hard. Apart from anything else, years at sea had meant sacrificing a wife and family. Although there were women who could stand to see their husbands away at sea for months on end, Greg had also seen too many marriages fail for that reason, including Jim's.

At six feet tall, with hair the colour of ripe wheat and eyes the colour of tiger-amber, his bachelorhood seemed to many women to be a personal affront. So, although his times spent at sea were always celibate (it was a sin of the highest order for officers to have romantic entanglements with passengers) his days on land were not without comforts.

Now, though, women were the last thing on his mind.

'Engineering next, I think,' he said to Jim, pushing the button that would send the lift to the lowest decks.

Contrary to popular belief, the chief engineer was the only one on board who could talk to the captain as an equal, for the engineer had a working knowledge of the ship equal to that of its captain, and his job was just as important. For that reason, Greg had asked Jock McMannon to come on board as chief. A wiry Scotsman, he had an affinity with machines that had to be seen to be believed. In the engine room, Greg could see that his calming, matter-of-fact attitude about the foul weather and its dangers had even the most inexperienced engineering lads feeling almost blasé about it all.

Jock spotted him quickly. 'A wee bit o' wind overhead, I take it?' he asked, for one seldom saw Jock above. He seemed to live in the engine rooms, like a mole.

'Just a bit,' Greg said. 'So why don't we check that all the gremlins have been ironed out, and see what kind of speed this young gal is capable of?'

36

Jock read easily between the lines. 'Yon boss has his eye on the Blue Riband, then?'

Greg smiled. The boss certainly did want to be holder of the Transatlantic Blue Riband, with top speed for any passenger liner. And although it was top secret, Damon Alexander planned to go for it, immediately after her maiden voyage. 'I just thought you might fancy a bit of bucking about – to make sure you've still got your sea legs,' Greg teased.

Jock grinned. 'I'll see what I can do,' he promised. 'Right then, laddies,' he turned to his now somewhat green-about-the-gills men, 'let's pull out all the stops, shall we?'

At that moment, in his Southampton office, Damon Alexander stared at the piece of paper in front of him. Seated opposite him, Ralph Ornsgood shifted uncomfortably. The letter he was reading was a request for a de luxe suite aboard the *Alexandria* on her maiden voyage. Normally such a simple request would never have reached him, but this 'request' was different. 'You've checked this out?' Damon asked, looking at the signature at the bottom of the terse letter. A Dr R. M. King. *King*. The name leapt at him off the page. A coincidence. Probably.

'Yes. Her claims are valid. She does own the per cent she claims to own,' Ralph confirmed unhappily. 'She's a Fellow. Of Economics,' the Swede said, putting off the moment when he'd have to tell his boss and friend what else he'd learned.

'How the hell did she get 5 per cent of the *Alexandria*?'

Damon asked gruffly. He had followed the flow of shares constantly. Every buyer had been checked out, with over 25,000 man-hours already dedicated to making sure no one shareholder became too big, without Damon knowing about it. Especially one shareholder in particular . . .

Ralph Ornsgood frowned. 'We still don't know for sure. Apart from the fact that she inherited it from a dead fiancé.'

Damon stared at his right-hand man. 'This fiancé. Who was he working for?'

'We don't know. He sank all his own money into it, certainly, but that would have been less than half a million. He must have got in over his head somewhere along the line,' Ralph said heavily, 'because he shot himself last month.'

Damon shook his head. 'Was he very young?'

'Twenty-eight.'

Damon winced, then grimly turned his attention back to the letter in hand. There were no polite references to looking forward to the voyage, no expressions of pride in being a part of the event of the decade. None, in fact, of the usual gushings and self-congratulatory back-slapping he'd come to expect from shareholders. 'I don't like the feel of this,' he said quietly. 'Could Treadstone have got the rest of the money from this Dr King?'

Ralph shook his head, and began to look extremely troubled. 'No. Not Dr King herself. She lives with her mother in a nice enough place, and her stipend as a fully-fledged Fellow of an Oxford College isn't miserly, but still . . .'

'Not in the *Alexandria* league?'

'No.' Ralph looked down at his hands, which were twisting about in his lap. Damon, who knew him well, read the signs easily. 'Ralph,' he said, his voice a low, warning rumble. 'What aren't you saying?'

Ralph Ornsgood met his unflinching eyes, stared at his twiddling thumbs for a brief moment, and then took a deep breath. 'This Dr King . . .' Ralph began, and then stopped.

Damon's eyes widened for a fraction of a second, and then narrowed. Slowly, something deep, something dangerous, stirred in their steely depths. 'Are you trying to tell me that this . . . Dr King . . . is . . .?'

Ralph nodded. 'Yes. I'm afraid so. His daughter.'

Damon sat slowly back in his chair, his face slightly pale. He'd thought he had safeguarded himself against King. He glanced at the letter again and after a long, painful silence, he said grimly, 'Send her a reservation.'

Ralph started. 'Do you think that's wise?'

Damon snorted. 'I'd rather have a King where I can keep an eye on him . . . or her. You know the old saying, Ralph. "Keep your friends close, but your enemies even closer."'

Ralph nodded. He sighed. But he didn't like it.

Damon Alexander didn't like it either. But he had no other choice. At least, not at the moment.

Joe King looked out over the London skyline from the window of his office, his hand curled so tightly around a telephone that his hand ached. Usually he wallowed in his wealth, and gloried in his power. But today he felt none of the complacency his vast business empire usually instilled in him.

He was not, at that moment, a happy man. Not happy at all.

'You're sure there's been no mistake,' he asked with gritted teeth. With narrowed eyes he listened to his underling confirm, yet again, that Keith Treadstone *had* made another will, breaking a clause of their contract. That he *had* bought extra shares of his own on the Q.T. That he *had*, unbelievably, bested him.

Joe King grunted and hung up, not bothering to say goodbye. With gimlet-eyed precision he clipped and lit his cigar and began to gently swing the chair back and forth, a habit of his when he was thinking deeply. Damn Treadstone. Why had he dragged his daughter, Ramona, into all this? How much did Alexander know? As *unthinkable* as it might seem, could Ramona and Damon Alexander be in on this thing together? Ramona could get herself very seriously hurt, if she carried on meddling. Joe King bit down angrily on his fine, expensive cigar, his eyes narrowing into almost invisible slits. Everything had been going so well and now his perfect plan had gone up in smoke. And now there was a new player on the scene – his own daughter! A woman he had never even met.

Verity Fox left her job at the hospital for good on December 10th, and one week later, she was very comfortably installed at her mother's house in Belgravia. Lady Winnifred Fox was very rich, and a still quietly grieving widow of ten years, who nevertheless lived life to the full in the heart of London's elite. Verity had not told her about her illness, and didn't plan to do so until nearer the end.

They'd just spent the morning Christmas shopping at Harrods, and buying themselves designer dresses galore. Now, Winnie watched her daughter come down the stairs in an oyster silk shift, and felt her breath catch. 'Darling, you look marvellous. You should have no trouble at all catching a husband.'

Verity laughed. 'Mother, what makes you think I'm taking this cruise of Damon's just to catch a husband?'

'Well, darling . . . why not?' Winnie asked innocently, taking her daughter's arm and companionably tucking it under her own. 'I do wish I'd invited Celia Fortesque's son over for dinner. Ah well, let's indulge ourselves, and have a champagne cocktail instead.' She led the way to the library, where Verity wandered around the room, fond memories of her father coming back. He'd loved to sit in here, surrounded by all the books and smoking his favourite pipe. Suddenly, Verity froze. She'd been glancing down at the small Chippendale coffee table when her eyes had fallen to a magazine and the picture of a man on the front cover. But not just any man. *The* man.

It had been two years ago when Verity, due to a big motorway pile-up, had been the only surgeon available to do an emergency appendectomy. In the theatre, she had taken one look at the face on the operating table, and felt her heart leap. Something primordial and deeply feminine screamed at her that this was him. This was the one. She found herself memorizing every

41

inch of his face as if her life depended on it. The moment, though brief, had terrified her, and afterwards she'd immediately handed the case over to someone else before even finding out the patient's name. She firmly told herself that she'd imagined it. But the fact was, the feeling had been too animal. Too instant. Too overpowering. She just hadn't known what to do with it. Besides, her logic had screamed at her, you couldn't just look at a man and love him. Love was . . . friendship. Trust. Loyalty. Fidelity. It could not happen with just a single glance. Far better to forget him. Forget the moment had ever happened. But now she was seeing that face again, when she'd thought she'd never see it again. And the feeling was instantly upon her. With hands that shook she picked up the brochure, and looked at the picture longingly, her breath coming in a series of tiny gasps.

'I picked that up when you told me you were going on the cruise,' her mother said. 'Isn't the *Alexandria* simply beautiful? I'm so pleased for Damon. And Joceline say's she can't wait for the maiden voyage to begin.'

Verity hardly heard her mother's voice. Instead she continued to stare down at the picture of the *Alexandria*'s captain. The last time she'd seen him, she'd been cutting into his firm flesh with a scalpel, fighting to keep herself from looking longingly at his face above the green hospital cloth. And she hadn't even known his name . . . Her eyes slid helplessly to the bottom caption. Captain Gregory Paris Harding. The man she loved. She would see him again. Might even talk to him. It sent her heart hammering in her chest.

Then her mother's words filtered through, and she felt her heart contract. Joceline! She was going to be on the ship too. The thought that she might run into her, even for a moment, filled her with cold dread. She shivered as a memory, dark as midnight, flittered across her mind like the touch of a batwing, and she quickly pushed it away, leaving only a fleeting impression. Joceline. Blood. Screaming . . . and murder.

She took a deep breath and shook her head. No. She couldn't go. Not if Joceline was to be on board. Then she looked once more at the picture of Greg Harding, gasping at the colour of his eyes, which she'd never seen opened. Who'd have thought they'd be so amber, so beautiful and full of fire? Her throat went dry, and her heart thumped, making her head spin with a dizzying kind of pleasure. But this time there was nothing to be afraid of. This time she would not let the thought of impetuous love frighten her. She looked deeply into the amber eyes and felt her heart surge with life. Greg. No matter what, she had to see him again. And if she *did* happen to run into Joceline . . . Well, she'd just have to cross that bridge when she came to it. God help her.

CHAPTER 4

Florida: The Maiden Voyage

Joceline Alexander stood at the vanity table and brushed her cheeks faintly with rouge. Looking back at her from the mirror was the reflection of a deeply troubled, sixty-year-old woman. Just a week ago, Mollie Granger, a member of Joceline's bridge club, had very tactfully given her the name of her own plastic surgeon. Cheek! Joceline turned sideways, checking that the two-piece Chanel suit was not too 'young' for her. Dove grey, with dark blue piping, it suited her perfectly. Slipping on a pair of cluster-sapphire and diamond earrings, and a brief spray of Christian Dior's 'Dioressence', she was ready. The ship was due to sail any moment.

Straightening her shoulders and picking up a grey leather purse, Joceline walked purposefully through her suite, barely noticing the luxury around her. She had not come on the cruise to enjoy herself, but to perform a long-postponed task. A very dangerous task . . .

Jeff Doyle took a sip of Mouton Rothschild champagne and nodded. It was perfectly chilled, and sparkling with bubbles. Giving the gaggle of acolytes surrounding Damon Alexander a wide berth, Jeff glanced around him at the splendour that was the Grand Salon, noting every feature. He'd done his homework with meticulous care, of course. It always paid to be prepared. Especially in Jeff's line of work.

The Grand Salon was the heart of the ship, two decks high, with an Italian marble dance floor, old-fashioned bandstand, and huge, impressive chandeliers of unbreakable glass that could be retracted into a ceiling cavity, where sliding panels would cover them completely. The captain had insisted on it for safety's sake, knowing that in high seas they couldn't be guaranteed to be secure. Huge, original seascapes adorned the walls, and Jeff knew an original Turner when he saw one, even if he did come from humble, working-class origins. What a pity it would be, he mused cynically, if his employer was forced to go to plan B. To destroy such loveliness . . . Ah well. Jeff drained his glass, and reached for another one, contemplating his 'boss'.

Joe King. It had been Joe King who'd first recognized the scope of his talents. Joe King who'd met the thirty-two-year-old, fit, psychotic man outside the prison gates, and offered him a unique niche within his empire. Jeff grinned. And now here he was, rubbing shoulders with the beautiful people, his brown hair carefully cut, his suit hand-tailored. He wondered what his fellow passengers would do if they knew who, and what, he was. With an ironic twist to his lips, Jeff silently saluted Damon Alexander just a few feet away.

'To the *Alexandria*,' Jeff muttered. 'She'll soon be all ours.' Or nobody's.

Verity Fox stood in the middle of her modest, single cabin, her mouth agape. The walls were papered in flock velvet, of a pale blue and silver design that was reminiscent of the French fleur-de-lis. The carpet under her feet was inches think and smoky-grey. Long, billowing white silk curtains framed a window, not a porthole, and her bed, although called a single, was in fact a full, three-quarter size bed. The huge room easily housed a settee and pair of chairs, a writing desk, drinks cabinet, television and video unit, and hi-fi.

Verity walked towards a door of solid English oak and ran her hand over the fine grain. All the wood on board the *Alexandria* had been treated with a special varnish that made it fire-resistant. Classified a Method-1 ship, it was also, she knew, festooned with sprinkler systems. Nice to know she was safe, as well as cossetted.

Pushing open the door, Verity gasped. She'd been expecting a shower, loo, and washbasin. Not a sunken bath, a Jacuzzi, shower, full toilet set (including bidet) and again, carpet that you sank into up to your ankles. One entire wall was made of painted tiles depicting a tropical island at sunset. Backing out, she shook her head. Too much, Damon, she thought, grinning widely. Way over the top, my old friend!

Suddenly, the massive whistle blew, the sound reverberating in the air in one long, haunting blast. With a little laugh, the first sound of genuine joy she'd made in over three months, Verity ran to the door and made for the nearest lift. She got out on the fourth deck, where a discreet sign on the side of the bulkhead read Peacock deck.

The railings nearest the docks were lined with waving passengers, but Verity had no trouble finding a space. A bowl full of streamers had been provided, and she reached for a handful and threw them into the air, laughing as they unravelled in spools of red, green, blue and gold. Some fell into the ever-widening gap of water, but some landed on the pier, disappearing into the crowd waving off their loved ones.

Slowly, Verity rested her arms on the railing, her smile fading. Thoughtfully, she looked towards the bow of the ship, and up to where she imagined the bridge to be. He was there, of course. Where else would a captain be as his ship began her maiden voyage, and tugboats pulled their mammoth charge out into the Atlantic Ocean? Verity smiled, imagining him giving orders, his eyes swivelling, watching everything and any-thing. Then she shook her head. She wasn't going to talk to him, though. She'd come to terms with that. Although she expected to be invited, at some point, to sit at the captain's table, she'd decline. She hadn't come on board this ship to try and recapture what might have been if she'd had enough guts and sense to have given it at least half a chance when she'd first set eyes on him. It was too late for that.

She was now more or less reconciled to her fate. She'd had her Christmas with her mother. Now it was her cruise with the man she loved. Although he'd never know it. No, she'd be happy just to be around him. To lie in the sun. To say a long, bitter-sweet farewell to life. There was no need, and she had absolutely no intention, of dragging anybody else into her own tragedy. So she resolutely turned back to the pier, and waved, and laughed, and threw the last of the streamers.

She didn't notice that Joceline Alexander, who was standing on the deck above, was staring down at her, her face a picture of dismay.

Only one passenger never went on deck to wave Miami goodbye. In the sitting room of her de luxe suite, Ramona King sat calmly in a real leather, English-made armchair. The walls of the study were covered in rich old teak. The carpet was oriental, the writing desk Chippendale, the sideboard Sheraton. In her bedroom was a Queen Anne four-poster bed with a Gainsborough portrait hung opposite it, so that it would always be the first thing she'd see on waking. The curtains were maroon velvet, the predominant colour scheme that of maroon and soft, muted grey. Ramona hadn't been able to bring herself to look into the bathroom yet, for all this beauty only served to remind her that this was what Keith had died for. She may not know why, yet, but she would. Oh yes, she would. She'd had three months to recover from the shock of Keith's death, and now anger was predominant. That, and a determination to have justice.

She sensed, rather than felt, the ship begin to move, and walked out onto her balcony of elegant black wrought iron. At the moment there was only the harbour, but a while later she again sensed, rather than heard, the mighty engines turn over, and within minutes the *Alexandria* was heading out to sea under her own power. Where was the noise, the vibration, she had expected? They seemed to be gliding along effortlessly. Ramona shook her head. There was no doubt about it, the *Alexandria* was a jewel of a ship. But if it, or its owner, had been responsible for what had happened to Keith . . .

Unknown to her, her fingers curled around the wrought iron railing until her knuckles gleamed white. For a long while, she watched the coastline of America slowly falling away, and turned her face into the sun and salt wind and made herself a promise. Before the ship returned to this place, she would know everything. And if Damon Alexander was to blame for what had happened to Keith, he'd wish he'd never been born.

The first night out at sea was always informal, just as the second night out would always be one of the grandest of all. Even so, the guests who began to wander into the *Alexandria*'s six restaurants wouldn't have looked out of place on the cover of *Harpers* or *Vogue*. Designer labels and discreet jewellery was the order of the day.

Every restaurant had a senior officer's table. Tonight, the Saint George restaurant played host to the captain's table, but tomorrow it would be set in the Tahitian Gold restaurant, and so on. Likewise, the passenger list would also rotate until, at the end of the voyage, every single passenger would have dined, at least once, with the captain.

Greg Harding stood by the bar, drinking tonic. He wanted to be on the bridge, but knew that a large part of a captain's job, like it or not, was to entertain. Apart from hosting dinner every night, it was his duty to dance with the ladies and charm, with a capital 'C'. The ship's hostesses would have a fit if he tried to sneak back to the bridge before midnight.

He glanced at his watch. Just coming up to 8 p.m. The dog watch was almost over. He only hoped his first lieutenant, who was today's officer of the watch, was on his toes. Not that he didn't trust his bridge crew completely, of course. And the ship had two radar screens, two gyrocompass repeaters, a magnetic compass, a radio direction finder, an automatic course indicator and an ultrasonic depth finder, to keep them afloat, heading in the right direction, and off the reefs. Still. He wanted to be on the bridge.

Greg walked towards his table, took and kissed the hand of an American multi-millionairess, and shook the hand of an English ex prime minister. He didn't notice the woman who had quietly seated herself on a table to his right, but in all the hustle and first-night excitement, he distinctly felt her eyes upon him. Briefly, he glanced around. He was the centre of attention, of course, just as Damon Alexander undoubtedly was, over in the Aurora restaurant. Even so . . . .

Greg felt a strange trickle climb up his spine, using tiny grappling hooks of excitement and curiosity to scale the heights to the back of his neck. Once again he looked around, wondering who was playing such havoc with his hormones, but the introduction of an

Indian princess took precedence. The restaurant was intimately lit with low, glass-covered flickering wall-lamps, so there were plenty of dark corners in which honeymooners, or the merely bashful, could safely hide. It was no good. He couldn't find the owner of the eyes. With an effort, Greg turned his attention to the Amsterdam diamond magnate who was complimenting him on the restaurant's decor.

'All of the *Alexandria*'s six restaurants have a pastel theme, Mynheer van der Falken. Our interior designer insisted on light, discreet colour schemes.'

'But why so many, Captain?' his wife asked flirtatiously, her blue eyes running happily across the captain's wide shoulders. She'd always admired a man in uniform. Especially one who fit it so well.

'Mainly for variety, madame. Also to cut out the wearisome necessity for a first or second sitting. No one will have to sit, cooling their heels, whilst early birds hog the "first sitting".' He smiled, and the diamond-covered woman laughed. She put a long-nailed hand on his arm.

'Captain, you are naughty . . . calling your passengers hogs.'

Greg inwardly winced. Oh hell. He was going to have to be careful. 'That was very indiscreet of me. I shall have to throw myself at your mercy and beg you not to tell anyone I said that.'

The woman laughed. 'Your secret is safe with us,' she husked, patting his arm playfully, nevertheless managing to run her fingernails lightly over his wrist.

From her table, Verity Fox saw the beautiful blonde

put her hand on his sleeve, and heard their combined laughter. She bit her lips and reached determinedly for the menu. This was not going to be as easy as she had thought.

In the Tahitian Gold restaurant a band was playing Gershwin melodies. Waiters in impeccable black and white tuxedos moved busily with fluid ease around the tables. Jeff Doyle sat with his eyes glued to the doorway. Where was she? He knew from the list of diners posted outside the door that she was booked in at this restaurant, and at Damon Alexander's table. Each passenger had had a Daily Programme waiting for them in their suite, giving details, amongst other things, of the dining arrangements, so she couldn't have made a mistake.

At the centre table, Damon Alexander, too, wondered where Dr King was. On the table to his left he saw Ralph Ornsgood glance at him questioningly, and Damon gave a barely perceptible shrug in reply. He was not looking forward to meeting Dr R. M. King, Fellow of Economics, Oxford. Still, the sooner he got it over with, the better. He and this Dr R. M. King had some serious talking to do. If she thought she could buy her way onto his ship with who knew what kind of mischief in mind, she had another damned think coming.

Damn the woman, where was she?

Ramona King was in her suite, eating an excellent Dover sole. She'd requested a tray be brought to her room as soon as she'd checked in. She wanted time to get over the jet-lag. Time to re-read all the data she had collected on the Alexander Line. Time to digest it's unexpectedly personal history. A history that all began with Michael Alexander and her own father . . . She had started out expecting to digest dry and statistical information about a company. Not unearth an old family feud.

Michael Alexander and Joe King had been bitter rivals, although exactly why, she hadn't yet been able to discover. They had both started out in the cross-channel ferry business, but Michael Alexander had succeeded where Joe King had failed. The fact that her father had gone on to succeed in Paper, then Construction, then Imports and Exports, making a fortune in each, was, to her, neither here nor there.

But could this old Alexander/King rivalry have had anything at all to do with Keith? It seemed unlikely, as Michael Alexander had been dead for some years, murdered by a burglar in his own home. And yet . . .

She sighed deeply. Keith's personal papers had yielded no clues. The answers didn't lie in the anonymous sheets of paper in front of her. Or in the past. The answers lay square with Damon Alexander. Just what in the world did he have against the Kings? Against Keith?

She didn't know. But tomorrow, when she was better prepared, she'd start to find out.

CHAPTER 5

The Grand Salon easily accommodated the entire passenger list of the *Alexandria* the second night out. Even Ramona couldn't help but be impressed by the spectacle of her first ship-board ball. Women wore nothing but designer gowns, of course, and their necks, wrists and ears dripped diamonds, emeralds, rubies, sapphires and pearls.

The party was in full swing when she arrived. On the bandstand a twenty-piece orchestra was playing 'Blue Guitar' and the centre of the dance floor was a gently swaying mass of people. Lining two sides of the Grand Salon were wide, covered decks, giving a panoramic view of the moonlit ocean. At the moment these decks were laden with buffet tables. Where the desserts were congregated, flowers made of icing festooned the tables in ropes of gentle pastel colours.

Ramona spotted a relatively unoccupied space of bulkhead, and moved thankfully towards it, unaware of being watched.

Damon Alexander was leaning casually against one of the deck's Gothic veranda columns, a glass of fine burgundy in his hand. It was ten-thirty, and he'd begun to relax. Everything was running smoothly. The orchestra, one of twenty-two that had been auditioned, was perfect. The ship was right on schedule, and the purser had reported absolutely no complaints at all – an almost unheard of occurrence on a maiden voyage.

He was just beginning to wonder if he could get away with sliding off in an hour or so, when he saw her. The sight of her, absently twirling an unwanted glass of champagne, hit him like a physical blow, and he felt his mouth drain of all moisture. He swallowed. Hard. And suddenly he was sure of two things. Firstly, she was the most beautiful woman he'd even seen. And secondly, that he hadn't seen her before. Except in a very blurred picture that Ralph had shown him of Joe King's daughter, which had done her no justice at all.

He took a sip of burgundy and without a moment's thought, began to work his way across the room towards her. He had things to say to Dr R. M. King. But the nearer he got, the more slowly he began to move. From across the wide width of the room, he'd thought she couldn't possibly be as beautiful as distance had made her appear. But he was wrong. Heart-stoppingly wrong. She was wearing a simple, shimmering, electric-blue sheath that was a mere tube of material, hanging from delicate spaghetti straps that showed off her naturally wide but elegant pale shoulders. She was wearing a simple silver rope chain around her neck, the only jewellery she had on. But it was her hair that made the breath leave his lungs in a rush. As he closed the final yards between them, his eyes were drawn helplessly to the nearly waist-length curtain of water-straight, silvery hair that was the exact colour of very old, white gold. Since her face was turned away from him, it hid her profile behind a curtain of glory.

Damon, still holding onto his glass of burgundy, felt his hand tremble slightly and frowned. Unbelievably, his heart was beginning to thump with a forgotten excitement, something he hadn't felt since he was a giddy teenager.

Ramona felt the fine hairs running the length of her spine come to rigid attention and quickly turned around, unaware that her hair, washed only an hour ago, swirled out around her like threads of spun gold, a few strands clinging to her cheek.

She knew him at once, of course, and her eyes widened.

Damon Alexander said nothing. He was sure he'd been about to say something; 'What the hell are you doing on my boat?' perhaps. But her eyes had burnt every word he might have said into a pile of cinders, for they were the exact same colour of her dress. An unbelievably pale, electric blue. Almost silver.

Ramona looked at his strong, handsome, confident face, and felt anything but confident herself. Now that she was face to face with the enemy, she suddenly wished herself elsewhere. Looking into Damon Alexander's steely-grey eyes, she felt suddenly naked.

Damon loved her face; from the high, intelligent forehead to the fine, straight nose, the perfectly-shaped lips and strong, attractive chin. He had hoped for something to save him. Two buck teeth. A pimple.

Something. The fact that she was so perfect made him want to take her by the shoulders and . . .

He took a deep, solid breath. 'I think it's about time we met, don't you?' he asked, his lips curling into a challenging smile. No doubt Dr R. M. King was used to curling men around her little finger. The sooner she knew better in *his* case, the better he'd like it.

Ramona blinked. 'Is it?' she asked, her voice impossibly husky. Fright, she supposed, defensively. He'd taken her by surprise, turning up like that right out of thin air, like some damned genie out of a bottle.

Damon's smile turned wolfish. He held out his hand. 'Damon Alexander,' he said ominously, and waited.

'Ramona Murray,' Ramona said, holding out her hand. Murray was her maiden name, but she'd chosen to use it for no other reason than she thought she might learn more from Damon Alexander if he believed her to be just another pleasure-seeking passenger, and not a legitimate shareholder.

Damon's eyes narrowed, but he forced a pleasant smile onto his face. Fun and games so soon? he mused. How interesting . . . 'Care to dance, Miss Murray?' he asked, and saw her eyes flash in . . . fear? Or anger? Before she could do so much as blink, he snaked his hand around her waist and all but carried her into the dancing throng.

Ramona felt her heart leap into her throat as his powerful arms swept her away. Her thighs trembled as they were pressed against his solidly-muscled legs, and she dragged in a deep, trembling breath. Never before had she felt a man's strength as forcefully as she

57

did at that moment. Her knees turned to jelly, and for one awful moment she thought she was going to fall, like a bad soufflé, at his feet. But he was holding her much too closely for that.

'Aren't you supposed to wait for the lady to say yes?' she snapped, angling her head up, her eyes shooting sparks.

Damon looked down at her and felt his heart stumble at the sight of her. Her eyes seemed to shoot their fire right into his blood, and he felt his loins harden in unbidden, helpless desire. 'Oh, I never do what I'm supposed to do. Miss Murray,' he added softly.

She saw his eyes darken, felt the hard surge of him against her, and felt a swift surge of power flood her bloodstream. At the same instant, some deep, dark, female part of her seemed to melt. To cover the mortification she quickly dipped her head and rested her cheek against his lapel. Her hands, which had been resting lazily against his back, suddenly curled into fists.

Damon stared down at her, his face tight and pale. Her pale head rested against his shoulder as if it belonged there. The thought sent a small shudder rippling through him. Suddenly, he knew he'd wandered onto a minefield. And if he didn't watch his step . . . His hands tightened ominously on her waist, and when she glanced up at him, his eyes had turned smoky, but the look within them was pure steel.

She gasped as she felt her nipples burgeon to sudden attention, and since she wore no bra, she knew that he must be able to feel the buttons of flesh digging into him. Damon promptly missed a step, and drew in a quick ragged breath.

Damn her! He had to keep his mind on business, or he was lost. He was being hunted by a very beautiful, very dangerous tigress, and he'd better do some stalking of his own.

'You know, it's very strange that I don't remember seeing your name on the passenger manifest,' he said blandly.

Ramona shrugged. 'Perhaps I came as someone's . . . guest?' she said. Half the millionaires on the boat had brought a 'guest' who was not their wife, on that she'd bet any amount of money. As she said it, she looked up and smiled. She mustn't, ever, let him suspect her lack of experience with men. He'd eat her alive.

Damon splayed his hands against her lower spine suggestively, only the thin material of her dress between his palm and her bare skin. Deliberately, he leant forward. 'I don't believe you,' he whispered softly into her ear, his breath blowing against her delicate lobe, sending shivers down her back.

Ramona swallowed. Hard. And quickly changed the subject. If this carried on for much longer, the only thing she'd learn about Damon Alexander is that she wanted him. Desperately.

'You must be proud of this ship,' she said, her voice much too husky for her liking. 'But I'm surprised at all this extravagance. It must have taken an awful lot of money?' she probed, knowing she had to start somewhere. And if he thought she was naïve in financial matters, all the better. She knew men liked to boast about how clever they were. Give him enough rope, she thought grimly, and he's be bound to hang himself.

Damon smiled, his smile pure wolf. He knew damned well she was playing with him, but he didn't mind. Never before had he been so stimulated by a conversation. Never before had a woman been able to push his buttons so thoroughly. His every sense was on super-alert. He was acting like a teenager with hormones that had gone rampant, and that gave her way too much power. Like the cavalry coming to the rescue, the orchestra finished the last strains of 'Strangers in the Night' and he pulled away before he made a total idiot of himself.

'I'm sure you've read the brochure,' he said evasively, smiling widely as her eyes flashed her annoyance. 'And I do so hate to talk business around any woman as beautiful as yourself,' he added, deliberately lowering his tone and, raising one of her hands to his lips, he kissed each finger in turn, his eyes glinting up at her sardonically. But who could resist playing the willing mouse to such a sensuous, dangerous cat? he wondered. It would be oh-so-sensible to just tell her that he knew who she was and demand to know what kind of game she was playing. But then it would all be over. And Damon knew, with a frisson of fear and pleasure, that he was already hooked. Dangerously, deliciously, hooked.

As his lips closed over her fingers, and her body spasmed in helpless, sexual arousal, Ramona knew only that she was way out of her depth. What the hell was she doing, playing the *femme fatale* when she was such a total novice? Especially when, with his every word, his every scorching look, it was obvious that Damon Alexander was a master at the game. She was way out of her league, and knew it. She looked around, hoping for a way of escape.

'Have you eaten yet?' Damon asked, smiling at her obvious desire to get away. Ramona chose that moment to decide it was safe to look at him again, and felt her hackles rise. Just what was so damned amusing? She shook her head reluctantly, and he led her to the buffet, heaping a plate with salad and leading her onto the open deck, to an empty table by the rail. As he helped seat her, he couldn't help but feel as if he were handling volatile gelignite. One wrong word, one wrong move provoking a stray spark and . . . *whoomph!*

He shook the intoxicating thought away, and grinned. Well, why not give TNT a little poke? 'So,' he said, sitting opposite her, marvelling at the way the moonlight turned her hair to silver. 'Tell me all about yourself. Do you have any family?'

Ramona shook her head, and reached for a fork to stir the lettuce around her plate. 'Not really. Only my mother,' she said. She felt unutterably weary. As if she'd just run a marathon. She had no idea that verbal fencing could be so draining.

'Oh?' Damon said cynically. 'No father? Brothers or sisters?' He watched her closely, waiting for the wariness to leap into her eyes, or the colour to leave her face as she scented danger. Instead, she merely shook her head.

'No brothers or sisters, and my father left us when I was born.'

Damon knew as much, but that meant nothing. 'But surely he kept in touch?' he prompted, waiting, once again, for the performance to begin.

Ramona smiled. 'No. I think I was the final straw that broke the camel's back,' she said sadly. 'My mother always denied it, but I think he left because she couldn't have any more children, and because I was not the son and heir he wanted. My father was, no, *is*, a big businessman. It's ironic to think that I . . .' She stopped abruptly, aware that she'd been about to admit to going into the field of economics. That would never do. Instead, she shrugged.

For a long moment, Damon stared at her, his eyes narrowing. Now what game was she playing? But he was willing to play along. 'Didn't you keep in touch at all?'

Ramona shook her head. 'There seemed no point,' she said. 'I asked my mother about him often as a child, of course, and she told me all about him. I used to keep a scrapbook about him when I was in my teens. You know, newspaper clippings from the papers, that sort of thing.' And when she'd been working towards her D.Phil. she'd done an in-depth study of King Enterprises, her father's company, as part of her theories. 'But we never actually met,' she carried on, unaware that he was staring at her intently. 'Oh, he left us well provided for,' she added quickly, aware that she might be coming across as little orphan Annie. 'I went to some good schools, and we had the house . . .' Suddenly, she was aware that she'd been gabbling on like an idiot. For pity's sake, *shut up*, Ramona, she told herself. 'But that must all sound pretty boring to someone like you,' she said, firmly bouncing the ball back into his court. 'The glamour of the high seas and all that,' she teased.

Damon said nothing. He could think of nothing *to* say. Did she really expect him to believe all that? he wondered. And then, a moment later, he found himself almost wishing he *could* believe her. And she'd sounded so sincere. He'd have to remember just how good a liar she was, he thought grimly. When he got back to his cabin, he'd phone head office and have their investigators fax out everything they had on every meeting they could find between Joe King and his daughter. When the time came, he wanted proof of her lies to throw back in her face. Her beautiful, incredibly lovely face.

'Do I have dust on my nose or something?' Ramona asked, half frost, half exasperation. Then, as he smiled and shook his head, she added angrily, 'And will you please stop that? You've done nothing but laugh at me since we met.'

Damon's smile abruptly disappeared. 'Sorry, I'm not laughing at you. I'm laughing at myself. Please, believe me,' he added quietly, his voice suddenly grim.

Ramona looked up quickly. His last words had sounded so . . . not desperate, but . . . sincere. Important. It was as if they were doing more, much more, than indulging in mere big-bash meaningless chit-chat. And it unnerved her.

'Oh . . . What's so funny, anyway?' she asked curiously.

'Nothing that I can't laugh over,' Damon assured her quietly, but even as he spoke, he wondered who he was hoping to convince. 'It's just that ever since I saw you, I've been feeling as if I was sixteen again,' he said, and could have kicked himself. Good going, Damon. Why not just give her a big club to hit you with? he wondered, his lips twisting ironically.

Ramona blinked, totally surprised. 'Oh,' she said. 'That . . . er . . . must be very interesting for you,' she replied, in her very best sophisticated and amused drawl.

'Oh it is, Ramona,' he said softly, suggestively. 'It is.'

He watched, amazed, as a tide of pale pink flooded into her cheeks and she quickly looked away. Was it actually possible she could be shy? Had he actually found a woman who could blush? Surely not. Not Ramona King, of all women.

Time to get back to the business in hand. Dangle a little more bait. He looked around, at the swell of the ocean, the white wake of the ship stretching out behind her. 'I love this ship,' he said, watching as her head lifted swiftly, like a hawk scenting prey. 'I only wish she was all mine. I hate having to share her, even with my shareholders.'

Ramona felt her heart leap. Play it cool, she warned herself quickly. Don't seem too eager. 'Oh? Who?' she asked casually. She knew all their names of course; had, in fact the list of major shareholders memorized.

'Oh, a banker here, a business magnate there. Who knows, maybe even your father bought the odd share or two,' he mused, his eyes watching for the slightest flicker. But again, nothing. Blushes one moment, and iron-clad control the next. It didn't seem to make sense. Damon frowned.

Ramona had no idea if her father had shares in the *Alexandria* or not, nor did she care. She didn't like all this lying and scheming, but at the same time, she knew she had no choice. Damon Alexander was obviously a complex man. A clever, and devious man. And if she was to get to the bottom of Keith's death, she would have to be just as clever and just as devious.

Damon beckoned a waiter, who brought an ice bucket and bottle of champagne over, and left as silently as he came. Wordlessly, Damon poured them both a glass, and leaned back, trying to get things into focus. 'So, what do you do, Ramona Murray,' he asked, watching as she took a small sip from her glass.

'I'm in education,' Ramona said, and Damon almost choked on his drink. *In education?* Lord, she had some gall, this woman. He grinned, and found himself admiring her more and more. He had no doubt that it had taken guts, brains and dedication to succeed in Oxford, and whilst most men felt threatened by a successful woman, Damon had always admired them. 'I can see why,' he said, and when she looked up inquiringly, said softly, 'You've already taught me a thing or two.'

'Is that all?' she shot back, not caring over-much for the teasing tone of his voice. 'Stick around,' she advised, her voice hardening, 'and I just might teach you a lesson you'll never forget.'

Damon felt a rock hard punch of desire thump him solidly in his lower stomach. Her words and her hard, challenging eyes were like aphrodisiacs, raging in his bloodstream. He felt his breath burst out of his lungs as his loins stirred in instant pagan reaction to an age-old feminine sexual battle cry. To cover it, he reached for the bottle. 'More champagne,' he murmured, handing her a fresh glass. His blood was still boiling. 'To education,' he said softly.

Reluctantly, Ramona clinked the glass. 'To education,' she said, wondering why she seemed to be having so much trouble breathing. Her nipples were tingling as if they'd been electrified . . . She felt, quite inexplicably, terrified. And suddenly Keith's face was in front of her. Had he been scared, at the moment he'd died? But she didn't want to think about that terrible moment of self-destruction.

Restlessly she turned, and Damon's face was filling her vision once more, his eyes radiating a strange alluring heat, his glance both possessive and confident. She could not imagine this man ever killing himself. He was too damned cocky. He'd always find a way out of any trouble he got himself into. And suddenly she felt a wall of rage rise up out of nowhere, and knew that fear had caused it. Fear of his eyes that seemed to reach down into her and rip away her every defence. Fear of the heat he could instil in her blood by just a touch. Fear of his voice, that could send snaking shivers down her spine. But she must not ever let that fear stop her.

Damon Alexander might think he could get away with murder, and no doubt, he usually did. Women, especially, would let him get away with anything, she thought angrily. But this time, he would have to pay for his mistakes.

She smiled gently and took a sip of her champagne. She leaned close, her eyes glittering, looking deeply into his. 'You're never too old to learn, Damon,' she said softly. And laughed.

Damon caught his breath, then leaned forward to meet her gaze, clinking his glass against hers. 'And neither are you. Ramona,' he said softly. 'Neither are you.'

CHAPTER 6

Trinidad and Tobago

The *Alexandria* arrived at its first port of call at dawn, and by nine o'clock most of the passengers had already gone ashore. In a nearly empty restaurant on the stunningly beautiful Hummingbird deck, one of the ship's topmost decks, Ramona bit hungrily into a slice of tender and juicy ham and reached for a slice of toast and the butter dish. Although the Alexander Line offered a wide variety of organized excursions, she had decided to 'do' the island on her own.

The tropical sunlight pouring through the wide picture-windows reminded her with a delicious tingle of excitement that she was now in exotic climes. Usually her travelling had been work related, and nearly always in Europe. Suddenly, a shadow fell across her and she looked up quickly, her lips falling open and her heart hammering.

Damon smiled. 'Enjoying the meal?'

'Very much. Please, join me.' Ramona was glad her voice sounded so steady. She had hardly slept, for her wayward mind would insist on remembering the sensation of being held in his arms, and she was determined that this time she was not going to let her opportunities slip away from her due to her lack of self-confidence.

As he sat down in front of her, she noticed that his simple white shirt was unbuttoned at the top, revealing a strong corded column of throat and the beginnings of a broad, tanned chest, sprinkled with just a few dark hairs. Immediately the hand holding her coffee cup began to tremble.

'Mind if I filch a slice of your toast?' he asked, one eyebrow raised.

She shrugged. 'Go ahead.'

She watched him butter a slice and then bite into it with strong white teeth. From out of nowhere the image of those strong teeth nibbling at her bare breast shot into her mind, and she felt her whole body turn rigid. At the same time, heat, stronger than the equatorial sun outside, rushed into her blood and her breath burned in her lungs. She coughed and looked away from him. Her mother had been right, she thought wryly. She was a passionate woman. Oh Keith, why couldn't you . . . ? Abruptly, she snapped the thought off.

Damon watched her, fascinated by the wave of colour that flashed across her pale, creamy skin. His eyes fastened on her mouth, which was touchingly free of lipstick. They were a perfect bow-shape, full and soft, he noticed, and could imagine the padded feel of them under his own mouth.

Ramona looked up and found him staring. 'Is . . .' She had to cough, for her voice sounded like a strangled cougar. 'Is something the matter?'

'No,' he said quickly, harshly. Then, more softly, 'No. Nothing's the matter at all.' For a moment they stared at one another, then he smiled and held out his hand. 'Since you've finished breakfast, can I escort you to the tender?'

Ramona smiled, reached for her beach bag and stood up, whilst Damon ran his eyes over her hungrily. She was wearing shorts that showed off her long, exquisitely-shaped legs to perfection. She didn't realize that the looseness of her blouse, being ruffled by a breeze from the open window, would occasionally cling to her full breasts, outlining her nipples perfectly. She caught him staring again.

Damon smiled an apology and stood up. And up. And up. Ramona, who at five feet nine had never considered herself tiny, found her chin doing a steady upward sweep as he rose, and nibbled on her lip. She had forgotten how tall he was.

Damon, before he could stop himself, found his index finger resting on her bottom lip. 'Don't do that,' he said softly, and then his eyes widened. Damn her! For all of his life, he'd kept himself strictly under control. Even his women, he realized now with a jolt, had been selected on a careful, even if subconscious, level. They'd all been his social equal, attractive, intelligent and worldly. And whilst Ramona King surely fit into all those categories, she was different in one very obvious way. He had *chosen* his past lovers with a mutually satisfying affair in mind.

Now, suddenly, in Ramona King, he had stumbled upon an unknown quantity. He had not chosen her at all.

Instead, he found himself swept up on a tidal wave of desire, intrigue and, yes, sheer compelling need. He was in foreign territory and although it needed to be trod with caution, it never once occurred to him to try and back off. He was going to have her. Soon. No matter what it took. No matter how dangerous the game . . .

Ramona blushed under the heat of his gaze, and turned away abruptly. 'Well, this is what a cruise is all about,' she said, sweeping her hand across the exquisite view of the island. 'If I don't get a move on, I might miss Trinidad altogether.'

Damon escorted her to the tender, for once strangely silent. His brooding presence, confidently striding beside her, made her more nervous than ever. 'Do you know Trinidad, Mr Alexander?' she asked, and saw his head swivel and angle down at her.

'Damon,' he said sharply. The formal sound of his name on her lips somehow hurt him. 'Please,' he added, as an afterthought. 'And no, I can't say as I do. But you attended the lecture last night on all it had to offer. Perhaps you could show *me* the sights?' he purred.

Ramona gulped.

On the lower deck, two tenders were waiting to transport the last of the *Alexandria*'s passengers to Port-of-Spain, Trinidad's capital, and the warm wind blowing in off the island was redolent of fruit, and salt and sun. Damon leapt lithely on board the tender, then helped her down, his hands possessive and caressing on her arms.

Once on land, she half expected him to leave her, but he showed no signs of doing so, and she didn't know

71

whether she was glad or sorry. Although she knew he was attracted to her, she wasn't sure if that was a good thing or not. Her knowledge of men was practically zero. But, at the same time, the thought of *not* being near him left her feeling hollow.

'Listen,' Damon said. They'd been walking steadily away from the docks and into the centre of town. Somewhere ahead was the unmistakable, evocative sound of steel band music, Trinidad being the birthplace of that very Caribbean form of music. It got louder as they moved further into the town, and then, from around the corner, a parade was suddenly filling the streets. Dressed in the brightest of colours, men and women danced their way past, a slow-moving float being pulled by a dilapidated car painted all over with white daisies. Almost as soon as it had come, it was gone, leaving behind only the haunting notes of the music and the sound of echoing laughter.

'Wow,' Ramona said. She had not expected to be introduced to the Caribbean quite so quickly, or so forcefully.

Beside her, Damon grinned. 'Welcome to the Caribbean, Ramona . . . Murray.' He'd very nearly said 'King' and he warned himself to be careful.

The sound of the false name on his lips made her wince, and she quickly turned away. 'Well, now that we're here, what shall we get up to?' she asked, and then wished, whole-heartedly, that she'd phrased that better, as Damon looked down at her, his eyes seeming to do some strange melting trick from hard steel to liquid pewter. Her breath caught, her knees did a lovely little melting trick of their own, and she quickly looked away. The town spread out around her looked slightly sleazy, but at the same time it was magical. Tropical. Exotic. *Different*.

'Let's explore,' she said firmly.

'Yes, miss,' he said meekly.

Ramona shook her head exasperatedly and strode briskly away. Grinning openly now, feeling happier than he ever had in his entire life, Damon Alexander followed. She was like a gold mine, full of precious gems, buried in deep rock. But instead of being hard work, chipping away at her was proving to be immense fun, and, he was sure, promised jewel-like rewards.

They bought a map of the town in the tourist office, and set out on a walking tour that made Damon glad he was as fit as he was. From the King's Wharf where they had disembarked, they crossed Wrightson Road into Independence Square. They duly inspected the Cathedral of the Immaculate Conception, and then, barely pausing for breath, headed up Picton Road to the Forts Chacon and Picton, built to ward off invaders by the British and Spanish regimes respectively. The magnificent Red House, a Renaissance-style building that took up an entire block, and was Trinidad's House of Parliament, followed. Eventually, when even Ramona seemed to be running out of steam, they found themselves in Queen's Park, known more commonly to the locals as Savannah. There, he took her hand and forced her to a halt.

'Alright, enough's enough,' he said firmly, leading her to a bench and collapsing beside her. 'Where do you get your energy, woman?' he growled. And immediately wondered what it would be like to release that energy of hers in his bed. The thought made him giddy. He leaned back against the bench and groaned, running one hand through his hair, grinning ruefully, and shaking his head.

Suddenly, she began to laugh. She just couldn't help it. The whole situation was so . . . *bizzare!*

'That's better,' Damon said softly. There was no thought of practised seduction in his head. His arms just moved naturally, his hands cupping her waist and pulling her forward onto his lap, almost as if his limbs were entities with a mind of their own. Ramona, too, seemed to have trouble understanding what was happening. It was only when she felt the heat of their bodies touching, and realized that his eyes were so much closer than before, that she knew what he was going to do. She had time to gasp a startled breath of air, and then he was kissing her.

The city she had been so determined to put between them abruptly faded away as if it had never been. The strange sounds, the unusual, exotic scent of flowers and tropical fruit, the odd, very un-English strength of the sun, the rolling, easy-going drawl of Caribbean voices . . . all of it just went, as if somebody had turned off a cosmic switch.

There was only herself, and him. His breath tasted cool and clean, but his lips seemed to scorch her. She tensed and then shook, as if hit by an earthquake, as his tongue darted into her mouth. Her first reaction was to pull away, and she felt her back strain against his arms as she shot into reverse. Instantly, his hold on her tightened. He was not about to let her go. Her body reacted to his mastery in a pagan, erotic, totally spontaneous way. Her nipples began to ache, crushed as they were against the solid wall of his chest, and she felt her thighs tremble against his. His tongue was on her teeth now, flicking against them, and she could hear the pounding of her heart . . . or was it his? . . . echoing in her ears. She groaned against his lips as his tongue found hers and a bolt of heat shot into her womb and made her loins churn. Shocked at the shaft of desire that pierced her, she pulled away, this time with a harder and more determined movement, catching him unawares. Damon felt her slip away, and he reluctantly opened his eyes, looking and feeling physically pained.

Ramona took a step back, and then another. She shook her head. Damon's eyes narrowed as he saw how pale she was. 'Are you alright?' he asked, his voice suddenly harsh with concern. He'd only kissed her! But now he remembered how unprepared she'd seemed. Her response had been whole-hearted but clumsy. Unsure. Almost as if she'd never been kissed before . . . Damon smiled crookedly. As if!

She flinched, not understanding his tone but recognizing the cynicism of his smile. Hell, she was reacting like a schoolgirl on her first date! Pull yourself together, girl, she berated herself. Her chin lifted. 'Yes. Fine. Of course I am. Why wouldn't I be?' she challenged. Not for anything would she let him know just how . . . shaken . . . she felt.

Damon stood up slowly, and walked towards her, something in his loping, silent gait reminding her of a hunting animal. A *male* hunting animal. And something deep inside her responded to it instinctively. An opposite, but an equal response. A *female* hunting animal. Suddenly, she wanted his lips on hers again. His hands on her. She wanted to feel his body, naked, sweating, writhing . . . She shook her head, and turned, wanting to run away. To hide. To build herself some deep, protective walls. But how could she? She had no time for all that.

Damon ran a distinctly shaky hand through his hair, looking harassed. 'I don't get it, Ramona,' he said softly. 'Why did you pull away like that, so suddenly?'

Ramona flushed angrily. Had her inexperience been so damned obvious? 'Perhaps I just don't like being grabbed and kissed without any warning,' she snapped.

Slowly, Damon lowered his hand. Around them, Port-of-Spain carried on its usual, busy business. In the park, flowers bloomed and birds sang. 'I see,' he said at last. This 'little innocent' act she was putting on had to be part of the game she was playing. It might have nothing to do with the shares themselves, or her deal with her father, but it was part of the game alright. It had to be.

'Look, let's start again, shall we,' he said gently. Two could play games, after all. 'It's nearly noon, why don't we find find somewhere to eat, and then find a nice beach somewhere and just relax; take a swim. What do you say?'

Ramona nodded. 'OK,' she said. She would go along. After all, she might learn something. But if he thought he was going to kiss her again, she'd . . . she'd break his kneecaps.

Damon reached out and took her hand. One thing he knew for sure. He was never going to be bored around Ramona King.

Neither one of them noticed Jeff Doyle, sitting on a bench several yards away, staring at them in slit-eyed amazement.

Slowly, very slowly, he began to smile.

Twenty-two miles away, on the smaller, quieter and much less-commercialized island of Tobago, Verity Fox smiled blissfully as she contemplated the nearly deserted beach stretched out ahead of her. She'd spent the morning in a beach-front bar sipping fresh, deliciously chilled pineapple juice. Around noon, she'd wandered around a small shop and gathered together a few picnic items before hiring a car. A quick check of the map showed her that Great Courtland Bay was the nearest beach. Now she surveyed the sweeping curve of near-white sand, the blue ocean and swaying palm trees with a sigh of pure satisfaction. She literally couldn't remember the last time she'd taken a holiday to anywhere nearly as lovely as this.

Quickly, she put up a big striped umbrella, under which she'd retreat after half an hour or so, then under the cover of a huge beach towel she struggled somewhat awkwardly into her bikini. Even though the beach was large enough to make it feel deserted, there were still a few sunworshippers dotted about here and there.

With the sun warming her through to her bones, she headed for the sea. She'd been braced with typical British fortitude for cold water and uncomfortable pebbles, only to find that the Caribbean sea lapped around her like a warm gentle bath, and beneath her feet the sand was as smooth as silk. With a sigh of happiness, she pushed forward in an easy but not very expert breaststroke. She was careful not to swim out too far, then turned onto her back and stared up at a sky so blue it was almost painful on the eyes.

Greg Harding, dressed only in black shorts and sunscreen, strolled up the beach with a towel, looking for a spot away from it all. He'd spent the morning ensuring everything was running smoothly with the ship, and had decided to listen to Jim's advice to take a few hours off. He'd been working like a dog for weeks now, and a little relaxation wouldn't hurt.

Unwilling to risk Trinidad, where he might run into passengers, he'd chosen the smaller, less busy island of Tobago to catch some sun and iron out the kinks.

Seeing a deserted umbrella nearby, Greg spread out the towel and stretched out, sighing blissfully. The sun felt good. The quiet felt even better. No passengers to entertain. No ship to worry about. At least for a few hours . . .

Within moments he was asleep.

When Verity, tired from the swimming, waded ashore, she grabbed the towel she'd left at the water's edge and started to dry her hair. Walking without looking where she was going, she almost fell over him. As it was, her foot connected with his ankle, and she quickly pulled the towel off her head. At the same moment, Greg sat up with a start.

Verity, her hair in spikes from the brisk rubbing, stared down at him, mouth agape. Greg looked up at her, his eyes instantly taking in the trim figure in a small but modest blue and red striped bikini. He looked up into her midnight ebony eyes, and smiled. 'Sorry. Am I in your spot?'

Verity gave a small mental groan, and quickly ran her fingers through her hair, attempting some sort of order. 'No, of course not. Sorry if I trampled all over you!' Without being able to stop herself, her eyes dropped to his abdomen, her practised eye quickly finding the almost invisible scar of his appendectomy. She had done good work. If she hadn't know it was there she would probably never have noticed it.

'Sorry. I didn't mean to intrude,' Greg said, and looked as if he was about to get up.

'Oh, but you're not!' she said in a rush, and quickly dropped down onto the sand beside him. And then, just as quickly, wondered what the hell she was doing. Hadn't she promised herself she would never talk to him? Never give herself even half a chance to capitalize on whatever it was that she truly felt for him?

Greg couldn't drag his eyes away from the sea-nymph who had almost fallen right into his lap. He held out his hand. 'Greg Harding,' he said simply, omitting his title as Captain.

'Verity Fox,' she said, likewise omitting her own title of Doctor.

'Have you been on Tobago long?' he asked, wishing that he wouldn't have to leave in just a few hours. He could spend that time just lost in the dark depth of her eyes and never notice the passing of the minutes.

Verity shook her head. 'Only since this morning,' she

admitted. She started to open her mouth to tell him that she was, in fact, a passenger on his ship, then abruptly changed her mind.

'What's the water like?' he asked, his voice deep and forceful without being loud. She found herself unable to look away from his eyes, which were a strange combination of amber and brown, like a tiger's. The look in their depths made her heart pound.

'It's lovely,' she said, her voice no more than a breathy huskiness.

He stood up lithely, using just his legs, a mute and unintentional testimony to his physical fitness, and looked down at her. Slowly, he held out his hand. 'Want to swim again?'

Verity, almost as if in a dream, found herself lifting her own hand to meet his. The moment she felt his fingers close around hers, her heart began to beat again, for what felt like the first time since she'd met Gordon in that small, depressing little room and learned the results of her blood tests.

As she let him pull her easily to her feet and lead her into the water, and as she began to do a slow crawl, feeling inadequate as he swam – literally – rings around her, she felt once again like crying and laughing.

Only this was nothing like before, when shock had been the main instigator. This time she wanted to cry because of the sheer, beautiful perfection of the moment. And laugh, just because she felt like it.

She did neither of course.

But later, much later, she would do plenty of both . . .

CHAPTER 7

The sea was in a competition with the sky to see which could be the bluest, whilst the *Alexandria* skipped across the ocean like a craft from a poem. On the Serenade deck, Joceline Alexander pulled her silk jacket a little tighter around her and stared out to sea.

'You're up early!' The sound of her son's voice had her spinning around, an instant sensation of guilt rising up within her. Quickly, she swallowed it back down and smiled, but Damon felt that instant barrier come up between them and sighed. He wasn't sure why he felt that his mother was always a million miles away from him, even when he was standing right next to her. As a boy he'd been packed off to boarding school, and later he'd been too busy working his way into a position of power within the company to spend much time at home. Now he felt he should be immune to their lukewarm relationship, but every time he and his mother met up, the little-boy part of him half hoped that it would be different. But it never was.

Now Joceline looked away from her handsome son and gazed out over the ocean once more. 'Yes, it *is* hideously early,' she admitted in her usual, cool precise way. 'But I have trouble sleeping these days. I must be getting old.'

Damon laughed. 'You, Mother? Never.'

Joceline winced. She knew how she must appear to her son. Dressed in a youthful trouser suit, fully made up and wearing her diamonds. But it was all camouflage. The barrier she erected whenever her son was near. The charm, the precise manners she used. All were designed to keep her child safe. But now she must hurt him. Like it or not, she had no choice. Things were getting out of hand, and it was time that he knew the truth. All of it, no matter what it cost her. No matter how it terrified her . . . 'This is a wonderful boat, Damon,' she said quietly, trying to sidle into the subject carefully.

'Ship, Mother,' Damon corrected, his lips twisting wryly. As the widow of a shipping man, Damon often found her lack of interest in the business a little annoying.

Joceline bit her lip, sensing immediately his censure. She wanted to weep and curse at the same time. But how could she possibly explain the reason for the distance she'd been forced to keep between them? She turned and found her lips parting, an impassioned plea for understanding ready on her tongue. Then her son turned to her, and she saw Michael in his strong jaw, his deep, grey eyes, and the pain and guilt punched the words right out of her mouth. Hastily she turned back to the sea, her spine ramrod straight. Her knuckles, clinging to the rail, were white. 'I hate boats,' she said distinctly, her voice cold and somehow terribly hollow.

Damon stared at her, his face as shocked as he felt. 'What? Why? Since when?' For all his adult life he'd never known her say such a personal or revealing thing. In fact, it was the first time he could ever remember hearing any emotion in her voice at all.

Joceline swallowed hard, and raised a hand to her head. The moment for confessions had passed. She could no more blurt out the truth now than she could fly in the air. 'Damon, not now. I have a splitting headache,' she said coolly.

Damon shook his head, exasperated. But he knew better than to try and make her talk to him. He knew his mother in this mood. Untouchable. Unreachable. Shaking his head, Damon turned and left her.

Joceline watched him go, her carefully-painted lips crumpling, her eyes filling with tears. She was not going to be able to go through with it after all. And it was not the fact that she might go to jail that stopped her. It was not even the fact that she'd be branded a murderess . . . It was the thought of the sadness she'd just seen in her son's eyes turning to . . . what? Disgust? Hate? Contempt? Yes, probably all of those things and more. Her son might not love her, and who could blame him for that? But at least he didn't hate her. Perhaps she should settle for that much. Except . . . time *might* be running out. If what her private detectives had told her about Joe King was true . . .

Jeff Doyle stepped out of the shower, dressed, and reached hastily for his amulet. He hated taking it off, but the medium who'd given it to him had told him never, ever, to get it wet, or else the protection it gave him would turn against him.

Things were beginning to happen. And happen so fast he wondered how Joe King would react on hearing the news. He checked his watch, and quickly dialled a London number into the phone. It rang only twice before it was answered. 'Yes?' The voice was curt but not disgruntled.

'Our lady, Ramona. She's just one big surprise after another. You never told me how beautiful she was. That very subfusc picture of her you had did her no just–'

'Stop babbling.' The voice was like a diamond – cold, sharp and incredibly hard. 'You've contacted her?'

'No,' Jeff admitted bluntly.

'Why not? I told you that was our first priority.'

'I know you did,' Jeff gritted, 'but you never told me she'd make a beeline for Alexander.'

'She did *what*?'

So the great man was not infallible after all, Jeff thought with a sneering smile. The great man could actually be surprised by something.

'Tell me, exactly and precisely, what you mean by that statement,' the voice said, once more its cold, precise, unnerving self, and Jeff could just picture him, swivelling in his chair, his eyes narrowed into slits.

'The first night out she didn't come out of her room, although she was booked on Alexander's table.' He began his report with the clear precision that Joe King preferred. 'I was going to approach her at the ball on the second night, but before I could do so, Alexander moved in. The next morning, she and Alexander were together again, so I followed them around Port-of-Spain, and that was no damned picnic I can tell you. I don't think they left a tourist attraction unseen . . .'

'Doyle.'

'OK, but it's relevant. After all this sightseeing crap they stopped in a very romantic park and shared a very romantic kiss. I could feel the heat from where I was. It was a scorcher. Since they were stuck together like glue after that, I gave it up as a bad job and headed back for the boat,' he lied. He had, in fact, headed for Port-of-Spain's red-light area.

There was a long, long pause from London. Then, 'You're sure about this?'

'Very. I didn't know what to make of it, so I decided to hang back and wait to hear from you.'

'You did right,' Joe King said bluntly. 'This does change things,' he added quietly. Indeed it did. The reports from the private investigator he'd hired had been thorough and exhaustive. Ramona had never met Damon Alexander before the voyage. She probably knew nothing of Keith's involvement with himself in purchasing the *Alexandria* shares. Both pieces of news had almost made him wilt with relief. But now it was obvious that Ramona was becoming involved. Now, it seemed to him, his intelligent and very capable daughter was following some plan of her own. But what? And how did it affect him? On the other end of the line, Jeff waited patiently.

'We must find out exactly what is happening. Perhaps Alexander is after her for her shares,' he mused aloud, 'or . . . think back, Doyle. Who did all the running? Alexander or my daughter?'

Jeff's brow wrinkled with thought. 'The first night, he went to her. No doubt about it. Like a homing beacon.'

'And after that?'

'I'm not sure,' Jeff said slowly. 'You're thinking that maybe our lady has designs on *him*?'

'I think,' the voice said flatly 'that we shouldn't underestimate *either* one of them.' And Joe had no intention of doing so. It was not just Ramona's obvious academic brilliance that intrigued him. Her sheer single-minded determination worried him. He was not about to underestimate her. Or Alexander.

Abruptly, he made up his mind. 'I'm coming out there,' he said, and hung up.

Doyle shrugged and walked out onto his balcony. At the deck rail below and to the right of him, he saw a woman in a lime-green trouser suit leaning against the rail and it took him only a moment to recognize her. Joceline Alexander. Yet another wild card in their little game of poker.

There was a cabaret of steelband music in the main theatre, but Verity didn't plan to go. She'd gone to the cinema in the afternoon to watch the latest American blockbuster, then played some traditional quoits up on the top deck, and missed every one of the skeets when she'd tried her hand at shooting. That was quite a full enough day for her. The last thing she wanted was to overdo things. The ship's surgeon was fully cognisant with her leukaemia, but she hadn't felt the need to check in with him yet, and the last thing she wanted to do was spend the cruise in the ship's hospital.

Now, after dining on fresh red snapper and Caesar salad, she had no intention of undoing all her relaxing work to go and sit in a packed, noisy theatre – no matter how good the band was rumoured to be.

It was nearly midnight by the time she'd finished reading her Jane Austen book, and she was no closer to sleep. She put on a light white linen jacket and headed for the top deck. There, she walked to the rail and took a deep breath of air, looking out at the breathtaking beauty all around her.

The moon was out and nearly full. A few clouds scudded across the sky, their greyish forms only accentuating the stars, which were out in force. Moonlight reflected off the waves in silvery streams of twinkling light. The bow of the *Alexandria* cut smoothly through the waves, ploughing a path and forcing white, rushing water to stream away to either side of her. There was no sound of her powerful engines, just the rushing water beneath her and the silent, moon-washed night all around her.

On the bridge, the officer of the watch straightened as the captain entered. Midwatch had just started, and he checked the log automatically. They were due to pass another cruise ship any minute. Contrary to what many passengers believed, 'the rules of the road' were generally very simple, and Greg knew he didn't have to remind any of his crew to check that the navigational running lights were operational, or that the correct colour for passing the ship on the starboard (which should be green) was already being shown. At the appropriate time a blast on the horn would also confirm their direction (one blast for starboard, two for port). Satisfied that all was well, Greg walked to the wide windows, which gave a 180-degree view all around, and nodded. It was a beautiful night. They'd make Grenada right on time. He was just about to leave and get some much-needed sleep, when a glimpse of white caught his eye. When he turned back to the window he saw a woman strolling slowly along the deck.

Greg warned the bridge crew to contact him should anything unusual occur, then stepped out into the night. He moved quickly and easily down the wide, steel staircase and onto the deck. He'd had no intention of seeking out the lone female passenger, but suddenly, there she was, and he found himself frowning. There was something very familiar about her. As Greg felt his steps begin to falter, she suddenly became aware of his presence and spun around.

'Oh. Hello,' Verity said, her voice sounding as surprised and dismayed as she felt. And yet, at the same time, she felt herself beginning to glow. Hastily, she turned a little away, resting her back against the rail and staring, with apparent fascination, at the quoits markings on the deck.

Greg smiled, in spite of his own surprise. 'You could sound a little happier to see me,' he admonished, and then wondered why she should. Then, hard on the heels of that thought, came another. Why was he so damned glad to see *her*? True, their afternoon together at the beach had been very, very nice. They'd lain in the sun and talked about anything and everything. She'd offered to share her picnic, and the wine had been deliciously cold. She was beautiful and he was attracted, but there it had ended. Or so he'd thought.

Suddenly Greg felt nervous. 'What are you doing on board?' he asked, his voice sounding far more harsh than he'd intended, and Verity flinched. He cursed quietly. 'I'm sorry. I didn't mean to sound so . . . accusing. It's just that . . . on Tobago you didn't mention you were from the *Alexandria*.'

Verity managed to shrug. 'I didn't really think you'd be interested,' she said. 'After all, you were obviously having the afternoon off, and if I'd told you I was one of your passengers, you might have felt the need to be a captain again. And you seemed so . . . I don't know. So glad to get away from it all, I didn't have the heart to put you right back in the thick of it.'

Greg smiled and shook his head. Wryly, he acknowledged she had a point. 'Thank you,' he said. 'It would have ruined the afternoon.' Verity winced at his choice of words. No doubt it was all 'ruined' now. 'I'm surprised you aren't at the cabaret,' Greg said, also feeling suddenly awkward. He was becoming aware of too many things. On the beach, Verity Fox had been a dishevelled, unknown, beautiful companion who posed no threat whatsoever. Now she was suddenly looking very groomed, still very beautiful, but a distinctly 'known' element. In one word, a passenger. And a passenger on board the *Alexandria* was as far out of his reach as the moon. And it was not only the etiquette

89

of the sea that made her so. To be on board this particular ship at all, let alone on her maiden voyage, meant that this woman must be very rich and very powerful, or knew someone who was. The thought that she might be with a man, a wife or mistress of one of the rich, arrogant, powerful men he'd come to recognize so well, made him actually want to double over. He took a deep breath and turned away sharply. As he did so, his eyes caught the lights of the other ship a mile out to one side of them. 'We're about to pass her,' he said softly and Verity turned, a look of pleasure crossing her face as she watched the liner, ablaze with lights, sailing past in the darkness.

'It's so wonderful out here,' she said, then added softly, 'You're very lucky to do what you do.'

Greg nodded. 'I know. This is where I've always wanted to be, ever since I was a boy.'

Verity nodded. 'I know. You told me,' she reminded him gently, as he looked at her sharply.

Greg sighed angrily. He'd told that waif on Tobago a whole lot of things. Things he'd never, in a million years, have told a passenger. Time to do some damage control. 'Well, I mustn't bore you any further,' he said, and smiled charmingly.

'Don't!' Verity said sharply, then shook her head as he stared at her. 'Sorry. I just don't like being talked to like . . . like . . . a customer in a shop,' she finished lamely and then jumped as the *Alexandria* let out a blast on her horn.

'It's OK,' Greg said instantly, stepping forward and taking her arms gently in his hands. 'The other ship will answer with the same signal in a moment.' Right on cue, a haunting blast came across the sea as the two liners passed each other in the night.

'Sorry,' Verity smiled. 'My nerves aren't . . . what they used to be,' she finished, her voice catching as she suddenly become aware of the tingling sensation of his hands on her arms. Suddenly she wished she weren't wearing the jacket, and that she could feel his fingers against her bare flesh. Her heart hammering, she looked up at him. The moon bathed one side of his face in pale light, turning his hair silver and his eyes a mysterious bronze, leaving the other side of his face in dark shadow.

Greg looked down into wide, midnight soft eyes and felt himself being drawn closer to her. It felt so right, so perfect that it took him a moment to realize that he was actually holding her in his arms. The shock of it rippled through him, and he abruptly let go of her and took a step back.

Verity's eyes widened. She sensed fear in that moment. Sharp and distinct, but not her own. But what could *he* possibly be afraid of?

'Well, I have to get some sleep,' Greg said, his voice sounding strained, even to his own ears. 'Docking in Grenada can be tricky . . . so I'll say goodnight, Miss Fox.'

She started to open her mouth, but the request that he call her Verity died before it had ever been uttered. She watched him turn and walk away, her eyes swimming in tears. Quickly she turned back to the rails. His withdrawal couldn't have been more obvious. And she knew she should be pleased. After all, he was doing her job for her. Ensuring they stayed stangers, keeping them both safe.

She should be glad.

But the trouble was, she wasn't glad. She wasn't glad at all.

CHAPTER 8

Grenada

Grenada lived up to its title of the island of spice, Ramona mused, as she strolled around one of St George's many outdoor markets, the pungent aroma of nutmeg, cinnamon, mace and cocoa wafting tantalizingly from huge burlap bags.

How different it all was from Oxford! Especially the heat! Gratefully, she caught a bus that would take her to Grand Anse, the most popular beach on the island. The ten minute ride, however, felt more like ten hours, due to the terror factor. When she finally got off, her head was filled with vivid memories of oncoming cars (horns blaring), and reckless overtaking on corners (on tires that she was convinced were mostly flat).

She was still laughing at herself when she stepped onto the beach. As she began to unbutton her blouse, it occurred to her that this was the first holiday she'd taken from Oxford since she'd become a Don. It was a sobering thought.

Damon, leaning against a palm trunk only a few yards away, caught his breath. He watched, mesmerized, his heart pounding as she pulled the flimsy material off her shoulders and let it fall onto the sand beside her. Although she was totally unaware of his presence, and undressed as functionally as anyone else might, it affected him as strongly as the most seasoned of strip-teases. When he swallowed, his throat was bone-dry.

Ramona untied the strings of her yellow wrap-around skirt and felt it fall to her feet. Quickly, she kicked off her sandals and headed for the surf. The elegant loose-limbed grace with which she moved and the long, silky curtain of silver-gold hair rippling over her shoulders and back, drew every male eye around. Damon noticed two young men of the dark-haired beach Lothario type zero in on her from different directions, and quickly shucked his own clothes to follow her in. He'd hired a car right after disembarking, and had been following her shamelessly ever since. He saw no reason to break the habit now.

Ramona neatly duck-dived into a swell, swam under-water for a few yards, then turned right, to stay parallel with the beach. Consequently, when she at last came up for air, she was a long way from where Damon expected her to be. But when she surfaced, she was not alone. On either side of her were the seal-dark heads of two young men. Used to teaching students of that age, Ramona was not worried. Not at first.

''Allo, pretty lady,' one of the boys said, showing a row of gleaming white teeth.

'Hello,' she nodded back, prepared to be polite.

'You come in on the big British ship, yes?' the other one asked, his eyes flashing as they glanced down her cleavage.

Ramona began to feel a bit uneasy. She had some money on her, wrapped in a plastic bag and tucked into her bikini bottom. Nervously, she took a quick look around. It was a working day for the native Grenadians, and only a few tourists littered the beach in depressingly far-away groups.

'Your first time on the island, yes?' one of the boys said. 'I am Phillipe. And my ugly friend over there is Jean-Paul.'

'Look who he calls ugly,' his friend guffawed, splashing his friend in the face, and for a second or two, Ramona began to relax again. They were just boys, after all, enjoying some high spirits. But Jean-Paul's next words put the worry right back into her. 'You want a good time on Grenada, yes?'

Ramona began to feel annoyed. 'Of course. Who doesn't? But I have my day all planned,' she lied and began to move away in a cautious crawl. She felt like a cat surrounded by two dogs. As she'd guessed, they swam after her, easily keeping up.

'Oh, but it is no fun to be alone,' Phillipe pouted. 'Jean-Paul and I know all the best spots in town. All the best hotels . . .' He let his voice trail off knowingly.

Ramona felt her face flame as she finally twigged. They were gigolos! 'Look, why don't you boys try somewhere else, hmm?' she suggested, her voice both firm and a little nervous.

'An excellent idea,' a deep voice agreed loudly, and all three of them jumped. The two young men faced off Damon for a moment or two, but after one long look from the steely eyes, they quickly shrugged and headed back for the shore.

Ramona, now that the potentially nasty incident was over with, laughed. 'I thought you were going to challenge them to a duel next. Honestly, they were only boys.'

'Boys with a habit,' Damon said grimly, then glanced at her. 'Didn't you notice their arms?'

Ramona paled and shook her head. 'No. No, I can't say as I did. Even paradise has its serpents,' she murmured, and shuddered. 'I thought they were only after . . .' She stopped abruptly, and blushed.

Damon saw the blush, and couldn't help but laugh. 'They probably were "only after",' he agreed. 'Let's head back for the beach. You're not safe to be let out on your own.'

Once on the sand, Ramona reached for her towel. 'Bit of a coincidence, you turning up like a white knight just when the damsel got into distress, wasn't it?' she asked casually, flicking back her long, dripping strands of wet hair, unaware that the gesture thrust her breasts forward.

Damon swallowed hard, then grinned. 'Is it?' He managed a wonderfully careless shrug.

Ramona gave him a long, level look, then turned and walked to one of showers set up along beach. She let the clean water saturate and cleanse her hair and bikini, then stepped back out into the sun. As she did so she noticed Damon at the next shower, doing the same. As he lifted his hands to run them through his hair, she noticed the way his muscles rippled under his skin, and she felt her breath catch. A solid wave of desire hit her, making her nipples tighten into a pleasingly painful ache, and a molten moisture erupt low in her abdomen. At that precise moment, Damon turned. For a long moment they stared at each other. Then, without a word, he turned off the spray and began to walk towards her. His eyes were darker than she could ever remember them, his face taut with an answering desire.

Quickly she turned and walked back to her bag, and pulled her top and skirt back on over her bikini. Damon watched her, his fists clenching and unclenching by his sides. If she had been anyone else, he thought savagely, they would be checking into the nearest hotel to enjoy a morning of long, satisfying love-making. But, when she turned eyes on him that were at once pleading for understanding and at the same time flashing warning electric-blue fire at him, he knew he would have to be very careful, if he wasn't to frighten her away.

'So, what now?' he asked, his voice just a little rough.

'Whatever I want,' Ramona snapped back, quickly.

'Can't you just relax for once, like any normal person would?' he asked, half exasperated, half curious to hear how she would react to his question.

In response, she turned and glanced at him over one shoulder, the gesturely supremely provocative and completely guileless. 'Whoever said I was a normal person?' Ramona asked bleakly, smiled somewhat sadly, and turned away.

Damon nodded, very slightly. In those few words, and in that very telling smile, she had revealed more to him of her personality than she could ever have guessed.

What's more, he'd heard back from his investigators in England, who'd assured him that that was no evidence whatsoever that Ramona King and her father had ever met. Joe King had left the marital home less than a week after her birth, and had never been back. They'd found no photographs, no society clips, no hearsay, to confirm that Joe King had ever kept track of his only child. They'd also told him that Barbara King's maiden name was Murray. Was it possible she preferred to use the name Murray, and that she was not in league with her father after all? He could almost believe it. Except for Treadstone, and 5 per cent of the *Alexandria*. The 5 per cent that was now hers . . .

The mystery only made him more determined than ever to win her trust. To know her every secret. To become her lover. To carve a place for himself in her life, no matter what it took or however painful it might prove to be for both of them.

When she looked up and found him holding out his hand to her, she took it automatically, and without a thought. And Damon's quest had begun. 'Where to now?' she asked, taking it for granted they would be spending the rest of the day together. His fingers felt warm against her hand, and not even she could possibly misinterpret the look in his eyes as he kept glancing over at her.

'How about we explore the Levara National Bird Sanctuary?' he offered, his mind still stubbornly picturing a quiet hotel room, and a big, big bed. Just what was it about her that made him feel so damned young and in love? Abruptly he pulled in a large gulp of air. Steady there, he thought shakily.

'If we have to go by bus, do you mind if I make out a will first?' she asked, and suddenly they were both laughing.

'No need. *I* had the sense to hire a car.'

'Well bully for you, cleverclogs.'

The sanctuary turned out to be at the northern tip of the island, where the Caribbean met the Atlantic. The first of the Grenadines was visible in the distance, but a thick fringing of mangroves made it ideal as a sanctuary for birds.

'No wonder you chose these islands for the *Alexandria*'s maiden voyage,' she said casually. 'But I dare say the board of directors had to agree with it?' she probed, wanting to know just how much power the board had. If the worst came to the worst, and she found herself taking on Damon Alexander as an adversary, she wanted to know just how much support he commanded in his own company.

Damon laughed at the thought of the board dictating anything to him. 'Not really. The only man who's opinion means anything to me is Ralph Ornsgood's.'

Ramona nodded. She'd read all about the indispensible Swede. She'd have to meet Mr Ornsgood. He might be able to give her some interesting insight into the inner workings of the Alexander Line. 'So you tell the board to go to hell, do you?' she asked, her pulse rate beginning to rise.

'More often than not,' he admitted, wondering, exactly, what information she was angling for. His eyes became wary, but when she looked up at him, he was smiling easily.

'So you feel safe, then?' she asked, her heart soaring in sudden hope. If Damon was *that* confident of himself and his position, perhaps he wasn't behind Keith buying the extra shares after all. In which case . . .

'You're never safe in business, Ramona,' he said quietly, and stopped. Suddenly, she realized that they were now deep in the trees, off the path and hidden from sight. Slowly, Damon took her chin in his palm and tilted her head up. 'There's always someone out there trying to take away what's yours,' he said, his voice cold now, and hard.

Her heart plummeted. 'So what do you do?' she asked, her voice cracking just slightly. Suddenly she could sense the ruthless businessman in him and she shuddered.

'You make damned sure nobody gets what's yours,' Damon said. 'If someone is out to get you, you make sure you get him first.' Like your father, he added silently, bitterly.

Ramona felt her breath wither out of her. She should have known that a man as clever as Damon Alexander was bound to have an ace up his sleeve to ensure the *Alexandria* remained his. Namely, more stock under another name, just in case he should need it in a proxy fight or takeover bid. But Keith had ruined it all by killing himself and leaving her the shares. But why?

As she looked up at him she saw his eyes darken. Some powerful emotion she couldn't name swept across his face. Her heart began to pound as he pulled her into his arms.

'You're becoming very important to me, Ramona. You know that, don't you?' he said softly.

Her heart did a gleeful sommersault at the same moment that her brain kicked into overdrive. 'You're never safe,' he'd said. And he was right. He certainly wasn't safe – not from her. Not now she was becoming convinced he was somehow responsible for her fiancé's death. She wondered what he'd do if he knew that she had a handy amount of shares in his precious ship. Or, a suspicious little voice said, perhaps he knew already? Ramona felt a jolt of shock run through her. Perhaps he'd known all along who she was, and all this time, when she'd thought she'd been hunting *him*, he'd actually been hunting *her*.

But then he was kissing her, and it suddenly, terrifyingly, ceased to matter. Ramona gasped under his lips as her body melted around him. She felt herself leaning into him, her breasts crushed against his, her legs turning to jelly where her thighs and knees brushed his. Dimly she was aware that her arms had somehow got curled around his neck and her head was going back, back, back, against the powerful force of his kiss. The molten heat had returned and seemed to be flooding her insides. She moaned. There was no other description for the wanton sound that escaped her lips as he slowly lifted his mouth from hers. Her eyes snapped open. When had she shut them? She couldn't remember. Suddenly the steel in his eyes was melting all around them, and when he lowered his head, this time to nibble on her throat, his tongue following the curve of her neck, she moaned again, louder this time. Suddenly she was moving backwards and then her shoulders were pressed up against something solid. Unknown to her, they had reached the site of some Arawak ruins, and she was leaning against an ancient stone. Once, Dr R. M. King might have felt her academic soul stir at the sight of the fine Indian ruins, but the woman now in Damon Alexander's arms couldn't give a fig.

She gasped as his lips moved from her throat to her ears, and his breathing magnified against her sensitive eardrums. Her heart began to pound and when his hand moved down and cupped her breast through the thin cotton top, her knees gave out. Luckily she was pinned between the rock and the solid wall of his chest, otherwise she would have crumpled. She gasped as she felt his fingers tweak her nipples, intensifying the ache deep inside them until she felt like screaming. She wanted his lips on those buttons of flesh. She wanted . . . she wanted . . . She just *wanted!* Ramona shook her head, forcing him to abandon her ears and nip the side of her neck. She drew in a deep, shaky breath and felt her hands on his back. His flesh felt smooth beneath her hands, and unbelievably hot.

If she didn't do something soon, they would both burn.

Shakily she got one hand between them and pushed weakly against his chest. Reluctantly, so reluctantly it was frightening, he pulled away. A line of red lay high across his cheekbones, and his eyes had darkened to the colour of old pewter. They were both breathing heavily. Damon took another step back. She looked so beautiful, leaning against the ancient stone, her hair breeze-dried and swirled around her, her nipples thrusting against the cotton, her long, lovely legs, bent at the knee.

'I'm sorry,' he said, then knew immediately that he wasn't. Not sorry at all. He'd been wanting to do that ever since that first night he'd seen her.

Ramona drew in another shaky breath. 'Forget it,' she said, and knew that she herself never would. Not for as long as she lived. It was terrifying to be affected so overwhelmingly by a man who was now, without doubt, her enemy.

Shakily, she scrambled to her feet, and by mutual consent, they went back to his car to play tourist again, taking snapshots of the Concord Falls, then going on to the Grand Etang National Park. Afterwards, they drove out to the district of L'Anse aux Epines, where they dined in style at the Calabash, enthusing over the Jab Jabs, pork coated in a black tamarind glaze.

Later they returned to the beach, to watch the perfect sunset. But as he took in his arms and slowly, tenderly kissed her, Ramona knew only two things.

She wanted him.

And she wanted him to pay.

CHAPTER 9

Verity opened her eyes and yawned. They were at sea again, her favourite time. She loved the sense of elegant movement, and the inaudible power of the mighty ship's engines. It gave her a wonderful sense of peace, mixed with excitement.

She pushed aside the covers, anxious to rise and breakfast, and see what the day had in store. But as soon as she got up and took a step forward, a wave of dizziness hit her that had nothing to do with the ship's motion. Reaching for her watch on the pretty carved bedside table, she took her pulse. Carefully, she walked into her bathroom and went straight to the mirror, where she checked her pupils, her tongue, throat and neck glands. She sighed deeply.

Back in her bedroom, she picked up the Daily Programme and idly ran her eye over the seemingly never-ending list of activities. She dialled room service and ordered a cup of coffee, some fresh pineapple juice, half a grapefruit and a round of toast with apricot jam. Whilst she usually breakfasted in one of the many restaurants on board, liking the convivial atmosphere and the spectacle of food that was so much a part of ship life, she had to admit that her confidence had taken a nose-dive. She also had to admit the time had come to see the ship's surgeon.

Ramona King was in her cabin, re-reading her research notes. There was an obvious rift between Damon Alexander and his board. The board feared that the new ship was bound to over-extend company borrowing, leaving them vulnerable to takeover. He'd beaten them down by the simple expedient of putting all his own personal money into it, to ensure that he owned just over 40 per cent of the new ship. And, no doubt, he'd watched the share flotation with an eagle eye, to ensure that no one investor amassed more than a small percentage.

And as the biggest shareholder, he'd be getting the biggest share of the profits. No doubt he intended to go on raking in huge piles of money, and who was to stop him? The *Alexandria* was obviously a huge success. Already everybody she'd spoken too had said they'd be back for another cruise soon. Word of mouth alone would ensure that the *Alexandria* was *the* ship for the elite for decades to come.

But if she knew Damon, and she was sure she did, he wouldn't be satisfied with just that. He'd have to capitalize on it. Build or buy more huge ships to add to his fleet and his empire. The question was, what could she do about it? She had to stop him, that much she owed Keith. He just couldn't be allowed to crush people and get away with it.

But, a little voice insisted, deep inside, Keith was not the only reason for her outrage. Hadn't her own mother said she knew nothing about life? And hadn't Damon Alexander made her feel more alive in the past few days than she'd felt for the last eight years at Oxford? And wasn't that scaring her?

Dammit, yes. Ramona almost smashed her fist against the table in frustration. She hated him! She detested this damned ship, and these beautiful, exotic, alluring places it was taking her to, forcing her to confront the emptiness that had been her life until now. She hated him for it. And . . . something else. She felt something else that was even more terrifying. Something so deep, so dangerous, that it made her only more and more determined, more and more obsessed with bringing him down. And that had nothing to do with Keith, but more to do with self-survival . . .

Slowly, forcing herself to relax, she leaned back in her chair and took a long, deep breath. OK, so she was out of her depth with Damon. OK, so this cruise was turning into a voyage of self-discovery as well as of the Caribbean sea. But that didn't really *change* anything. She still had a job to do. It only made the stakes that much higher . . .

Determinedly, she turned back to the paperwork, and acknowledged angrily that she would need help. She needed someone who knew the cruise ship business inside and out. In short, she needed a partner, and moreover, someone with a lot of shares in the *Alexandria* as well. Perhaps, if she could rally enough investors, she might be able to organize a takeover of her own? To take away Damon's pride and joy would surely be a step in the right direction.

Quickly, she checked the passenger manifesto, and wrote out a list of investors who owned at least 1 per cent. She decided to start with Gareth Desmond, a man who had even more shares than herself. Carefully and thoughtfully, Ramona put away the papers and locked them in her briefcase, then glanced at her watch. She had work to do.

Joceline Alexander chose a lounger that didn't catch the slight breeze toying with the promenade deck, and sat far away from the pool. Consequently, it was quiet and bakingly hot. Settling back down, she lifted her face to the sun, sighed and slowly closed her eyes. It was a mistake.

Instantly she was back to that night nearly twenty-five years ago. So long ago, and yet she could recall every detail as if it had been only yesterday. The look of hate and rage in Michael's eyes. Her own fear . . . the terrible, blinding, helpless fear. The violence. She shuddered. Oh, dear God, the *violence* . . . Quickly she snapped her eyes open again, but although the scene faded, chased out by the bright and cheerful Caribbean sunlight, the feelings stayed.

The guilt. The pain. The fear. The betrayal.

Wordlessly she sat up, bowing her head, one lone tear running down her wrinkled cheek. At that moment, Verity reached the top of the stairs and stepped out onto the promenade deck. She'd called the ship's surgeon before leaving her cabin and he was expecting her in half an hour. Before that, however, she wanted a dose of the Caribbean, and she walked to the rails to take a few, deep breaths. Everywhere she looked was ocean. Grenada was left far behind and the next stop was somewhere on the horizon. Gulls followed the ship hopefully, and alongside the bows, dolphins raced and played in the ship's wake.

Then she turned and froze.

Lying on a sun lounger not a foot away, was a woman. She was leaning forward with her head bowed, grey hair hiding her face, but Verity knew instantly who it was, and her whole body turned cold. She turned away quickly, wanting only to be somewhere else, but her sudden movement had Joceline's head snapping up. Verity's head spun at the unexpected surge of emotion that hit her like a tidal wave, and she swayed precariously for a moment. Helplessly, the two women stared at one another. Finally, Joceline felt the tears on her face and brushed them away frantically. 'Hello, Verity,' she said, her voice cool and composed.

'Hello, Mrs Alexander.'

Joceline smiled. 'I think you're old enough now to call me Joceline, don't you?'

Verity blinked. She wasn't sure why, but there was something in the older woman's smile that made her feel sorry for her. Which was ridiculous. The last thing she could see Joceline Alexander wanting or tolerating, was pity.

'Alright . . . Joceline,' she said reluctantly. She glanced at the stairway. Could she possibly just walk away?

'Are you enjoying the cruise, Verity?' Joceline asked politely, her throat dry. 'I must say, I was surprised to see you aboard,' she added wryly. Which was something of an understatement. 'How is dear Winnie nowadays?'

'Mother's fine,' Verity said restlessly. Winnie and Joceline had gone to the same school together, and later to Cheltenham Ladies College. When they'd married and had children, they had each been godparents to the other's offspring, and in the early years at least, Winnie and Verity had spent a lot of their summer holidays with Joceline at the Alexander country estate in the Cotswolds. Damon had been ten, Verity six, when she'd tried to ride 'Ironsides', Damon's pony, and had fallen off. Damon had carried her all the way back to the house, and they'd been inseparable for the rest of the holidays.

But later, after that one, awful night, Verity had screamed and cried, and begged her mother not to take her back to the Alexanders ever again. And although Winnie had been puzzled and hurt, and tried to get her hysterical six-year-old daughter to tell her what had happened, Verity never had.

'I'll have to find Damon and catch up on old times,' she said stiffly now, and began to sidle desperately towards the stairs. Joceline took her wrist in a firm grip.

'Verity, please, I need to talk – '

Verity felt instant fear rise in her chest, a fear that belonged to a terrified six-year-old who didn't understand what was happening, and she gave a small cry of alarm.

Joceline's jaw fell open in surprise. Then she saw the terror in the younger woman's eyes and felt sick. Quickly she let go, as if Verity's hand had turned to fire. 'I'm sorry,' she said, moving back on the lounger, her eyes pleading. 'I'm really sorry, I never meant to . . . frighten you.'

Verity took a deep, shaken breath. 'I'm sorry,' she said huskily. 'I don't know why I did that,' she added lamely, and promptly wished she hadn't. For they both knew exactly why.

'That's alright,' Joceline said quickly, wishing now that she'd left well enough alone. Quickly she donned her sunglasses, needing to hide behind something. Coolly, she turned her head away. The dismissal was unmistakable.

Wordlessly, Verity turned and headed for the stairs. But as she did so, she suddenly realized that she was no longer afraid of Joceline Alexander. Somehow, in those few brief moments, Joceline had ceased to be the monster of her six-year-old nightmares and became instead just another woman. A human being, prey to a human being's frailties and weaknesses.

Ramona approached the second man on her list, a New York banker, relieved to see that the sun lounger next to him was free. He was forty-eight, and a top executive in New York's Breaker Manhattan Bank. And he owned 3 per cent of the *Alexandria*.

'Hi there,' he said, slowly taking off his sunglasses. The effect, Ramona supposed, was meant to make her appreciate the blueness of his eyes, so she smiled as if she was duly impressed. 'Hello. Ramona King,' she held out her hand, and he all but fell over himself to take it. She was wearing a simple white one-piece swimsuit with a long, see-through lounge jacket over it.

Dwight J. Markham III had never seen a more beautiful woman. 'Can I get you a drink?'

Ramona asked for fresh lime juice with lots of ice and waited until her drink had been delivered before stretching out on the lounger beside him. 'Well, Mr Markham, it seems we have a lot in common,' she said, and saw his smile widen.

'We sure do,' he drawled, looking at the length of her legs and then hastily dragging his eyes back to her face. Up close, her eyes were a fantastic silvery blue . . .

'Yes, we do,' Ramona said. 'We both own a share of this ship, for a start . . .'

Greg was half-way through his daily inspection, and stopped the lift one floor below the games deck. The hospital had deliberately been located here, since most injuries were going to occur as a result of sporting accidents.

Greg, like most men, felt uncomfortable in the antiseptic surroundings, but he had to admire the efficiency of the clinic. There was a dentist's surgery, an operating theatre, an X-ray room, an isolation unit, and sixteen cabins for the patients. He nodded to the nurse on duty, and was about to ask if there was anything he needed to know when the door to the surgery opened.

Verity stopped dead at the unexpected sight of him,

her eyes running hungrily over his tall, vital frame. Dr John Gardner, the fifty-eight-year-old eminent ship's surgeon, nearly cannoned into the back of her. He looked over her shoulder and smiled.

'Oh, hello, Captain. Doing your daily rounds then?' Gently he put his hands on Verity's shoulders, sensing her unease. Gently he steered her away from the captain. 'Don't worry about a thing, Verity,' he said quietly. 'Sea sickness affects us all from time to time,' he added, knowing instinctively that she wanted no one to be aware of her condition. She gave him a quick, grateful smile, silently thanking him for him understanding and hurried away. Greg watched her go, only then realizing they'd not spoken a word to each other.

'Captain?' John said, once more business-like, and Greg quickly pulled himself together and followed the doctor inside. He watched as the ship's surgeon put away the blood-pressure equipment.

'I've never seen you use that on seasick patients, John,' Greg said softly, and watched the older man stiffen.

'I don't. I had it out to check it was in working order. Now, has Hannah filled you in on the latest mishaps?'

Greg didn't reply. Instead his eyes fell on a small tube of blood set in a small rack. He didn't know much about medicine, but he knew phials of blood samples were never kept around in the surgery. They always went straight to the ship's lab. That meant the blood had only just been taken. That it was Verity's.

Greg felt his insides tighten. 'John. Miss Fox . . .' he

began, but the doctor sensed where he was heading, and quickly cut him off.

'Captain, Dr Fox came to me for treatment, and that's what I gave her. Now, if there's nothing . . .'

Greg blinked. 'She's a doctor? Of medicine?'

John nodded, but remained stubbornly silent.

'Is it standard practice to take blood samples from seasick patients, John?' Greg asked, unwilling to let it go.

John Gardner stiffened. 'You're the captain of this ship, Greg . . .'

'Yes I am,' Greg interrupted, his voice firm. 'And I need to be kept fully informed of any . . .'

'But I am the ship's surgeon,' John cut in, equally firm. 'And consultations with me, as with any other doctor, are strictly confidential. You know that.'

For a second the two men stared each other out. Then, slowly, Greg nodded. 'You're right. Forget I asked.'

John smiled. 'Already forgotten,' he said, relieved. Like the rest of the crew, John liked and respected Greg Harding. He was an exceptionally fine and able captain, and it was not like him to make the mistake of . . .

Quickly, John looked again at his captain. Greg's face was stiff and pale, and there was an unmistakable look of fear in his eyes. Oh, it was well hidden, but John was a doctor with many years of experience. 'You know Dr Fox well, Greg?' he asked casually.

Greg shook his head. 'No. I've only just met her,' he said absently, then, as if aware of danger, suddenly snapped his eyes back to the doctor. 'She's just a passenger, Dr Gardner. That's all,' he added, his voice coldly forbidding.

John nodded. 'I hope so, Greg,' he said gently, holding the captain's eye with a level glance. 'I really do hope so.'

Greg paled. Were his feelings so damned obvious? He nodded once to John, then strode out of the hospital without a word of goodbye for the nurse, who watched him go. She looked surprised. In the doorway, John Gardner too, watched him go.

He looked worried.

CHAPTER 10

Barbados

Barbados had one of the most stable governments in the Caribbean, and as Ramona and Damon wandered around Bridgetown, its capital, she could see at once that the difference between the have's and have-not's was not nearly as obvious as on the other islands.

They were right in the centre of the town, overlooking the picturesque harbour, known as the Careenage. As they continued walking, Ramona cast a quick glance at him. 'You look distracted, today,' she said quietly, and felt his hand on hers tighten, fractionally.

'I suppose I am. It suddenly occurred to me how little I know about you.' He glanced at her, amused. How would she cope with that little bombshell?

Ramona shrugged. 'There's not much to know. I've led a very boring life.' And it depressed her, suddenly, to realize just how true that was.

'That, I find hard to believe. A woman as beautiful as you?' he gently mocked.

Ramona shrugged. 'It's a fallacy that blondes have more fun,' she said with asperity. 'I've spent most of my life in the pursuit of knowledge. And now I find I know next to nothing.'

Damon grinned. 'Poor thing. And men are a total mystery too, I suppose?'

Ramona frowned and cast a quick look at him. Just what was he getting at? 'In many ways, I suppose so. My fiancé and I were together for many years. There was no one else but him,' she found herself confessing, and then could have kicked herself. Whatever he was angling for, it could hardly be information about her love life. Or lack thereof. 'But he . . . died recently,' she finished quietly.

Damon took a swift breath. Treadstone! He'd forgotten he had been her fiancé. Now, the thought of some other man knowing her, and for so many years, made him angry. Or rather, he thought grimly, jealous. And the fact that he was jealous of a dead man showed him just how deep in he was.

'I'm sorry,' he said softly. They'd moved on from Trafalgar Square to the war memorial and the three dolphin fountain. Now, he stood watching it in silence for a while. 'And there's been no one since . . .?' he asked gently, turning to face her, wanting to look in her eyes.

Ramona shook her head. 'No one before and no one since,' she admitted, staring at the water and horses.

'You're still grieving?' he said quietly, his eyes thoughtful. That had not occurred to him before.

But Ramona shook her head. 'No. No, that's over,' she said, surprised at the truth of it. And in a blinding flash, she knew just why it was true. She'd never loved

Keith. Oh, she'd cared for him, deeply. And needed him, in an odd sort of way. But she'd never loved him. And, she could face it now, Keith had never loved her, either.

Damon took one look at her ashen face and wide, haunted eyes, and took her gently into his arms. For a second she resisted, but then she allowed herself to lean on him. After a long, long, while, she drew back and gave him a shaky smile.

'What say we give Broad Street a miss, hmm?' he asked, since neither of them were in the mood for shopping. Eagerly she nodded, and instead they hopped aboard a tour bus, determinedly lightening the mood.

The tour took them past all the sights, including the House of Assembly and Parliament buildings, which turned out to be a collection of oddly out of place Victorian Gothic structures. They opted to get off at Queen's Park, home to some of the island's largest trees.

'They're magnificent,' Ramona murmured, staring up at the trees around her.

'You should know,' Damon replied, his voice dry. 'You're magnificent yourself.' He looked her over, unable to deny the punch of desire that the sight of her caused. She was wearing a simple silvery-green light silk dress, that left her arms bare. Her hair was caught back in a pony-tail, emphasizing the tenderness of her temples, and the clean, beautiful lines of her face. And suddenly he knew that he was in much, much deeper than he'd ever thought. *Too* deep. He had to get out. And quickly, before it was too late.

'The way you lie is nothing short of brilliant,' he said suddenly, harshly, and watched her head snap around, her lovely eyes widening.

'Sorry?' Ramona said, her heart thundering in her chest. Suddenly she was on quicksand, and she had no idea how she'd wandered into it without seeing the signs.

'I'm talking about your magnificent game plan, Dr King,' Damon said grimly. Now that he'd started, there was no going back. He had to cut her out of his heart with the sharpest scalpel he had, and damn the pain.

'I haven't got the faintest idea what you're talking about,' she said lamely.

'No? I think it's a little too late to play the innocent now, don't you? *Dr King*,' he added. 'I've enjoyed the game, while it lasted, but it's beginning to wear a little thin.' He smiled wolfishly down at her, his eyes like flint. Only a tiny nerve, ticking in his jaw, gave him away.

Ramona realized two things at once. That the look in his eyes hurt her to the quick, and that she had to do something quickly. 'You say my name as if it should mean something,' she said, lifting one eyebrow questioningly.

'And it shouldn't?' he asked, his voice like raw steel.

She looked him straight in the eye. 'I can't see what,' she said bluntly.

'Then why introduce yourself as Ramona Murray?' Damon pounced.

Ramona lifted one shoulder and one corner of her

mouth, in a wonderfully nonchalant gesture of amused exasperation. 'Because that's my name. Or rather, the name I use whenever I'm not playing the Oxford Don.' She looked into his disbelieving eyes, and sighed. 'Let me tell you something about Oxford, Damon,' she said quietly, and took his arm. At first she felt his resistance, but then, slowly, they began to walk through the palms, his head angled down to catch every word she said.

'It's a wonderful place in many ways, but exhausting in others. And the back-biting that goes on is something you just wouldn't believe.' She glanced up at him to see if he was still with her. He was. She could see the interest stir behind the ready-to-kill look in his eyes. 'Oxford is no ordinary university – it's the best in the world. And when I'm there, I'm very much Dr King, B. A., M. A., D. Phil., and all the rest. I'm the author of much-vaunted textbooks. I've gone to Radcliffe and Harvard to lecture. I've taught politically active students from China, princesses from Arabia, Right Hon's. from some of England's finest houses. All as Dr R. M. King . . .' she trailed off, unaware of the unmistakable weariness in her voice.

Damon found himself, very much against his will, believing that she meant every word she said. 'Go on,' he said briefly, not sure he liked where all this was going. He'd started all this in an effort to push her away. Not understand more about her. And yet, he wanted to know. He *needed* to know.

Ramona had no choice but to carry on to the bitter end. He was forcing her to face up to facts she'd never wanted to acknowledge before. What was it about this man that he could unlock the deepest, darkest secrets of her soul?

'At Oxford I have to be Dr R. M. King all the time,' she said simply. 'I can't let the mask slip. One hint of academic hesitancy, and the knife goes in. There are always research Fellows who want to be fully-fledged Dons. Always graduates who are trying to disprove some of my theses in the books I've written. Always someone, wanting to bring you down.'

She stopped for a moment, unaware of how large her eyes had grown, or the trapped look that had appeared within them.

She looked at him, so vibrant and alive and desirable. And she wanted to touch him. No, she wanted more than that. She wanted to rip the damned shirt of his back and rake her nails across his skin. She wanted to see his lips fall open and hear him moan with the desire that she wanted to plant in him, like a Judas seed. But most of all, she wanted to make him pay for making her want to do all those things. Shakily, she took a deep, calming breath, pushing the ridiculous thoughts away. She simply had to concentrate on winning his trust again. It was vital she did so. 'So, you see, whenever I can get away from all that, I become Ramona Murray,' she explained, the lie slipping off her tongue like honeyed acid. 'Just in case there's an ex-student on board the *Alexandria*. Or an academic from Oxford now living in Barbados, eager to talk shop. You'd be surprised how many Oxonians there are, scattered around the globe. The last thing I want to do is spend my holiday discussing Oxford! Can you understand that?'

Damon looked down at her, his mind racing. He wanted to believe her. He wanted to so badly it was frightening. 'All very plausible,' he said, forcing sarcasm into his voice. 'But why didn't you tell me about the shares?'

Ramona rocked under the second assault. He knew about those too? She already felt battle-weary. Trying to best him was absolutely exhausting. He was so damned sharp. So damned . . . sexy.

'The *Alexandria* shares you mean?' she asked, dragging her mind back to what was important. 'I don't know if I can explain that any better. I don't know why Keith bought so many. But he was the stockbroker, after all. I suppose he thought you made for a good investment,' she said, and this time it was her turn to watch him with eagle eyes.

But she saw no guilt in them, just a sudden look of unmistakable jealousy. She felt a vicious, victorious stab of pleasure at this evidence of his feelings, quickly followed by a frisson of shock. She had no damned business being so pleased. Keith, poor Keith was dead. And, dammit, Damon *must* be made to pay, a desperate voice screamed at her. He must . . . 'I had no idea he'd bought so many shares until . . . his will was read out,' she continued.

Slowly they made their way out of the park. She looked and felt utterly drained. Holding her hand, Damon wanted to comfort her and shake her at the same time. He'd wanted them to split. To drive a wedge between them that would keep him safe from her, and from his own feelings, for good. Instead he was more intrigued by her than ever.

They took the first bus to stop, sitting in silence for a while, both needing a breathing space. Ramona stared out of the window at the passing countryside, then said softly, 'Keith killed himself. And I still don't know why.'

But she did know why. Now. He'd done it because someone had driven him to it. And she had to remember that. *Always*. She turned and looked at him, unaware that her eyes were swimming with unshead tears. 'I took a sabbatical and decided to take the *Alexandria*'s maiden cruise. Oh, I don't know,' she sighed, and looked back out the window. 'I thought this would make me understand, somehow, why he did it.'

She felt her hand being lifted from her lap, and a long, strong finger turned her chin to face him. 'You really don't know what it's all about?' he asked quietly, a strange look of defeat in his eyes.

She shook her head. 'No. That's why I asked you so many questions about everything.'

Damon sighed helplessly. 'Tell me about your father, Ramona,' he said quietly, looking deeply into her eyes. And his heart soared, for it was impossible to miss or mistake the genuine puzzlement that flickered across her electric-blue gaze.

'My father? Joe King?'

'You have another?' he asked teasingly. Nevertheless, he waited, tense as a bow-string once more. What she said next would make all the difference in the world . . . all the difference in his *life*.

Ramona shook her head, frowning, genuinely non-plussed. 'There's not much I can tell you. He left Mother and me when I was just a baby. Why the interest in him?' Suddenly she recalled that his own father, Michael, had beaten her father in business all those years ago. But what the hell did that have to do with anything now? The puzzled frown on her face owed nothing to acting, and again Damon found himself believing her. He sighed in heartfelt relief and slumped back in his seat, utterly spent. They were both surprised when the bus started to empty around them. 'We're here,' she said automatically.

'Here' turned out to be the Flower Forest off Highway Two. As they stepped down from the bus and followed a small crocodile of people into the eight acres of flowering fragrant bushes, Ramona was relieved when his hand slipped back into hers.

Instantly, the day became somehow perfect. The bushes of pungent fragrance were all new to her, and totally beautiful. Damon pointed out the ones he recognized – the canna, ginger lilies and puffball trees. The view of Mount Hillaby was breathtaking. In a deserted thicket, slowly, gently, Damon pulled her into his arms. He hesitated, expecting at any moment a wave of caution and suspicion to flood over him, but no such feelings came. It felt natural, and good, and right. Her eyes were wide and blue and hopeful, and as he lowered his head he saw her lips part in a gasp of expectation. Then he was kissing her, and thoughts of shares, of schemes, of the *Alexandria*, faded. For both of them. Ramona felt herself being lowered to the

123

ground, which was soft and springy with moss. They had moved off the path for a better view of the mountain, and now she could sense the bushes around them, screening them from view and providing a natural bower for lovers. She felt his hand slide over her bare arms, then smooth down over her hips to caress her bare calf. She moaned beneath his lips and felt her legs move open of their own accord, a throbbing weakness pulsing in her blood. Her body was on fire wherever his hand touched her, and alien, wonderful sparks errupted in her bloodstream. Damon felt her smooth skin shiver delicately under his fingertips, and he slid his hand upwards, to the soft white skin of her inner thigh. He released her lips from his own and buried his mouth in her neck, nibbling and teasing, before going lower. Against the cool silk of her dress he kissed her nipples, the buttons of flesh burgeoning beneath the material, making her moan in desire. He licked them and the silk become cool with his saliva, clinging to her flesh, the hot darting tip of his tongue making her head thrash from side to side in heedless pleasure. But it was more than just her body that responded to him. She felt herself opening up, like a flower in its very first dawn, petals opening to the unknown, but wonderful rays of the warming sun. She wanted to cry, and at the same time scream aloud her joy.

'Damon,' she said his name, her voice thick and unheeding. When his hand moved across her thigh to cup her womanly mound, her back arched off the ground, her eyes closing out the vista of sky and bright pink and purple blooms. Instantly her world narrowed to his tongue on her breast and his hand on the centre of her throbbing, needy passion. With one finger he began to delicately and remorselessly rub the burgeoning nub of her clitoris, the totally new sensation making her gasp out loud. He was the expert, she the novice, but somehow it didn't matter. They came together like the two halves of a coin. 'Damon,' she said again, not sure what she wanted to ask. His mouth covered hers passionately as his finger began to move more quickly and firmly, and she felt her whole body moving in time to his stroking. A tightness was spiralling ever outwards in her stomach, and her legs thrashed helplessly against the grass.

He lifted his head. 'Open your eyes,' he demanded, his voice coming in pants, and she obeyed thought-lessly.

He watched her eyes as he stroked her, their electric blue sparks turning to silver as she began to writhe. A look of surprise, almost of fear, darkened her eyes as she sensed the coming explosion, and her lips fell open in surprise. She stared at him, loving the tightness of his jaw, the dark, brooding passion in his eyes, and she wanted suddenly to have him inside her, filling her, driving her on and on . . .

'Damon,' she cried out one last time, his name both a curse and a plea, then her head fell back helplessly as she gave herself up to the gift he had forced upon her, the gift that she had so greedily and so needily accepted. Her neck thrust forward in graceful abandon, her eyes closing helplessly as her first orgasm overtook her.

Damon didn't move, his eyes glued to her face, a tender smile coming to his lips as she shuddered and collapsed panting onto the cool moss. Her face was flushed with wild heat, and a small droplet of perspiration trickled across her forehead. She looked beautiful and magnificent, like a wild tigress, and at the same time, she looked hopelessly vulnerable. For a long while they lay together in the fragrant bushes, Ramona with her eyes closed tightly once again, trying not to think about what had just happened to her, and Damon watching her, seeing the flush of passion slowly fade from her face. At last, slowly, she opened her eyes. 'I don't know what to say,' she said, truthfully. 'No man has ever done that to me before.'

'Not even Keith?' he heard himself say, and tensed as he waited for her reply.

She shook her head, her eyes incredibly sad. 'No,' she said, and swallowed hard. 'Not even Keith.'

Damon looked away. He was glad. He couldn't help it.

'You're a strange woman, Ramona,' he said at last.

She turned her head slightly, aware of a satisfied throbbing deep in her stomach. She tried to ignore it. She tried, too, to ignore what she had just done. Or rather, what she had allowed *him* to do to *her*.

'What do you mean?' she asked instead, genuinely puzzled.

Damon tenderly pushed a strand of hair off her perspiring forehead, his fingers incredibly gentle. 'Dr King, you're a fraud.' He smiled tenderly. 'I'll bet underneath that black gown and that ridiculous flat hat, you wore scarlet underwear.'

126

'Now you're sounding like a chauvinist,' she snapped, caught on the raw. 'I'm not some bimbo panting for a man to make me whole.' She pushed him away, intending to get up and stride away, but he wouldn't budge. His hands shot out, pulling her back down. He leaned over her, his eyes liquid steel. She stared up at him.

'Calm down,' he said, his voice firm. 'That's not what I meant at all. You're a woman, Ramona,' he said softly, his voice thickening. 'I think I just proved that to you. You're made of emotion, as well as intellect. You have a heart, as well as ambition. You have needs, emotional, physical, natural, the same as the rest of us. You're a woman. Admit it.'

Ramona turned her head away, a slow, lone, miserable tear running down her cheek.

'Oh no, Ramona, don't,' Damon groaned and gathered her into his arms. 'Don't cry, sweetheart. It's alright. Everything's going to be alright.' For a long while he held her in his arms, stroking her hair as a wave of protectiveness washed over him. She was such a contrast, this woman. Beautiful but shy. Intelligent about some things, but so foolish about others. Innocent and yet sensual. And, quite simply, he wanted to make love to her, and be loved by her.

For the first time in his life, Damon knew that he was in love, and it felt wonderful.

Dry-eyed now, Ramona stared blankly over his shoulder. For the first time in her life, she too knew that she was in love.

And she was terrified.

127

CHAPTER 11

Jeff Doyle glanced over his shoulder, but the companionway was still empty. It had taken him only two minutes to get from his cabin to the captain's office, but a steward could pass by at any moment. Extracting a gadget that looked a bit like a remote control for a TV, he made short work of the electronic lock. Quickly, he stepped inside.

His search was quick, thorough, and fruitless. But then, it had always been a long shot. Jeff, however, quite liked long shots. More often than not they paid off for him. His mother had told him a gypsy, a true Romany gypsy, had given him a charm as a baby that had brought him good luck ever since. But not this time. If there was something going on between Ramona King and Damon Alexander, the captain knew nothing about it.

He made his way back to his own cabin, and headed for the drinks cabinet. He selected a fine malt Scottish whisky and poured himself a good slug, then glanced at his watch. The boss would be on his way to St Lucia by now. He picked up the phone and within minutes was connected to the private jet that was winging its way swiftly across the Atlantic.

'Doyle?'

'Yes. Nothing.'

Joe King grunted. He too, knew it had been a long shot. Still, it didn't do to leave any possibility unchecked. Especially when you were dealing with Damon Alexander.

Verity had spent four hours getting ready for dinner, trying on every evening gown, and experimenting with her hair in what felt like hundreds of different ways. She'd also exhausted every combination of the jewellery she had, including using one necklace as a headband. And all because tonight it was her turn to dine at the captain's table in the Tahitian Gold restaurant.

She'd finally selected a Maurice Francais caftan in jewel-like colours of green, gold and white. The low, square-cut neckline was the perfect foil for the lavish emerald necklace her mother had insisted on buying her for Christmas from Asprey's, and the loose, raw Indian silk of the material alternately clung to her body and floated around it, whenever she moved. Tonight, she had donned high heels of a perfectly matching gold, with a handbag to match. Her hair was swept back at the temples and held behind her ears by two matching hairclips of diamonds and gold, which sparkled like stars against the midnight of her hair. She'd kept her make-up light but effective, with dark gold eyeshadow lending her ebony eyes an exotic look.

She wanted to be beautiful for Greg.

But was that fair? She hadn't been able to mistake the look of concern in his eyes when he'd seen her emerging from the doctor's office the other day. Deep down she knew he was attracted to her in more than just a casual way, as women for centuries have always known which men might fall in love, and which wouldn't. Now, as she stared apprehensively and indecisively at her reflection in the mirror, Verity wondered if she was doing the right thing. But the cruise was almost a third over. And she had so little time. If Greg could be persuaded to have an affair, and if she made it quite clear it would last only as long as the cruise, perhaps he'd feel safe enough to take her in his arms and into his life? Just for a while. And then, with the next cruise, he could forget her and go on to the next woman. She winced at the thought, but it made her feel less guilty. So long as Greg wouldn't be broken-hearted after it was all over, what harm would she be doing to either him or to herself? Verity met her dark eyes in the mirror, and shook her head. 'You're heading for trouble, Dr Fox,' she said softly.

But what, really, did it matter? By next winter it wouldn't matter. Nothing at all would matter.

With a deep breath Verity headed for the restaurant.

In her Belgravia home back in London, Lady Winnifred Fox was suffering her usual insomnia. Now, at nearly three o'clock in the morning, she was sitting in her favourite lounge, a real fire roaring away in the hearth, and a cup of hot chocolate by her side. Tonight she had felt nostalgic and had retrieved the family albums.

She smiled over Verity's baby pictures and sighed longingly at her husband as a young man, stiff and handsome in his Royal Horse Guard's uniform. Once more she was transported back to those halcyon days of summer at Joceline's estate in the Cotswolds. There was Verity, on Damon's pony . . . what was his name now? Something amusing . . . And there again was Verity taken on that very last visit. Slowly Winnie let the album fall back onto her lap. That last visit. When Michael, poor Michael, had been killed. So long ago now . . .

As she recalled, she herself hadn't been there that night. She'd gone down the Friday before with Verity, and then something had called her back to London the next morning. But Verity had wanted to stay behind, and Joceline hadn't minded. But then, that same Saturday night, there'd been a break-in and the burglar had killed Michael. How terrible it had all been. Michael still only in his early forties, and Damon just a young boy. How Joceline had coped, Winnie couldn't imagine. To have your husband killed by some villain out to rob the family home . . . Winnie shook her head and her gaze fell once more onto her daughter's laughing, pixie-like face with the big mischevious brown eyes. She'd been such a handful at that age. But when Michael had died, it had affected the poor child deeply. Although Joceline had assured her Verity had been tucked up safely in bed when it was all happening, the sounds of the gun-shots must have frightened her much more than they realized, for Verity had flatly refused to go back.

Winnie sighed. Who knew what demons a six-year-old might imagine? Perhaps she'd heard about Joceline firing the gun at the fleeing thief, and that had made her see her godmother in a different light? Perhaps it was just the sudden, uncomprehending loss of her beloved 'uncle Mike'. Ah well, Winnie sighed, putting the album away. Whatever it was, it was all in the past. But, who knows, with both Joceline and Verity on board the same boat, they might even be able to put the past behind them.

Winnie hoped so. She rather missed her old friend.

Greg stood out in the crowd. It was not just his height, or the crisp whiteness of his uniform amidst all the dark tuxedos and dinner jackets. It was something else. Some indefinable aura that marked him as the man in charge. Verity noticed it as soon as she stepped foot into the sumptuously decorated dining room. Her legs felt a little weak, and her heart began to pick up a beat as she approached the centre table.

Greg looked up. He thought he was ready for her, for he'd noticed her name on the list of dinner guests that had been given to him that afternoon by his yeoman secretary. But he wasn't nearly as prepared as he'd thought. She looked stunning. As she moved, the silk of her caftan shimmered around her and clung to her firm, up-tilting breasts. A long slit to mid-thigh revealed then concealed a long length of leg as she walked forward, and her smile, although shy and hesitant, easily out-sparkled the diamonds in her hair.

Greg, and the other four men seated at the table, rose

to their feet as Verity joined them. 'Dr Fox,' Greg said, making her blink in surprise. 'I'd like you to meet . . .' He introduced the rest of the guests with effortless ease and charm. They were the usual bunch – a senator from Kansas and his very ambitious wife, a famous Italian tenor and his very charming wife, a Nobel-prize-winning husband-and-wife team who were very big in astro-physics and a run-of-the-mill multi-millionaire and his fourth wife, who looked about sixteen.

Verity was disappointed to find that she was sat between the Italian tenor and the senator, with Greg opposite. Suddenly, the silver candlesticks and the chic crystal bowl centrepiece with its armada of floating, breathtaking waterlilies ceased to be beautiful and became a barrier between them.

Verity felt a growing sense of anti-climax as Greg played the perfect dinner host, giving her no more time or attention than anyone else. The Italian tenor told them a lovely story about the time he was singing Carmen in front of one of Italy's many *principessas* and nearly fell into the orchestra pit, and the multi-millionaire boasted of the six-million dollar scoop he'd just made in dog biscuits. From the scientists came a dry but interesting discussion on the differences between a white and blue quasar.

As her choice of coconut curried shrimp and filet of grouper marinated in fresh herbs was placed in front of her, she looked up and found everyone looking at her expectantly.

'I was just telling everyone how comforting it was to have an extra doctor on board,' Greg prompted, aware that she had been caught napping, and smoothly coming to her rescue.

'I expect you have a lot of people come up to you and ask about their varicose veins and things,' the Italian tenor's wife helped ease her embarrassing inattention, her kind brown eyes twinkling in understanding.

Verity cleared her throat. 'Not really. I'm a surgeon, rather than a GP.'

'Really? Do you specialize?' This from the senator.

Verity smiled. 'I worked . . . work at the John Radcliffe, in Oxford. I do it all – heart transplants, key-hole surgery . . . But I'm sure this isn't a topic for the dinner table,' she laughed, feeling gauche.

'I was taken to the John Radcliffe with appendicitis once,' Greg said thoughtfully.

'Who knows, perhaps it was Dr Fox who cut you open,' chipped in a tactless voice, which, not surprisingly, belonged to the millionaire's child-bride. Everybody laughed politely, but Verity looked quickly away, a flush staining her cheeks and so missed the stunned look Greg gave her. Jumping once more to the rescue, Maria Fermintino launched into a story about entertaining a senile cardinal, and Verity was relieved when the attention moved on from her. But she could have kicked herself for being such a fool. What had she expected, a table for two, with just her and Greg? And Greg, just falling over himself to be seduced?

When dinner at last was over, the Nobels and the Italians went off to watch the 'Mousetrap', which was being performed in the ship's theatre at ten-thirty. Verity excused herself quietly and headed back for her cabin, her shoulders slumped just a little in an unknowing show of defeat. Ten minutes later, Greg excused himself, murmuring vaguely about the bridge and navigational channels. He didn't go to the bridge, of course. Cursing himself for his stupidity all the way, he made his way to her cabin.

Verity had kicked off her shoes and taken out the hair clips when the knock on the door surprised her. When she answered it and saw him standing outside, her heart stood still and then leapt into her throat. She swallowed once, a single, convulsive movement, her hand fluttering to her neck.

'Dr Fox,' Greg said stiffly. 'May I come in for a moment?'

He looked so ill at ease that Verity almost smiled. 'Of course. Come on in, before a steward spots you and reports you to the headmaster.'

Greg blinked, then grinned. Nevertheless, he stepped quickly into the room. 'That obvious, is it?' he asked, his eyes crinkling attractively at the corners. It was almost as if they'd been friends all their lives. And yet there was all the excitement and anticipation that came with meeting someone new. The satisfaction of mutual attraction. It was a heady, dangerous combination for a bachelor in his thirties.

'I always thought captains were masters of their ships,' Verity said, still teasing. 'Captain Bligh, and all that.'

Greg laughed. ''Fraid not. It's all rules and regulations, even for me. One of which,' he said quietly 'is the very strict rule about not mixing with lady passengers. Except whilst on social duty, of course.'

Verity felt her smile fade. 'I see,' she said quietly, and did. Greg was taking a big risk coming to her room like this. 'Is there . . . something wrong, Captain?'

Greg shrugged helplessly. 'I just wanted to ask you something. Something that's been bothering me all night.'

Her eyes were enormous and he felt a warmth seep into his body, making his breathing difficult. She was so damned beautiful and contradictory, stood there in her bare feet and fabulous emerald necklace, with those wide, vulnerable eyes. 'About the hospital,' Greg said, then sighed. 'Oh hell, Verity, did you operate on me in Oxford?' he blurted out at last.

'Oh, that! Yes, as a matter of fact I did,' she admitted.

Greg stared at her, dumbfounded. 'You did?' The thought of him, lying naked on an operating theatre flashed into his mind. And this woman, standing over him, taking his life into her hands. The thought was giddying. It hit him with such a strong sexual punch that his hands actually began to shake. Suddenly the room crackled with electricity. Verity too, remembered that moment when she had first seen his face. Her eyes dropped to his abdomen, where the scar would be, and Greg felt his stomach quiver.

'Verity,' he said, his voice thick, and somehow he was moving towards her, and she was stepping into his arms, lifting her head, silently demanding that he kiss her. And he, like a slave, blindly, willingly, obeyed. Their mouths touched, the heat scorching them with a fire that instantly demanded more fuel. Verity put her hands on either side of his face, frightened he might pull away, but she needn't have feared. His strong lips prised hers apart, allowing his tongue to dart into her honeyed mouth. She moaned deep in her throat. She could feel her heart beating strong and defiantly under her breast, and her fingers ran up his cheeks to his temple and then into his cool, thick hair. His scalp felt hot under her fingertips. Greg groaned, holding her closer. She felt so small in his arms, and yet her hands, moving across his shoulders and down over his back, felt strong and urgent, her fingers digging into his muscles, making his legs go weak. He stumbled, and they fell back on her bed. Verity still clinging to him fiercely, their mouths locked in a kiss that was almost ferocious in its hungry need.

His weight felt glorious on top of her, and Verity hooked her bare feet around his calves, her vagina flooding with molten heat. When he opened his eyes they looked dazed, and the desire in them made her want to shout in female triumph. With one hand she grasped the back of his head, lowering and guiding his lips toward her breasts, and with the other hand she thrust the low-cut neck of her caftan even lower, exposing one cherry-tipped nipple. Greg gasped at the lovely sight, aware of the hard pressure of her hand at the back of his skull, demanding and urgent. With a gruff moan he fastened his lips onto her breast and felt her strain against him. She tasted warm and wonderful and his big body shuddered as she clung to him. The inarticulate cry that escaped from her lips sent blood pumping into his loins.

Feverishly he pushed aside the rest of the caftan so

that he could kiss her other breast, and a slight but painful scratching on his hand distracted him. It was the necklace, lying like green flame against her skin. The sight of its hundred-thousand pound brilliance brought his sanity rushing back. He closed his eyes briefly, and shook his head. 'What the hell am I doing?' he heard his own voice, despairing and angry, interrupt the intense silence, and his eyes snapped open again. As did Verity's. She felt the heat drain from her as he pushed himself away and stood beside the bed, staring down at her. His white shirt was half undone, and she had vague memories of her own hands feverishly undoing the buttons. He looked bemused, but even as she instinctively pulled up the caftan to cover her nakedness, she could see reality returning to his eyes.

'I'm sorry,' he said. 'I just can't . . .' Something in her eyes stopped the words dead. Something understanding and sad. So incredibly sad. He shook his head. Slowly, not taking his eyes off her, he walked backwards towards the door, then turned, and left.

Verity stared at the ceiling above her for a long, long time, tears flooding her eyes and rolling down her cheeks.

Far away, in a small research annexe at the John Radcliffe Hospital in Oxford, Dr Gordon Dryer was staring incredulously at the meticulous research notes of a doctor from Venezuela, a specialist in AIDS. But it was not the notes on that disease that interested him. Instead, he concentrated on an obscure but potentially pioneering off-shoot of his research, that could drastically alter the treatment for a variety of blood cancers the whole world over. Provided the tests done in Venzeula could be duplicated successfully here.

But it would be far too late for Verity, Gordon knew, his excitement fading. *If* he waited. But did he have to? Here, at the John Radcliffe, he had access to the experimental Venezuelan drug that was probably the only batch of its kind in the world. He could easily assign himself to oversee its preliminary testing. No one would know how much he used if he doctored the medical logs. Gordon felt himself begin to sweat. If he were caught . . . if the drug proved to have some fatal or hideous side effect on human beings . . .

But . . . *Verity*. If he could *save* Verity . . .

CHAPTER 12

St Lucia

As Greg stood watchful and alert on the bridge, he couldn't help but feel a thrill of pleasure at the sight of the island. The twin peaks of the Pitons, the Petit and Gros, rose more than 2,400 feet into the clear, sunny sky.

'Watch out for the yachts coming out of St Marigot's Bay,' he said quietly to Jim. 'And tell the harbour pilot we're ready for him,' he added, then checked with engineering to see that all was in perfect working order in Jock McMannon's engine rooms. It was. The passengers would be rising in an hour to take breakfast, and he always liked to be docked well before then. Squeezing a big boat into a relatively small harbour could look nerve-wracking enough to put anybody off their eggs and bacon.

In her cabin, Verity Fox was mulling over a brochure, trying to work up some enthusiasm for her day's exploring. But the look in Greg's eyes yesterday, as he'd left her, kept flashing into her mind. She'd just ringed the Falls and Mineral Baths site in Soufriere and

140

had her pen poised over the Drive-In Volcano and Sulphur Springs site, when the telephone rang. Surprised, she picked it up, her heart hoping it was Greg, her head telling her it was more likely to be her mother, wanting a gossip. It was neither.

'Verity? How are things going out there?'

'Gordon?' The voice from what now felt like her past and very-long-ago life, shocked her back into reality.

'Yeah, it's me.' There was a long pause, and then Gordon said quietly, 'I need to see you, Verity. It's important. Very important. Where's your next port of call?'

'Er . . . Martinique. Gordon, you're not going to fly all the way out here for nothing. What's going on?'

Gordon coughed. 'I really can't say on the phone, Verity. You're just going to have to trust me. Where can we meet on Martinique?'

Verity had no idea. She'd never visited the place before. 'You'll have to come to the ship. I'll arrange a pass for you with the bursar. Everybody and his aunt wants to see this ship, she's a floating palace, so you won't be the only one.'

Gordon breathed a sigh of relief. 'Oh, that's good. What time do you dock?'

Quickly she checked with the Daily Programme and gave him the details. A cold, hard, tight feeling was beginning to make her limbs shake. 'Gordon . . . something's happened, hasn't it?' she asked warily, not sure that she wanted to know.

'Yes. Something totally unexpected,' Gordon admitted.

'Good or bad?' she forced herself to ask the question, and took a deep, steadying breath.

'Good. I think,' Gordon qualified. 'It's hard to say. Look, I'd better go. I've got a hundred things to arrange. I'm really sorry I can't say more, Verity. I know this is leaving you dangling on a string, but I have to be careful.'

Verity nodded. 'You're doing something . . . unethical, aren't you?' she said at last, slowly.

'Let's just say, you won't find it in the Hippocratic oath,' he answered grimly, and hung up. For a long while Verity stared blankly at the receiver still clutched tightly in her hand. Just what the hell was going on?

Anse Chastanet was a grey-sand beach north of Soufriere that boasted the best reefs for snorkelling and diving. The wooden gazebos and Anse Chastanet Hotel nestling in the trees were a picturesque delight for the revellers on the beach, but that morning, one temporary resident of the hotel didn't give the view even the merest glance as he climbed into the back of a lush, black Jaguar. 'Castries, sir?' the chauffeur asked.

Joe King nodded, then smiled. 'I have a ship to meet.'

Ramona and Damon never noticed the black Jaguar that followed them, always two or three cars behind as they headed out of town. Driving up the Hill of Good Fortune, Ramona gasped at the sight of frangipani, lilies, bougainvillaea, hibiscus and oleander that thronged the roadside. They were in banana country, and she was almost sorry when Damon finally turned into Marigot Bay and cut the engine. 'I know a man here who has a yacht. If you wanted, we could hire it for the day and sail to Anse-La-Raye.'

'That sounds wonderful,' Ramona agreed, but she felt butterflies invade her stomach as she got out of the car and walked with him down to the harbour. Not surprisingly, since Damon was an expert yachtsman, his old friend agreed they wouldn't need him aboard to keep them off the reefs, and within half an hour they were headed out to sea. Alone.

On the rise, Joe King trained his binoculars on the yacht, the lenses fixed on the blonde woman on the deck. She was beautiful. Much more beautiful than he'd expected, even though he'd seen all the photographs that his private eye had unearthed of his long-forgotten daughter.

As he watched, Ramona casually slipped off her sunny yellow dress, revealing a long, slim, shapely body covered by a modest white swimsuit. She made a stunning contrast to Alexander's dark and brooding good looks. The couple on the boat looked so damned *right* together, he could feel his fingernails digging viciously into palms. But he needed to see more, just to make sure, before he made his move.

It felt good to sail with the wind in the canvas and the sun on his face, but Damon anchored in the first rocky, deserted cove that he came to, and went eagerly forward. Where Ramona was waiting. He stood for a long time looking down on her. She was lying on a huge navy blue towelling robe that made her skin look creamier than ever. Her long, silver hair swirled around her like old gold, and as the yacht bobbed gently at anchor she stirred, as if feeling his gaze on her body. Suddenly she opened her eyes and Damon gasped. 'I'll never get used to your eyes,' he said softly. 'They're the colour of blue lightning in the summer-time.'

Ramona swallowed, her throat going dry.

'I'd better put up a sun-shade, before you burn.' Quickly he opened up a huge red sun-shade, the parasol immediately hiding them from view from any passing para-sailors or tourist helicopters. Ramona shivered just slightly at the loss of the warm sun, but then Damon knelt down beside her, and, not bothering to undo the buttons, just pulled the shirt over his head. Ramona's heart thumped. His eyes were dark, like molten lead, and she felt an answering rush of molten desire bubble deep in her vagina. Her lips fell open as breathing suddenly became difficult. She'd always know it would come to this. When he'd hired the yacht for just themselves, she'd known. That first night she'd ever seen him, and they'd danced together, she'd known. It felt as if she'd known all her life. Slowly he moved over her, his eyes watching her face as he put his hand lightly on her stomach, and then splayed his fingers, moving over the thin white fabric and sliding up to cover one breast. She gasped, her back arching automatically, like a cat being stroked, his touch so sensual, so deeply erotic that she thought she must surely scream aloud. Under his palm Damon could feel the sharp, urgent thrust of her nipple burgeoning to life and he caught his breath yet again as her eyes seemed to sparkle silver.

144

With a moan he lowered his head and kissed her, his mind reeling at the softness of her mouth, his senses immediately drowning in the sweetness of her tongue and the scent of her hair. He loved the soft, warm sensation of her bare flesh against his palms as his hands moved over her bare arms and up to cup the back of her neck, bringing her closer to him as he deepened the kiss. He lifted his head at last and ran one finger over her chin, down her throat, then across to the strap of her swimsuit. Wordlessly, their eyes locked, he pushed the strap away and down her arm, his gaze dropping to the exposed mound of flesh that looked, if possible, even more creamy white than the rest of her body, which had at last began to tan slightly. His jaw clenched as desire belly-thumped him, then he walked his fingers across her breastbone, listening to the tiny gasps of pleasure she gave at every touch, until he pulled the other strap away also. Lying on the warm wooden deck, her arms held prisoner at her sides by the swimsuit straps, Ramona shuddered in anticipation as his lips lowered and pincered around the button of waiting, quivering, yearning flesh. A long, low, animal groan suddenly errupted into the silence of the deserted cove, and it took her a confused moment to realize the sound came from her own throat. Then his tongue was on her, laving the tiny button of flesh, the very tip of his tongue digging firmly down and she jerked spasmodically, her legs falling apart, moisture flooding between them. Feverishly she reached for the elastic waist of his shorts, pushing them down, and Damon rolled with her, helping her push them away. He wore nothing underneath, a fact she became only too aware of as she felt the strong, long, hard and hot length of him pressing against her thigh. Her insides clenched, as if anticipating his invasion and she moaned loudly, any lingering inhibitions now gone, swept away on a wave of core-deep passion.

'Damon,' she murmured. 'Oh Damon.'

She had never known her body could feel like this. Had never expected to feel so completely the desire that was raging in her like a floodtide. And with it, around it, through it all, was a deep vein of tenderness and heart-stopping love that transported it beyond the mere physical. Damon sat back on his haunches, withdrawing slightly, and her eyes flew open in disappointment. But then his strong and agile hands were tugging her swimsuit down, exposing her navel and then the triangle of silver-gold hair at the junction of her thighs. At the sight, he hesitated a moment, his breath catching in his throat at her loveliness, and then he impatiently pulled the white nylon from her legs and threw it carelessly behind him along the deck. It landed on the picnic hamper, a white flag of surrender in the strong, midday sun. With his gaze magnetized onto hers, Damon lifted one of her feet and planted a kiss on its instep. Ramona gasped as a jolt of pure, undiluted want shot up her leg and lodged in her vagina, her whole lower body throbbing to the siren song of sexual passion. She could feel liquid heat melting inside her, and her breath came in great, ragged pants. Her whole body quivered to his slightest touch, like a finely-tuned instrument responding to the deft handling of a maestro.

Damon felt the warm flesh of her calf quiver as he lifted her leg higher and felt fierce triumph, and humble joy, at her reaction to him. Eagerly he moved forward, planting a kiss at the tender point at the back of her knee. Her muscles jerked in instant reaction and her free leg thrashed spasmodically against the deck. She watched him, mesmerized, over the length of her naked body as he worked his way up to her thigh, planting tiny, minute kisses on her skin. She watched, wide-eyed, as he gently but firmly spread her shaking legs apart, and she had one last glimpse of eyes, dark as a thunder-cloud and just as powerful, before he bent his head and buried his lips against the very core of her womanhood. Ramona gasped and jerked convulsively, her head falling back against the deck, her back and neck arching upwards. She flung her arms wide, her fingers clawing helplessly against the hot wooden planks of the deck. She moaned as she felt his tongue delve deeply into her, and moaned again when she felt him take both her knees firmly in his hands and hoist them either side of his head, lifting her lower body completely off the deck and giving him greater access to her exposed feminity. Nothing mattered now but his tongue and the powerful sensations it provoked. Nothing mattered but this man, and his wonderful, exciting, dangerous, addictive loving. Nothing mattered but that he never stopped. She would die, if he stopped . . .

His tongue delved ever deeper, a hot, seeking probe that had her head thrashing from side to side, tangling her long gold hair all around her. And then his teeth found and nibbled at that tiny button of flesh, usually so ignored and protected, and Ramona almost screamed at the bolt of ecstacy that shot through her, as unexpected and as devastating as fork lightning. Ramona thrashed in pleasure, her heels drumming harmlessly and helplessly against his strong, sun-warmed back as orgasm, for the second time in her life, claimed her, driving away rationality and sanity, leaving only sensation and glorious, mind-blowing ecstacy in its wake.

It took a long, long while for the spiralling pleasure to recede, but as it did so, she felt his lips on her belly, his tongue dipping into her navel, and the roller-coaster began to build all over again. By the time his lips were on her breasts and then her throat and finally her lips, she was on fire again. One part of her silently begged him to stop, but a greater, more needy part, silently begged him to go on, and on, and on . . . And damn the consequences. She felt him push one knee between hers, forcing her legs apart, and gasped as the hot, hard tip of his manhood brushed against her inner thigh. His weight was heavy but pleasing on her body, and she felt her nipples tighten and tingle as the soft hairs of his chest teased them, brushing against them as he moved to kiss her once more. She felt the nakedness of her exposed womanhood, knew that he was only moments away from claiming her, and her eyes widened. 'Damon,' she said, wanting to warn him, to explain. But when he lifted his head and looked at her, she knew she had no need.

'It's alright,' he said softly, and reaching for her hand he brought it down between them, guiding her to him. She gasped as her fingers curled around his member, marvelling at the iron hardness of it that nevertheless seemed to be sheathed in hot velvet. It was so big, and much longer than she'd expected, and her eyes widened even further.

'You know . . .' she began, and gasped as her vagina clenched fiercely, demanding its presence inside her.

'It's nothing to be afraid of, Ramona,' he said softly, his voice thick and taut with controlled passion. 'It's an instrument of pleasure,' he said, gasping as her exploring fingers found it's tip, her little finger flicking over it and making him shudder. His eyes darkened to midnight, his lips falling open in wordless ecstacy, and she felt a thrill of primordial triumph at this evidence of her feminine power over him. But she knew that soon, so very soon, what she could feel in her hand and imagine in her mind would be buried deep within her, stroking, filling, tormenting her with pleasure, and the thought sent hot waves of desire rippling through her, bringing every part of her body, heart and her mind to glorious, vibrant life. Safety was gone. Years of self-protection fell away. There was only Damon Alexander and his body, and his love, and her own want and need of him.

'Make love to me, Damon,' she said at last, shocked but thrilled at the huskiness of her voice. 'I want you to make me scream.' Damon gasped, his self-control at breaking point. He could feel her heat and moisture and knew she was ready. Wordlessly he gripped her hands in both of his and pushed their arms far above them. Taking his full weight now, Ramona thrilled at the primeval glory of it, and her legs, either side of his muscular thighs, shivered deliciously as she lifted her hips slightly. And then she could feel the tip of his manhood seeking entry to her, and she groaned, her whole body quivering with expectation. Then he was inside her, moving deeply, and her muscles were expanding and contracting around him, welcoming him as a beloved invader.

Nothing in her life had prepared her for the sensation now exploding in her body. He was big inside her, filling her, but after a first stab of pain there was only delight. She felt her hips begin to move as he withdrew slightly and then plunged into her once more, making her gasp all over again with renewed pleasure. And it continued, time suspended, each thrust driving her pleasure a little higher, each thrust pushing his length a little further into her until it felt as if he were filling her entire body, threatening to make her explode with pleasure. She was unaware that her fingers were scoring deep scratches into his shoulders, and the tiny lacerations of pain only made Damon groan with heavy desire. She was so tight around him, her fit and healthy body producing muscles that gripped him like steel, making him growl low in his throat, like a trapped animal that wanted to stay trapped forever. He felt his climax clamouring for release, and he gritted his teeth in an effort to hold it back. His thighs strained, sinews standing out in stark relief as he plunged into her again and again, her legs thrashing on the deck, her hands curved like claws, digging into his shoulders in unheeding ecstacy as she suddenly bucked one last time and screamed her pleasure into the sky. It was pagan. It was glorious. It was dangerous.

It was living.

CHAPTER 13

Kitted out in a white sports kit, Jeff Doyle took the lift to the games deck and strolled casually outside onto the veranda that looked down at the squash courts, which were now empty. Slowly he made his way to the men's changing rooms, his eyes constantly on the move. But he'd picked his time well. The place was deserted. Quickly now, he walked over to the furthest set of lockers and glanced at the key he had purchased for the day. On the back of the key were four digits, the combination to the stout padlock on the locker door. Jeff opened it and looked inside. A rail with four coat hangers hung at the very top, and gave way to two shelves. A built-in shaving unit complete with razors (electric and traditional) also housed a small collection of French fragrances for men. There were three towels, huge and fluffy, and two sets of expensive soap, shampoo and deodorant.

Jeff's smile widened when he saw the enclosed box right at the bottom. Inside, it was completely bare and made of plain metal, obviously a recepticle for sweaty and odorous trainers. Jeff laughed softly. Just what the doctor ordered. Quickly, he opened his bag and lifted out his squash racquet and a towel. Underneath was a featureless black box, about one-and-half feet by one foot, made of some kind of metal that had no visible means of entry. Carefully, Jeff put it into the locker shoebox, breathing a sigh of relief at the snug fit. He lifted the box out and carefully put it back in his bag.

He left, choosing a slow meandering path out onto the open deck. He was sure nobody was taking undue notice of him, but Jeff had lived as long as he had only by being very careful. Only when he was ultra-sure of himself and those around him, did he let his eyes lift to the bridge, mentally gauging it's geography. Slowly moving along the rail, he began counting off his strides. That done, he counted again until he was level with the entrance to the inside games deck, and then counted back until he was once more in the locker room.

The room was still deserted now, but Jeff waited a moment, ears pricked for the slightest noise. When he was sure there was none, he glanced up at the ceiling and began counting off again. When he was sure he was directly under the bridge, he took out a little notebook and looked at the rough plan of the bridge sketched inside it, which Joe King had given him in St Lucia. He hoped it was accurate. Moving sideways and backwards like a crab, one eye on the plan and one eye counting off the strides, Jeff selected the locker he was sure was most directly under the piece of equipment on the bridge that mattered, and noted the locker number. He smiled. It was 13, the traditional number of bad luck, and it gave him an added confidence to see it. Numerology was important.

He played one game of squash, just in case some instructor had noticed him, and might later remember that a passenger, dressed for squash, hadn't actually played. In Jeff's field of work, you quite literally couldn't be too careful.

He was just leaving the courts when he saw Ramona King walking towards him. The bright sunlight turned her hair to liquid silver, and Jeff felt his breath catch. He'd never seen her this close up before. She cast him a brief, uninterested look in passing, but Jeff knew he had never seen eyes so blue they were almost silver. They were supernatural eyes . . . Jeff shuddered as an icy hand gripped his stomach. In some mythology, a woman with eyes that were too blue to be true could represent anything from a witch to an agent of Nemesis, the goddess of retribution. And, suddenly, Jeff was scared. It could be no coincidence that the woman with eyes the colour of electricity should turn out to be the lover of Jeff's enemy. It had to be a warning. Jeff tried grimly to shrug off his feeling of unease, and headed back to his cabin. By the time he'd poured himself a drink he'd almost succeeded in putting the incident from his mind. Almost.

Greg entered the bursar's office and a young steward on the way out nearly cannoned straight into him. Flushed and unnerved, the youngster saluted. Greg, amused, nodded and stood to one side to let him out. From his desk, the bursar smiled. 'Stop dancing with the captain,

Jimmy, and get that visitor's pass to Dr Fox. I damned nearly forgot it,' he muttered, putting some paperwork into a file and slamming shut the drawer. When he looked up there was a strange look on the captain's face. 'Everything's alright at this end, Captain. Looking forward to the captain's cocktail party tonight?'

Greg managed to smile, but if felt stiff and uncomfortable on his face. 'I never look forward to the captain's cocktail parties,' he said dryly, and got bruskly down to business.

Greg tried to concentrate. Verity was fully entitled to have boyfriends come on board. It was none of his business. Quickly he took a look in the log, demanding an explanation for every small mishap. As soon as he was gone, the bursar reached for the telephone to spread the word. The captain was on the warpath. In engineering, Jock gave his beloved machines another check. By the time the captain had found his way there Jock had already upbraided one of the men for not wearing his 'whites'. White was always, but *always*, worn in engineering. But Jock needn't have worried. The reason for the scowl on the captain's face had nothing to do with the *Alexandria*, her running, or her crew.

In her cabin, Joceline Alexander was feeling nervous. Damon had asked her to lunch in his cabin to meet someone special and she couldn't help but feel a rising sense of excitement. By 'someone' he must surely mean a woman. And although Joceline knew that Damon had had several relationships before, she also knew there had been no one 'special'. This, as the old cliché would have it, was the first woman he'd 'brought home to mother' and Joceline wasn't quite sure how she should handle it. If only she didn't have so much else to think about! Should she tell her son about his father after all? When she'd boarded this ship, she'd been determined to do so. Joe King had been up to his old tricks, and Damon needed all the ammunition he could get. But now, when he'd found the woman of his dreams, did she have the right to bring his happiness crashing down? She thought not. At least, not yet. After all, that night had been so long ago . . .

It had been summer-time, and the big French windows had stood open to let in the cooling breeze. Upstairs, little Verity Fox was tucked up in bed. Joceline, too, was dressed for bed, in chiffon lounging pyjamas and a matching coat. It was nearly midnight, and still Michael hadn't come home. At last, she heard the sound of the car and saw its headlights sweep over the rhododendron bushes at the front of the house. With a relieved sigh she stood up and went to the open windows, looking over the patio to the garages where the big Rolls Royce pulled to a stop, half on and half off the lawn.

Joceline frowned. Michael was usually such a neat and careful driver. Abruptly, Michael flung open the door, lurched to his feet, and began to walk away from the car, leaving the Rolls Royce door open. He was drunk! For a while, Joceline just stared at her husband as he weaved his way towards her. It was so unlike her husband to get in this state that Joceline didn't even think to get angry. Instead she backed away as her

155

husband stepped into the lighted room, and then gasped as she saw his face.

He looked so angry she almost didn't recognize him.

'Michael?' she said softly, and took another step back. As she did so, a savage sneer appeared on her husband's face. It was so very much the opposite of his usual, easygoing nature, that Joceline felt a shiver of very real fear begin to creep up her spine. 'Michael, you're drunk,' she said, trying to force some firmness into her voice.

'*Drunk!*' Michael roared, so loudly that it woke the little girl upstairs. Quickly, she pushed the covers away and walked to the door of her room. She wanted Auntie Joceline. She wanted her mommy.

Downstairs, Joceline recoiled as if bit by a snake. 'Keep your voice down, Michael, for heaven's sake,' she hissed, glad that Damon was away on a two-week school trip. Damon worshipped his father. To see him like this . . . Well, it wouldn't have been good for a twelve-year-old boy.

'Keep my voice down?' Michael mimicked, lurching forward and crashing against a table. An expensive Lalique glass toppled and fell, smashing with a loud and distressing explosion.

Upstairs, Verity opened her door, curious about the sound of breaking glass. If she ever broke anything, her mother was usually cross. Once though, when she'd broken that 'hideous thing Aunt Mabel gave us as a wedding present', her mother had brought her an icecream. Now, Verity crept onto the landing. If someone was in trouble, perhaps she could help.

'Michael, what's got into you?'

That was Auntie Joceline's voice. Was Uncle Mike home? Verity got to the top of the stairs and then stopped. The door to the salon was open and she could see Uncle Mike swaying against a table, and he looked . . . funny. Slowly, Verity sank onto the top step and peered through the banisters. Something told her she shouldn't go downstairs now. Not when Uncle Mike's face looked so strange, and all twisted up.

Joceline stood with her back against a bureau, not sure what to do. Her husband looked so wild-eyed and out of control. 'Michael, what's wrong?' she asked, her throat unbearably dry. She tried to swallow, but couldn't.

'Wrong, dearest?' Michael hissed, his lips curling back to bear his teeth like a very vicious, snarling dog. A dog that was about to attack. Her heart thumped in her chest, making her feel physically sick. She was drenched in icy sweat. 'What could be wrong?' Michael sneered. 'My wife is only screwing the man who's trying to take away my company,' he shouted, leaning back and nearly falling.

Joceline gasped, going white. 'Oh my God . . .'

Michael laughed. 'He has nothing to do with it, my dear,' he said, his voice lowering. Before he had looked red-faced and out of control. Now, suddenly he was pale, and deathly still, his eyes like murderous pools of dark water. Joceline felt something deathly cold touch her. She began to shake.

'Michael, I . . .'

'How long?' he interrupted, staring at her and blinking, as if trying to get her into focus. 'I want to know, *how long*?'

157

For someone so drunk, he enunciated each word so eerily and clearly that Joceline flinched. 'Let me explain . . .'

Michael Alexander laughed. It was a sound that made Verity, still sitting on the stairs, begin to cry. Her tiny knuckles were white where she was gripping one of the stair rails, and her little body began to tremble. Michael's maniacal laughter affected Joceline too. She stared at her husband in growing horror. 'Michael . . . Michael, please. I . . .'

Joceline stopped dead, the reason being that Michael was picking up a large piece of jagged glass from the broken vase. It was a long, spear-like spike that was cutting into his hand even as he held it. But he seemed obvious to the little trickle of blood than ran down his hand and stained his white cuff a scarlet red. Joceline stared at the glass, mesmerized.

Michael looked from it to her, his eyes still blinking slowly, in that owl-like, terrifying way. 'I'm going to kill you,' Michael said softly. 'I know I'm drunk, or else I wouldn't be able to,' he explained, so reasonably it was hideous. 'So I'm going to to take advantage of my inebriated state. Isn't that what *he* does? Take advantage of things?' he asked, one raised eyebrow and a lopsided, cold smile transforming his face. Slowly he began to move around the table. Joceline could only stare at her husband. Her whole body felt frozen. Michael, moving slowly, had passed the table now and he was swaying slightly as he walked, but the purpose in his face was impossible to ignore.

'I am going to kill you, Joceline,' he said again, that

one thought clear in his otherwise befuddled mind. He turned the glass in his hand until it was pointing at ninety degrees, the perfect angle with which to stab her.

Joceline knew with crystal-clear clarity that she was only moments away from death. Her instinct for survival suddenly vaulted over her paralyzing fear and took complete control. Her mind, that only a split second ago had been bogged down by shock, suddenly became sharp and determined. Her husband intended to kill her, and she must stop him. She needed a weapon. Michael kept a German luger in the bureau behind her, a souvenir from the war. It wasn't even registered. She remembered him telling her that he now kept it loaded, ever since their friends and near-neighbours, the Hornsby-Pikes had been burgled last year. Blindly, she reached her hand behind her and fumbled for the drawer, never taking her eyes off her husband. Michael was still coming towards her, his arm lifting, getting ready to strike. The light overhead glinted off the expensive glass and it glittered like a living, evil thing. Joceline could almost feel it lacerating her skin, plunging into her flesh, ripping apart her organs.

The drawer behind her opened and she delved into it, her fingers feverishly searching. Nothing! She opened the next drawer, and suddenly there was something cold and slightly greasy-feeling against her hand. In that instant, Michael lurched forward, his eyes widening, his mouth stretching into a deep, gaping hole, transforming his face into something horrible. He screamed, a sound she had never heard before, or would ever hear again. It was like death itself, and it echoed from the ceiling, up the stairs, seeming to permeate the whole house.

His forward momentum took him out of sight of the little girl sitting frozen on the stairs, and Verity clamped her hands over her ears, trying to shut out Uncle Mike's horrible, horrible scream. She didn't know she was holding her breath until it shuddered out of her as a loud *bang* came from the room. Verity stumbled back onto the landing and scuttled back a few feet. Even so, she still saw her Uncle Mike stagger back into view. He was holding his hand over his tummy, and his shirt was all red.

Michael felt himself falling back onto the sofa, and he stared at Joceline, who was moving forward, walking on stiff legs, her face a mask of shock, the gun, forgotten now, hanging loosely by her side. For a second or two Michael stared at her, his eyes at last clearing, and a look of horror coming into them. Joceline dropped the gun and put her hand over her mouth.

'Joceline,' he said simply, then his head fell back, his eyes closed, and his shuddering chest was suddenly still.

Verity got awkwardly to her feet and went back to her bed. She crawled under the bedclothes and pulled them right up over her head. She stayed like that until morning, when her mother came to take her away. Downstairs, Joceline continued to stare at the body of her husband. She felt totally numb. Then, walking on legs that felt like stilts made out of rubber, she went to the phone. She must call the police. But the voice that answered was not that of the desk sergeant at the local police station in Stowe-on-the-Wold. It was the voice of her lover. Joe King. Her subconscious had done the dialling for her. Slowly, as if speaking through cotton wool, she told him what had happened.

Joceline opened her eyes and stared at herself twenty years on. All the love and passion that had once been hers and that had led her into an affair and its shattering aftermath was now gone. Burned away by her guilt. It was only the fact that she had known, as surely as day followed night, that Michael had really been about to kill her, that had kept her sane all these years. Even so, in the depths of some very bad nights, she couldn't help but wonder if she hadn't deserved to die. She should have just let Michael kill her. Except then Damon would have lost his mother, and his father would probably have gone to prison, and his life would have been ruined by scandal.

Shakily Joceline left the cabin to keep her appointment with her son. Since that night, she'd had hardly been able to look at him without drowning in a wave of guilt and pain. She knew he thought her cold and unloving, and was powerless to explain. She had kept the secret for years, until Joe King had once more come back into their lives. Trying, once again, to take over the Alexander Line. He'd failed to best Michael, now he was trying to best her son. Which was why she'd taken this voyage, determined to tell him the truth. Joe King was an accessory after the fact. He could go to prison. As could she. So long as Damon was kept safe. She would die, or kill, for her son. So when she knocked on Damon's cabin door she was ready to welcome her son's choice of wife into the family. Ready to keep her secret to the grave. Ready to take whatever punishment was coming to her and never complain.

Damon opened the door, and smiled. He was so tall and handsome, so much like his father, that Joceline had to take a deep steadying breath.

'Come in, Mother.' Damon opened the door and gestured inside. Joceline turned to look at the woman who got slowly to her feet. She had never seen someone so lovely. Dressed in a simple white dress that reached to mid-calf, and a simple gold chain, she screamed class. Her hair was swept back in a very elegant and becoming chignon and was of the whitest shade of blonde that Joceline had ever seen. She walked forward, her smile just a little nervous, which made Joceline like her at once. That touch of nervousness offset what might have been too much perfection. She became aware of the woman's very blue eyes as she came closer, and Joceline smiled as Damon slipped a comforting arm around the young woman's waist. She only had to take one look at her son's face to know he was head over heels in love.

Damon looked at his mother and smiled. For a second it was as if the intervening years of separation and aloofness had never been. This was her son, introducing the woman he loved to his mother. Joceline felt tears of gratitude clog her throat. After all this time, something good, at last.

And then he introduced them.

'Mother, I want you to meet Ramona King. Ramona, my mother, Joceline.'

And suddenly, without any warning whatsoever, Joceline's world had turned into a living hell once again.

CHAPTER 14

Martinique

Gordon Dryer landed at Lamentin International Airport just as the *Alexandria* was due to dock. In his bag, hidden in a tube of sweets, were the pills he'd made up out of Dr Annazwala's formula. But he got through customs without a hitch, and soon he was in a taxi headed for island's capital, Fort-de-France.

The name Martinique meant Island of Flowers, and Gordon had no problem seeing why. The island had to be one of the most beautiful and lush in all the Caribbean, with wild and exotic orchids running rampant, battling for supremacy against frangipani, anthurium, jade vines, flamingo flowers and what seemed like hundreds of varieties of hibiscus. In the distance were the towering mountains of rain forest.

In the city, he tipped his cheerful driver and looked around, noting the French influence everywhere. Not surprising, since the island still belonged to France.

Quickly he unfolded a large street map of Fort-de-France. With it's pastel buildings and ornate ironwork balconies, the city reminded him of the French quarter

164

in New Orleans. Except that Fort-de-France was hilly. Resolutely, he hefted his single backpack onto his shoulders and set off, pausing to linger in the landscaped park across the street from La Savane. There he admired the statue of the Empress Josephine, who stood gazing towards Trois Islets across the bay.

At the docks, people were wandering in from the marketplace, cheering. And it was a sight well worth cheering. The huge, magnificent, beautiful *Alexandria* had already berthed, and Gordon wished he'd been on the dock to see it sail in. It must have been a magnificent sight.

He gave his name to the officer at the bottom of the gangplank, who checked his name off on the visitors' list and handed him a white, lamenated card. He also briefly checked inside his backpack, but the guard saw nothing wrong in a tube of sweets. A minute later, Gordon walked up the companionway and stepped onto the ship, feeling a distinct thrill.

'Gordon.' The voice was warm and familiar. He wheeled around and stared at her. Verity Fox looked more vibrant and alive than ever. Dressed in a see-through pair of gauzy green trousers and a matching top, with a deep sea-green bikini underneath, she looked like a model stepping from the pages of *Vogue*. The sea breeze ruffled her clean, dark cap of hair, and her deep dark eyes smiled at him from a suntanned face.

On the deck above, unable to stop himself, Greg Harding's eyes narrowed on Gordon. He was young, fair, good-looking. Greg sighed. Officially it was his day off, and he was not even in uniform, but it hardly mattered. The day had suddenly become flat. Grim-faced, he made his way to the bridge.

Verity led Gordon to her cabin, giving him a run-down on all the ship's rooms they passed. Once in her cabin she fixed him a long, refreshing glass of ice-cold, fresh pineapple juice and sat down carefully on the bed. Gordon pulled the table between them and then spread Dr Annazwala's notes and his own onto the table. 'I think you should read these first,' Gordon said. As she did so, Gordon began work on the pills, using a saucer and the end of a paperweight as a makeshift pestle and mortar to grind the pills into powder. Since they'd have to decide on dosage together, it would be easier for Verity to handle it in this form. When he'd finished, Verity was looking at him. Her face was tight and pale, but her eyes sparkled. Without a word, Gordon handed her the results of the drug as tested so far on laboratory mice, rats and monkeys, then showed her his own calculations and theories. Eventually, drained and emotionally ex-hausted, Verity leaned back onto the bed and stared up at the ceiling. Gordon watched her, then took a deep breath. 'Verity, you have to think long and hard about this. The possible side effects . . .'

Verity nodded. 'I know,' she said grimly. 'But I'm going to die, Gordon. In my place, who wouldn't take the risk of trying an experimental drug?'

'You're definitely going to go through with this then?' Gordon said at last.

Verity sat up slowly, and looked him straight in the eye. 'Yes,' she said. 'I think I am.'

Gordon nodded and let out a long, shuddering sigh. The dye was cast. 'Then I think we'd better arrange for some proper tests. Can we trust the ship's surgeon here?'

Verity nodded cautiously. 'He'll do the tests for me, but we can tell him nothing about the drug.'

Gordon nodded. 'Agreed. But he'll be suspicious. Especially if the drug works.'

Verity laughed. 'Suspicious? He'll be amazed.' Suddenly, she couldn't stop laughing. She had a chance again. A long shot, to be sure, but a chance. A chance of life where before there had been only the certainty of death. 'Oh Gordon,' she said, wonder in her voice.

The first person Verity saw when she and Gordon walked into the bar and grill on the Peacock deck was Greg Harding. Most passengers had already left, and the room was deserted. As Greg looked up and saw them, and she looked helplessly back, there was an awkward silence. Then she took a deep breath (no use arguing with fate) and moved forward, Gordon by her side. She walked straight up to his table. 'Hello, Captain.'

Greg rose. 'Dr Fox.'

'If we're disturbing your free time, please . . .'

'Not at all. Please, won't you join me? It's my day off and I'm feeling at a loose end.' How polite they all sounded, Greg thought, his lips twisting into a smile.

'Thank you. This is Dr Dryer, a colleague of mine. Gordon, Captain Harding.'

Gordon took Greg's hand and sat down. In honour of

being at Marinique, the chef had outdone himself with a French menu that made Gordon's eyes pop. Verity opted for the Ecrevisses, a freshwater crayfish, whilst Gordon chose the boudin, a Creole blood sausage. Greg, she saw, had been very adventurous and was already half-way through the oursin, which, if her French didn't let her down, was sea urchin.

'Are you in Marinique long, Dr Dryer?' Greg asked, trying not to stare too hard at Verity's visitor. Even so, Gordon looked up to find eyes boring into him like drill bits and nearly choked on his lovely French Beaujolais.

'Er, no. Actually I'm . . . touring the Caribbean,' he lied. 'And since Verity and I were going to be in the same place at the same time, I thought I'd drop off some research notes for her.' Gordon believed in keeping as close to the truth as possible. And unless he was totally off-base, the good and very handsome captain and Verity Fox were striking sparks off each other like dual Catherine wheels.

Greg felt the tension begin to seep out of him. 'It's a business call then?'

Gordon took the hint, and then some. 'Oh yes. My girlfriend is lounging by the pool, no doubt totally fed up with me. But you know what we doctors are like . . . Oh, and that reminds me. I hadn't better stay for dessert. She'd kill me.' As Greg beamed, Verity gave her friend a long, level look out of the corner of her eye. Girlfriend indeed! Gordon, who was already on his feet, missed it. 'Well, goodbye, Captain. It's been a pleasure meeting you. You really must be proud of this ship of yours.'

168

Greg smiled. He wondered what Damon Alexander would have said to that statement. 'Well, I like to think of her as mine, and yes, I am proud of her,' Greg admitted freely.

Gordon turned to Verity. 'Since I'm doing the full-blown tour of the islands, we might meet up again somewhere . . . The Virgin Islands, perhaps?' His eyes spoke volumes, and Verity nodded. It would need two of them to analyze the data, and he'd need to give her a thorough medical.

'Yes. We'll do that,' she promised. By then she would have taken ten doses of the drug. If there were going to be any problems, they would probably have surfaced by then.

Greg's eyes narrowed as he recognized a silent communication passing between them. He stiffened, like a dog scenting danger. Then Gordon said a cheery goodbye and left, and Greg felt relief wash over him. But why should he worry about Dryer at all? Verity was young, beautiful and free and could have any man she wanted. So long as it was him.

Greg drew in a sharp breath as he realized just how fast and deeply he was falling in love. And at that moment Verity turned back round in her seat and looked at him. Instinct recognized the slightly shattered look in his eyes, and she felt her heart pound.

'So,' she said softly. 'I really should get going and see something of the island.' She paused delicately. 'Did you say it was your day off too?'

Greg stared at her. His heart began to thud in his chest. 'Yes. It is.'

Her eyes were glowing like jet. 'Do you recommend anywhere specific?' Her voice, that had been growing quieter and deeper, was now no more than a husky whisper.

Greg swallowed. Hard. 'They say the fishing villages are nice. Case-Pilote, and Bellafontaine. All pastel houses on a hillside and colourful boats.' He was talking jerkily, as if he couldn't string a proper sentence together.

'Sounds lovely. Shall we go?' she added softly.

Greg nodded. Quickly they left the ship, where Greg was the captain and she was a passenger. Now, on the island, they were alone and equals, free and clear. They both knew, too, what the consequences could be. No captain's reputation could survive an affair with a passenger. And the *Alexandria* was the pinnacle of his career. Blow this and . . . On the other hand, Verity was beginning to feel like life itself to him. Suddenly, with Verity, he had a whole other life that could run parallel with his career. A wife, children. Love.

Love. That was what defeated everything else, Greg thought. Caution. Plans. Ambition.

Quickly he hired a car and they headed inland, away from the popular beaches, where they might easily be spotted by eagle-eyed passengers. In St Piere, where, in 1902, Mount Pelee had erupted, destroying the whole town and calcifying its inhabitants, they found a small hotel, opposite the Musee Volcanologique.

Verity had supposed she would feel clandestine, or guilty, or faintly ridiculous, booking into a hotel for one afternoon with a man, but she felt none of those.

Instead, as she waited in the quaint, very French-looking lobby, her eyes caressed Greg's broad back as he signed them in. She smiled, wondering if had registered them as the traditional 'Mr and Mrs Smith', and when he turned back to her, she laughed softly. With his face relaxed and tender, and a warm, answering smile playing with his lips as he joined her in the lift, every trace of the captain of the *Alexandria* had disappeared. He pushed open the door to their room, stepping aside to let her enter first. She looked around her with the eyes of a woman in love, about to become the lover of the man she adored. The room was small but beautiful, with a large bed that dominated one wall. Then she walked to the windows and closed the pretty floral curtains on the Caribbean sun.

Greg shut the door behind him and leaned against it wordlessly. Verity, who'd changed for lunch, lifted her simple yellow sundress over her head. She was wearing no bra and only the sheerest of panties that clearly showed the dark mysterious triangle at her thighs. She kicked off her simple sandals as Greg dragged in his breath.

She was beautiful. Her eyes were full of a love so pure and uninhibited that for a moment he could only stare at her.

Then he moved across the well-worn oriental rug and fell to his knees in front of her, his lips fastening onto her breast, his hands splaying around her naked back and pulling her close. Verity threw back her head, her neck arching, and closed her eyes. Above her, an old-fashioned propellor fan stirred the spicy, Caribbean air into a cooling breeze.

Ignoring the bed, Verity pushed Greg backwards until he was lying on the carpet, and her hands went to his shirt, eagerly undoing the buttons and pushing the flaps away. His chest was broad and strong, with a smattering of golden hair and she leaned forward and bit one nipple, hard. Greg gasped and jerked, his loins hardening. He helped her shuck off his trousers, their movements fast and awkward, and yet leant a kind of grace and elegance by the sheer frenzy of their passion. Verity pulled her panties off and stilled as Greg's hands cupped her naked buttocks, his fingers both strong and gentle. Her eyes opened wide as he guided her to his upthrusting manhood, and she quickly speared herself upon him, a willing sacrifice. They both gasped and cried out as they joined, and Greg felt her knees clench either side of his hips, imprisoning him in a strong, erotic clamp.

His hands held her waist as she began to move up and down, his own breathing sounding like ragged gasps in his ears. He watched, fascinated and humble, as her face became flushed, and her mouth fell open as she began to moan. When she looked at him her eyes were darker than midnight, and he felt his whole body shudder in reaction to the look in their deep, dark depths.

'Verity,' he gasped, his big body beginning to buck, and suddenly they were both crying out in ecstacy as the world receded around them and they rode the wave of passion together. Afterwards they lay together on the carpet, a single ray of sunshine that had cunningly found its way through a chink in the curtains warming their naked bodies. She was lying half on top of him, one of his nipples making an indent in her cheek. He was running one hand over her back in lazy, wonderful circles.

'Verity,' he said, his voice hesitant.

'Hmm?' she mumbled against his chest, and ran one finger over his other nipple. She felt fluid and content. She never wanted to move ever again.

'We . . . It's not just me, is it?' Greg asked, staring at the ceiling. 'I mean . . . We have something together, don't we?'

She smiled against his chest, incredibly touched by his insecurity.

'Yes,' she said softly. 'We do.'

'It's serious.'

Again she smiled. 'Yes,' she assured him. 'It's serious.'

She felt him take a deep breath, and her head rose and fell with his chest. 'Marriage, and children, and all the future together. That kind of serious. Yes?' Greg felt the seconds stretch and felt a cold shiver begin to replace the warming sun. 'Verity?' he said, hearing the fear plainly in his voice.

Verity stirred. 'Yes,' she said. 'Marriage and children, and . . . the future.'

Greg relaxed. His hand curved around her waist. 'Good. We'll have to wait until the cruise is finished to get married of course, but then . . .'

She listened to his happy and excited plans for the future in a miserable silence.

But what else could she have said? That she wasn't even sure there was going to be a future?

CHAPTER 15

Verity loved the early morning. She showered quickly and changed into her bikini, leaving her room and stepping confidently out into the corridor. As expected, there was no one in sight. It was wonderful to have the *Alexandria* all to herself. If she closed her eyes she could almost imagine it was a ghost ship, with only herself and Greg aboard. She was still laughing at her fantasies as she stepped out onto the deck and walked to the rails. With the sun still young she made her way to the pool and dropped her towel onto a deck chair.

Executing a neat duck-dive, she sank beneath the water with growing skill. On the bridge, Jim Goldsmith saw a flash of movement and walked to the window. He cursed gently beneath his breath. Greg glanced up, and then checked his watch. Two hours into the morning watch. He walked up beside his second in command. 'Trouble?'

'A passenger in the pool.'

Greg frowned. 'What time do the lifeguards come on duty?'

'Not for another hour.'

Greg sighed. 'I'd better go down and explain about the safety factor.'

Jim smiled. 'A captain's work is never done.'

Greg scowled good-naturedly and left the bridge. It wasn't until he was half-way down the stairs that he recognized the svelte, dark-haired figure, and his heart jumped.

He walked across slowly, aware that he was probably being watched from the bridge. Nevertheless, the smile that came to her face when she saw him made his breath catch in his throat.

'Hello,' he said softly, and hunkered down beside the pool, his broad back to the bridge.

'Hello yourself. I didn't know you would be up and about,' she said, and meant it. She knew how careful they had to be.

Greg smiled, loving her all the more for her understanding. 'I know. My staff captain spotted you. You're not really supposed to swim when there isn't a lifeguard on duty.'

Verity flushed. 'I'm sorry. I didn't think. And especially since I . . .' She'd been about to say that she had to be very careful now that she was taking the new drug, but stopped herself just in time. Instead, she added, 'I'm not the world's greatest swimmer. It's just that I love having the place all to myself.' Gently and bravely, the way new lovers do, she told him about her little daydream of that morning, and Greg smiled. 'You're a closet romantic, Dr Fox. Who would have guessed?'

'You might,' she said. 'Especially when we reach Antigua.'

Greg's smile faltered. 'I'm on duty all that day.'

Verity took a deep breath, then shrugged one shoulder. 'The Virgin Islands then,' she said, and then chuckled. 'How very inappropriate.'

Greg grunted a laugh and held out his hand, tugging her easily out of the pool. 'You're as light as a feather. You should put on some weight.'

Verity laughed. 'How very unromantic you are, Captain Harding.' She batted her eyelashes at him and he found himself once more laughing, then abruptly remembered they were standing in full view of the bridge.

Verity saw the realization hit him, and half turned away to pick up her towel. 'Well, I'd better go and get changed,' she said, hoping she didn't sound as disappointed as she felt. She loved this man, and wanted the whole world to know it.

Greg read her like a book. Regardless of any watching eyes, he reached out and touched her shoulder in a wordless gesture that pleaded for understanding whilst offering comfort.

She turned to him, her eyes so vulnerable that Greg, for the first time in his life, wanted to curse the ship he was on, and the job he was doing. 'It won't always be like this,' he said softly, his jaw tightening. 'As soon as we make Miami, we'll be married. This ship has officers' married quarters on board. These *are* the 1990s, you know.' He smiled briefly as he recalled his thoughts on married captains at the beginning of

177

this trip. How cocksure of it all he'd been then. How little he really knew. Gently, he ran a finger under her chin.

Verity nodded and quickly turned away so that he shouldn't see her guilt. She should have told him on Martinique about the leukaemia. She should have explained everything right then and there. She reached for a towel and began rubbing her hair briskly. 'Oh Greg, I'm sorry,' she said, and hoped that, between the layers of towel and the ocean breeze, he hadn't heard. When she came out from under the towel, he was gone. She cast one, brief, agonized look at the blank, impenetrable glass of the bridge, then turned and walked back to her room.

Once there she mixed a tiny portion of the powdered drug into a glass of water and drank it without a qualm. If it was able to keep her white and red blood cell count in enough harmony to live a normal life, she'd happily devote that life to Greg. There would be children, and Christmasses together when they would make up their own, special, family traditions. But if the drug didn't work . . . Then all Greg would have would be a funeral to arrange. In the warm and beautiful cabin, on the huge and wonderful ship, in the beautiful and breathtaking Caribbean, Verity Fox shuddered.

Two decks above, in one of the *Alexandria*'s major suites, Joceline Alexander stared up at the ceiling. She hadn't slept at all. How could she, when her son was in love with Ramona King? She sighed and turned restlessly. She had to do something, that was obvious.

But what? Nothing she could say would make Damon change his mind about Ramona, that had been made obvious to her yesterday. Damon had immediately launched into singing her praises. She was an Oxford Don, no less. And, although he never said so, it was obvious he believed that this Ramona King woman had never loved anyone else but him in her entire life. As if *that* could possibly be true. A woman as beautiful as that. And yet she had made Damon, usually so worldly-wise, believe it.

How could she fight a woman like that? With a sigh, she pushed back the bedcovers and ran hot water into the basin. Was she just projecting her own fears, her own betrayal, onto Ramona King? Was she being totally unfair, visiting the sins of the father onto those of the daughter?

Dressing in the first outfit she came across, she dressed wearily and stepped out to meet her son and his girlfriend for breakfast. Ramona, watching the older woman approach, felt a familiar tightening in her stomach. She wasn't sure why, and she had not mentioned it to Damon, but she was sure his mother didn't like her. The restraint was still in Joceline Alexander's eyes as they met her own. Ramona glanced at Damon quickly, but he seemed to see nothing wrong. With a sigh she reached for the menu and quietly ordered muffins. After several pots of tea and polite conversation, Joceline excused herself, and left. Miserably, Ramona stared into her cup.

'Don't let my mother worry you,' Damon said softly, and she glanced across at him. Dressed in a simple pale blue T-shirt and white loose-fitting slacks, he looked so handsome, Ramona never wanted to look away. Immediately, the old familiar battle began. Love versus hate. Need versus trust. Want versus common sense. Would it never end, she thought wildly. If only she could be *sure*. Sure of Damon's guilt. Sure of her own feelings. Sure of her own motivation . . .

Oblivious to her confusion, he ran a harassed hand through his hair and sighed. 'I've got so used to the way she is, I forget, sometimes, what other people must think of her.'

Ramona was glad he'd brought the subject up. It gave her something else to concentrate on. 'I don't think she likes me,' she said bluntly, waiting for him to make the usual, placatory noises. They never came. Instead, Damon smiled ruefully. 'I don't think she likes me, either.'

'Damon!' Ramona said, sincerely shocked.

'Don't look so appalled,' he said gently. 'My mother and I . . .' he sighed. 'It's hard to explain.' But he gave it his best shot. As the restaurant slowly emptied around them, he told her about his often lonely childhood. She felt for him as he told her about the death of his father, and his rage and hate for some unknown burglar. And she felt sad for him as he talked with obvious bewilderment about his mother's reaction to it all. 'She just seemed to get further and further away from me,' he finished, his voice sad but not self-pitying.

Worldlessly, she reached across and took his hand in hers. He looked at her, love in his eyes, and she felt a fist punch her straight in her guilty heart. One moment she hated him for making her take risks. The next, she so vividly wanted to sample everything he was teaching her, showing her . . .

After their wonderful, unexpectedly passionate and fulfilling love-making, she had drifted with the tide, very much as the *Alexandria* rode the currents. One moment she was sure she loved him as much as he seemed to love her, the next moment she was suspicious of his every move. Now, here he was pouring out his heart, and she felt both sorry for him, and protective of him, and so very, very guilty.

'Nothing I did could bring her back,' Damon sighed, shaking his head. 'I even thought that somehow she might blame me for what happened to Dad. Eventually, I just stopped trying.'

Ramona shook her head sadly. What life did to people . . . 'Grief affects different people in different ways,' she said softly. 'Perhaps she retreated so far, and pushed you so far away, that when she'd finished grieving, she didn't know how to get you back?'

Damon looked at her, his throat tight. With Ramona, he knew he could open up every secret in his heart, and they'd be safe with her. She understood things in a way nobody else could. Looking into her kind, troubled eyes, he felt a swelling, wonderous kind of happiness. 'I love you,' he said softly.

Ramona took a deep breath. 'I love you too,' she acknowledged. But she wished with all her heart that she didn't.

Damon suddenly realized they were the only ones left in the restaurant. With a wry grin, he got to his feet.

'Come on. We can't sit here discussing my sad childhood all day long. It will have us both blubbering into our napkins.'

Ramona smiled, relieved to be out of such dangerous waters, and let herself be led back to his cabin. Once there he shut the door and simply watched her, the moments stretching into infinity as her body flamed wherever his eyes touched her.

In the heavy, pulsating silence she stared back at him, her heart thumping as he slowly pulled the T-shirt off his head, the cotton tousling his hair as it came away, his bronzed muscles rippling with telling ease. Her throat went bone-dry as he slowly, very slowly, walked barefoot towards her, his eyes holding hers prisoner as surely as chains. When he lifted her, her body shuddered in expectation, and as he carried her to the bed she felt her vagina flood with molten heat. She lay looking up at him as he gently lowered himself over her, his eyes darkening as his hands moved gently but possessively up her rib-cage. His lips parted on the softest of sighs as his two thumbs rubbed across her stiffening nipples. Ramona gasped and then closed her eyes as he lowered his head and kissed her, his tongue delving deep into her mouth, his hands quickly stripping them both of their confining clothes. It felt so good to feel his naked flesh against hers, and seemed as natural as breathing. She ran her hands along his back, loving the feel of firm warm skin over muscles that clenched spasmodically at her touch. She traced the indentation of his spine and moaned as he nudged her legs gently apart with his knees, his movements both tender and yet brooking no refusal. She could feel the power in his thighs as they parted hers, and her womb contracted sharply in sudden, intense desire.

They both cried out as their bodies came together, and nails dug into his shoulders as he plunged deeply into her. Of their own accord, her legs locked around his, holding him prisoner inside her honeyed depths, and within moments she was eagerly, unthinkingly, moving in time with the rhythm he set. The minutes rushed by in spiralling pleasure, their soft cries and their thrashing bodies performing their own dance to their own music. When she cried out, her whole body locking briefly into a vice of ecstacy, she felt the world slip away from her, and didn't care. It came back in a slow, throbbing ebb, bringing her into awareness of his heavy, manly body on top of her, his head cushioned on her shoulder, his lower lip a fraction of a millimitre away from her nipple, his panting breath making it tingle and tighten with delicious pleasure.

For a long while she lay absently stroking his head, his scalp warm against her fingers, his hair cool on her palm. Eventually he rose and stood looking down at her for a moment, and then without a word, walked to a desk and opened the top drawer. Puzzled, she raised herself on one elbow and watched him. When he came back he was carrying a small box that bore the logo of the ship's jewellery store, a branch of one of the most famous, family-owned jewellery stores in the world.

Her heart stopped then began to beat like a sledge-hammer. Before he spoke, before he even opened the lid, she knew what it was. 'When I saw this, I knew it had been made especially for you, Ramona,' he said gently, kneeling down carefully astride her legs and sitting back on his heels. His shoulders and chest were slightly sweat-slicked from their love-making, and his face was still a little flushed with passion. He seemed totally at ease with his nakedness, and she felt her body tremble with remembered passion. His eyes never leaving her face, he flipped the lid. 'Will you marry me, Ramona?'

He had thought, when asking her this most ultimate of questions, he would feel a little apprehension. Perhaps a little surprise. But he felt neither. He'd never been so sure of anything in his life.

Her eyes, unable to meet his, fell to the box in his hand and she gasped. The engagement ring was very different from the traditional, round diamond. Instead, the ring was a large oval, and although it contained diamonds, they formed a glittering, silver-white edge around a large stone of the lightest but most vibrant blue she'd ever seen.

'It's a Ceylon sapphire,' he said. 'I got it because . . .' he retrieved the ring from its cream velvet and held it up to one cheek. 'Yes, it is,' he breathed, a delighted smile creasing his handsome face. 'It's exactly the same colour as your eyes.'

Still she said nothing, and he reached, a little hesitantly, for her left hand and held it for a moment in his. The moment seemed to hang in eternity. Ramona had never needed to rely on instinct before, but in that moment that was all she had, and as she looked down at their joined hands, she saw her fingers fall apart, freeing the third finger of her left hand as if by magic. From under her eyelashes, she saw him smile and his eyes flash in happiness, and her own heart leapt but then quickly subsided, unable to beat with all the happiness it, too, felt. She just couldn't allow it. How could she let him put the ring on her finger? But he was doing just that, and she was doing nothing to stop him. As she stared at the ring on her hand, it felt cold and heavy and alien. And yet she lacked the strength to reach out and take it off.

She looked up, her mouth open to say something, but then he was kissing her, and the passion flared again, and she could do nothing, say nothing, except moan, and gasp, and scream as he made love to her.

Joceline walked down the corridor, feeling numb all over. Neither Ramona King nor her son had mentioned the ring at dinner, but Joceline had noticed it at once, on the third finger of Ramona's left hand. It had seemed to wink and catch the light every time Ramona moved. The beautiful blue stone seemed to be laughing at Joceline. If they were engaged, why didn't Damon say something?

Joceline didn't like it. It was all happening too fast. It couldn't be coincidence that Joe King's daughter was on board, getting her claws into her son. And if Ramona broke Damon's heart . . . Joceline's hands clenched into fists. If she hurt her son . . . Joceline would kill her.

John looked up as Verity walked into his surgery and rose with a smile. 'Verity! How are you today?' he asked, his kind face darkening with concern. 'No relapses?'

Verity quickly shook her head. 'No, no, nothing like that. I came because I have a friend meeting me in the Virgin Islands. A blood specialist. He wants to take and analyze some of my blood samples. You can do that here?'

'Sure, no problem,' John said easily. 'We have a quite sophisticated lab on board.'

Verity smiled, somewhat wryly. She wondered if he'd be so casual once the results came in. The very nature of the drug she was taking would ensure that the changes would be enormous, and occur very quickly. Be they good, or bad . . .

Jeff dialled his boss, his brows furrowed into a frown. When Joe King answered, he said simply, 'She's got engaged.'

In one of the finest hotels on Antigua, Joe King straightened stiffly in his chair. 'Ramona?'

'I was just in the dining room. She was wearing a ring on her left hand and they were acting . . .'

'You're talking about Damon Alexander?'

'Yeah. I thought you were going to approach her on Martinique,' Jeff said flatly.

'I didn't get the chance,' Joe snapped, his thoughts racing.

Jeff smiled. The old man was rattled. 'What do you want me to do about this engagement?'

'Don't worry about it. I'll see to that from this end.' Abruptly, there was only the dialling tone left in Jeff's ear, and he slowly hung up. He shook his head. He didn't like it. He didn't like it at all.

In Antigua, Joe King slammed the phone down and immediately redialled. This time he reached London. 'Get onto Treadstone's firm. Tell his boss that there will definitely be no repercussions for his firm. We won't be suing for the money back. He can inform Ramona King of that fact. What? That's none of your business. Just do as you're told.'

Angrily, Joe King hung up. He had to sit for a long time before he could bring his temper under control. Eventually, though, he smiled. Things were back on track. And tomorrow, when he finally met his wayward daughter, things would get even better.

Damon Alexander's days of glory were well and truly numbered.

CHAPTER 16

Antigua

'**W**ith three hundred and sixty-five beaches to choose from, I think we can manage to find one we like,' Damon said wryly, glancing at Ramona's stuffed beach bag as they disembarked and strolled casually to a waiting taxi. Ramona felt him take her hand in his, and glanced down, her eyes skidding off the twinkling Ceylon sapphire on her finger and up into his eyes. In the cab, which set off on the left-hand side of the road, they quickly travelled through St John's, the capital city that was home to nearly half of the island's population.

'I never get tired of these islands,' Ramona said softly, glancing out at the passing scenery. 'They're all so different. Every one seems to have something special.'

Damon grinned. 'I know what you mean.'

'Where to, man?' the lazy, ultra laid-back drawl of their taxi driver asked.

'The best beach you've got,' Damon said.

'You lovely people want a beach with a view? Carlisle Bay has a bluff on the peninsula that looks right out over the Atlantic.'

Damon smiled. 'We were thinking of something more . . .'

The taxi driver's eyes twinkled. 'Ah, of course. Young people such as yourselves . . . You want the sports, yes?' he teased the obvious lovers with a gleeful smile. 'Moon Bay is three quarters of a mile long and is prime snorkelling and windsurfing territory.'

Ramona largely ignored them, too busy thinking of other things. She was relieved that Damon had agreed to keep their engagement under wraps, just for the duration of the cruise. He had wanted to throw a big party and announce it to the whole ship, but the thought had made her shudder. It would have made it so . . . final. So *established*.

'Very funny,' Damon muttered. 'This is supposed to be an island of beaches. Surely you can think of one that is nice and quiet and out of the way?'

The driver's cheerful dark face sobered. 'Yes, man. There are plenty of beaches like that on Antigua. Johnson's Point, for instance, over on the south-west coast. That's usually deserted.'

'That's fine.'

'Or there's Lignumvitae Bay, just south of Jolly Bay, on the edge of the saltwater swamp. Not many people go there.'

'I think we'll give the swamp a miss, thank you,' Damon said archly, but with a grin. He was in such a good mood he could take teasing from anyone.

The taxi driver, glancing in his mirror, frowned. The big black expensive-looking car was still with them. He remembered it following them all the way out of the city. The driver shrugged. There were so many expensive cars on Antigua these days. So many rich tourists.

The teasing by-play was totally lost on Ramona. Only when the taxi pulled to a halt under a stand of palms, did she realize she had allowed herself to be steered to a quiet, sparsely-populated beach in the middle of nowhere. Briefly she recalled passing an odd, now unused, old sugar plantation. As she stepped out, the warmth hit her, along with the cry of the gulls. As she watched, Damon paid the driver, asking him to come back at midday. Seeing the size of the tip, the driver cheerfully agreed. When the car was gone, Damon held out his hand and she could do nothing else but take it. Then he was pulling her close, and bending down and kissing her, and she was glad there was nothing else she could do.

Half a mile down the deserted road, the taxi passed the expensive black car parked on a layby of compacted beach sand. As he passed he thought he saw the tip of a pair of binoculars poking out from the back seat's open window. He frowned, and wondered if the beautiful blonde lady was married. And if so, did she know her husband was on to them? The taxi driver smiled gently and a touch sadly. Ah well, such was life.

Verity Fox was at Nelson's Dockyard. According to the pamphlet she had picked up, Horatio Nelson had headquartered here for his forays into the Caribbean to do battle with the old traditional enemy, France. The English harbour just south of Falmouth was one of the island's greatest attractions and had only recently been restored, and the old forts and eighteenth-century naval base was obviously a history buff's paradise.

She wished Greg was here to share all this atmosphere with her. Things improved 100 per cent when you were with someone you loved. She'd just decided it was time to head to the beautifully-restored Cooper and Lumber Store Hotel for a cold drink and a relaxing half an hour in the welcoming shade, when she felt a hot flush suddenly swamp her. Verity paused, caught by surprise. As people moved around her, like a river finding a path round a pebble, she swallowed hard, her throat suddenly dry. The flush, she knew instinctively, had nothing to do with the heat. It was as if her whole body had suddenly risen in temperature like mercury in a thermometer. She looked around and spotted a bench and slowly, carefully, made her way to it. Her whole body felt tight and hot, as if she was suffering from indigestion all over. She got to the bench and slowly lowered herself down. The flush was burning her face, her hands, arms, legs. And yet it wasn't painful, as such. Oxygen. She knew it was imperative she regulate her breathing. Slowly, carefully, she spread her legs a little and lowered her head almost onto her lap, leaning forward to prevent her from passing out. She began to do breathing exercises, almost like a woman in labour. Slowly, her heartbeat began to return to normal, and after a while, very slowly, the heat too, began to fade. Very carefully, she sat up. She looked at her watch and made a mental note of the time. She was keeping a careful and complete diary of her progress; when she took the drug, and how much. Until now, she'd had no side effects to report.

She told herself it was useless to worry. Practically every strong drug had side effects. And really, the hot flush wasn't so bad. So she told herself. But when she stood up and found herself feeling almost normal again, she did not head back into the most famous tourist attraction on the island. She headed for a taxi and the ship. She might not be able to see him or talk to him, but right now she only wanted to be near the man she loved.

The black car followed them all the way back from the beach. Francis, the taxi driver, had not been surprised to pass the black car still parked in the layby, and wondered if he should warn his passengers that the lady's husband was on to them. Francis sighed. No, it was none of his business who was following the lovely rich couple. He'd just drive, and take the tip, and go home to his wife. Better not to get involved.

They didn't go back to St John's, but instead went to Falmouth, past Monk's Hill and Fort George and what was the base of the old Flagstaff.

Falmouth itself, Ramona saw immediately, was sited on one and a half miles of a lovely bay, backed by former sugar plantations and sugar mills. When Francis dropped them off, he noticed the black car pulled in three places behind them, parking outside a pleasant little open-air café. Francis sighed, took the man's money a little guiltily and pulled away.

Damon and Ramona walked slowly along the pavement, admiring the colonial feeling of the small town and the views. 'I'm starving,' Damon said. 'For food as well,' he added, laughing as she blushed and playfully thumped him. Spotting a café with it's higgledy-piggledy collection of odd chairs and tables she took a seat under a sun-shade.

From the car, her father watched her, his admiring and proud eyes running over her. She was so beautiful. His daughter. Intelligent. Perhaps a little dangerous. But his daughter.

Oblivous to everything but one another, Damon ordered the Mediterranean seafood terrine, sprinkled with saffron, whilst Ramona opted for the soufflé of scallops with a basil puree.

In the car, Joe King nodded to himself, smiled, and reached for the telephone.

On board the *Alexandria*, Verity Fox reached her cabin and sank gratefully onto the bed. Now that she was resting, she felt paradoxically even more tired than before. Her legs felt a little rubbery, her stomach a little fluttery. Nothing to worry about. Nothing too out of the ordinary.

She reached for her diary and wrote out her notes, took her pulse and temperature and recorded that too.

She lay patiently still for a long time, staring at the ceiling, waiting to feel better.

'Is there a Mr Alexander here?' the proprietor of the café called from inside. Damon looked up from his long glass of pineapple and rum, his eyes widening in surprise. 'How the hell . . .?' he said then shrugged his shoulders at Ramona's lifted eyebrows and went inside.

From the back of the car, the man waited.

Damon lifted the receiver. 'Yes?'

On board the *Alexandria*, Jeff Doyle quickly put a handkerchief over the mouthpiece. 'Is that Mr Damon Alexander?'

'Yes. Who is this? How did you know I was here?'

'I'm sorry to bother you, Mr Alexander, there seems to be a problem at the ship, sir. Captain Harding asked me to find you and request that you return immediately.'

Outside, Ramona glanced briefly through the window and saw Damon talking into the phone, his back towards the window. She frowned, but was relieved at the interruption. It was too easy to fall deeper and deeper under Damon's seductive spell. The telephone call, whoever it was from, had probably saved her sliding yet another notch down into the beckoning but dangerous abyss that was love without trust. The problem was, she couldn't seem to make herself care. The downward journey into love was too wonderful for her to want to fight it. Her mother had been right, about everything. Life had been passing her by, and now it had caught up with her with a vengeance.

And what of Keith? Where did he come into this new-found life of hers? He was dead . . . Suddenly, in the bright and cheerful Caribbean sunlight, she went utterly cold. Had Keith had to die in order for her to live? Was this new, heady, wonderful, brave new world of hers being built over the foundations of his grave?

She was still no further towards avenging him. Distracted, bemused and confused, she was letting him down.

She heard the door of the car parked almost opposite her open and close, but didn't realize she was no longer alone until a shadow fell across the table. She looked up into the sun, blocked by a large and solid form, and put her hand up to her eyes. The man moved, stepping out of the glare and moving across to sit briefly in the chair Damon Alexander had just vacated. As he did so, Ramona opened her mouth to say that the seat was taken, then abruptly changed her mind as she recognized him from his newspaper photographs. Joe King. Her father. Her mind went suddenly blank, the shock was so profound. As a child, she'd felt his absence keenly. But her mother had made it plain, as gently as possible, that her father just wasn't going to be in their lives. And she'd grown to accept it. But now . . . Ramona shivered. He was a vital looking man, with an invisible aura of power. In his sixties, with silvery-grey hair and wide, hazel eyes.

'Hello, Ramona,' Joe King said simply.

'Hello, Father,' she returned, just as simply.

Joe King glanced casually over his shoulder into the café, seeing with relief that Damon Alexander still had his back to the window. 'I need to speak to you,' her father said. 'There's a lot to be explained. Can you get away from your young man and meet me somewhere?'

Despite the sheer surrealism of the situation, Ramona felt utterly calm. 'Can you give me one good reason why I should?'

Joe King smiled sadly. 'No.'

Ramona blinked, a little surprised by the simple admission.

'But I am your father,' Joe King added gently.

'A little late in the day to remember that, isn't it?' Ramona said, no bitterness in her voice. In truth, she felt none. This man was a stranger to her.

'Perhaps it is,' Joe King said gently, never taking his eyes off her. 'Perhaps it isn't. Perhaps I'm just in time.'

Ramona's eyes sharpened. 'What do you mean by that?'

Joe King knew he didn't have much time. Doyle couldn't keep Damon talking forever. Quickly he took a card from his pocket and wrote a phone number on it. 'This is where I'll be staying in the Virgin Islands. Call me there tomorrow at ten. It's important, Ramona.'

Ramona reluctantly took the card. 'Why now?' she said, suspiciously. 'Why after all these years?'

Her father shook his head. 'It's a long story. And it's a story you have to hear, Ramona. For your own sake.' His eyes seemed to bore into hers, and with a start Ramona felt herself responding to the compelling stare. Blinking, she drew back.

'I'm not sure,' she murmured, and Joe stood up, knowing his time was running out.

'Call me,' he said again. 'And Ramona . . .' he hesitated, glanced once more over his shoulder, and then back at her. 'Don't trust Alexander.' Quickly he held up his hand, seeing she was about to launch into an avalanche of questions. 'I'll explain it all when you call. Just . . . don't trust him.'

196

Satisfied that he'd planted the seed of mistrust just deep enough to keep her from talking about him to Alexander, Joe walked back quickly to his car and closed the door, just as Damon stepped onto the pavement, a frown on his face.

'There's something going on back at the ship.' He looked down at her, seeing her pale face and wide eyes, and mistook her shock. 'I'm sorry, I didn't mean to blurt it out like that. I'm sure it's nothing serious. But I'd better go.'

Ramona turned sharply as the black car pulled smoothly out onto the road. She stood on legs that felt slightly shaky, and picked up her bag. 'I'll go with you.'

Together they rode the taxi back to the harbour, and while Damon strode anxiously off to the bridge, Ramona walked quietly and thoughtfully back to her cabin, where she slumped down onto the couch, her mind spinning.

Her father, after all these years. Warning her against Damon. Asking her to call him, as if he had every right in the world to expect her obedience. What did it all mean?

She reached for the phone and dialled her own number in Oxford, drumming her fingers against the table as she waited impatiently for her mother to answer. 'Hello?'

'Mother?'

'Ramona. Do you have any idea what time it is?'

Ramona flushed guiltily. 'Sorry, I haven't.'

Barbara King laughed. 'Forget it, darling,' she said,

sitting up straighter in her bed and yawning. 'How are things going?'

'Fine. I've . . . met Damon Alexander.' And perhaps, she thought bitterly, it would have been better all around if she had just stayed at home and tried to forget everything. But then a little voice said wickedly, there would have been no love-making on a yacht in a deserted cove. No wedding ring . . .

'What's he like?'

Her mother's question jerked her back from her thoughts, and she almost laughed aloud. What was Damon like? 'If only you knew . . .' she said softly, almost to herself. 'Oh, Mother, it's all so complicated. Let's forget about him for a moment. I called about something completely different. Although perhaps it might all be connected.' Romana broke off for a moment, and laughed out loud. 'I'm not making much sense, am I?'

Barbara King's voice had a smile in it when she answered. 'Not much, no. I take it this Damon Alexander has had something of an effect on you?'

Ramona bit her lip, and sighed. Sometimes her mother seemed to have an uncanny sense of perception. 'You could say that,' she admitted wryly, then quickly changed the subject. 'I called about . . . my father,' she said instead.

There was a short, telling silence on the other end, and then Barbara said cautiously, 'What about him?'

'He met me on Antigua today. Just a few minutes ago in fact. That's why I called. Mum? Are you OK?'

Barbara roused herself, sitting up straighter in bed

and trying to keep calm. 'Yes I'm fine. I'm just . . . a bit surprised, that's all. You're sure it was him?'

'Positive. And he introduced himself.'

'What did he want?' Barbara said quickly, and far more sharply than she realized.

Ramona felt her hand tightening on the receiver, not missing the sharp fear in her mother's voice. 'I'm not sure. He said I wasn't to trust Damon and to call him. He said it was important that we talked. I think it's about the *Alexandria*, but I'm not sure. In fact, I think I'm becoming obsessed with this damned ship,' she admitted grimly.

Barbara was silent for a few moments more, then said quietly, 'What else did he say?'

Ramona could hear the tension in her voice, and felt guilty for bothering her with all this. 'Nothing really. We didn't have much time. Mum, you never really did talk about him much. How does he think? Do you know anything about his feud with Michael Alexander, and can that have anything to do with why he's warning me against Damon?'

Barbara King sighed deeply. 'I only know he despises the Alexanders. But why . . . It could be anything. Ramona, be careful of your father. Joe was . . . Well, he always was a man who simply *had* to get his own way. He always had such a *forceful* way about him.'

'I know what you mean,' Ramona said gruffly.

Back in Oxford, Barbara sighed. What did Joe want with his daughter after all these years? Could he really want a reconciliation? And if so, did she have any right to try and put a stop to it? 'After a while, we drifted

199

apart,' Barbara began cautiously. 'I think he had another woman.' But she would not say who she suspected Joe of having an affair with. She really *hadn't* had any proof and yet it could have something to do with the *Alexandria* and what was going on now. But after twenty odd years? 'Just be careful, Ramona, that's all I ask. Your father is a complex person. He likes to win. He's tough and . . . Well, when he was younger, he could be quite ruthless.'

Ramona licked her suddenly dry lips. 'I see.'

And she did. Her father was a man used to getting what he wanted. She'd have to be wary. 'OK. I'll be careful, I promise. And don't worry, Mother, I'll call you back when I know more.'

Barbara sighed gratefully. 'I know you will.' It was at times like this that she blessed her daughter's extraordinary intellect. Not wishing to dwell on Joe King, but knowing that she'd nonetheless lie awake all night thinking about him, she adeptly changed the subject. 'Oh, before I forget. I got a phone call myself earlier tonight, from Keith's old boss on the stock-exchange. Something strange has happened.'

And with those ominous words, Joe King was quickly delegated to second place in Ramona's mind. 'Oh?' she said sharply. 'What did he want?'

Barbara King's voice had lost it's anxiousness now, and was more alert. 'It's really odd. It's that client that Keith borrowed from.'

Ramona ignored her mother's tactful use of words, and felt a cold slithering up her back. Her heart began to race. She could feel cold fear uncoil in her stomach and she licked her painfully dry lips. Something awful was about to happen. She just knew it. 'What about it? Are they suing me for the money now?'

'No, darling, just the opposite,' Barbara said happily, but obviously still puzzled. 'He's pulling out of Keith's firm, yes, but he's made it clear that he's more than happy with the service they received.'

Ramona gasped, for a second too stunned to take it all in. 'But that doesn't make sense. Keith must have used millions of his money,' she murmured.

'I know. That's what we can't understand. It doesn't make any sense at all, does it, just giving up on all those shares like that?' Barbara agreed, her voice perplexed. And in the back of her mind, she wondered. Joe King. Was it just a coincidence that he had reappeared in their lives just at this moment?

'No,' Ramona said automatically, her voice barely audible. 'It doesn't make sense.' But it did. It made perfect sense. With a sudden clarity that was brutal, she understood it all, and the truth was so hard it almost smashed her to pieces.

The mysterious client wasn't suing for the money back that he had given Keith to purchase shares, because the client knew full damn well that those shares were all his, after all. They were, in fact, perfectly safe.

He was marrying them.

After everything that had happened, it was, it *had* to be, Damon after all.

201

CHAPTER 17

Jeff Doyle checked that the stopper on a bluish-white phial of innocuous looking liquid was tightly sealed, then put it in his coat pocket. When Joe King had given it to him yesterday afternoon, he'd asked what it was. His only answer had been a warning glare. Obviously, it was better not to know. Which was fine with Jeff. He opened his cabin door and stealthily crept down the passageway. It was three-thirty in the morning.

He had to consult a map before he found the galley entrance, a part of the ship normally off-limits to passengers. Once inside, Jeff paused. He daren't put any lights on, but his torch, sweeping in arcs, picked out what looked like acres of top space, rows of ovens, and gadgets galore. It was nearing four before he found the temperature-controlled wine room, and stepped inside. It was unlike any wine cellar he'd ever seen. Every bottle hung in a hammock-like construction. It took him a while to realize that these were the gyroscopically-controlled wine bins. If the ship rolled, the 'hammock' rolled counterwise to it, so that the precious, fizzy champagnes and sparkling wines were not tossed about, but kept on an even keel.

He glanced at his watch. Joe King's instructions had been very clear. Find the batch of champagne that was to be used on the final night's cruising. There was to be a special champagne masked ball to celebrate the end of the cruise, with fancy dress available from the ship's own fancy-dress store.

Jeff had immediately understood his thinking, of course. What was in the innocuous looking phial now in his hand would make everybody ill overnight. Then, when the *Alexandria* sailed majestically into Florida, with hordes of press photographers and media waiting, the big story would not be the successful end to a triumphant voyage, but the sight of stretcher after stretcher of groaning passengers being rushed off to hospital. And with the ship disgraced, Damon Alexander would be ousted by his outraged board, and the Alexander Line itself would be ripe for a takeover. By Joe King Industries, of course. Jeff smiled and got out a long, sharp syringe that had been safely nestled in its case. Then he ran his torch over the neat labels on the sides of one batch, which was set just a little apart from the rest. Very nice of them, he mused, to label them all as 'Masked Ball'.

Jeff carefully counted the bottles, eyebrows rising at the vintages. Wines so exclusively expensive that only the super-rich ever drank them. Carefully, he divided the number of bottles with the tiny marks on the syringe. The maths done, Jeff inserted the hyperdermic through the cork of the first bottle. Eyes glued to the tiny marks along the side of the needle, he began to press. Very lightly. A miniscule amount went into the champagne. One down. Two hundred and nineteen to go . . .

In her cabin, Joceline Alexander slowly hung up the phone. She'd been talking to a very reliable little man her son had put her in touch with years ago, when she'd wanted a little discreet private investigation to be carried out.

Lately, she'd set him the task of keeping an eye on Joe King. And what he had had to tell her was not good. Not good at all. Joe King was in the Caribbean. Worse, he and his daughter had met for a few minutes, right under Damon's nose. The *nerve* of that man! And as for her . . . Ramona.

Joceline felt helpless, hot and despairing tears slid down her cheeks, and she quickly rubbed them away. She had been hoping against hope . . . But Ramona King was as rotten as her father. Together they were up to something. Of that she had no doubt. She already knew Joe King was making a move on the Alexander Line. Her little man had quite a few contacts in the commercial world, and she already knew that Keith Treadstone had been in bed, so to speak, with her former lover. No coincidence, surely, that he had been Ramona King's fiancée.

And if Joe King had been gathering shares on the quiet, using Keith Treadstone, who else on the shareholder's list was really Joe King in all but name? Was a takeover imminent?

Now, more than ever, it was imperative that she give Damon the ammunition he needed to destroy Joe King once and for all. Even if she had to destroy herself in the process . . .

Jeff watched the last drop of blue-white liquid disappear into a bottle of Mouton Rothschild, and sighed. Finished. And not a moment too soon. He went quickly to the wine-cellar door and opened it. The galley was still deserted. He crossed the dark room and opened the outer door, squinting into the crack along the corridor. His heart leapt and he quickly shut it again, wincing at the small clicking noise.

Greg, walking briskly along the deck, stopped abruptly. He glanced around, but saw nothing amiss. All the doors were shut but he moved back a step, sure the sound had come from the galley. He glanced at his watch and saw it was five-thirty. Still very early. But then the executive chef probably got off to an early start.

He shrugged, a frown crossing his face. Into his mind, he saw again a picture of Verity leaving the surgery, and the blood-pressure equipment, and sample of blood she'd left behind. He wasn't sure why, but that scene kept coming back, thrusting its way into his consciousness, unwilling to leave him alone.

With a shrug in the galley's direction, he set off down the corridor once more.

With his ear pressed to the door, Jeff waited, then slipped out. It had been close. But nothing he couldn't have handled. A ship could be a dangerous place, and if the captain were to have an unfortunate, and fatal, accident. Well . . . there was always the staff captain who could take over.

It was raining. For the first time since the voyage began, the water fell from the sky like a torrent. But far from depressing the passengers, it delighted them. The tropical rainfall was nothing like the cold, damp rain back home in England. This was a warm, gushing torrent that every steward on board seemed to reassure them would soon be over. Tropical storms were wet, but brief, and everybody knew the hurricane season was months away. As Ramona and Damon chose a table next to the window and looked out over the deluge, Ramona smiled at the almost festive mood on board. 'Everybody suddenly loves the rain,' she murmured, determined to keep her smile and loving look firmly in place.

She'd put him off staying with her last night, claiming a mild bout of seasickness. His solicitousness would once have made her feel even more guilty, but not this time. She'd had the whole, sleepless night to make her plans, and this morning she'd been nervous, wondering if she could possibly look him in the eye and not betray her rage and determination.

But it had been easier than she'd thought to react to his kiss, to smile into his eyes, to talk the talk of lovers.

He smiled directly into her eyes. 'Mmm,' he agreed. 'If I was sure I could find a place where we could be guaranteed privacy, I'd like to make love to you in the rain,' he said, his eyes smouldering. 'All that warm water, the open air, the sea breeze, and us . . .'

Her heart leapt at the words and she reached out her hand to let it rest briefly, lovingly, over his. When she looked at him, she wanted to simultaneously kill him and make love to him. But on the outside at least, she was perfectly in control and could just about step back and watch herself play the besotted, foolish puppet. No doubt he thought he had her thoroughly under control. How did he have it planned? Marry her first, then ask her to place all the financial aspects of their marriage into his hands? Yes, no doubt something like that. It was what you got, a small voice crowed at the back of her mind in a twisted kind of triumph, when you decided to 'live' instead of opting for safety.

'We could always go to my room and take a shower,' he said, laughing as she gave him a speaking look.

Yes, Ramona thought. Laugh, my darling. Laugh while you can. Because soon I'm going to wipe even the tiniest of smiles right off your face. The sweet savagery of this thought was abruptly suspended as the captain smoothly appeared at their table.

Damon frowned slightly. He didn't like being interrupted when he was with Ramona. He wanted his attention to be totally free to enjoy every second. 'Yes, Greg?' he asked, his impatient tone not lost on any of them.

'I need to speak to you, Mr Alexander,' Greg said, a little stiffly. He, like everyone else, knew about the 'Romance of the Voyage', as everyone was calling the love affair between the handsome, bachelor owner, and the very beautiful and slightly mysterious passenger who seemed to have captured his heart. As Greg might have warned him, on a ship, even one as big as the *Alexandria*, secrets were impossible to keep. And the ring Ramona King had suddenly started wearing had not been lost on the crowd. Although there were strictly no reporters on board (the super-rich didn't like to have their pleasure spoiled by picking up a paper and seeing their drunken faces splashed across the gossip columns) the press had somehow got wind of it, and already the London papers that were flown out to their every port of call were beginning to speculate that *the* bachelor of the year might, at last, have been caught.

And the last thing Greg wanted was to interrupt his boss's *tête-à-tête*'s. Damon frowned. 'Is it about yesterday?'

When Damon had rushed onto the bridge and asked Greg what he wanted, Greg had only been able to stare at him blankly. When Damon told him about the phone call, and Greg had denied asking for it to be made, it immediately became clear that some sort of practical joke had been played. It had worried them both. Damon still couldn't figure out how anyone had known where he was, unless he was being watched. And Greg wondered if the spitefulness of the joke might spell future danger for the ship.

Greg nodded. He hadn't been able to let it rest.

Damon didn't miss the seriousness in the other man's tone, and he knew how cool Greg was under fire. Whatever it was, it had to be bad trouble. He glanced at Ramona, but she smiled sweetly. 'No need to apologize. You go ahead.'

As she watched the two men disappear, her smile

vanished. If it was ship's business they were discussing, they would soon have to discuss it with her.

For, come what may, and no matter what she had to do, she was going to take this damned ship away from Damon. It was the only thing she *could* do, because it was the only thing he seemed to care about. If he was willing to drive a man to suicide over it, and marry someone he didn't love just to ensure it stayed his, then it was the only way to attack him.

Besides, a small, weary voice piped up, somewhere from deep inside her weary soul. Isn't that what you've always wanted? To attack him. To be safe from him. To crawl back into your oh-so-safe little shell . . . Angrily, she pushed the thought aside. *She* didn't matter any more. What she wanted was insignificant. It was Keith who was dead. Keith who couldn't seek his own justice, making it imperative that she did so for him. And so she *was* going to attack Damon Alexander, and make it count. Just like he had attacked her. Making her fall in love with him. Oh yes. She was going to take the *Alexandria* away from him alright.

Even if the thought of his pain did cripple her with anguish.

Mentally and physically she straightened her shoulders. Tomorrow, in the Virgin Islands, she was sure her father was going to get in touch with her again. She deliberately hadn't called him, as he'd asked. What she wanted to ask him could not be said over a telephone. It had to be said face to face.

Briefly she remembered her mother's warning to be

wary of Joe King. And wary she would be, even though it was Damon who was the real snake in her garden . . .

Greg steered Damon to a quiet corner, and cast a look around. 'I traced the call made to you at the restaurant.'

Damon blinked. 'Traced it? How? Unless . . .'

Greg nodded, his face grim. 'It came from here. From the *Alexandria* herself. From one of the booths in the casino, to be exact. I questioned the staff, but nobody noticed anyone acting suspiciously. It was too much to hope for, I suppose.'

Damon stared at him gravely. Neither spoke for a long, long while. 'It doesn't make sense,' Damon said at last.

Greg sighed. 'I know. But we have to face facts. Someone on board is up to no good.'

CHAPTER 18

The US Virgin Islands

The mixture of the familiar and the exotic made the American passengers feel right at home, and Ramona had heard several departing passengers call the islands the 'American Paradise'. The *Alexandria* was at anchor far out to sea, in between the islands of St John and St Thomas, and north of the largest island of St Croix. Tenders were standing by, ready to ferry passengers to their choice of island.

Standing at the rails, Ramona watched the carefree departure of the first tenders. Feeling very much aware of his presence beside her, stood her new fiancée. Even now, she knew she wouldn't have felt complete if Damon wasn't near.

'She's late,' Damon noted, leaning against the rail, his bare arms a golden brown, his hair tousled in the breeze.

Ramona smiled. 'We women like to take our time, you know.'

Damon grunted. 'You don't. I've never known a woman get her act together so quickly.' He was

211

referring, she knew, to the way she had quickly showered and dressed this morning, before he could awake and reach out for her. Now, she smiled provocatively. 'I'm different.'

Damon smiled, his eyes gentle. 'You can say that again. Are you sure you don't mind my taking mother to St Croix? Only she said she wanted to talk to me. Alone.'

Ramona almost laughed aloud. Mind? She was over the moon. She'd been racking her brains for a way of wangling the whole day to herself in order to meet with her father, when, over breakfast, Damon himself had solved the problem for her.

Now he suddenly turned, his face shuttered, as Joceline appeared on the deck, a vision in peach lace.

'I hate leaving you on your own!' Damon said possessively, causing a thrill to shoot through her.

'I'll survive without you for one day, at least,' she laughed, turning those blue eyes towards him, her eyes challenging. Damon's lips twisted grimly. It had hardly been what he wanted to hear, as she knew only too well, damn her.

'But only a day,' he growled. 'Tonight, we'll dine in my cabin. I'll have the chef prepare something special. Just for us.' He moved closer and ran the backs of his knuckles lightly across her cheek, his eyes devouring her.

Ramona looked into his pewter-grey eyes, and felt her womb contract. She knew what would come after dinner, of course. But could she go through with it, now that she knew for sure that he was the enemy.

She'd put him off last night, but he'd still insisted on sleeping with her in the same bed, and this morning she'd made a quick exit before he awoke, but she couldn't put off love-making forever.

And if her talk with her father went anywhere near as well as she hoped, it would be more imperative than ever to keep him off his guard and his mind occupied elsewhere. Like in her bed, for instance, an eager, salacious little voice demanded, shocking her momentarily. For the idea of playing the *femme fatale* was so absurd, and yet so exciting, that she didn't know whether to laugh or cry. Slowly, feeling her way like the novice she was, she let her lids lower just a fraction, and then moved a step closer, instantly gratified at the way his eyes darkened to iron and he drew in a ragged breath. 'I look forward to it,' she said softly.

But then Joceline reached them, her eyes, as usual, skittering off Ramona, and fixing at some point just over her right shoulder. 'Good morning, you two.'

'Ready?' Damon asked with a sigh, trying to get his breathing back under control. Joceline nodded and Ramona stayed by the rail, waving cheerfully as they descended to the St Croix tender and stepped aboard. She herself was headed for St Thomas. She glanced at her watch, sure that the main tourist destination was where she would find her father. Or, more accurately, where *he* would find *her*.

She felt her stomach lurch. Now that the time had actually come to set the trap, she felt ridiculously guilty. But it wasn't even as if Damon really loved her, she quickly reminded herself.

One deck above her, Verity Fox stepped out of her room and glanced at her watch. She still had plenty of time to catch the second tender to St John. It was where she and Greg had arranged to meet, Greg, of course, taking the last boat out. Just so they wouldn't be seen together.

She still hadn't settled on an excuse for going back to the boat so early in the afternoon. She knew that Greg would want to spend the whole day together, away from the *Alexandria*, but she had already arranged to meet Gordon in Cruz Bay. And they would need the medical facilities on board ship. With a sigh, she headed for the boats, and made a determined effort to push any unpleasant thoughts away. As the tender motored across the sea to the small island, the sun was shining, and soon her lover would be with her. It was more, much more, than she'd ever hoped for. It might have to be enough.

As Damon and Joceline walked along the harbour of St Christiansted, he looked at her curiously. 'So. What's up?' he asked quietly, since she'd made no attempt to explain.

Joceline looked at him briefly, then looked quickly away. Where did she start? 'Let's find a nice, quiet spot. There, by those trees,' she said fatalistically. Slowly they made their way through a park to a stand of enormous silk-cotton, or kapok trees, and sat on a shady bench.

'Damon,' Joceline began firmly, then sighed. 'I've been having Joe King watched,' she started, bluntly enough.

By her side, Damon jerked in surprise. '*You* have? Why?'

Joceline glanced at him, then quickly looked away again. 'I . . . I used to know Joe King quite well. When you were very young.' Her voice became strained as she strove to keep it steady. She stared dead ahead, unwilling to see the pain in his eyes.

Damon stared at her, eyes wide. 'I . . . never knew that,' he finally said. 'How . . . well, exactly, did you know him?'

Joceline took a deep breath. 'Very well. He . . . hated your father because I wouldn't leave him. For a man like Joe King . . . Well, it was a serious blow to his ego.'

Damon shook his head, unable to believe what was she was saying. He felt anger on his father's behalf rise to engulf him. Coldly, he said, 'Did Dad know?'

And now, Joceline knew, was the moment to tell him. She stared at her shaking hands, willed the memory of that awful night to come back, but she just couldn't bring herself to say the words. 'I . . . no, he didn't,' she lied, her breath gushing out of her. 'But, Damon, I know Joe King so well,' she reached out to grasp his hand. 'I know how his mind works. He's always wanted what Michael had. Me, the Alexander Line . . . And now he's making a move on it. I wanted to warn you. Joe's been buying shares through intermediaries. One of them was a man called Keith Treadstone. He . . .' Joceline took a deep breath. 'He was engaged to . . .'

'Ramona,' Damon said flatly. 'Yes, I know.' Slowy, unable to help himself, he disentangled his hand.

She winced, knowing she'd alienated him forever,

but too stunned by his answer to do anything about it. 'Then, why . . . with Ramona . . .' she whispered, unable to finish the question.

Damon smiled grimly. 'I love her,' he said simply.

St John was very American, Verity thought, as she noticed a McDonalds rubbing shoulders with a Pizza Hut in the capital town of Cruz Bay. And yet, along with cable TV and US dollars, came green hillsides rife with the orange of the flamboyant tree, red with the flower of the hibiscus and magenta with the myriad blossoms of the bougainvillaea. Scattered throughout it all were the blue-stone ruins of sugar mills, whilst the town itself consisted of pastel-coloured European-style villas with decorated wrought-iron balconies and narrow streets climbing up from the harbour.

Consulting her map, she mused on their options. Hawksnest Beach was narrow and lined with sea-grape trees, and the thought of making love under the trees was tempting. She glanced up as the familiar tender from the *Alexandria* disgorged the last of its passengers onto the quay. Her heart leapt as she easily picked out Greg's figure amongst the crowd, his head towering several inches above the others. Discreetly waiting until all the other passengers had dispersed, she walked up to him, ignoring the slight weakness in her limbs. Another side effect of the drug.

Greg watched her approach, his eyes slowly going down her body, not missing a thing. She was wearing a light, floral dress and no bra. Her legs were brown and bare, her sandals open-toed. The sea breeze had got at

216

her hair, blowing the dark cap into a confused mop on top of her head. 'You're beautiful,' were his first words, and Verity laughed.

'I was going to say the same thing about you,' she said. And in loose-fitting white slacks and an open-necked black shirt, he really did look like a sculptress's ideal model for a Greek nude.

Greg glanced at the map she was holding, and his eyes darkened. 'Figured out where we're going yet?' he asked, his voice husky.

'We could go shopping,' she said, her lips twitching.

Greg laughed. 'Tormenting wench. The moment I set eyes on you, I knew you were going to be trouble,' he growled.

'Not fair,' she cried. 'I've found a perfect place already. Somewhere where there are a lot of sea-grape trees. A deserted beach. Did you bring a blanket?' she added huskily.

He nodded at his bag. 'Iced champagne too.'

Verity took his hand, all thoughts of that afternoon's appointment with Gordon completely gone. 'Then what are we waiting for?' she asked throatily.

St Thomas, only thirteen miles long, was a bustling island, a paradise for shoppers, full of discos and glitz and hopelessly over-commercialized. Ramona ignored the lures of Coki Beach, next to Coral World and stuck to Charlotte Amalie, wandering slowly around the hilly town, with its Dutch-named streets and cobble-paved alleys. She paid scant attention to Blackbeard's Castle, and climbed the ninety-nine steps after Kongen's Gade

217

without even noticing. By eleven she was beginning to think she'd read the situation with her father all wrong. Surely he should have contacted her by now? Back on Dronnigens Cade, the main street, she desultorily hailed a cab and asked to be taken to a recommended restaurant. The Fiddle Leaf, packed with vibrant art, and set in a covered pavilion overlooking town, was ideal. In more ways than one.

Ramona spotted her father the moment she stepped inside. She wasn't niave enough to think that this meeting was accidental. A slightly nauseous feeling settled into the pit of her stomach. But when he stood and lifted one hand, she walked towards him without a second thought.

Verity Fox gasped as Greg pulled the dress over her head and bent instantly to take one pert nipple into his mouth. They were in the dense, cool, covering shade of the sea-grape trees, whilst a few hundred yards away, people swam and snorkelled in the sea. She moaned as he lay her gently back onto the blanket, and she closed her eyes as his warm hand curved around her calf, then moved up her thigh, his fingers feathering over her feminine mound. Raising her head to kiss him, she pulled him down and over her with eager hands, wriggling out of her panties as he shucked aside his slacks. She moaned again, a low, soft, wanting sound, as his knees nudged hers apart. They both cried out softly as they came together, the sound of the surf and the wind in the trees keeping them hidden and private, in the world that was all their own. Greg's hands dug deep into the soft sandy soil either side of Verity's head as he slowly thrust into her, and he grunted in quiet but extreme satisfaction as her long, supple legs twisted around his own. His jaw tightened as the sweat poured down his back and the pleasure became near-pain. He felt her small hands gripping his shoulders, felt her teeth nibble on his ear and his whole body began to tremble on the brink of ecstacy. Staring up at the canopy of trees above her, her whole body spiralling in an ever-increasing surge of pleasure, Verity cried out and arched into his strong body, never feeling more alive than in that moment.

Her whole being seemed to crystalize in that passionate instant. The harsh sound of her triumphant breath. The intense heat of her inner body. The overwhelming love that flooded her heart. Suddenly she knew that even if she did die, right now, there was nobody else in the human race's entire history who had lived more than she. The last few weeks with Greg had made sense of her life – however long it might last. Unaware that slow, grateful, slightly sad tears were running down her face, she slowly lay back against the blanket, smiling at the weight of him atop her. Wordlessly, she stroked his sweat-damp hair, pushing it back off his temples. Greg sighed, and slowly rolled over, not wanting to crush her. In the distance he could hear the laughing shouts of the beach revellers, and he smiled. Throwing caution to the winds was a new experience for him, and he liked it. He had become so dedicated to his career, so tied to his ship, that he had forgotten what it was like to actually live dangerously once in a while.

'I'm starving,' he said prosaically, and laughed when she groaned teasingly. He sat up and lifted his beach bag closer. 'Chicken, madam?'

Verity smiled. 'I thought I was being rather brave.'

'Oh, ha-ha, very hilarious. Here, have a drumstick,' he leaned over and summarily stuck a chicken leg between her teeth. Verity munched happily, getting up on one elbow and looking through the trees to the beach.

'I wish I could stay like this forever,' she said softly, and Greg glanced at her naked body, her skin still glowing, her hair mussed, her hand holding the drumstick with one clean bite taken out of it, and his throat constricted as love flooded over him. He'd never felt the emotion so precisely before. It was so sure it made him feel almost humble.

'I wish you could too,' he said gruffly, and leaned across and kissed her collarbone. As he did so, Verity saw the time on his watch, and it felt as if a dark cloud had suddenly blocked out the sun.

'But I can't,' she said, then took a deep breath. 'Gordon's meeting me back at St Cruz.'

Slowly, Greg lifted his head. 'Gordon?'

Verity looked casually down at her chicken leg, all appetite gone. 'Hmm. You remember him? The blood specialist.'

Greg's eyes narrowed. 'I remember. The man with the research notes.'

Verity nibbled a piece of chicken. 'Hmm. Only this time *I've* got some notes for *him*. I've left them back on board ship.' She executed what she hoped looked like a successful shrugging grimace. 'Sorry.'

Greg silently slipped back into his slacks. Verity watched him and bit her lip. 'I know what they say about all work making Jack a dull boy, but . . .' She shrugged.

Greg nodded, his face impassive. 'We'd better make for the town then. The first tender back to the ship leaves at two.'

Verity pulled her dress back over her head and got to her feet. She swayed, feeling a little light-headed. She held out her hand, glad when he took it, and she clung on to him all the way back to St Cruz, hoping he didn't notice how much she physically needed his support.

Joe King thrust some folders across a table now empty of the lamb and polenta soup Ramona had ordered, and his own swordfish medallions sautéed with green tomato and asparagus. The eyes that watched his daughter glowed with satisfaction. Although they'd only talked of general things over their meal, it had been Ramona herself who had brought up the subject of the *Alexandria*.

Naturally he had feigned great surprise and some concern as she'd told him about the shares she owned. It had been the perfect opening, enabling him to tell her that he, too, had shares in the *Alexandria*, about 4 per cent worth. He hadn't missed the disappointed look on her face as he mentioned the amount, and was reassured he'd read her motivation correctly. From the moment Jeff Doyle had told him about the 'Shipboard Romance of the Century' (as one tabloid had put it yesterday) he'd guessed his lovely, clever daughter was up to something. Now, he was sure he was right.

221

'What's this?' Ramona asked, but was already opening the first folder. It was a profile on Gareth Desmond, a major shareholder, and top of her own list. The folders detailed others, the amount of shares they controlled varying. But all, according to her father's research, might be willing to sell.

Ramona's face was totally inscrutable. 'All very interesting,' she said carefully, as she closed the last folder and handed it back. The eyes she turned on him were like mirrors. He could see nothing in them but his own reflection. Immediately, Joe knew he'd have to be very careful indeed. She'd spot a lie a mile away.

Joe leaned back in his chair and smiled. The game had begun. 'I want the *Alexandria*,' he began simply, looking at her from under his brows. Her face didn't alter one whit and Joe felt a sudden rush of pride. She was such a chip off the old block. He could see in her eyes a burning look that had the sharp radial spokes of hate and obsession, two emotions he knew only too well. He'd always suspected she was out for revenge for the death of Keith Treadstone, and for some reason blamed Damon Alexander. Now, he was sure of it. The irony was so delicious it made him want to laugh out loud. If only she knew . . .

'About twenty years ago, Michael Alexander and I were fighting for the same company,' he began. 'The . . .'

'I know,' Ramona said, and saw his eyes sharpen on her. Then a small, reluctant, but genuinely admiring smile came to his rather thin and cruel-looking lips.

'You have done your homework well,' he drawled.

222

Ramona nodded once in acknowledgement. 'You're still after the Alexander Line, I take it?'

Joe King smiled. 'Of course.'

Ramona nodded. 'I want it too,' she admitted coolly. 'But with our combined shares, we still don't have nearly enough.'

Joe smiled, and reached over and tapped the folders. 'If we bring these into a cartel, with me at the head, we will have.'

Ramona corrected him gently but firmly. 'With *me* at its head, you mean. I *will* be the majority shareholder.'

Joe King laughed. He couldn't help it. The cheek of the little madam! 'Alright,' he agreed. 'With *you* as head of the cartel, we'll have enough to take over the company.'

'If we can get them to sell,' she amended.

Joe smiled. 'Oh, we'll get them to sell alright.'

For a second, Ramona shuddered as something cold and ugly skittered across her skin. She glanced sharply at her father, her eyes narrowing suspiciously.

Joe cursed slowly under his breath. Careful! 'They're only interested in money, of which I have plenty.' He shrugged.

Ramona slowly began to relax. Of course that's what he meant. So why had she felt so . . . uneasy? As Ramona watched him smile, and did her best to hide a shudder that rippled through her, Joe King laughed. Things were once more going his way.

In her cabin, Verity Fox took off her dress and Gordon bent close, professionally and clinically examining her skin. They had to be wary of skin cancer with her type of leukaemia. 'Hmm, your back's clear,' Gordon said, with evident relief. 'Turn around.'

Verity did so, not in the least embarrassed. Years as a doctor had all but erased any feelings of inhibitions when it came to dealing with naked bodies, (her own or somebody else's) and she felt not the slightest qualm when Gordon carefully studied the mole on the left side of her left breast.

It was at that moment that the door suddenly opened and Verity jumped back in shock. Gordon, surprised at the interruption, did the same.

Verity's mouth fell open in surprise as Greg stared back at her from the open doorway. His mouth, that had been open to say something, suddenly snapped shut and his eyes became enormous. Abruptly, Greg's face drained of all colour.

Suddenly, Verity realized what he must have seen. Or *thought* he'd seen. Gordon's face, close to her naked breast. His hand on her shoulder . . . She cried out. 'Greg . . .'

'I'm very sorry,' Greg cut across her, his voice icy. 'I had no intention of interrupting your . . . work.' Not trusting himself to say more he quickly backed out and all but slammed the door after him.

Inside, both Gordon and Verity winced. Gordon had summed it all up in a second, of course. 'Go after him, Verity,' he urged. 'Quick!' And, indeed, she had already taken one step to the door, but then suddenly she stopped.

She shook her head. 'No.'

224

'But he thinks . . .'

'I know what he thinks,' she said, her voice stiff. 'But if I go after him I have to explain what's really going on. And I can't do that. Not until I'm sure myself exactly what's going to happen.' She glanced at the phials of blood samples Gordon had already taken. 'We'd better get these to the lab. John's expecting us. You're going to like him.'

'But Verity . . .' Gordon said helplessly, his eyes concerned as he watched her dress, his sensitive nature easily reading the set, pained look of determination on her face. 'If things are serious between you and him, don't you think he deserves to know?'

Verity reached for her shoes. 'I know what I'm doing, Gordon,' she said crisply, in an effort to stave off the tears she could feel welling perilously close to the surface. 'If those tests – ' she nodded to the phials 'don't show any improvement, then I'm leaving this ship at Miami, and I'm never going to see him again. In the long run, it'll be easier for him.'

She brushed a tear away and determinedly stepped into her shoes. 'Eventually he'll come to see me and what we had as just another passenger romance. I'll just be someone who was out for an on-board fling, and then went home to her real life. He'll forget me all the more easily that way. And if . . . well . . . if it comes to it, I don't want him to suffer more than he has to,' she said, her voice as shaky as she felt.

Gordon nodded, and looked away. What could he say? They both knew that she was right.

CHAPTER 19

The Charleston Club, tucked neatly away on Halcyon deck, reminded Ramona instantly of an elitist London men-only club. It had very high-backed, winged chairs, an authentic oriental rug that covered almost the entire floor area, and paintings of fox-and-hounds scenes on the wall. She strolled casually to the bar, and ordered white wine. Casually, she half turned and did a very convincing double-take. She let a cautious smile of recognition cross her face, and as she'd hoped, the New York banker she'd seen come in only minutes before, leapt straight to his feet. Within a moment he was by her side, his eyes, predictably, going straight to her legs.

'Hi, again,' Dwight J. Markham III smiled charmingly at her. 'Please, let me get this.'

Ramona watched as the banker took her wine and nodded confidently to his table. Two high-backed chairs surrounded a solid walnut table, and she allowed herself a gracious nod and meekly followed him to his table.

'Well, now, I can't tell you how upset I've been not to

see you before now,' Dwight Markham said, grinning charmingly.

Ramona fought back an itch of irritation and wished with all her heart that she could feel the same sort of amused indifference for Damon Alexander that she felt for the man opposite her.

'Never mind,' she forced herself to smile sympathetically. 'I'm here now.'

Dwight grinned. 'So you are,' he purred, and Ramona saw lust in his eyes. It didn't surprise her, but it made her feel dirty. The thought of him even touching her with his handsomely-manicured hands made her want to heave.

Because you know what it is to be made love to by Damon, a small voice piped up, deep in her soul. Quickly, she took a deep breath, and concentrated with almost manic determination on the task at hand. Ramona leaned back, suddenly brisk. 'I wanted to ask you about something, Dwight. Something I'm sure you're very good at.'

Dwight's eyes sharpened. He couldn't deny it, she had him hooked.

'You remember telling me about the 3 per cent you own in this lovely ship of ours?'

Dwight blinked. He didn't remember telling her that. Discretion was his middle name. 'No, I can't say as I do.'

Ramona laughed. 'I think you were too busy looking at my legs,' she said softly, and crossed them elegantly at the knees. Nonchalantly, she swung one foot and distinctly heard him gasp. So too, did the man sitting at

227

the next table, who was totally hidden by the high-backed chair. Now he leaned back, his ears straining.

'You also told me how much you paid for them,' Ramona carried on, very softly. She definitely did not want anybody overhearing what came next. If she had only known who was sitting right next to her, completely unsuspected, she would never have gone near Dwight J. Markham III in the first place.

Dwight stared at her, his mouth hanging open. 'I did?'

'You did. But don't worry. I wouldn't dream of telling anyone else. We shareholders have to stick together.'

Dwight smiled, but he was no longer staring at her legs. She now had his undivided attention. Ramona smiled. Good. She was talking to the banker at last, and not the lech. 'How would you like to sell your shares for 20 per cent more than you paid for them?' she asked him quietly.

Dwight swallowed. They were talking about a lot of money. 'I would like to sell them a lot more for 40 per cent.'

Ramona laughed. 'I should think so. But that's hardly realistic. How about 22 per cent?'

'Thirty,' Dwight said.

Ramona uncrossed her legs, but he wasn't biting. She thought about it. Her father had told her he could go to twenty-five, no more, and in fact believed the banker would settle for just that sum. And who was she to argue with Joe King's business acumen? She shrugged. 'Twenty-five per cent, and that really is my final offer.'

Dwight knew a final offer when he heard it. And a good price. 'Done.'

'Good.' Ramona opened her beach bag and extracted a very legal-looking document. Once again Dwight's mouth fell open. He took it from her and quickly read it. It was already typed and made out, the figure mentioned being the 25 per cent they had settled on. Dwight looked from it to her, his eyes narrowing. 'Got a pen?' he asked, his voice dry.

Ramona smiled, her first genuine smile of their whole encounter, and handed over a biro. Dwight signed and handed it back. He'd just made himself another million. He reached for his tequila and Ramona lifted her glass. Solemly, they toasted each other. Then Ramona rose, her prize clutched in her hand, and walked away. If she had looked back, she would have seen Ralph Ornsgood watch her go, a look of fury and dismay etched into his Nordic features. But she didn't. And it was a mistake she would come to bitterly regret.

Heathrow in February was hardly an inviting place, and Gordon was glad to leave it behind and catch the train to Oxford. He felt vaguely jet-lagged, but he was also excited. The preliminary tests they'd done on board the *Alexandria* had been very, very promising. As Verity had predicted, Gordon had liked John Gardner from the moment they'd met and the three doctors had worked in close harmony in the lab, dividing tasks and using the sophisticated equipment with an ease that spoke volumes of their respective expertise.

It was John's sample that had produced the first

result, and Verity and Gordon had only had to take a look at his stunned face to know it had to be good. And it was good. Better than Verity could have hoped for, even in her wildest dreams. Her white blood cell count was down by 5 per cent.

John had stared at her, and then at Gordon. 'I don't understand,' he'd said, and neither Verity nor Gordon could do anything to help him understand. Naturally, he'd been angry at first, demanding to know, pointing out that such a medical breakthrough deserved proper and world-wide investigation. Only by hinting at the trouble Gordon could get into, did John eventually back down.

But there was still a long way to go, Gordon acknowledged wearily as he alighted at Oxford Station and hailed a cab to take him to the suburb of Headington, and the big white building that sat on top of the hill. First they had to isolate the exact cause of the change. What dosage produced what effect, and what elements were likely to cause the hot flushes that Verity had outlined to him? They would need to do a lot more tests, which meant flying out to the Caribbean again, possibly when the *Alexandria* docked in the Dominican Republic, or Jamaica.

Paying off the cab, John trudged wearily to his small home in a cul-de-sac within walking distance of the hospital. Sometimes it was a pain, living so close to work, but today he was glad, since he could just drop off his luggage and then go straight to the labs, with the rest of the blood samples. It was nearly 7 pm. With luck, Dr Annazwala would have left for the day.

When he got there, there was only one dim light burning, towards the back of the labs where the animals were stored. Curious, knowing he had to be very careful, Gordon stored the blood samples and walked into the animal house.

He jumped as a loud clang echoed around the walls, and he heard a muffled curse. He walked carefully around the rat enclosure, and smiled as he saw Philip Knight retrieve a large metal tray from the floor. 'Hello, Phil. Having fun, I see.'

Philip, an orderly, seconded to the lab for the duration of Dr Annazwala's visit, looked around. 'Oh, hello Dr Dryer.'

'Has Dr Annazwala gone for the day?' Gordon asked casually.

'Sure has.'

Gordon nodded, turned, and then stopped dead. He was facing an empty cage. A cage that had once held a very large, very healthy rabbit. 'Where's Hercules?' Gordon asked, hoping his voice didn't sound as strained as he felt.

Phil looked up, and sighed. 'We lost Hercules, I'm afraid. Yesterday. Dr Annazwala's doing the autopsy tomorrow.'

Gordon felt his breath lock in his lungs and struggled to let it out. He felt icy-cold. 'Did . . .' he cleared his throat. 'Did Dr Annazwala say what he thought caused it?'

'Nah. Not really. He was the rabbit taking that AIDS drug thingy, wasn't he?'

Gordon nodded bleakly. 'Yes,' he said hollowly. 'Yes, he was.'

Stumbling out into the lab, Gordon made for his bench on shaking legs. Phil left, saying a cheery goodnight. For a long, long while, Gordon sat staring blankly at the walls. Eventually he stirred, grimly urging himself to pull himself together. *Think!* There were plenty of reasons why a rabbit might die. It didn't have to be the drug that had killed it. Gordon sighed. Dr Annazwala's notes on Hercules would surely help. Detailed notes were kept on all the test animals, and it didn't take Gordon long to find Herc's particulars. For the first few weeks, nothing untoward. Then, five days ago . . . Gordon stopped running his finger down the list of data, and stared at the entry.

An abrupt but temporary rise in temperature. A hot flush.

Gordon closed his eyes. 'Oh God, Verity,' he whispered. 'What have we done?'

Damon stepped out of the lift and walked slowly along the corridor. He didn't feel his individual steps. He ignored or gave a bare smile to those that greeted him as they passed. His eyes were dark, his jaw clenched. He felt . . . distinctly weird. When Ralph had found him at the gym, he had recognized immediately the signs of Ralph's unhappiness. The twiddling thumbs. The shifting eyes. The inability to get to the point. Pumping iron, Damon had grinned and tried to put him at ease, expecting him to come out with some minor problem. He was not prepared for what Ralph had told him. Not by a long shot.

If it had been anyone else doing the telling, Damon

wouldn't have believed it. As it was, after listening with growing grimness to Ralph's report of the transaction between Ramona and Dwight Markham, Damon knew his worst nightmares were coming real. He had slowly sat up, pushing the barbell away, a spiralling coldness falling down into the pit of his belly. Ralph had looked more and more miserable. He knew he was bringing his oldest and dearest friend the worst news of his life, and he was feeling acutely unhappy. Damon's grim-faced pat on the shoulder and his muttered, 'It's alright. It's fine,' did nothing to help him.

Damon had left the gym and was now on his way to his room. He showered, turning the spray to needle-cold, but it didn't help. He poured himself a straight scotch which settled on his stomach like a sour promise.

Grimly he left his cabin and when he stopped at her door the feeling of detachment was still there. It was stupid, he knew, for a grown man to react this way to a woman's treachery, but he felt gutted. Grimly, he raised his hand and knocked on her door. He had no clear idea what he was going to do or say.

Inside, Ramona's head shot up. She was staring at the document in her hands, feasting her eyes on Dwight's signature. She and her father now had another 3 per cent. It was a beginning. She quickly thrust the document back into her bag and pushed the bag under the table. She looked around, saw nothing out of place, and walked to the door and opened it.

Damon saw her. The white gold of her hair. The piercing blue of her eyes. The overwhelming power of her presence. The feeling of being cocooned left him abruptly, and for the first time he felt the danger that had been hidden before. Something inside him stiffened, like the hackles coming up on a cat, or the snarl of power that came from a wolf. It was an animal feeling, a pure feeling of instinct. At the same time he felt the vulnerability of loving someone who was out to destroy him. But most of all, he felt calm, because now he knew that she would not succeed. He could and would fight back and defeat her.

The thought hurt him.

Ramona stared up at him, every cell in her body leaping to life. Her whole being seemed to go up a gear, as if she had only been cruising along and now she was actually racing. She loved him. She hated him. He had dragged her out of her safe and comfortable shell, and made her feel. But at the same time he had put a great weight of responsibility on her shoulders, one that she didn't want but couldn't ignore – she must teach him that he was not impervious to justice. That people like Keith, little people, weaker people, counted. And the fact that she was the only one who could do it made her want to cry and tear at him in screaming rage at the same time.

The thought hurt her.

For a second she didn't think she could do it. For a moment she just wanted to give in. To whimper in surrender and drown in his love, even if it was false. Then she felt herself smile as her backbone and resolve simultaneously hardened. Her clever, calculating brain was back. Only now it was accompanied with a passion that was a stranger to her, yet very welcome. The passion of love and hate.

'Hello.' Lover. 'Come on in.' Said the spider to the fly.

Damon stepped across the threshold, and turned to watch her close the door. His head was perfectly clear. She had chosen the game. Now it was time she learned that he knew how to play it as well. He said gently, 'I'm sorry about last night.'

Ramona turned, a puzzled frown on her face. 'What?'

'About missing dinner,' he prompted, his eyes watching her reactions like a hawk.

Ramona nodded. 'Oh that. It doesn't matter.' She had been glad of the respite. Obviously his day with Joceline had been very important indeed. Briefly, she wondered what she'd said to him. 'How is Joceline?' she asked, just to be polite, and then stared as he seemed to stiffen like a puppet having a string pulled. His dark eyes narrowed.

'Fine. Why do you ask?' His voice had the hard edge of a diamond.

Ramona blinked. 'I just . . . I was just asking,' she said lamely. Was it her, or was he jumpy today? Surely it was she who should be nervous. She knew this man inside and out. Knew his passion and knew his surprising gentleness. Knew his humour, and knew the darkness it could hide. She also knew his ruthlessness. If he should ever find out what she was doing . . . She shuddered. She had no doubt he'd flex his mighty financial muscles and crush her. Just like Keith. Except she was not Keith. She would not crumple. Even if she longed just to have him take her in his arms and . . . *No!*

235

She turned away abruptly. 'Would you like a drink?'

Damon watched her move towards the bar and relaxed slightly. Her inquiry about Joceline had caught him on the raw. But he knew that she couldn't be interested in his mother at all. Joceline didn't have the money and power she craved. He did.

And the really sad thing about all this, Damon thought bleakly, the really ironic thing, was that she could have had it all anyway. Once they were married he would have handed her all the riches and status she so obviously desired, and been glad to. What rich man wouldn't want to give the woman he loved all that she longed for? Diamonds and rubies. Ships. Power. Wealth. His grim thoughts shifted quickly as she turned to look at him, one eyebrow raised curiously, her hand hovering over the drinks tray. He pulled himself together quickly. 'Thanks. I'll have rum.'

'Pineapple juice? Blackcurrant?'

'No. Straight.'

He watched her pour, then turn and walk towards him, the drink in her hand. She was so beautiful, so deadly. Like a leopardess. Or some Greek goddess, offering her mortal lover a taste of ambrosia before she had him killed. His eyes darkened and Ramona's heart lurched as a sudden, pagan excitement seemed to leap and crackle in the air. Their eyes met – hers electricity, his molten metal. Something elemental grabbed her by the throat and shook her and her lips fell open as she gasped, totally unprepared for it.

Damon growled. There was no other word for the savage sound that rumbled in his throat. His hand shot out and dashed the drink away, the glass bouncing off the thick white carpet, the rich and dark Caribbean rum quickly seeping into the pile. In the same movement, he reached out for her and yanked her to him, her feet actually leaving the floor. Ramona's eyes widened briefly, but she didn't cry out. An answering savagery was in her too, and when his lips swooped down on hers, the pressure almost cruel enough to split her lip, she found her mouth opening wide, her tongue darting out into his mouth and clashing with the hot spear of his own.

Damon groaned and pulled her closer, his hands cupping her buttocks, holding her tightly against his body, wanting to absorb her, to trap her inside him forever. Her short skirt rode up and she felt volcanic heat flow into her vagina, causing tiny whimpering sounds to escape her parted lips. Her hands rose to his head, her fingers digging into his temples as she pushed away, thrusting his head back. His eyes gleemed down into hers and he felt her fingers curl into talons. There was an echoing snarl of warning and desire on her face, and he felt the blood rush to his loins at the paganism of their fierce desire. He almost moaned out loud as the eroticism of their heat hit him like a physical blow. Quickly, his hands rose to her waist and his fingers dug into her flesh, making her wince. She tightened her own grip on his vulnerable temples and her nails scored the skin, a tiny drop of blood appearing in his hairline. His eyes turned to liquid pewter. She gasped in near-pain as she felt him pull her body even closer to his, as if he wanted to crush her, punish and love her, in the same instant. Her breasts, mashed against his chest, felt tight with a mix of aching pain and pleasure, and she could feel her nipples burgeon, digging into his chest like fierce little warriors.

Damon felt them too and dragged in a ragged, heaving breath. With a sudden movement, he knocked her hands away and lifted her, carrying her to the bed and dropping her so hard that she bounced. Before the rebound had her back on the mattress, he was on top of her, a tiny trickle of blood running down his temple. She knew she herself would have finger-mark bruises on her waist, but she didn't care. Love and hate were so indistinguishable now, she wasn't sure if they could be separated ever again. Feverishly, she reached up for him, thrusting her hand inside his shirt and yanking it open, buttons scattering onto the bed and rolling into the carpet.

Never taking his eyes off her, he ripped her blouse right down the front in one movement of his strong hands, the shocking tearing sound of rending material making her eyes open even wider. Looking down, she saw that the tattered scraps of the silk blouse still annoyingly clung to her breasts and with a small angry cry, brushed them away, exposing her tight, aching nipples. Instantly, her hand snaked out to the back of his head and she pulled him down to her, her eyes flashing electricity, her primitive female power demanding he pleasure her. She gasped and then yelped as he bit her nipple, almost hard enough to cause real pain. With a cry she pulled his head feverishly across to the other nipple as her whole body convulsed in total, wanton need. Damon felt his self-control desert him. Suddenly they were tearing at the rest of their clothes, and then naked flesh touched naked flesh, scorching them, tormenting them to greater, more passionate savagery. He was aware of the soft, silken sheen of her creamy skin touching every atom of his being.

She ran her hands through dark body hair, loving the sensation of rippling muscle under her palms. Her hands curved around his waist, cupping his buttocks as he had once cupped hers. Only this time she dug her nails in, intending to hurt, and gave a triumphant laugh as he gasped.

Then he was lifting her, thrusting apart her silken legs with his strong, hair-smattered legs, and it was her turn to gasp. Her thighs locked around his, and he suddenly looked down and into her eyes. For a split instant they were statue-still, staring into each other's eyes, their taut, straining, fit bodies, poised, like snakes ready to strike each other. And then he plunged into her, hard and fast, not caring if he hurt her. She screamed in ecstacy, her whole body curving around him, her legs around his legs, her arms around his back, her inner vagina muscles cradling and squeezing his manhood, as if her whole being was trying to absorb him, to drag him, screaming and struggling in ecstacy, into the molten heat that would melt him down and imprison him in her cells forever. Damon never allowed himself to look away from the flashing blue lightning of her eyes, his body pistoning into her, sweat running down his spine, dripping into their merged pubic hair, his feet digging deeply into the mattress as he prepared himself for yet another mighty lunge into her. Ramona scored his back time and time again, until sweat and blood merged and still the ecstacy fountained higher and higher. She moaned, groaned, growled and screamed as he clung and bucked, twisting her head from side to side and becoming blinded by her own, long silver-blonde hair. Then he was brushing it away from her face, one rough hand bringing her head off the pillow, until their noses were almost touching. As the world began to fall away, as she thought her body must surely perish in payment for the pleasure it was receiving, she saw his eyes suddenly sharpen into focus.

'I want to see you,' he gasped, panting and heaving as he felt his loins threaten to burst. 'I want to watch your eyes as you go crazy,' he rasped. 'I want to see you . . . *disintergrate!*' With his last, crying, savage word, Ramona screamed, her whole thrashing body arching in a pleasure so strong she never expected to open her eyes again. Damon saw her eyes turn to darkness as her pupils expanded, and then screamed himself as his whole body errupted, flooding her, his seed pouring out of him like life's blood itself.

They clung together then, as pleasure tormented them in wave after rippling wave.

They were lovers.

They were enemies.

And one of them must, inevitably, be defeated.

CHAPTER 20

Puerto Rico

It was true what they said, Ramona mused, looking
around. There was no city in the Caribbean more
Spanish in tradition and style than that of Old San
Juan. Posters for festivals littered the streets, celebrating even the most obscure of saints. The seven-square
block of the old city contrasted sharply with New San
Juan's sophisticated Condalo and Isla Verda areas, and
she was glad that he had steered her to the old part of
town, but not surprised. His taste was impeccable, as
was, if she had but known it, his acting. Not by so much
as a strained smile or a hard-edged word had he given
away the fact that he knew exactly what she was up to.
But soon she would. Soon, he would have to make
counter-moves of his own in this game of cut-throat
chess she had instigated.

As the trolley they boarded trundled happily along
the streets, she noticed that the buses were run in
exclusive lanes, and against the traffic! Briefly she
recalled her other terrifying bus ride, and laughed.

'What?' he asked, made curious by her sudden gaiety.

Ramona smiled. 'I was just thinking. I nearly died the last time I was in a bus, but if it had gone against the traffic as well . . .' She shrugged, and he laughed with her, one thumb absently rubbing against her palm, enjoying her ability to laugh at herself. Not many of the women he had known had been able to do that. It was just one more thing he loved about her. One more nail in his coffin . . .

From the back of a dark blue, rented limousine, Joe King impatiently waited for them to alight and make definite tracks. He had to separate them, if only for a few minutes, and he was so busy thinking and waiting for his opportunity that he didn't notice the more ubiquitous, rented Fiat following him.

Oblivious to her father's angst, Ramona sat back and admired the authentic and original sixteenth- and seventeenth-century Spanish colonial architecture that had to be some of the best in the New World. Against her will, a kind of peace and happiness seemed to seep into her. As they left the trolley to stand on a rocky promontory on the north-west tip of the old city in San Felipe del Morro, a fortress built by the Spanish in 1540, she found him looking at her, his eyes level and unflinching. And suddenly, miraculously, in that place of medieval times, with its labyrinth of dungeons, ramps, barracks towers and turrets, she was at last able to accept her own passionate nature. People had loved and hated for centuries. Why should she be any different? At last, as he reached for her and took her into his arms, as she felt his strong arms around her and felt her heart leap, she accepted the fact of loving. Now, she knew, she could never go back to Oxford and her old, safe but dull way of life. Damon, whatever else he had done, had freed her.

His mouth slowly, savouringly, covered hers, no trace of the angry passion of yesterday in his lips. Instead, there was something almost . . . sad . . . in the way his lips gentled as they parted hers. Something almost longing in the way his tongue lightly traced her teeth then slid deep into her mouth, making her shudder.

She half stepped away, throwing a patently insincere smile his way. Suddenly he wanted to wipe that falsehood off her face with a kiss that would make her bones melt! He wanted to scream at her for showing him a mask, when all he wanted was the real thing. For a single, blinding instant, he almost hated her. Taking deep, slow breaths he managed to get his furious frustration under control.

In the limousine, Joe King's knuckles had gone white as they had clutched the binoculars. He hated the sight of Damon Alexander kissing his daughter. Even though he revelled at the thought of the man's pain when he discovered he'd been duped, he still hated to see his hands on her. But the Alexanders would not win this time. And not even Joceline Alexander herself would be able to spoil his plans again.

A hundred yards away, parked in the shadows and almost disappearing into them, an unobtrusive little grey Fiat went unnoticed, and for that the occupants were grateful. Although they were working with the full co-operation of the Puerto Rican government, they were very much aware that they were far from home.

Damon firmly vetoed the Miensal Building, La Casa de los Contrafeurtes on the Calle Sebastian and the Butress House, and Ramona smiled wryly, beginning to get desperate. If she didn't know any better, she would think he was deliberately keeping her a prisoner by his side, a not unpleasant thought. But unless she could get him into the crowds, she would have no excuse for 'losing' him. She had to meet up with her father to give him the Markham papers.

'You're ignoring all this Puerto Rican atmosphere, you Philistine,' she said cajolingly.

'Easily,' Damon agreed.

'What do you want to do then?'

'I want to drink something cold. You're dehydrating me, woman.'

Ramona went hot all over, as, unbidden, she saw them locked together, thrashing in wild abandonment on the bed, their bodies sweat-slicked and twisted in ecstacy. 'Oh.'

Determinedly, Damon dragged her laughingly away along Calle Beneficincia to Casa Blanca, and there to the first watering hole he found. Ramona ordered a papaya freeze for herself, ignoring the pitcher of Mexican sangria that was looking more and more tempting with every smouldering glance from his darkening eyes.

Parking across from the café, Joe King watched them, hating every moment. They looked so damned good together. No wonder Alexander hadn't been able to keep his hands off her, touching her all morning, as if he had a right. Holding her hand. Stroking her arm. Strolling along with a hand at her waist. And now he was leaning across, taking a bite out of the ice she was holding. Something about the intimacy of the scene, about the way she smiled into his eyes, made him thump the door of the limo viciously.

In the Fiat, the man sitting behind the wheel raised an eyebrow as his companion, rather facetiously, wrote a note of it in his notebook. As he did so, he muttered under his breath, 'Subject thumped his car door, 11.45 a.m.' He was a tall, thin man, with thoughtful pale green eyes. 'How long has the Met been trying to get something on our Joe?' Detective Inspector Les Fortnum asked, the question almost rhetorical.

Seargent Frank Gless shrugged. 'Since before my time,' he acknowledged bluntly.

Les Fortnum nodded. He himself had only been a PC back in the late sixties, when Joe King had first come to the attention of the police. Then it had been insider trading. Not proven. Since then there had been a whole string of cases that grew in seriousness as Joe King grew in riches. Fraud. Not proven. Blackmail. Not proven. Conspiracy to defraud H.M. Tax Inspectors. Not proven. Aiding and Abetting. Not proven. Grevious Bodily Harm. Not proven. He seemed to get away with everything. But . . . 'I've got a feeling this time Joe is going to make a big mistake,' Les said, more to himself than to his sergeant.

'Yeah? How so?'

'For a start, this is personal.' He swung his intelligent light green gaze back to the couple in the café, who were rising to their feet. 'Heads up,' he warned softly, and Frank sat up straighter, turning on the engine.

245

As expected, Joe King followed them as Damon Alexander hailed a taxi. In a cat-and-mouse game, the two cars followed the taxi as it drove through New San Juan to the Puerta De Tierra, Puerto Rico's capital, a white marble building flanked by the Grand Rotunda with its mosaics and friezes.

'Fall back,' Les said, a little sharply, as they left the city behind and found themselves heading out into open countryside. They couldn't afford to blow it. They both knew how important this trip was. If they could actually nail Joe King for murder . . .

After a while, the taxi pulled up across from Luquillo Beach. Ramona was happy to be out of the confining space of the taxi and looked around at what had once been a flourishing coconut plantation. In the pretty little beach hut where she changed were posters advertising the lures of the El Yunque Rainforest nearby, set in the Luquillo mountain range. But as she stepped from the hut, she had no idea so many people were watching her. She was wearing a new bikini, one she'd purchased from the ship's boutique. It was ice-blue in colour, the perfect foil for her hair and tanned skin, and a perfect match for her eyes. It felt good to have so much sun on so much skin, and she stood on tiptoe and stretched, an errant sea breeze catching her long, free hair and blowing it away from her head, like a cascade of silvery-gold water.

Damon felt his breath catch, and walked quickly towards her. Whatever happened, he was determined to keep her. He was beginning to think, rather frighteningly, that he couldn't live without her. Once this whole mess with the shares was over, once she'd learned that she couldn't win by fighting him, he'd do anything to make sure that she wanted to surrender. One part of him winced at his obsession, but another, stronger part, gloried in it. He had never been so dangerously ensnared before. Never felt so damned *happy*. He was meant to feel this utter abandonment to his senses and the woman of his desires. Instead of being scared of it, he embraced it, eagerly.

'Ramona,' he said softly, reaching for her, unable to stop himself from kissing her, the need sparking between them the instant they touched. She felt her knees go, and clung to him, instantly lost in the sensation of mutual desire, her every other thought and aim drowned by the sheer power of their passion. With an enormous surge of willpower, he lifted his head and looked down at her, watching her eyes change from a look of dazed desire, to confusion, and back to her usual wary caution. 'Oh Ramona,' he said again, his voice almost a groan. 'You don't have to take, my darling,' he said softly, pushing his hand under her hair to cup the back of her skull, one thumb rubbing her chin. 'All you have to do is ask.'

Ramona felt a cold deluge wash over her. He *did* suspect something! 'I . . . I'll try to remember that,' she said, in what she hoped was a light and teasing voice, and gently but firmly stepped back out of his arms. Damon let her go, but his eyes were dark, his face strangely shuttered.

In his limousine, Joe King gritted his teeth. In the now baking Fiat, Les unwound a window, hoping for

247

some air, and watched Ramona King thoughtfully. If only he could be sure what game she was playing . . .

The Met had an extensive file on Joe King's latest adventure, and his plans to take over the *Alexandria* followed his usual pattern. And yet . . . Les shook his head. 'I don't know. This latest caper of Joe's still feels different from all the rest.'

Frank watched Ramona admiringly until she and her lucky boyfriend had disappeared into the sea. 'Oh? How so?'

Les turned to him, his pale green eyes serious. 'Gut instinct. I've followed King more times than I can remember. I know the bastard. And right now he's more uptight than I've ever seen him. Like I said before, this time it's personal. That's his daughter over there.'

Frank sighed. 'Yeah. Pity she's in on it.'

Les looked at him curiously. 'I'm not convinced she is. There's been no contact between father and daughter since King walked out on her when she was a few months old. With all the tails we've kept on King over the years, we'd have known about any moves he made in his family's direction. But now, suddenly, he shows up. And why would Treadstone leave the shares to Ramona if she was in league with her father? It makes no sense. I can't help but wonder what she'd do if we told her that her father killed her fiancée because he found out Treadstone was about to shop him.'

Frank sighed. 'I'd give my eye teeth to know what Treadstone found out that scared him so much.' Frank frowned. 'But if the daughter's not in on it with her father, why is she sucking up to Damon Alexander?'

Les nodded. 'Now that,' he said softly, 'is a very good question.'

On the beach, Damon leaned across and poured suncream onto his hands, his eyes on Ramona's lovely expanse of back. 'Hot?'

'Hmm. Very,' she murmured, then held her breath as cool, cream-covered hands suddenly slipped over her warm skin, massaging into her spine, making her nipples tingle against the blanket. She kept her eyes firmly closed. 'That feels good. I could stay here all afternoon.'

'Aren't we going to?' he asked casually, but his eyes were sharp as they watched her restlessly flickering eyelashes.

'Don't I wish,' she forced herself to sound regretful, then sat up. 'But I really must do some shopping. I promised my mother I'd bring her back something nice.'

'San Juan isn't a free port.'

'Oh?'

'So perfume and all the rest isn't as good a buy here as, say, in Jamaica.'

'Oh.' Reluctantly she lay back down again, then opened one eye. Why was he being so obstructive? In spite of herself, she shivered. Damon was a dangerous man. Time and time again he had her almost convinced that he really did love her, even though she knew that he was only lying, his every kiss only meant to ensure his precious shares remained safe and under his control. But if Dwight Markham let it slip that he had sold out to her, what would Damon do then? Uneasily, Ramona stared out to sea. The voyage was nearly over. She could last another week. She would have to. Surrender was unthinkable. Wonderful, he would make sure of that, but unthinkable. Oh Damon! How I love you. You bastard!

In the car, Joe King's gritted teeth actually began to ache. Never had he hated a man so much as he hated Damon. The Alexander whelp reached for the sun-cream again and began lathering her legs, his long fingers curving sensually around her calf. 'Get your hands off her, you son of a bitch,' he muttered. 'I'll bloody well kill you.' And, before he'd finished the last word, Joe King was already leaning back and smiling, his frustration abruptly draining away.

Why not? Yes. He would do exactly that. He would get some stuff to Doyle and order him to put an extra slug of poison in Damon's glass on the night of the masked ball. He'd kill the bastard.

It was obvious Ramona was not going to be able to get away from Alexander on this stop-over. Impatiently he tapped the glass separating him from the front. 'Drive me to Pier Three, where the cruise ships dock.' There was a man he wanted to talk to.

'King's moving,' Frank said. 'Do we stay with the girl?'

Les was tempted. His gut instinct told him Ramona King had her own reasons for being with Damon Alexander. Although he knew she was up to something, he was becoming more and more convinced she could be a valuable ally. But he couldn't risk blowing the whole deal on a hunch. Reluctantly, he shook his head. 'Stay with our Joe. I want to see what he's up to.'

As the cars disappeared, Damon put the top on the bottle of suncream and lay back on the blanket. Beside him, Ramona stirred restlessly. 'Something wrong, Ramona?' he asked softly, hiding a smile. No doubt she had wanted to post those Markham papers to a safe place. She probably felt very vulnerable having to keep them on board ship. Poor baby.

Ramona bit back a sigh of frustration. 'No. Nothing's wrong.'

Damon smiled, turned, kissed her shoulder, then settled down to some serious sunbathing. 'Good,' he said, sighing in contentment. 'I'd hate to think you weren't enjoying yourself.'

CHAPTER 21

Ramona felt a little foolish donning a sophisticated cocktail dress at two-thirty in the afternoon, but the casino was a *very* glamorous place, at any time of day. In a short, ruby-red satin dress that fell to just one inch above her knees, and matching, sequinned shoes, she supposed she looked the part. Dwight Markham had happily informed her that his bank had received the funds for his shares, so Gareth Desmond could assure himself of her *bona fides*.

Straightening shoulders which the high halter-neck dress left bare, she turned on her fancy shoes and walked to the door.

The casino came as something of a revelation. It was larger than she had expected, and simply eye-catching. Lush deep-red carpet drew the eye and pulled one in the moment one set foot inside. Brushed velvet gold and royal blue lined the walls and the chairs were sumptuously upholsterd in matching red and blue. Croupiers were dressed in white tuxedos, handling chips worth thousands of pounds with total ease.

Slowly, Ramona wandered around. At the roulette

wheel, she was fascinated by the intent looks on the people's faces. One man, dressed in a rumpled evening suit, had over £100,000 riding on red number fourteen. She shook her head as red twenty-two came up, and the man's £100,000 went to the croupier. And, by association, to Damon Alexander.

Deciding that pontoon was the game for her, Ramona cashed in a meagre £200 worth of chips and sat at an empty space. She began playing cautiously, all the while looking about her. But Gareth Desmond was not there. She sighed and placed another bet. As she did so, she felt someone sit beside her and glanced across, smiling at the woman, who, like her, was dressed in a cocktail dress. She had a shiny cap of raven hair and big, very brown eyes. She looked tired. 'Hello.'

Verity Fox smiled back. 'Hello.'

She knew who the blonde was, of course; who on the ship didn't? Rumour had it that Damon had given her the ring she now wore on her finger and the grapevine insisted that wedding bells were eminent. Everybody was talking about this woman who had finally hooked Verity's old childhood friend, and she could well understand why. She was easily the most beautiful woman Verity had ever seen. She half expected the other woman to turn coolly away, as only breath-taking blondes could, but she didn't. Instead she glanced ruefully at her diminishing pile of chips and shrugged a shoulder.

'Omar Sharif I'm not,' she said, her voice dry, and Verity found herself laughing, quite unexpectedly. She could sense at once that there wasn't an arrogant bone in this woman's body. Her years as a doctor had honed her ability to read personality, and she found herself liking the mysterious Ramona King right away.

'I don't expect I shall be, either,' Verity agreed, equally wry. 'Actually, this is the first time I've set foot in this place.'

'Really? Me too. But don't tell anyone,' Ramona said. 'I'm supposed to be the blonde equivalent of Mata Hari, or so I've heard.'

Verity burst out laughing. So she knew how the other passengers gossiped about her. 'Your secret is safe with me,' she assured her, then dithered over her cards, asked for another, received the nine of spades, and broke.

'I can see you're even better at this than I am,' Ramona said wryly, as the banker overturned two face cards, beating her seventeen and two eighteens. 'When I lose, I lose three at a time.'

Verity grinned, then groaned, as her chips were pulled away. 'Why am I doing this to myself?' she laughed, and suddenly her smile faltered, for she knew exactly why she was doing this to herself. To try and forget the look on Greg's face the last time she'd seen him.

'I'm Ramona King, by the way.'

A long white hand was extended, snapping Verity out of her morose thoughts, and she took it. 'I know. Verity Fox. Doctor. If the rumours are true, then you and I are neighbours. I work . . . worked . . . at the John Radcliffe.'

Ramona shook her head. 'Really? A small world.' She

looked around again, but without much hope. There was still no sign of her quarry. 'I think I need a drink,' she said dryly, and Verity quickly slipped off the stool.

'Me too.'

'In here, or have you had enough?'

Verity looked down at her small pile of chips and laughed. 'I think we'd better make it somewhere else. I can't afford this place much longer!'

Ramona blinked a little in surprise. She had assumed she was the only one on board this floating palace who wasn't a millionaire at least twice over. They found a sparsely populated bar on the top-most deck, the intriguing decor that of an Arabian café, all secluding rattan divisions, heavy and ponderous propeller fans, pastel walls and plenty of greenery.

'*Casablanca*,' Verity said, reading her thoughts, as they both ordered long, lime cordials with a dash of sherbert.

'Wasn't that a great film?' Ramona said, stretching out on her chair and shucking off her shoes with a sigh. Verity grinned and did likewise. A kindred spirit at last.

'It was a *fantastic* film,' Verity averred blissfully. 'I had a crush on Humphrey Bogart that just wouldn't quit.'

Ramona grinned. 'I'm a Burt Lancaster girl myself.'

In perfect harmony, the two women grinned at each other, neither of them realizing what a fierce jolt they had given one of the sunbather's outside. Joceline Alexander had been sunbathing for hours. Now, as she sat up slightly to sip her drink, her eyes fell on the two women sat behind the big picture window, the sight of them together making her heart almost stop. She swallowed dryly. What were they doing together? After talking to Damon in the Virgin Islands, she had set her little man on researching her son's lover. Naturally, she'd been delighted to learn that Joe King had never even been in contact with Ramona since he'd left Barbara. But now her terror was back.

Slowly, carefully, she got to her feet. She had to find out what they were talking about. By the time she'd made her way to the door of the bar, and concealed herself next to a huge, leafy fern, the two women were already fast friends.

'So you can see, there's nothing especially interesting about me,' Verity was saying, after finishing a brief description of her life history, minus the leukaemia.

Ramona shook her head. 'I don't know. It must be very satisfying being a surgeon.'

'I would have said the same thing about you. Not many people have it in them to be a Don at Oxford.'

Ramona shrugged and ordered them both another lime sherbert. 'I thought it was all I wanted. For a long time.'

Verity sat up straight, not missing the sudden sadness and disillusion in her voice. 'Oh? And it turned out it wasn't?'

Ramona gave a half-sigh, half-grunt of ironic laughter. 'No. I think now I rather made Oxford my prison, instead of my career. It took the death of my fiancée to figure it out.'

In the doorway, Joceline Alexander looked as shocked as Verity felt.

Verity's face creased with sympathy. 'I'm sorry. I didn't mean to pry.'

Ramona shook her head. 'You're not. To tell the truth, it's good to have someone to talk to.' And it was.

'I know what you mean. It's good to let people in, once in a while,' Verity said, wishing that she could repay the compliment and confess her own troubles. 'So, this trip is a breaking free trip, is it?' she asked, lightening the mood.

Ramona laughed. 'It was, but it's beginning to look as if I jumped right from the frying pan into the fire.'

Verity frowned, puzzled for an instant, then realized she was talking about Damon. 'Ah yes. But what a fire, hum?'

Ramona laughed. She couldn't help it. 'I suppose so. Are you here alone, or – ' she glanced at Verity's bare ring finger – 'are you married?'

Verity shook her head. 'No. I'm as free as air. My mother might have come, but London society would fold without her.'

Ramona grinned. 'Like that is it? My own mother doesn't get to London much. Not that she misses anything by it.'

Verity smiled. 'I'll bet your father's glad to keep her to himself.'

Ramona's smile faltered. 'Hardly. He left when I was just a baby.'

'Oh, that's tough. But you must see him sometimes?'

Ramona shook her head. 'Until five days ago I'd never set eyes on him.'

Verity blinked. 'I'm sorry,' she finally said.

Ramona looked up, her frown disappearing. 'Don't be. I never felt his loss as a child, and now . . . Well, we're both adults. We found we had mutual interests . . .' She shrugged, obviously reluctant to discuss it further, and Verity took the hint.

'Have you seen the film they're showing in the cinema yet?'

Ramona shook her head. 'I don't suppose it's *Casablanca*?'

Verity laughed. ''Fraid not. Not a glimpse of Burt Lancaster either, but it's supposed to be a good comedy. Fancy it?'

Ramona nodded. She could do with a laugh. And how!

The two women left, neither of them noticing the woman who watched them go, her face as pale and yellow as old parchment, her eyes wide with horror. Exactly what 'mutual interests' could Ramona King have with her father? She had to get Ramona on her own and warn her about her own father. She had to convince her somehow that he was poison. Joe King wrought havoc and destruction wherever he went. He had already taken everything she had . . .

Greg was walking with Jock (on one of his rare forays up from the engine room) when the cinema let out, and Jock's eyes widened at the vision two of the women made. He recognized the beautiful blonde in red at once, of course. Even in the bowels of the engine room, rumour had it that the big boss had fallen for a blonde to beat all blondes. At first, Jock thought Greg was merely

258

responding to the boss's lady, but then he saw that it was not the blonde Greg was staring at like a pole-axed ox, but the woman beside her. With her dark glossy hair and big brown eyes she was a sight to warm any man. Even as he thought it, the brunette glanced across and saw them, and the same look of frozen pain spasmed across her own face. Quickly she looked away, and the moment passed. Greg moved off, and Jock kept pace, his face wearing an unhappy frown. It had been bound to happen, of course. Greg was good-looking and at just the right age. But, dammit, a *passenger*! Didn't he know how dangerous that was? Jock sighed. Of course he did. He had a beer with his friend and captain in the crew's club, and kept his mouth firmly shut.

Greg was vaguely aware of Jock taking his leave a few minutes later, and for a long time he sat staring morosely at his beer. When he'd walked in on her and her doctor lover, he'd felt at first only shock and then anger. Later, he told himself he was lucky – he'd had a narrow escape. Or so his reasoning had gone. Until he'd seen her again. Until he'd looked into those big brown eyes, and seen his own pain mirrored there. His own lost hopes. His own helpless love . . .

With a huge sigh, Greg ran a hand through his hair. With a muttered curse he pushed his beer away and strode out of the club. He felt horribly exposed as he stopped outside her door and knocked.

Verity had been shaken by the encounter with Greg and had left Ramona King straight after the film, making plans to meet up with her again during the next day's full sailing.

Now she clucked exasperatedly at the knock on the door, and in her bare feet stalked across and flung it open. The angry 'Yes?' she'd been about to utter died on her lips, as the colour rapidly died in her cheeks when she saw him. For a moment, neither of them spoke, then Greg said stiffly, 'May I come in?'

'Of course,' she said, just as stiffly, and stood aside. Immediately, she felt a sense of *déjà vu*. Hadn't they done this before? She felt the old familiar longing creep over her. Verity sighed deeply. 'Oh, what a mess this all is,' she said simply.

Greg felt his heart plunge with her hopeless words. 'Yes,' he agreed grimly. 'I suppose it is. I just wanted to apologize,' he said stiltedly.

Verity stared at him, her eyes wide. '*You* apologize?' she said bemusedly. 'What on earth for?'

Greg sighed. 'I wanted . . . I expected . . . too much. I have no right to expect you to be faithful . . .'

'Oh Greg,' Verity wailed, 'you've got it all wrong. I love you,' she said simply.

Greg's head whipped around. 'What did you say?'

'You heard me,' she said softly, suddenly becoming very calm. 'I love you.' And it truly was as simple as that.

Greg let out a long, shuddering breath. 'If only you knew how much I wanted to hear you say that,' he said, his voice wavering wildly with unexpected hope. Wordlessly he held open his arms and she walked into them, tears flowing freely from her eyes. She felt his arms enclose her, their strength so welcome it made her realize exactly how much she needed it. In a blinding flash of revelation she acknowledged her self-sacrifice was only self-defeating and, worse, insulting to *him*. She needed him, as well as loved him. And love itself was composed of many varied things. Trust, need, friendship, understanding . . . Gordon had been right. She should have told him. He deserved it. Hadn't her silence done the very thing that she had hoped to avoid, and hurt him? She stepped back and looked up at him. She started to open her mouth to tell him about her leukaemia when the telephone rang.

For an instant they froze, then Verity's lips turned up in a reluctant smile. 'I don't believe it,' she said exasperatedly, and above her head, she heard Greg's throaty chuckle.

'You'd better answer it. What I want to say . . . I want to say without interruptions.' He looked down at her, his amber eyes glowing. Any part of herself that she could give him, he would accept and be grateful. He could ask for no more.

Verity nodded, her heart so full she could barely speak. Reluctantly she left his arms, then knelt across the bed and lifted the receiver. 'Yes?'

'Hello. Verity?' The voice was instantly familiar.

She closed her eyes. Oh Gordon. *Not now!*

'Hello,' she said cautiously, and glanced back over her shoulder at Greg. He looked so wonderful. She couldn't wait to rip his clothes off, and then later, explain everything . . .

'Verity. I . . .' In Oxford, Gordon slumped defeatedly at his desk. He'd gone through every item of information and had waited in an agony of suspense for the autopsy reports to come through before contacting her, but now there was no excuse to wait any longer. 'Verity,' he said again, and something in his voice made her drag in her breath harshly. She felt her heart do a curious flip, and land upside-down somewhere. Somewhere far away.

'Just tell me,' she said flatly. Greg took a step towards her, then stopped. He was close enough to recognize the voice on the other end, but not close enough to make out the individual words, when Gordon spoke again.

'Verity, I've got bad news. Very bad,' Gordon began in a miserable rush. 'One of the lab animals has died. It was being tested with . . . you know.'

'The autopsy?' Verity whispered, white-to-the-lips now. But she was facing away from Greg, who was puzzled by the obvious shop-talk.

Gordon sighed. 'It's related, Verity. No doubt about it.'

Verity felt as cold as ice. 'I see.'

'Verity, it could be controllable. We don't know yet exactly why . . .' Gordon's voice rose as he tried to convince her, and Greg took a step back, suddenly, ragingly jealous. He wanted to snatch the phone from her and beg her to tell him to go to hell. He wanted to scream at Dryer that Verity belonged to *him* now, and that he had no right to just ring up and expect her attention.

'Verity, you'll have to leave off taking the drug, at least . . . for a while.'

Verity said nothing. They both knew that she didn't have 'a while'. It was the end. It was all over. 'I

262

understand,' she said, her voice hollow. 'Goodbye, Gordon,' she added mechanically and hung up, her movements stiff and robotic. For a long while she stared at the telephone, and then sensed movement. Quickly she turned around. 'Greg,' she said. She'd forgotten he was there.

Greg, in that instant, knew she had too. One phone call from him, and . . . 'It's hopeless,' he said. He could not compete with Gordon Dryer, that much was now patently obvious.

'Yes, my darling, I'm afraid it is,' Verity said, her voice small and empty.

Greg nodded. 'I'm sorry,' he said stiffly. 'I . . . won't bother you again.' He turned for the door. It felt as if his heart had been torn out and he was leaving it behind, but he knew when he was beaten. If only she had wanted him more than Dryer then he'd have fought to his last breath for her. But she'd been mistaken when she'd said she loved him.

And anybody could make a mistake.

'I'm sorry,' he whispered again and shut the door, very quietly, behind him.

CHAPTER 22

Dominican Republic

Frank Gless quite liked the place. Perhaps it was because the Dominican Republic sprawled over two thirds of the Island of Hispaniola, and so felt less claustrophobic than the other Caribbean islands he'd visited in his pursuit of Joe King. Perhaps it was because he was a bit of a history buff, and in Santo Domingo, the capital, he'd found a city that had been continually inhabited since the sixteenth century, and looked like it. Many of the natives spoke a rudimentary English, which made their job a lot easier. They were in a little hardware-cum-repair shop on a tiny, cobble-stoned alley off the Calle Emiliano Tejera. How Les Fortnum had found the shop, or knew about the rather wizened and continually grinning store keeper, he didn't know, nor did he particularly want to.

The store keeper looked eighty if he was a day, and his eyes had an all-knowing look that made Frank feel distinctly uneasy. Suddenly he remembered that Haiti, that hotbed of voodooism, lay just across the border, and he shivered.

Watching his superior and the little old man haggle in pidgin English made him wonder if maybe some Haitians hadn't migrated east. Eventually the little gnome agreed a price and handed over a small package. It wasn't until Les had handed over a great wad of the coin of the Realm, the Dominican Peso, that Frank felt able to ask his superior what he was up to.

Les didn't answer until they were back in the car and driving back to the docks where a statue, only slightly smaller than the Colossus of Rhodes, stood staring out to sea. It was, in fact, Montesina, the Spanish priest who had come to the Dominican Republic in the sixteenth century to appeal for the human rights of the native Indians. Frank could only admire his optimism. Now, as they tucked themselves thankfully away in the shade of a huge, madly-blooming tree and awaited the arrival of the *Alexandria*, Les carefully unwrapped the tiny bundle and let it lie in the middle of his palm.

Frank stared at it, then whistled. He recognized it immediately, of course. It was a bug – the electronic recording kind, not the insect variety.

'We got a warrant for that?' Frank asked.

'Nope.'

'We got approval from London?'

'Nope.'

'Are we covered in any way?'

Les grinned. 'Nope.'

Frank grunted, but he was smiling. 'How are we going to get close enough to our Joe to plant it?'

'We're not. We're going to get close enough to his daughter.'

Frank blinked. 'Why?'

'Because we're going to tell her what we suspect her father of doing.'

Les had been thinking about it a lot since flying over from Puerto Rico. Nothing was going to happen unless they took a risk. Joe King was just too wily.

Frank twisted around in the cramped front seat. 'Do you think that's very clever, Les?'

Les shrugged. 'I don't think she's in on it,' he said simply. 'But even if she is, what have we lost? If she goes running to Daddy carrying this little bugger . . .' he patted the bug almost affectionately, even as Frank groaned at his atrocious pun '. . . and says, "Daddy dearest, the cops are onto us," we'll know for sure.'

'Not admissible in court,' Frank reminded him.

'No. But it makes for good leverage,' Les said shortly. There were few people who could listen to taped evidence of their own crimes and not break. If Ramona King was in on Joe King's murderous scheme, than the little object in his hand would give them just the edge they needed. And if she wasn't, then Joe King would have lost an ally and gained an enemy. Either way, the Met would win.

Ramona stood on the deck, admiring the sight of the city and its huge statue as the *Alexandria* came in to dock. There was, she knew, another statue, this time of Columbus, near Independence Square on the Calle el Conde in the Parque Colon. She supposed she should be looking forward to exploring the city, from the marble Altar de la Patria, to the Old Town Hall, but somehow she just couldn't work up the enthusiasm for it. The Markham shares were burning a hole in her big beach bag. If Damon should discover them . . .

The mighty ship gave a long blast on the horn, and the passengers lining the decks waved to the welcoming committee thronging the docks. Everywhere she went, the *Alexandria* was greeted like the queen she was. The glamour of sea travel had not gone, like the age of steam. It was still alive and very much kicking. Ramona glanced over her shoulder, half expecting Damon to appear like a genie. His absence, perversely, made her feel a little uneasy. Where was he? What was he up to? And was he still in that strange, watchful mood of his? Had she known where he was and what he was doing, she'd have felt more alarmed than ever. For Damon, at that very moment, was talking to Gareth Desmond, an old friend for many years, who listened with wide eyes that turned into a wider smile.

'OK, I'll do that. Are you sure she'll contact me?' Gareth asked, intrigued by his friend's dilemma.

Damon nodded grimly. 'Oh yes. She'll contact you,' he said wearily. 'With all your shares, you're the most obvious target. Just keep me posted, OK?'

Gareth nodded, and slapped him on the shoulder. 'I want an invite to the wedding, old son,' he said jovially. 'This is a match made in heaven. Or somewhere hotter . . .' He laughed heartily.

On the bridge, Greg and his officers watched the harbour pilot carefully and continuously checked the sonar but things were running as smooth as silk. At least, Greg thought miserably, *something* was going right.

On the deck, Ramona couldn't believe her luck. Damon was still nowhere in sight. She might have the whole day to herself if she was one of the first to disembark.

From inside one of the lounges, Damon watched her. Soon he would confront Joe King. And then, Ramona King, you'd better watch out, he thought savagely. Because I am going to get you . . . And he was never going to let her go again.

On deck, Ramona jumped as a steward lightly touched her shoulder. 'Miss King. I have a message for you. From Mrs Alexander.' Ramona thanked him, and quickly read the rather terse note. 'Ramona, I have to see you alone. Meet me at the Catedral Santa Maria La Menor, Primida de America at eleven-thirty. It's important. Joceline.'

Something was obviously wrong, Ramona mused. But she didn't know, yet, just how wrong things actually were.

'Just look at this crowd,' Frank grumbled as both men fought their way through the throng on the quayside.

'She's a real beauty,' Les said, his lean intelligent face wearing a very uncharacteristic look of awe and admiration as he gazed at the beautiful white ship.

'You see her?' Frank said, craning his neck, and frowning. The gangplank wasn't even in place yet.

'I meant the ship,' Les muttered and dragged his thoughts back to the task in hand. As Frank had pointed out, the crowd wasn't making it any easier. The sun grew fierce as it climbed slowly higher. At last, the *Alexandria* began to disgorge its passengers. 'You stand over by the taxi rank,' Les said, 'in case I miss her. Still no sign of our Joe?'

Frank grinned. 'None. Our phone call to his London office must have done the trick.'

Les hoped so. They had placed an anonymous call to one of King's many legal eagles, hinting at an informer within one of his London branches. King, much as he might want to meet the ship, wouldn't have been able to ignore such a potentially disastrous situation. Right now, he fervently hoped, King was at his hotel, pouring over his computer, faxes, and phones, and it would be a nice bonus if he happened to be sweating buckets while he did so. But if King had delegated the task, and was around to see them intercept his daughter, things could get rough. Very rough. He glanced around nervously, but saw, to his relief, no limousines. King would never rent anything less than a Mercedes.

He saw Frank standing over by the taxis, gesturing wildly. Following his pointing finger, Les saw her at once. He needn't have worried about missing her. She wasn't hard to spot – her long curtain of silver-gold hair made her stand out like a beacon. He felt Frank come up behind him as the passengers milled around and quickly passed him, all of them anxious to explore the island. As a particularly vocal group passed, chattering on about Laguna Gri-Gri, a swampland smack out of Louisiana Bayou country, with its Blue Grotto of Capri, he felt a moment of envy and pity. Envy of the people who were rich and carefree and on their way to Jarabacoa, known wistfully as the Dominican Alps. And pity for the girl who was even now closing the distance between them, unaware of what was about to happen.

Ramona didn't see them until one of them stepped out right in front of her. 'Miss King?'

Ramona blinked, then smiled. They had to be from her father. 'Yes.'

'Would you mind coming with us for a moment?'

Her smile faltered. There was something much too officious about these men. Instantly, she was on the alert, and took a backwards step. She glanced around and was reassured by the busy scene.

'There's no need to be alarmed, Miss King,' Les Fortnum said, instantly recognizing her fear, and feeling sick. He hated it when women had to be afraid of men. It was his job to ensure beautiful women didn't have to walk the streets in fear. Quickly he took out his identification and showed it to her. By his side, Frank did the same. 'We won't ask you to get into a car, or even move away from the crowds,' Les added. 'Perhaps a café?'

Ramona studied the identification closely and began to relax. 'Fine.' She glanced around, but Frank, who'd had a good scout around beforehand, quickly led them towards the Colonial Zone and to a wide open café facing the sea. Les was careful to lead them inside (just in case Joe King did show up and spotted them) and found a far, deserted corner. 'I hope you don't mind if we order breakfast?' Les said, more to put her at her ease than out of any pangs of hunger. 'The sergeant and I haven't eaten yet.'

Frank, brightening up at this largess, reached for the menu and scowled over the list of food, finally settling on a torilla de jamon, a spicy ham omelette. Ramona ordered a lemon and lime punch. Les solicitously took her big beach bag from her and placed it on the seat next to him. Frank very carefully looked away as Les slipped the bug out of his pocket. Ramona glanced at Les, whose left hand froze, then at Frank. 'Well, Inspector Fortnum, Seargent Gless. What's this all about?'

In the bag, Les could feel papers and the usual paraphernalia. Suncream. Sunglasses. What felt like a make-up bag. He also discovered that the whicker bag was lined with silk, and that right at the top, just below the handles, a little of the lining had come away. Very carefully, he slipped the flat, oval-shapped bug between the wickerwork and silk lining and then slowly withdrew his hand. He smiled. 'Miss King, I'm afraid . . .'

The waitress approached with Frank's omelette and the galletas that Les had ordered, and he fell momentarily silent. Ramona accepted her juice and took a sip, a little surprised to find that her lips, mouth and throat were unbearably dry. Her heart, too, was beating dull and heavy. Her hand shook just a little. Her instinct was screaming at her just one word. Trouble.

Les waited until the waitress was once more back behind the counter and far away. He glanced at Frank, who was taking a huge bite of omelette, and sighed. 'There's no easy way to say this, Miss King. I'm afraid I have bad news.'

Damon. The thought leapt straight into her head, and a terrible fear washed over her. If anything had happened to him, she'd just die . . . Her panicked thoughts screamed to a stop as sudden realization hit her. She loved him. She really, *really* loved him. More than anything else. More than her need for justice for Keith. More than her need to be safe. More than her own desires. More than anything. And here she was, about to betray him. She had shares in her bag and plans in her heart to take away the only thing he wanted, and all the time he was the love of her life.

'Dr King?'

She blinked, suddenly aware that the elder of the policemen was looking at her oddly. She managed to smile. 'I'm sorry. I wasn't listening.'

'That's alright. But I'm afraid it really is important. You must listen and understand what I'm about to say.'

Her heart lurched. 'He's alright, isn't he?'

Les blinked. 'Your father?'

This time it was Ramona's turn to look blank. 'No. Damon. We are . . .' She stopped, and determinedly pulled herself together. 'I think we're at cross purposes, Inspector. Why don't you tell me what this is all about?'

Les almost smiled at the sudden determination in the voice and the clear, probing intelligence that lasered into those extraordinary eyes of hers. For a moment back there, she'd looked as if she were about to fall apart.

Ramona suppressed a tiny shudder of apprehension and looked steadily at Les Fortnum. He had a good face, she saw absently. A strong, decent face. It was going to be bad, she thought. Whatever it is, it's going to be bad.

'Like I said, Dr King, I have distressing news. It concerns your fiancée.'

She paled instantly. 'Damon?'

'No, Dr King. Not Mr Alexander. Mr Treadstone.'

'Keith?'

'Yes.' Les took a deep breath and leaned back slightly. Without realizing it, Ramona did the same. 'At the time of Mr Treadstone's death, certain evidence was withheld from the public,' Les began. 'This was, of course, unusual, but since Mr Treadstone's death was part of an ongoing investigation by the Met – certain facts were deliberately supressed, in the interests of justice.'

Ramona stared back at him steadily. 'That sounds like police jargon for keeping the public in the dark,' she mused, her voice cool. 'So tell me. Exactly what was kept from us. From me?' Her voice went colder and became clipped, but she was in no mood to appease anybody at that moment. 'What happened to Keith that you didn't tell me?' she demanded.

Les did her the courtesy of not looking away and not mumbling. Instead his pale green eyes met her own without flinching. 'He was murdered, Dr King. He did not commit suicide.'

Ramona wasn't aware she was holding her breath until it exploded out of her. Briefly, she remembered her own doubts about the suicide, doubts shared by her mother. 'I knew it,' she said softly, missing the sharp look that passed between the two policemen. 'I just knew Keith wouldn't kill himself. But how do you know?'

Les shrugged. 'There were no powder burns on his hands. All guns discharge a tiny amount of cordite and powder when they're fired. They're microscopic amounts, to be sure, but they're there. Our pathologist could find no such residue on either of Mr Treadstone's hands. *Ergo*, he did not pull the trigger. Someone else did.'

Ramona stared at him, a deep, dark coldness beginning to stir in the very depths of her soul. 'He was . . . murdered?'

'Yes.'

Ramona licked her lips. They felt like desert furrows on her face. 'For his shares. In the *Alexandria*?' she asked, not wanting to hear the answer, already knowing what it would be.

'We believe so, yes,' Les said, satisfied that her pallor had proved him right, and that she really was just an innocent bystander in all this, after all. 'You had no idea of any of this, did you?' he asked sympathetically.

Ramona shook her head automatically, but she hardly heard him. There was a far distant buzzing sound in her ears, and her fingers curled around the seat of her chair. Keep calm, a voice screamed at the back of her head. *Keep calm.* 'No. I knew how obsessed he was about the ship, but I . . . never suspected he would go so far . . .' she heard her own voice say. Oh Damon! Damon, what have you done?

Frank nearly dropped his cup of coffee. He shot Les, who was looking equally stunned, a questioning look. Les quickly pulled himself together and took advantage of her obvious shock to probe her more. 'But you hadn't met him then, Dr King,' he said, letting his voice show his puzzlement. 'Had you?'

Ramona shook her head. 'No. That came later. When I boarded the ship.'

Les blinked. 'He was on the ship?' Joe King had been aboard the *Alexandria*? If the surveillance teams had screwed this up, so help him, he'd see heads roll. His vindictive thoughts skidded to a halt as he found her looking at him, her own eyes sharply observant now, and openly bewildered.

'Of course he was on the ship,' she said. 'Why wouldn't he be?'

'But . . . Dr King, that's not possible. We've been following him since he left England. Never once did he set foot on board.' True, Joe King had driven to the docks in Puerto Rico, and they had observed one of the ship's passengers get into his car. Unfortunately the windows were tinted, so they hadn't been able to see inside, but they had got a good photograph of the man, and London had given them a name. Jeff Doyle. But that was as close to the ship as Joe King had ever come.

Ramona shook her head, feeling as if she'd stepped into some surreal nightmare world. 'You've got something very wrong. He's on the ship right now.'

Frank opened his mouth to hotly deny it, but suddenly Les's hand shot up, silencing him. For a long moment, Les looked at her thoughtfully. Then he nodded. He said softly, 'Just who do you think we're talking about, Dr King?'

Ramona blinked. The words almost wouldn't leave her mouth. Everything in her cried out to protect him, but she knew she couldn't. 'Damon Alexander, of course,' she said at last, the Judas words tearing her apart. 'Who else?'

Frank gaped at her like a gob-smacked mullet. 'Alexander? But we're not talking about Mr Alexander, Dr King.'

Ramona turned sharply towards him. 'What?' The word was like a bullet, but even as she spoke, Les began to nod his head. Yes. Now, it was beginning to make sense.

'You thought Alexander was somehow responsible?'

Ramona turned back to the older man. 'He . . . isn't?' she whispered, trembling finely in every cell of her body, her voice dwindling to a bare breath.

Les shook his head. 'No, Dr King. He isn't. He had nothing whatsoever to do with Mr Treadstone. Believe me.'

Ramona slumped back, all strength seeming to leave her. 'Oh, thank God!'

At least one mystery was solved. They now knew why she was with Damon Alexander. For some reason she had been holding him responsible for Treadstone's death. Les saw the relief fade from her face as she began to think about what this meant, and then her blue eyes were once more back on him, the obvious question alive between them. 'Then who?' she said, her voice faltering even as she asked it. Because, suddenly, she knew. Les saw the knowledge creep into her eyes and nodded.

'Yes. Your father, Dr King,' he confirmed gently. 'We're talking about your father.'

★ ★ ★

Joceline glanced at her watch. Nearly eleven-fifteen. At last. She'd showered and donned a light, white linen jacket and matching trousers. Now she grabbed her handbag and headed for her cabin door. On the quay she took the first taxi she could find and gave him the address of the meeting place.

As she leaned back in the taxi, she took a deep, steadying breath. If Ramona King went straight to the police after Joceline had told her the truth about Michael's death, and Joe King's part in covering it up, she could count her remaining time of freedom in hours.

Ramona left the café feeling stunned. The two policemen had told her a lot about her father, about the list of crimes he'd committed and got away with, and about Keith being in league with him. The only thing they were not sure about was what had gone wrong between them. What had Keith learned that made it imperative that Joe King kill him?

Now, as she wandered absently back towards the quay, she felt split in two. On the one hand, she was elated. Damon was innocent. She had got it wrong, all the way down the line. What she had mistook for play-acting had been real. He really did love her. He really did want to marry her, and not just for the shares. She had let her own anger blind her. She had *wanted* him to be guilty, but all the time, he'd been truly falling in love with her. It was . . . joyous.

On the other hand, her father was now back in her life, casting a long, inky black shadow. Although they had never said as much to her, she knew the two police officers were hoping she would help them nail her father. But she had not told them she was due to meet him today, and now she wasn't sure that she was going to try and contact Joe King after all. She needed time to think. It was all such a mess. Although she had volunteered nothing, she knew she owed it to Keith to help them. And her father deserved everything that was coming to him. But she needed a little time to sort it all out in her mind first. Joe King was a very dangerous man. The consequences could be dire.

As she walked dazedly back towards the quay, she wondered what she should tell Damon. She owed him the truth, even if it meant risking losing him. There had been so many lies, so many schemes, that they had to have a fresh start. But would the police want her to bring him into it? After all, it was his ship her father was plotting to steal, and Damon had had dealings with her father before. Or at least, Michael Alexander had. She shook her head as she walked in the baking sun. There was so much to consider.

But she was to be given no time to recover. A taxi suddenly veered to a halt in front of her, and Ramona took a step back, thinking instantly of her father. Her murderous, extremely dangerous father. Perhaps he had seen her and the police.

But the head that leaned out the back was not that of Joe King. It was Joceline, peering at her out of the window, her eyes squinting against the light. Ramona's heart fell. She had forgotten all about Joceline.

'Joceline, I'm sorry but I forgot about the Cathedral.'

Joceline opened the door and moved across the back seat. Ramona leaned in, but made no move to join her. 'Joceline, can we do this some other time? There's something I have to do.'

Joceline smiled, a very strange, very alarming smile, and instantly, Ramona knew that this extraordinary day was not over yet. 'I'm afraid I must insist, Ramona,' Joceline said, and then nodded at the empty seat. 'It can't wait.'

Ramona got in with a sigh, and listened philosophically as Joceline changed their destination to the Parque Independencia. Once there, they walked very slowly to the nearest bench. In the bright sunlight, Joceline looked ghastly. Gently, Ramona took her arm and helped lower her onto the bench, then put her bag down at their feet.

In their car parked fifty metres away, Frank and Les put on their tiny earplugs for a routine equipment check. They needed to make sure the equipment worked.

Joceline leaned back on the sun-warmed wooden bench with a faint sigh. The sound came over loud and clear to the two policemen and was picked up by the silently turning cassette tape.

'Joceline, are you alright?' Ramona asked, her voice concerned.

Joceline smiled. 'No, not really. I have something unpleasant to tell you. It won't be easy.'

Ramona knew Joceline didn't like her, and up to five minutes ago, Joceline would have been quite right not to trust her. But now it had all changed. She loved

Damon with all her uninhibited heart and would do her best to make him happy. 'Joceline, there's no need to worry. . .'

'But I do worry,' Joceline interrupted, her voice sharp. 'I worry a lot about you and my son. Most of all, I worry about Joe King.'

In the car, both men shot up straight. 'That's Joceline Alexander, isn't it?' Frank whispered, and Les nodded.

Ramona stared at her, totally nonplussed. Whatever she had expected Joceline to say, it had not been that. 'I don't . . .'

Joceline held up her hand. 'Please, Ramona, let me get this over with. I don't know what you're planning, but I have to warn you,' she said urgently, 'if your father is involved somehow, then my dear, both you and Damon are in grave danger. Believe me, I know. Joe King is dangerous. He's . . . evil.'

In the car, Les watched the tape going round and round. 'You getting this?'

Frank nodded excitedly. 'Every word.'

Ramona couldn't think of a thing to say. Joceline nodded, satisfied she had her complete attention, and carried on painfully. 'I think, in spite of everything, you may love my son . . .'

'But I do,' Ramona said fervently, taking Joceline's hand and squeezing it. 'I really do. More than even I knew.'

Joceline looked into those remarkable eyes and suddenly smiled. She instinctively believed her, and it was as if a great weight suddenly lifted. 'I'm glad to hear that,' Joceline murmured. 'Because he's going to need

280

you. Wherever Joe King is, death and destruction follow. Damon is going to need a good woman by his side. Like Michael needed one. And I failed him. Totally.'

Ramona shivered. There was something so sad, so utterly sad, in Joceline's voice that it cut to the bone. 'I'm sure that's not true,' she denied fervently.

'But I'm sure it is,' Joceline countered wearily. 'You see, nearly twenty-eight years ago, Joe King and I were . . . lovers.'

Ramona gasped. 'He was still married to my mother then.'

Joceline nodded. 'I know. I'm sorry. I was happily married too, or so I thought. Then I met Joe and . . . things just happened.' Joceline shrugged her shoulders miserably, knowing how inadequate that sounded, but unable to do better. 'Before I knew it, I was seeing him secretly. And then we were in the middle of an affair. I don't know how it happened, even today. Joe never loved me, you see,' she said sadly. 'It was the Alexander Line he wanted. And like a fool, and without even knowing it, I helped by giving him little bits of information about Michael's business. His contracts. His business associates . . .' She trailed off, weakening for a second, then quickly carried on. 'Michael found out. He confronted me with a piece of broken glass one night. And I shot him.'

The two policemen in the car stared at one another.

Ramona gaped at her future mother-in-law. 'You shot Michael? But I thought Damon said it was a burglar . . .'

Joceline nodded. 'I know. Michael intended to kill me, of that I'm convinced. I shot him in self-defense. I wanted to call the police, to explain, but I called Joe instead.'

'And he stopped you?'

Joceline nodded. 'Yes. He knew a police investigation would reveal some of the fraud and blackmail he had used in his attempted takeover of the Alexander Line, so he came over and set up the burglary theory and told me what I had to say. He broke the glass in the window and took the gun. He threatened . . .' Joceline stopped.

Ramona took her cold, shaking hand into her own. 'It's alright, Joceline. I can imagine what he threatened.'

'That's why I've pushed Damon away all these years, you see,' she said bleakly. 'So he wouldn't be tainted by me any more. And that's why it's up to you, now, to protect him from your father. You have to. I'm getting too tired . . .'

Ramona nodded and squeezed Joceline's hand. 'Don't worry,' she said grimly. 'I'll see to my father . . .'

CHAPTER 23

Verity Fox hesitated at the drawer of her bureau, then slowly pulled it out. Carefully, she picked up one of the small squares of folded paper lying inside and put it on the table. For a long, long time she just stared at it, then, mechanically, she poured a half a glass of water and glanced at her watch. Eight-thirty. She'd taken the drug yesterday, just ten hours after Gordon had phoned, and her next dose was now due. She was not sure why she was still taking it. Almost absently, she watched herself competently empty the packet of powder into the water without spilling a single grain. With a swizzle stick, she stirred the powder into dissolvency, and then limply held the glass in her hands.

The last residues of shock had finally gone yesterday, in the Dominican Republic. The bright sunlight, the laughter, the busy streets, the quiet beaches, the eternally moving ocean, had all slowly brought her back from her cocooning little world of self-pity and denial.

As she absently swirled the glass she wondered if, in some small, stubborn backwater of her mind, she was refusing to accept defeat. Did she still believe that this drug could save her, no matter what Gordon said? Or was it the exact opposite? Did she have some kind of death wish? Did she want the drug to kill her, more quickly than the leukaemia would?

Verity sighed and brought the glass to her lips. She drank the slightly acrid-tasting brew in several quick gulps. Whatever the reason, she could no more resist the stubborn impulse to keep on taking the drug than she could stop herself from loving Greg. With a firm hand, she replaced the empty glass on the table with a solid thunk, and then stood up and collected her bag. She was going to breakfast. Then she was going to see her new friend, Ramona King. After that . . .

Verity shrugged. After that . . .

In the research annexe of the John Radcliffe Hospital at Oxford, Gordon Dryer watched the computer printer with a familiar feeling of hope, anticipation, and dread. Soon the final analysis from Hercules would be coming through.

After he'd hung up the phone from speaking to Verity he'd been inflamed by a sense of anger. He'd heard the defeat in her voice and something inside him had just railed at the injustice of it all. Consequently he'd gone back to work, fired up, determined not to give up the fight. They knew Hercules had died because of the drug, but now he would find out exactly *why*. Perhaps there was some way the drug could be moderated, or altered to prevent another death. It was the only chance Verity had. But, slowly, during the long, grinding hours, when he'd slept barely four hours in every twenty, and test after test proved unhelpful, his fire had gone and despair had slowly crept in. Now, as the printer sprang into life with the latest results, he felt again that dread and sick excitement unfurl in his stomach.

Standing, wincing at the pain in his stiff back, he removed the computer sheets and took them back to his bench. Quickly he ran his experienced eye down the list of figures and correlations, his heart sinking even further. It was as he'd feared. The drug itself, whilst bringing the white blood cell count down, destroyed too many reds at the same time. It was a form of chronic anaemia that had done for Hercules. He had hoped that that could be countermanded by transfusions, but this test made that hope look forlorn. The drug was not . . . Suddenly his dismal thoughts stopped dead. Scanning the lines quickly to get an overall view, he was only now reading, almost automatically, the separate processes gone through to achieve the end result, and there was something very odd and very interesting, about half-way down the page. Quickly, Gordon took a ruler and underlined the relevant information, his quick and brilliant mind jumping into overdrive. Perhaps. Just perhaps . . .

Verity glanced at her watch and frowned. It was already ten-twenty. Ramona was late. They'd agreed to meet up in the bowling alley at ten, both of them never having played the game and agreeing that they would make fools of themselves together. She wandered over to lane three. She had booked it when she came in, not that it mattered, since this early in the day the alley was deserted. Picking up a ball and finding it surprisingly heavy, Verity glanced around and saw with relief that the attendant wasn't watching, but was busy stacking balls at the far end of the court. Cautiously, she took a few awkward steps and let go of the ball. It rolled satisfactorily down the waxed runway for a few yards, then began to wobble, then dribbled miserably into the side gutter and rolled slowly to the end. The stack of skittles at the far end began to laugh at her, and Verity managed a smile and stuck her tongue out at them.

'They're insulted. I can tell.'

Verity very nearly yelped with surprise and spun around, her heart pounding.

She managed to swallow, but it was a dry and painful effort. 'Hello, Greg. I didn't know you were a bowling fan.'

Greg smiled. Keep it light and easy, he warned himself. 'I didn't know you were such an excellent player.' You're the captain of the ship, he told himself firmly, you're supposed to be good at socializing, at keeping things light. Except that this particular pep-talk didn't take into account that he wanted to push her back against the highly polished floor, strip her naked, and beg her to love him back. He took a deep breath. 'I have a message for you, from Ramona King. I understand you were supposed to meet her here?'

Verity felt as if he'd just punched her. The official politeness of his voice was like acid on her skin. She half turned and reached for another ball.

'That's right,' she said tightly. 'But I would hardly have thought she'd use the captain as a messenger.'

Greg drew in his breath harshly. 'You little . . .'

Verity swung her head around. At last. Raw emotion. If only it didn't have to be anger. 'Little what, Greg?' she asked tauntingly, wondering despairingly even as she spoke why she was doing this. But she knew why, of course, deep down. She couldn't bare to have him so near and not touch him. The white uniform looked crisp and clean and a direct challenge to her. She wanted to rip it off him. His cool eyes made her want to make them melt, and his cool voice was just asking to be turned into that gasp and tiny, strangled moan he gave whenever she cupped him in her hand and gently squeezed. His official reason for being with her made her want to scream and shout with frustration.

That was why she was being such a bitch.

Greg pulled himself together with an effort. 'I don't usually deliver messages from one passenger to another.' He heard his voice being hissed out through gritted teeth and forced himself to relax. The next time he spoke, his voice was oiled. 'But I happened to bump into her. She said to tell you she had something important to do, and could you make it another day.' And, Greg added silently, like a fool, I said yes, just so that I could see you again.

Verity sighed. 'Of course. I'm sorry, Greg,' she said. 'I . . .'

'Forget it,' Greg said briskly. Now he felt more of a fool than ever. As if this woman, who socialized with the likes of the Alexanders, would want to marry a post-man's son.

Verity reached for another ball and stopped. A tingle in her fingers warned her of what was about to come and sure enough she began to feel the heat start to build somewhere in the back of her neck. Oh no. Not now! She straightened quickly and gave a vague smile some-where in his direction. 'Well, thank you, Captain, for letting me know.' She turned and walked at a brisk pace to the door. She could feel her face begin to flame with heat, and knew it must be turning fever-red.

'Dr Fox.'

Verity stopped but didn't look around.

'Yes?'

Greg stared at her back, a frown of surprise and suspicion on his face. She was acting very strangely. 'Are you . . . feeling alright?' he asked, wondering why he suddenly felt so cold. Frighteningly cold.

Verity smiled grimly. 'Oh, I'm fine,' she lied savagely and took another few paces. Then she stopped and added more softly, 'Thank you.' And then she was gone.

Greg stared at the empty space where she had been, feeling frustrated and somehow cheated. He could not have said why, but he was sure there was more to this than just an awkward love affair gone wrong.

In her cabin, Ramona was half-way to the door when the phone rang and she cursed grimly. She'd told Damon she would only be a minute, and as she snatched up the receiver she barked out, 'Yes?'

'Dr King?'

Ramona almost groaned aloud. 'What is it, Inspector Fortnum? You must make it quick, Damon's expecting me.'

'I will, Dr King. I just wanted to ask if you've heard from your father yet.'

'No.'

'I see. If you do, will you call us?' He recited the number of his boarding house in Jamaica, and she jotted it down.

'Yes. Alright. I'll call you.'

'Dr King!' The voice was urgent, sensing she was about to hang up.

'Yes?' she snapped shortly, glancing at her watch. She was only supposed to be getting her bag.

'How is . . .' The voice, usually so sure and smooth, faltered, instantly alerting her. 'How are things on board? No problems?'

Ramona's eyes narrowed. 'What do you mean?'

In Jamaica, Les Fortnum could have kicked himself. Damn, but she was sharp. They had informed the Met of their latest discovery concerning Joe King, and had been told that if they could prove a case of accessory after the fact to murder, they would settle for that, as a starting point. With Joe King in custody, who knew what other worms might feel safe enough to come out of the woodwork? But it all depended on Joceline Alexander's testimony. Not that Les could tell Ramona King that. Not when things were getting so tricky. He thought quickly. 'We believe your father has a man aboard the ship,' he said, knowing he had to sidetrack her suspicious, and quickly. 'His name is

Jeff Doyle. Has he approached you, by any chance?'

Opposite him, Frank raised an eyebrow, but Les ignored him. It was just as well to warn her, but he was not about to mention the bugging device. Not when she was in this mood.

'No,' Ramona said, frowning. Jeff Doyle. She'd have to look him up, see if she could find him. 'Look, I have to go.'

'In that case I won't keep you. Can I ask you, if you meet your father in Jamaica, to call me immediately?'

'Yes. I will,' Ramona said, willing to promise him anything just then. 'Goodbye.'

Les hung up, his face thoughtful. 'I hope she's not going to try anything on her own,' he said thoughtfully. But that was exactly what he feared.

'You didn't ask her to take the beach bag,' Frank reminded him.

Les shrugged. 'It wasn't the time. Besides, she needs something big to hide the Markham papers in. Chances are she'll take the same bag.'

Frank grunted. 'I don't need to point out, do I, that so far our luck hasn't been exactly brilliant?'

Les gave a harsh bark of laugher. No. He didn't need to point it out. It was rapidly becoming very obvious. Joe King seemed to have more lucky lives than a basketful of cats.

In his master suite, Damon stood on the balcony, staring thoughtfully out to sea. He heard her walk up behind him, and turned. Just the sight of her turned his day brighter. He held out his hand and Ramona took it, her eyes brightening under a load of unshed tears. 'Oh Damon,' she said softly, leaning her head against him, her heart so full she felt it would surely burst.

'Hey, what's this?' he half laughed, bringing her into his arms and brushing away the tears that had overflowed and were running down her cheeks. 'This is the first time I've seen you cry. Is something wrong?'

Ramona laughed. 'No. Oh no. Just the opposite.' She looked up at him, for the first time ever free to love him without inhibition or fear. 'I love you. No matter how many times it's been said over the centuries, by men and women . . . I've never said it before. Not to anyone. And it means so much. Just three little words that mean the difference between a life worth living, and mere existence.' Slowly she reached up and touched his face, so familiar, so wonderfully precious. 'Damon, I love you.' Slowly, standing on tiptoe and leaning up against him, she kissed him, marvelling at the firm but softly padded texture of his lips.

Damon felt his heart leap. He curled his hands around the top of her arms and held her a little away, needing to plumb the depths of her eyes. Was this just another act? If so, he would die.

But she looked back at him, loving pouring from her eyes, from the pores of her skin, and he took a deep shuddering breath. Wordlessly, Ramona put her cheek to his shoulder and kissed him through the fabric of his shirt. 'Yes,' she said, as if he'd asked a question with only one possible answer.

Damon sensed the invisible bond tightening around them and accepted it gratefully. It was just one more aspect of love that he was beginning to learn, and he hoped he'd carry on learning for the rest of his life.

Ramona took his hand and led him to her bed. Gently, he stroked the hair from her face, looking down into her eyes, her lovely face, feeling at peace again. 'Thank you.'

Ramona gently pushed him back against the mattress, for the first time free to love him totally. Slowly, not taking her eyes from his, she slipped her fingers through the gaps in his shirt and slipped free the buttons, her fingers running across the smooth, warm bare skin to rotate gently against his nipples. She felt them harden and stiffen beneath her palms at the same time as his eyes darkened to a thundercloud grey. His lips parted slightly, and breath feathered past his lips to blow a stray strand of hair off her cheek.

Slowly she leaned forward, her knees on either side of his hips, and kissed his navel, feeling his flesh quiver, sensing the muscles tensing in his flat abdomen. Slowly, she worked her way up, to suck hungrily on first one nipple then the other. She heard a low, almost inaudible growl rise from his throat and smiled. His body was hers. All hers. His heart was hers, and she'd keep it safe. His love was hers, and she'd never let it go.

She closed her eyes as her tongue slid up the columns of his throat, and then her lips fastened hungrily on his.

Damon's hands went to her waist, drawing her close. It felt as if she were kissing his soul, drawing up the very essence of his being through his mouth and into her own. He wanted it to go on forever. Never before had their love-making been like this. The first time had been a revelation, and afterwards it had been passionate, very nearly savage, and thrilling.

This was different. This was love-making with unconditional love, and it was so poignant, so exquisite, he understood why the French called consumation a 'little death'. He opened his eyes and looked up at her, his hands brushing aside the curtain of hair that fell down to his own shoulders. His gaze bored deeply into hers.

'Ramona?' He said her name as a question. He had to be sure. And, again, she answered.

'Yes,' she said softly. 'Oh yes!' She drew off her clothes with quick, feverish hands and then reached for his belt buckle. Within moments, he was naked beside her, his hands on her waist, turning her onto her back, his knees nudging aside her own.

Her eyes widened as he plunged into her, her body bucking upwards to meet him, her blood singing in her veins. Her legs quickly scissored over his waist, imprisoning him between her thighs, capturing his long, hard pulsating shaft deep within her. Damon's jaw clenched, his dark hair falling across his forehead as he looked down at her with eyes now the colour of a snowcloud – deep, iron grey. His pupils were large black circles, mirroring her own.

Quickly his mouth swooped on hers as his body did the same, and Ramona cried out at the power of his loins. Her nails raked helplessly against his back as he began to drive her towards the edge of screaming, blissful ecstacy. She hugged him fiercely to her, her nipples hard buttons of flesh digging into his chest, her hair splaying out like a cloud of woven gold on the pillow.

He screamed, or she screamed, it hardly mattered which, as their world exploded on tidal waves of pleasure. She felt his collapsing weight on top of her and welcomed it, as she gloried in his harsh, ragged breathing, and the final spasms of his sweat-slicked body.

For a long time she lay supine beneath him, her hand absently stroking his damp hair, his face cushioned on her breast. She knew now why women throughout the centuries had killed and died for their lovers. Why wars had been waged because of a lover's betrayal, and duels fought for the chance of winning a lady's favour.

She would have gladly died, or killed, for the man now lying in her arms. She felt courageous, and defiant, and so dangerously determined, she could have shouted out loud.

And, a small voice warned her, she was going to need every last scrap of her new-found courage. Because, now, she had to save Damon from her father. And, after that, face a whole lifetime with him. There would be predatory women to fight off. Wolves to be held at bay. And all of life's sometimes spiteful little arrows.

But, now, she was ready for them.

CHAPTER 24

Jamaica

Verity Fox stared at the Dunn's River Falls at Ocho Rios, and couldn't help but be affected by the magnificent six hundred feet of cold, clear mountain water splashing over a series of stone steps to the warm Caribbean sea. Slowly wandering down, she saw people in swimsuits heading for the falls and, in a moment of sheer recklessness, quickly found the changing rooms, grabbed her own swimsuit from her beach bag, and changed. It took her only a few minutes to find another gaggle of holiday-makers and tag on, and soon they were introduced to their guide, who explained some of the geography of the island and the specific history of the falls, before telling them what happened next. And what happened next was a climb up the watery steps, forming a human chain by hanging onto the person in front and behind you!

After drying off and sipping a positively lethal combination of coconut milk, Jamaican rum and fresh pineapple juice, she changed and wandered off to the Old Fort, built in 1777, before finally giving up and admitting defeat. It was barely noon and it already felt as if she'd been on the island three days instead of three hours. It was not that she felt ill, exactly. Nor was she immune to the sheer beauty of the island. But she wanted Greg. She wanted him so badly she could hardly think straight.

She meandered along to the railway station and took one of the diesel trains run by the Jamaica Railway Corporation back to Montego Bay. She began to feel hot, and opened one of the carriage windows. Almost routinely now, she leaned forward and began to take deep breaths. She felt her heartbeat accelerate, as usual, and took her pulse. A few more minutes and the flush would pass. But it took the train another five minutes to pull into the station and still the flush was on her. She left the carriage quickly, desperate for some air, and stood by a pillar, absently listening to a group of laughing teenagers speaking Patois. Knowing she was attracting attention, Verity walked slowly to the exit. Her head began to throb. It had never done that before. The pavement under her feet seemed to undulate, as if she was in an earthquake movie, but she knew it was not the ground that was rocking. She managed to hail a taxi and slip in.

Her legs felt like rubber. 'The docks. The *Alexandria*, please.' Her voice sounded weak, even to her own ears, and she saw the driver's eyes go quickly to his rear-view mirror.

'You OK, lady?'

'Yes. Please . . . the docks.'

'How much?'

Verity blinked. 'What?'

'How much, lady?'

Verity groaned. She'd forgotten the warning by the ship's lecturer about setting the price of a taxi drive before setting off on a journey. 'Ten Jamaican dollars, alright?' She just wanted to get somewhere cool. Somewhere near Greg.

The driver nodded, the car moved off and Verity almost gasped. The sensation of movement sent her head into a tornado-like spin that had her grabbing the back of the seat in front of her. Quickly she closed her eyes, but it wasn't enough. With a hollow sense of fatalism, she realized she was passing out. She wasn't going to make it back to the ship . . .

John Gardner was checking off the drugs supply on his roster, something he did every day. It was not only to make sure they never ran low on the essentials. Some of the drugs in his cabinets were highly prized and he was not surprised that the captain had insisted on daily checks. John was able to spot a user a mile away, and as he checked off morphine, he shook his head. What made people who were intelligent enough to make themselves fortunes suddenly become stupid enough to get themselves hooked on drugs?

He almost dropped his manifesto as someone hammered on the door, the rapidity and loudness of the rapping setting his heartbeat racing. He was at the door in two strides. 'Yes?'

A steward was at the door, looking wan and just a little wild-eyed. But his voice was calm and he came right to the point. 'One of our passengers, Dr Fox, has been taken ill, sir. She's on the dock at the moment, in a taxi. We're not sure if we should move her without . . .'

John cut in quickly. 'Show me the way.'

The taxi driver was pacing helplessly up and down, and sighed in relief as the doctor arrived. John felt utterly calm as he walked to the back of the taxi, one look telling him she was deeply unconscious. He took her pulse, which was much too fast, and frowned. 'Help me get her out. Then go and tell the captain we may have a medical emergency.'

With two hundred miles of beach to choose from, they were spoiled for choice, but Ramona had opted for the Doctor's Cave Beach at Montego Bay, and now they walked leisurely, hand in hand, along the beachfront.

Damon couldn't keep his eyes off her. He'd never felt this relaxed and at peace with the world since their first, distinctly dodgy meeting! She was wearing a floatingly thin black dress, which contrasted sharply with her silvery hair. The wind caught the chiffon and pressed it against her body, clearly outlining her generous, thrusting breasts and hugging her thighs, whipping the black lacy material around her calves. He felt desire flood over him.

Ramona looked at him, caught the look in his eyes, and caught her breath. 'Shall we find a room somewhere?' she asked, her voice little more than a husky whisper. 'Find a quiet little inn someplace, far away from all this?' She glanced at the tourist-clogged beach, the gaudy umbrellas, the fast-food stands. Although it had only been a matter of hours since they'd made love, it suddenly felt like years.

Damon bent and suddenly gathered her close, swinging her around and laughing out loud. Then he held her so tightly that for a moment she thought he was going to crush her ribs. She did not see, over his shoulder, the long, navy blue Bentley parked beside a towering palm.

Damon sighed happily. 'Ah, Ramona,' he said huskily, leaning his head back to look at her, his eyes dancing once more. 'If you only knew how much I loved you, it would scare you silly.'

Solemnly, she looked up at him, her eyes shining. 'No,' she said softly, firmly. 'It wouldn't.' Not now. She laughed out loud. She couldn't help it. All the ugly intrigue of the last months was relegated into obscurity, warmed away by the hot look in his eyes.

'I could love you to death,' he warned, his voice impossibly husky, deepening with desire.

'Is that a promise?' she asked hopefully.

Damon grinned and bent forward to capture her earlobe in his teeth, nibbling around the jet earring, making her shudder.

'In that case,' she said, and swallowed hard as he raised his head, his eyes the colour of rain-clouds, 'let's get going.'

They left eagerly, never noticing the dark blue Bentley that followed them, or the commonplace little red Fiat that followed that.

Greg strode into the hospital and stopped dead. On the table, an oxygen mask over her face, was Verity.

When the steward had found him in his cabin and relayed the doctor's message, he'd hadn't elaborated. Greg had come quickly, mentally reviewing medical procedures for an emergency when the ship was in port. He knew all the people to contact, all the things that must be done, but at the first sight of her, all his training and professionalism fled, leaving in its place only a sick dread. John looked up and read his face quickly and accurately. He cursed inwardly, knowing he should have remembered his suspicions about the captain and Verity Fox. He should have made sure the steward had told him who it was. At least then he'd have been better prepared. He sighed deeply. 'Take a seat, Greg. Outside,' he added firmly, pointing to the waiting-room door.

For a second Greg looked as if he was going to argue. His instinct was to go to her, to hold her, to shake her, to demand that she wake up and that she be alright. Only by dredging up years of practised self-discipline did he manage to turn and walk away, shutting the door behind him. Outside he began to pace, as, inside, John slid a needle into her arm and waited. It seemed to him that he had to wait a very long time.

Slowly, the world came back. Verity heard first the sounds, a dull clanging that slowly identified itself as John, moving a saline-drip holder into position. Then vision. She blinked, watching and waiting patiently for the shapes to make up their minds what they wanted to be. A pale green blob became the bedside curtain. The moon-like round thing became John's face. 'Hello,' John said neutrally.

The voice seemed to echo, as if they were in a cave. She managed a smile. 'Hello. I'm thirsty.'

John nodded and poured some water and held it to her lips. She drank slowly and carefully, even though the thirst seemed to be eating at her. She finished the glass, looked at him, and knew better than to ask for another one. 'How long have I been unconscious?'

'We're not sure. A taxi driver alerted one of the stewards. You've been under at least ten minutes, as far as I can tell.'

Verity nodded. 'I see.'

But she didn't. Fainting fits were not a usual symptom of the type of leukaemia she had. And if she knew that, then John knew it too. She watched him nervously as he put down the glass, then turned to her, his face serious and grim. 'So. Are you going to tell me what's going on, or do I have to call that friend of yours? Dryer, isn't it?' John challenged firmly.

Verity swallowed, her mouth still feeling like sandpaper. 'There's nothing to tell. I overdid it, that's all. I climbed up the waterfalls this morning, then walked around in the Old Fort in the baking sun . . . it's probably only heat-stroke.'

John held her eyes, but she refused to look away. He nodded slowly, supressing a deep sigh. 'OK, Verity. OK. I'll keep you here overnight, just to keep an eye on you.'

Verity nodded, relieved. 'Fine. Thanks, John.'

John got up and walked to the door, drawing the curtains over the portholes as he did so, turning the cabin into a cocoon of greeny-blue light. 'I'll be back to

301

check on you in an hour. Meanwhile, you need anything, just press the buzzer, it's at the side of the bed within easy finger-reach. A nurse is always on call, just outside the door.'

Verity nodded and watched the door close. The silence lengthened. Slowly she turned back to face the blank ceiling.

'Oh damn,' she said, very softly.

The room was tiny and dominated by a four-poster bed. It looked as if it had arrived almost with the very first 5,000 British soldiers that appeared in Kingston Harbour in 1655. The huge, intricately-carved four corner posts were ancient cherry, the headboard equally impressive. There was one small window, wide open, and the surrounding jasmine growing around it wafted in with the breeze, tickling and pleasing their noses.

They had found the inn quite by accident, in a small village overlooking the Martha Brae River. Apart from the bar and small restaurant, the inn boasted all of three rooms. Now, as Ramona wandered to the window and looked out, the white starry flowers curling around her wrist as she leaned on the window sill, she was sure she'd never seen a more beautiful room. She turned and looked at him. He was standing by the door, dressed in the sombre black suit, his hands hanging loosely by his sides. His eyes were burning in his face, but his body was utterly still. She could feel raw energy pulsing out of him, and her heart began to hammer in her breast.

Wordlessly, she reached up and began to unwind her hair from its pleat. Using her fingers as combs, she pulled her hair free until it was its usual, water-straight curtain, falling to her waist. Damon swallowed hard and slipped off his shoes, at the same time shrugging off his jacket. The air pulsed with passion and something softer, something infinitely precious. She bent down and gracefully released the ankle straps, kicking off her own shoes as his hand went to his grey and blue tie and yanked it free. When his hands went to his cuffs she made a small sound in her throat and moved quickly across the small space, her fingers going to his wrist, her eyes never leaving his as she dealt with the gold and onyx cuff-links. Then, their eyes still locked, she unbuttoned the shirt, her fingers feathering between them, her fingernails lightly scraping his skin as her hands climbed higher. He gasped, a single indrawn breath, as she brushed against his nipples and then, slowly, only breaking off eye contact at the last moment, she leaned forward and kissed his collarbone, her hands clutching the silk sides of his shirt as she did so.

Damon moaned, low in his throat.

He tasted so good. Warm, slightly salty. Her tongue flicked out and touched his nipple where her finger had been only a moment ago. Sucking hard, she felt him sway slightly against her, and her hands tightened on the shirt, a small tearing sound testimony to her strength of grip. Leaning up against him to maximize her height, she pushed the shirt from one shoulder then dipped her tongue into the indent there, working her way along from the side of his neck to the top of his arm, letting the shirt fall off his back as she began to kiss his other shoulder, thrilling at the way he began to tremble.

Suddenly she grabbed him and thrust him away and Damon, taken by surprise, found his face and chest cannoning into the faded wallpaper on the wall. And then she was on him, her lips on the back of his neck, running down the length of his spine, her hands, as she knelt, running down his calves, slipping to his ankles then moving around, up his shins to his knees, and higher.

He gave a slow, lingering sigh as she moved back up, her lips on the small of his back, her busy fingers around his waist unbuckling his belt and pulling down, leaving him naked and vulnerable. Again, taking him by surprise, her strong hands whipped him around and pushed him firmly back against the wall once more. His lips opened on a gasp as she pressed herself against him, her tongue darting into his mouth.

She could feel his strong loins pushing against her, and her legs went weak. Slowly, ever so slowly, she kissed her way to his chin, down his throat, over his collarbone and down, dipping into his navel, the taste of him like nectar on her tongue. His knees, either side of her crouching figure, jerked in instant reaction. Then, without inhibition, without fear, without doubt, she went lower still.

Damon had time only to glance down in startled surprise to the top of her silver-gold head and then he moaned loudly, his strong, handsome head moving back, banging against the wall as his back arched and the pleasure hit him like a stampede. His eyes closed, his mouth fell open, his hands scrabbled against the wall, seeking but not finding a hold.

'Ramona!' He screamed her name, his neck arching, his throat tendons standing out as he began to feel pleasure such as he had never felt before begin to tighten in his loins.

He thought for a long, long moment that he must surely slip down the wall, so liquid did he feel. But, at last, the rippling sensations of pleasure began to fade and ebb and she stood slowly up, meeting his eyes with a kind of wild defiance that made him want to whoop for joy. He managed a crooked smile. 'Feeling pleased with yourself, aren't you?' he said indulgently, and she laughed.

'As a matter of fact . . .'

'Good. Because now it's your turn,' he growled, and suddenly grabbed her, carrying her to the bed and coming down on top of her, his eyes once more blazing. Holding her hands prisoner over her head he slowly lowered himself down onto her.

'Is that a promise?' she murmured, her thighs falling apart as his knees nudged her, her legs feeling deliciously weak.

'No,' he said huskily, and reached for the zipper at the side of her dress. 'That's a threat. And,' he added softly, his eyes infinitely gentle, 'another thank-you.'

Greg leapt to his feet the moment John rejoined him. 'How is she?'

John walked a few paces away from the door, looking like a man making up his mind. 'To tell you the truth, Greg, I don't know.'

'Don't know?' Greg exploded, the tension having

305

built up inside him to almost fever pitch in just the few short minutes he'd been waiting. 'What sort of answer is that?'

John didn't take offence. 'A truthful one. I don't know, because I don't think she's being straight with me.' The doctor took Greg's arm and led him out. 'I want you to come with me. I may need an independent witness.'

Greg followed him to Verity's deserted cabin. 'Alright,' Greg said grimly. 'Tell me straight. What's going on?'

John sighed. 'Dr Fox has leukaemia, Greg,' he said softly, as gently as he could. 'Some kinds of leukaemia can be kept under control with blood transfusions and drugs . . .'

Greg's eyes grew round and haunted. 'But not hers?'

'No. Verity has a terminal kind. Or so I thought.'

Wild hope leapt into Greg's eyes. 'For pity's sake, John, has she or hasn't she?' His voice was loud and anguished and he half turned away, running a hand through his hair.

'You love her, don't you?' John said quietly.

Greg, not looking at him, nodded. 'I know it's against all the rules . . . Oh, to hell with all that. Are you telling me she's going to die?' he demanded, his voice rising again.

John took a deep breath. 'When she first came to me, and I saw the dossier she brought with her, yes. I thought so. And so did she. This cruise was . . .' He stopped.

Greg nodded his understanding. This cruise was her

last chance for some enjoyment of life. He closed his eyes briefly, so many things suddenly making sense.

John sighed. 'What I'm about to tell you is in the strictest confidence. About tèn days or so ago, one of her colleagues came on board.'

'Gordon Dryer? Yes, I know,' Greg said, and suddenly, he realized what it all meant. Verity *wasn't* having an affair with him at all. When he'd walked in on them, and she'd been topless, he'd been examining her!

John nodded. 'Right. Last week, he returned and examined Verity and took more blood samples. Her white blood cell count was down. Way down. Which would normally be good, but Greg, I think she's taking some kind of experimental drug.' John made no attempt to hide his suspicions, and Greg stared at him, his eyes narrowing.

'Are you talking . . . illegal?'

John nodded. 'Yes. I'm afraid I am.'

Greg took in a very deep, very shaky breath. 'But if it's helping her, if it's curing her . . .'

John looked at him gravely. 'I'm not sure that it is, Greg. That's the whole problem. I'm not sure that it is.'

Greg thought of Verity back at the hospital. 'You think . . .' He didn't finish the sentence. Instead he looked around. She was everywhere. The rows of scent on her dressing table. The hairbrush with raven strands of hair. Her books. Her radio. Oh God, she might be dying. He shook his head. Don't break down. Keep calm. Think, dammit, *think*. 'We'd better search for it then.'

John nodded gloomily. 'That's what I came to find,' he admitted. But he didn't like going through her things any more than Greg did. Luckily, they didn't have to do much searching. John found it in the first drawer in which he looked. Silently Greg watched him unfold a little square of paper and together the two men stared at the white powder it contained. 'Oh damn,' John said. He hoped he would never find it. What the hell did he do now? Report her, and Dryer would be finished. Not report her, and watch her die?

'What do you think it is?' Greg said, his voice without strength. A creeping horror was beginning to climb over him, like fast-growing, clinging, choking ivy. Verity was really dying. She was really *dying* . . .

'I don't know,' John said, and very carefully re-wrapped the paper and put it back where he found it. He glanced up at Greg, wincing at the look of pain and horror on his face. He straightened briskly, all professionalism once more, and saw, with relief, Greg do the same.

The next moment, the very professional doctor of the ship looked at the equally professional captain of the ship, and sighed. 'I don't know what it is, Captain, or what it's doing to her,' John said grimly, 'but I'm going to find out.'

As he finished speaking, both men had exactly the same thought, at exactly the same time.

Yes. But then what?

CHAPTER 25

Jamaica

'This was a good idea,' Ramona sighed contentedly as they watched the *Alexandria* depart for Cuba, both of them struck by her beauty as she sailed out into the sunset. They'd both decided a little break from the ship would do them good, but they were due to fly to Cuba in two days time to meet up with the ship at her next port of call.

They spent the next morning having a lie-in at their hotel, and making slow, peaceful love. A late breakfast set them up for the day. Damon refused to tell her where they were going, and now, as he turned off the car engine and turned to her, his eyes were twinkling. In the last few days he had forgotten about the Markham shares, about Joe King, about the ship. Now only Ramona and the moment mattered. 'What's the matter?' he asked, as she stared at the notice board. 'Chicken?'

Ramona gave a grunt of indignation. 'We'll see who's chicken,' she muttered, squaring her shoulders and climbing out of the car, her lips twitching at the corners. Together they walked into the complex bearing the logo MOUNTAIN VALLEY RAFTING and quickly set things up. The river Lethe, they were told, ran through miles of unspoilt countryside. Donning bright orange life-jackets and meeting up with a gang of teenage boys from, of all places, Scunthorpe, they listened intently to their guide, who explained safety procedures and the route. With a slight feeling of trepidation, they followed their very capable-looking guide out to the round, bright yellow raft that bobbed lethargically in peaceful water at the docks. A few elbows nudged a few ribs, but no one seemed about to volunteer to get in first.

'Ladies first,' Damon murmured, *sotto voce*, and she glanced at him sharply, a wry smile tugging at her lips.

'You're *so* kind,' she said, ever-so-sweetly, and stepped into the raft. The swaying motion was a little unnerving at first, and the sensation of only a seemingly thin layer of flexible rubber between her and gallons of cold river water took some getting used to, but she made a passable job of getting in and sitting as they had been instructed. Damon, naturally, got in last with barely a ripple and she stuck her tongue out at him.

'You've done this before,' she said suspiciously, and indeed, there was something very capable about him. Perhaps it was the long, tanned limbs. Perhaps the dark hair and dark, confident eyes. Whatever it was, he had the same quiet, forceful quality as the leader of a wolf-pack, and the guide didn't hesitate to put him at the rear, the most responsible position for an amateur.

'Not fair! This is my first time in one of these things,'

he denied, but he took his place with a certain assurance. The guide, busy with the ropes, took up his oar and looked at them expectantly. Quickly, they all grabbed an oar and they were off.

It was an experience never to be forgotten. For the most part, the ride was peaceful and quiet, even the boisterous lads falling silent as the guide began to point out native plants and flowers, birds and even some of the water mammals that were usually never seen, even by locals. Some faster water half-way down raised the adrenalin, but Ramona enjoyed the bobbing sensation as the raft rode the currents, and she was unaware that her colour had heightened and her eyes were sparking electric blue fire every time she laughed. Damon spent more time watching her than the wondrous beauty of nature all around him.

The *Alexandria* sailed on smoothly. On the bridge, Greg listened to the weather forecast from Havana. Rougher winds, expecting to rise to Force Eight on the Beaufort Scale. Greg wasn't surprised, having already read the signs in the clouds. 'Tell engineering the stabilizers can expect to earn their keep tonight,' Greg told the officer of the watch, who nodded and lifted the radio mike.

Not that anyone was worried. The *Alexandria* had been designed to weather the worst that nature could throw at them, including Force Twelve, or hurricanes. Already the strong breezes were sending more and more passengers indoors.

Greg glanced once more at the radar scope. A couple

of freighters out to port, another larger tanker off to starboard. Nothing his extremely competent crew couldn't handle. 'Eric, I'll be gone about half an hour. You'll find me in the hospital if you need me.'

As expected, John was overseeing the nurses who were dishing out the dramamine to a small gaggle of green-about-the-gills passengers. 'Captain, not feeling the strain yourself, I hope,' he said, mostly for the benefit of the few passengers who looked at him curiously.

Greg smiled easily. 'An old sea dog like me? I need to see those manifestos, John.'

John caught on in a flash. 'Right. They're in my office. Nurse?' he nodded at a very comforting sister, whose reassuring manner calmed even the most ruffled of sick feathers. In the privacy of the doctor's office, Greg got right to the point. 'You called him yet?'

John shook his head. 'I was waiting for the time distance to even out. But he should be at work now. I got the number from the Jamaican exchange last night.' Greg nodded and sat down, twirling his cap nervously in his fingers as he watched the doctor dialling.

'Yes?' Gordon took the call, his voice short and sharp. Nevertheless, John sensed a bone-deep weariness, just from that one word.

'Gordon? John Gardner here.'

In the Headington hospital, Gordon tensed. 'John? What can I do for you?'

'Verity collapsed yesterday. I was wondering if you could tell me why?'

For a second, Gordon said nothing, then, 'But she
. . . can't have done.' There had been no indication of
any fainting spells when he'd seen her last, and since
she'd stopped taking the drug, there should be no
reason for it.

'But she did,' John said grimly. 'What's more we
found some . . . interesting things wrapped in tiny
squares of paper. Know anything about those?'

This time the silence was longer. Across the thousands of miles, John heard a long, wavering sigh. 'She's
still taking it,' Gordon said at last, his voice hollow.
'Oh, damn. Just when I might be . . .' Suddenly he
stopped, realizing he was talking on an open line. 'Look,
John, I need some time. I think I may have found the
reason for the hot flushes and the fainting. I think I *may*
have the side effects pinpointed. It was so simple I kept
missing it. It wasn't until . . .'

'Gordon,' John said warningly, and looked up to find
Greg Harding's eyes boring into him.

'John, please, I need a little more time.' Gordon
pleaded. 'Just twenty-four hours and I'll know, one
way or another. I don't think we should tell Verity,
though, not until I'm sure.'

John sighed. So Dryer had been smuggling an
experimental drug out of the country. Verity had been
taking it. Technically, they had both committed
criminal acts. 'Dammit man, don't you realize the
seriousness of all this?' he snapped.

Gordon, for the first time in weeks, actually smiled.
'Oh, I think so,' he said wryly. 'But would you play it
safe? Especially if that patient was the best friend you

313

had in the world, and a damn fine surgeon to boot?'

John slumped back in the chair with a defeated sigh. 'You're right. I apologize.' He saw Greg raise an eyebrow, and shook his head. 'What, exactly, needs to be done now?'

Gordon sighed. 'I think she's still taking the . . . stuff. Get it out of her room and lock it away somewhere safe. The side effects are obviously too dangerous.'

'But her white cell count is down another 4 per cent. I took a blood sample yesterday and had it checked.'

'That's great!' Gordon whooped, then groaned. It was only great if he had the side effect licked. He *thought* he had, but he wasn't sure. He could be wrong. It was all so simple that he felt, almost superstitiously, that it must be *too* simple.

'So don't you think she was right to keep on taking it? Surely, in her condition, the white blood cell count is the most important thing. Tell me more about these hot flushes she's been having.'

Across the desk, Greg sat up straighter, his face paling. She'd been feeling ill all this time, and had been hiding it from him? Suddenly he recalled all her hasty exits. Her odd behaviour. Her sudden mood swings. And he'd thought it was because she was tiring of him, getting restless, just looking for an excuse to end their affair. He shook his head despairingly. How wrong could one man be?

John listened intently as Gordon told him about Hercules. When he'd finished, John sighed. 'I don't like the sound of that either. So do we carry on? Or take

314

her off it, and watch her white cell count go sky high again?'

Gordon sighed. What could he say? 'It has to be up to her.'

'She's already chosen, hasn't she?' John pointed out.

Over the miles, Gordon nodded grimly. 'You're right. It's her life after all. Leave the stuff where it is. I don't think we have the right to interfere at this point.' John agreed. Then he looked across at Greg, knew he would have to explain it all to him, and wondered if he would see it the same way.

Somehow, he didn't think so.

After the wonderful rafting ride, Ramona and Damon were keen to keep up the river theme. An evening on the great river, so the guide book assured them, included a boat ride up the torchlit river, a full Jamaican dinner, a native folklore show and dancing to a reggae band. They were not disappointed. The boat was a flat-bottomed, wooden queen of her kind, slow, quiet and elegant. Ramona had dressed in a simple but elegant white pure silk dress, very Grecian in design and look, that left one shoulder bare and fell to her feet in a simple ripple of silk. In keeping with the ancient Greek look, she had put her hair up into a tall, elegant chignon, and wore only the simplest of silver and diamond drop-earrings at her ears, and a simple, silver plated chain around her neck. Damon wore a black evening suit, looking the epitome of male beauty, strength and elegance, and their appearance on the boat turned a lot of heads. Now, as they sat out on the deck, watching the torchlit night float by, a waiter handed over a menu and quickly left them, feeling like an intruder in their lovers' world. She chose the traditional Jamaican Coat of Arms to begin with (otherwise known as peas and rice), which was cooked with red beans, coconut milk, scallions and seasonings. Damon opted for the Pepperpot, the island's famous soup, a peppery combination of salt pork, salt beef, okra and the island green known as callaloo, which, once he had tasted it, he laughingly told her *tasted* as if it should be red!

She laughed and quickly poured him a glass of water, laughing harder at his suspiciously bright eyes. 'That'll teach you to be so macho,' she chided.

The evening passed by like a dream. At the railings, they watched the dark night vegetation glide by, the torches reflected in the water. It was a magical night. A night, she thought, meant only for them. A lovers' night. A night that nothing could spoil . . .

Joe King had watched the boat leave, feeling both furious and impotent. What, exactly, was Ramona up to? Why hadn't she tried to slip away from Alexander and hand over those Markham shares? As he watched the boat disappear into the torchlit night, he felt, unnervingly, as if it was all slipping away from him. He sighed and instructed the driver to return to the hotel. Now, everything depended on Cuba. As his car drove away, Joe would have felt even more worried if he'd realized just who was watching him, from the safe anonymity of a dock-side café.

'There he goes,' Frank said, sipping a bottle of

Jamaican beer. Les nodded. 'You have the route?' Frank did. The evening boat docked at a small club a few miles up river, where the folk dancing and reggae band were waiting. 'Come on.' Les got to his feet and threw some Jamaican dollars onto the table. 'It's time we levelled with Dr King.'

'What about Alexander?' Frank asked as the two men walked to their car and got in, quickly winding down the windows. Les said nothing. He wasn't sure, yet, where, or how, Damon Alexander *could* fit in.

Verity picked up her swimming costume and quickly changed. The decks looked deserted, the stiffening wind having sent the last of the pleasure-seekers indoors. Over her swimsuit she put on her heaviest beach-coat and set off to brave the elements. The moment she opened the door onto the Serenade deck, she felt the strength of the wind gusting against her, bringing snatches of music with it.

Mindful of yesterday's fainting spell, she never went near the rails, but made her way to the most protected side of the deck to an anchored-down sun lounger. She lay down and closed her eyes, sighing happily. It felt good to get out of the hospital. Then she jumped as a shadow fell across her and she looked up, her heart crying out at the sight of him.

'You shouldn't be out here,' Greg said softly. 'It's too cold and much too windy.'

Verity forced her joy into the deepest, most private part of her soul and managed to shrug. 'I like it when nature's being a bit antsy. It makes me feel more alive.'

Greg winced, but because he was standing with his back to the sun, she missed it. 'Verity . . .'

She looked up, frowned as the setting sun sliced into her eyes, and held her hand up for shade. His face looked dark and grim in the shadows. 'What is it, Greg?' she said softly. She wanted to reach out and comfort him, sensing he was in pain, and knowing she had planted it there. 'Oh Greg,' she said softly. 'I never meant to hurt you. Can't you just forget about me?' She saw him flinch, this time in what looked like physical pain. Her eyes widened. 'Greg?'

Greg shook his head. He just couldn't do it, not with her looking at him with those wide, vulnerable eyes. Now that he'd had time to think about it, he realized that everything she'd ever done, she'd done to protect him. How could he just blurt out that he knew everything and watch her back away from him, like an animal retreating into a protective shell? What right did he have to ruin this cruise for her when it might be . . .

'It's nothing,' he said, more crisply than he'd intended. 'I just wanted to warn you the winds are due to get worse. I really do think you should go inside.'

Verity slowly lowered her hand and then stood up. 'Alright . . . Captain.'

Greg said nothing as he watched her turn and walk away from him.

Ramona watched Damon fight his way to the bar. They had left the boat and watched the show, which had been very good indeed. Now, prior to dancing the night away,

318

they had both decided they would need refuelling. The club was packed, smoky and rife with atmosphere. Before long, Damon was swallowed up by the throng around the bar and she smiled, imagining him scowling as he was jogged and cursing as he spilled the long, rum punches they had both decided on.

'Dr King?' The voice was shouted, but sounded faint, so fierce was the noise. Ramona turned and found herself looking into a policeman's calm green eyes, and instantly the night lost its magic. Inspector Les Fortnum was pointing at the door. She sighed, but got up and followed him. Slowly, in unspoken mutual accord, they wandered away into the gardens of the club and towards a bench in the far corner, under a large, blossoming tree, giving off a faint aroma reminiscent of ginger. Les came straight to the point. 'I've come to ask you a favour, Dr King.'

'Such as?' she asked, but she already knew.

'In your beach bag, the one you had in Puerto Rico, is a listening device. I want you to take it with you to Cuba and meet your father,' Les said, grimly staring dead ahead. He held his breath, waiting for an anger that didn't come. At last, he looked across at her, half expecting a slap in the face. But she was looking at him with all the coolness of ice in her electric blue eyes.

'I see,' she said, her voice absolutely neutral. 'That was very clever and, I suspect, very illegal of you, Inspector Fortnum. I do hope that anything Mrs Alexander said is totally inadmissible as evidence?'

Les smiled grimly. 'It is. We will not be looking into any . . . er . . . irregularities concerning Mr Michael

Alexander's death.' The prosecuting lawyers had made it very plain they had no case.

Ramona wilted in relief. 'So, what, exactly, do you want me to do?' Ramona asked, but again, she already knew.

Les shifted uneasily on his seat. 'Dr King, I want you to meet your father in a public place. Frank Gless and I will be only yards away. I have no evidence, only gut instinct, but I think your father places more value on your blood-relationship than even he might be aware of. In short, I think he's vulnerable around you, Dr King.'

'So?' Ramona said softly, and Les sighed grimly. She was not making this easy, but then he could hardly blame her. He was asking her to trap her own father. 'We believe he is about to blackmail Gareth Desmond into selling his shares.'

'How?' she asked curiously.

'His daughter, Felicity, is at college in Oxford,' Les said simply, and Ramona nodded.

'Oxford has a bad drugs problem,' she said neutrally. Then, abruptly, she made up her mind. 'Alright. You want me to trap my father on tape, don't you?'

'Exactly. But it won't be easy,' he warned.

She was silent for a moment.

Les, obliged to be honest, said quietly, 'You will be called as a witness at the murder trial, and will need to confirm what you heard on the tape.'

Ramona paled. 'I see.'

'I hope you do, Dr King. We have a lot of circumstantial evidence against your father, and we think

Doyle will crack when we pick him up, probably at the end of the voyage.'

Just then a blast of music came from the opening door, and Ramona instantly recognized the man who stepped out, even before he called her name. 'Ramona?'

Les's head shot around and he got quickly to his feet. 'It's up to you, Dr King,' he said quickly. 'We want your father for the murder of your fiancé. Do you?' And with that very unfair parting shot, he turned and rapidly walked away.

From the door, Damon spotted his retreating figure, and in the moonlight her white dress and silver hair pinpointed her like a beacon. Slowly he walked towards her, eyes narrowed, senses alert, and put the two glasses down on the rustic-looking table nearby. 'Who was that?' he asked, his voice a little too netural.

Ramona looked up and smiled. 'Nobody. Just someone trying to pick me up. Jealous?'

Damon smiled. 'Not a bit.'

She laughed. 'Liar.'

He handed her the drink and took a sip, watching her over the rim, his eyes darkening. He sensed her unease, and wondered who the man had been. Another shareholder she was trying to sound out?

He had foolishly allowed himself to forget her hidden agenda. Perhaps it was time to start remembering it again.

CHAPTER 26

Cuba

They flew into Cuba, the no smoking sign blinking on as, ironically, Cuba's tobacco plantations, a 145-kilometer strip known as *vuelto abajo* country, sped by below them. In the Sierra Maestra range, Pico Turquino, the tallest, was clearly visible in the clear tropical sunlight. 'We're about ten minutes from Havana,' Damon murmured by her side, and Ramona shuddered theatrically.

'Weren't you worried, docking the *Alexandria* at Cuba?'

'I thought I'd give the American passengers a thrill.'

'Big of you,' she grinned. 'But what, exactly, do you know about the place?' she challenged, and promptly wished she hadn't as he gave her a very thorough lecture on it.

'Now if you want to talk about culture . . .' he offered, 'Or carnivals, which are held in July in Havana and Santiago . . .'

'I couldn't care less about carnivals.'

'Philistine! How about nature reserves then? Cuba has six national parks . . .'

'Damon?'

'What?'

'Do you want to carry on living?'

'Well, it would be nice.'

She leaned across and kissed the top of his arm through his plain white shirt. 'Then shut up.'

'Dr King! Such a temper. And here was I thinking you'd be fascinated by the thought of the Soledad Botanical Gardens, and all the butterflies? Cuba is overrun with them. Or perhaps the crocodiles are more your forte,' he added, some of the fun seeming to drain out of him. Not noticing, she turned, baring her teeth and sinking them into his arm, not quite enough to hurt. His eyes darkened as she looked up at him, her eyes shooting sparks as she sunk her teeth together just a little harder. Damon gasped, and bent his head closer. 'I think it's illegal in Cuba to make love in public places,' he said gruffly, 'so you'd better stop what you're doing, or we'll end up in clink.'

Below, the Sierra de los Organos slipped by to the west of Havana as the pilot banked for the airport. It took them a while to get through customs, but once outside, Damon beckoned a rather ancient and battered taxi that took them through the city. Many buildings, she noticed sadly, were shored up by wooden planks, but the parts of the Havana that dated back to 1515 were as beautiful as any she'd seen on the cruise.

'Fancy exploring the place?' Damon asked temptingly.

'I'd like to go back to the ship first,' she admitted. 'Just to freshen up and change.'

At the port, the familiar, gleaming white towering superstructure of the ship hove into view. The moment he saw it he felt better. On the Hummingbird deck she kissed him slowly and lingeringly. 'See you in an hour?'

'An hour? Why so long?'

Ramona smiled. 'I need to make myself beautiful.'

'You don't need an hour to do that. It only takes ten seconds to get undressed,' he added, his voice lowering several octaves. She flushed as a sudden thunderbolt of desire hit her, and then shook her head.

'You men,' she said, shaking her head. 'Only thinking about one thing . . .' She smiled and left, hoping she'd kept the atmosphere light and easy. If Damon found out what she was about to do, he'd certainly try and stop her. Inside her cabin, she locked the door behind her and went straight away to the coffee table and picked up the large beach bag. The listening device was so cleverly hidden it took her a while to find it. Then, for a few seconds, she stood staring down at the small object and smiling. 'Inspector Fortnum, you are a clever dog,' she murmured, then glanced at her watch. She wished she had a phone number for the policemen, but she was sure . . . well, *reasonably* sure, that they would have been there at the airport and followed her back to the ship. She hoped so, because she was not going to put things off any longer. She had to get it over and done with. She took a shower and changed into a simple green and cream sundress in record time. Running a brush hastily through her hair and leaving it loose, she grabbed her beach bag, with its restored listening bug, and headed for the door.

As she left her cabin and walked quickly down the corridor, Jeff Doyle followed at a discreet distance. Ramona, her thoughts intensely concentrated, barely acknowledged him. Instead, she headed for the nearest phone in a bright and sunny lobby. As she lifted the receiver, a ray of sun caught the silver chain at her throat and reflected it dazzlingly, right into Jeff Doyle's eyes. Silver! The thought hit him like a bullet, even as he raised his hand to shade his eyes. He shuddered, blinded by the light. Why wasn't she wearing gold, damn her? Every other damned woman on this floating palace did. Why did she, of all women, have to wear silver? And why had it shone in his eyes like that . . . Jeff hurriedly carried on across the lobby, almost running now. Only when he had turned a corner did he stop and lean against the cool bulkhead, panting and shaking. Silver. He *hated* silver. A medium had once told him that silver, which had such a rich and bloody history – much more so than gold – was the one metal that he should never, ever touch. It was, she had told him, a metal that signified his personal doom. He wiped a shaking hand over his mouth and managed to laugh. Stupid. He was being stupid. But when he turned and walked away, the hairs on his neck was still standing on end.

Ramona, totally oblivious to Jeff Doyle's plight, rang the most expensive hotel on the island (where else would her father be?) and took a deep breath. She didn't see the lift doors open at the end of the corridor, or Damon step out.

He saw her and his face instantly lit up, his gaze, as usual, stalling on the silvery curtain of hair. He loved to feel it running over his wrists in a cool and silvery curtain as he made love to her. He loved the smell of it against his nose, he loved to spread it over his shoulders as she lay sleeping, curled up against his chest. He loved . . .

The phone was answered and she was put through to her father's room. 'Hello, Father?' she almost choked on the word, but instinctively used it. She was totally unaware that Damon had stopped dead in his tracks.

'You weren't on the ship when it docked,' Joe King said accusingly. So he had been waiting for her. Good. 'No. I flew over with Damon. Listen, Father, we have to meet.'

Damon, hardly aware of it, moved to the side of the wall, behind a huge, anchored-down fern. His face tensed.

'Yes, we must,' Joe agreed. 'Take a taxi to the Bodeguita del Medio, near the Cathedral. And bring the shares with you.'

Ramona smiled grimly. 'Of course.' She hung up and glanced down at her bag. The Markham shares were not the only thing she'd be taking with her. From behind his cover, Damon saw her smile and felt something shatter inside him. Then she was walking away and he was following instinctively, careful to keep out of sight. He tailed her in a second taxi, cursing a small, battered-looking Volkswagen that pulled up in between them. Damon watched both Ramona's taxi and then the Volkswagen pull to a stop outside a building, and hastily paid off his own driver and stepped under the shadow of an awning. He saw her emerge and glance around.

Ramona spotted Les and Frank straight away. They were getting out of a Volkswagen beetle that looked as if it was about to fall apart at any moment. Carefully, she let her gaze pass over them. She walked to the restaurant. Unnervingly, she thought for the briefest of seconds that she could actually see Keith's face in the reflection of the plate glass. This if for you, Keith, she thought, and walked inside. Les and Frank followed, Damon slipping in last.

Joe King was already there and rose to his feet as she walked in. He saw the cool smile on her face, the predatory light in her eyes, and felt his chest expand with pride. She was hungry for money and power and it would be his pleasure to give it to her. Not all at once, of course. She'd have to learn the business, and obey him, but then . . .

'Hello, Father.'

Joe almost beamed with pleasure at the sound of the word 'Father'. 'Ramona. Sit down. I've ordered mojitos for both of us, I hope you don't mind?'

'Sounds fine,' she said coolly and took a seat. Three tables over, Les and Frank lifted a menu off the table and hid behind it the sensitive cassette player that Frank was anxiously watching turn, recording everything from the rustle of her dress to the faint ticking of Joe King's expensive watch. Damon moved to a corner table very close to them, but was obscured by a large dead tree-trunk that was kept permanently moist, and

327

festooned with orchids. He could hear their voices clearly, since the hour was early and the restaurant all but deserted.

'You have the shares?' Joe asked, and Ramona handed them over. Damon's hand curled around the glass of beer he'd ordered on entering, and a little trail of froth trickled over his thumb as his hand began to shake.

Joe King looked them over. 'Excellent . . .'

'We'll have the Desmond shares soon?' she prompted coolly and flicked her hair back off her shoulders as her father nodded. 'I dare say your Mr Doyle will be moving in soon then?'

At the table, Frank glanced across at Les, his look startled. Les blinked nervously. It was a bold opening. Too bold? She could blow it. He felt his nerves tense. They only had one shot at this. He glanced across as Joe very slowly lowered the Markham shares and stared at her. Ramona, who had already decided on her strategy in the taxi, knew she was now committed. If she had read her father's character wrongly . . .

'Doyle?' Joe repeated, his voice neutral.

Ramona allowed herself a small smile. 'Oh, come on, Daddy. I knew you had to have a man on board. Did you really think I wouldn't winkle your little mole out?'

In the corner, Damon frowned. What the hell was going on?

Joe slowly smiled. 'I should have known,' he said indulgently. She really was something, this daughter of his. 'He has his uses,' he agreed, and smiled even wider. 'But I have another man dealing with Desmond. A second man. I don't suppose you found him out too?'

Ramona hoped her face didn't register her shock, and simply smiled. 'Perhaps. Perhaps not. But whoever it is, I imagine he's using Desmond's daughter for leverage. Yes?' she purred.

Joe knew the blood was flooding from his face, and nonchalantly reached for his glass. 'Sorry?'

Ramona leaned back, a wry smile on her face. 'Come on, Daddy. I've done my homework too.' She had let her voice harden, become almost abrasive. It made her feel slightly sick to see that her father approved of her supposed ruthlessness.

In the corner, Damon dragged in a deep breath that sounded harsh to his ears. Rage hit him, but even as its heat flooded his veins he knew despair, for the rage was not born of outrage, but out of pain. Oh Ramona. *Ramona*!

'Gareth Desmond's business dealings are remarkably clean,' Ramona continued bravely, 'but his daughter goes to Oxford, and she's a bit of a mess. Nice and convenient, isn't it?' she said mockingly.

Damon wanted to march over there and shut her up, to stop the sarcasm, the ugly greed, the sheer malevolence that was pouring out of her. This was not the woman he loved. This was some evil bitch that he hardly recognized.

Joe King took a long sip of his drink. 'So what are you saying?'

At the table, Les Fortnum's hand curled into a fist. No, Ramona, no! *He* has to say it. If they could get this second man of King's, probably one of the ship's

329

stewards, to turn State's evidence, they could try Joe King for blackmail as well. He cast an agonized glance across the room, but, of course, he could do nothing but sit, and hope.

Ramona smiled. 'I'm not saying anything, Daddy.'

Joe King laughed. 'You're right, of course, my darling girl. We are going to use the daughter. She's a junkie, plain and simple. Desmond will sell the shares, if he wants his little darling to stay out of jail and avoid the scandal.'

Ramona absently swung the glass in her hand as, in the corner, Damon went pale. Blackmail. They were going to blackmail his old friend. As calmly as you pleased. His eyes went, fascinated, to her long slim fingers swaying the glass casually in her hand. He remembered those fingers on him, caressing . . . loving . . .

'Especially,' Joe carried on happily, 'when Desmond sees the photos.'

Ramona stopped swinging her glass for a fraction of a second. 'You have photographs?' she asked calmly. 'I'm impressed. I know those Oxford parties. Nobody but students allowed. Even then, they have to be vouched for.'

Joe King smiled, glad for the chance to boast. 'Oh, I have people everywhere. The photographer was also the supplier. Crack, mostly, I believe.'

Frank Gless drew in his breath sharply. This was explosive stuff. They had him on blackmail, procurement of drugs and extortion. Now, if only she can get the conversation round to the murder of Keith Treadstone. Over in the corner, Damon closed his eyes in utter misery. How much worse could it get?

Ramona tossed back her head, sure she was going to burst out screaming at any moment. Never had she felt such loathing for another human being in her entire life. But she forced herself to go on. 'So. Once we have the Desmond shares, we combine them with Markham's shares, yours and Keith's and launch a takeover bid?'

Damon bowed his head, the pain almost crippling him. For now he had no choice. He would have to sacrifice the love they had. The happiness that could so easily have been theirs. For a second, he hated her so much he wanted to kill her.

Ramona's heart thudded. Here it comes. 'Poor Keith,' she mused, laughing softly. 'He really didn't know what he was getting into, did he?'

Joe King laughed. 'No. I must say, I'm rather surprised you chose such a nonentity. You could have had anyone, Ramona.'

In the corner, Damon's head reared up.

Ramona shrugged. 'He was weak, which meant he was malleable. Also, from your point of view, he was ideal. A stockbroker can buy and sell shares without the least suspicion. That's why you chose him, right?'

Joe King almost applauded her. It was like watching your favourite race-horse win the Derby. 'Bravo.'

Ramona smiled grimly. 'But you were taking a risk, surely, Daddy. Keith could have cut you out of the deal at any time. In fact, he did buy quite a few shares under his own name.'

Joe King guffawed. 'No way, my girl. I had him sign

so many guarantees and contracts he got writer's cramp signing his signature. I even made him make a will, leaving the shares to me, just in case. I thought of everything. Those shares were always going to be mine. And it worked.'

'Well, almost,' she mused, her heart beginning to thump in her chest as she played her trump card. 'You didn't reckon on Keith's loyalty to me, did you? Do you still think it was a coincidence that he changed his will in my favour?' she challenged and laughed softly. Over the rim of her glass, she tried to gauge his reaction to her taunting. She took a deep gulp of the alcohol. She felt like she needed it.

Les risked a glance across the room and saw that King had gone ramrod straight. 'What . . . do you mean?' he asked, his small eyes narrowing, reminding her of the eyes of a rat.

She shivered. She was glad Les and Frank were only a few feet away. Briefly, she wondered if those were the eyes that Keith had seen just before . . . No. She mustn't think about that. Not now. She managed a smile, but it felt twisted on her face. 'Come on, Daddy, think,' she admonished. 'What was Keith's was mine. Do you really think that he kept it a secret from me that he was buying shares for you on the quiet? Do you really think I wasn't on to you right from the beginning?'

Joe King remained still and silent for a long, long time. Suddenly, his thoroughbred filly was looking more and more like a beautiful but deadly poisonous snake. Yet, even as the evidence of her unexpected ruthlessness unnerved him, it also thrilled him. What a team they would make. Father and Daughter. Unbeatable.

In his corner, Damon winced at the sound of her mocking laughter. He'd gone white to his lips listening to the story of how she had used Keith Treadstone. And, like night following day, his thoughts skipped to how she had been using him, Damon Alexander. Just another fool to use and suck dry. He shuddered, remembering their savage love-making. The laughter. The love, that had seemed so real. Oh God . . .

'What you have to remember, Daddy dearest, is that he was reporting to me all the time,' she lied. 'You really thought you had him?'

Joe King smiled appreciatively. 'I did, as a matter of fact,' he admitted. 'But all the time, you were controlling both of us,' he added admiringly. He raised his glass. 'I have to hand it to you, girl,' he said, his voice a mixture of anger, envy and admiration. 'Cheers.'

'Cheers,' she said, and in the corner Damon Alexander stood up. He'd heard enough. He'd taken as much as he was going to stand. He would get to Gareth and make him testify to the blackmail. He'd see Joe King ruined. He'd see *her* jailed. The thought haunted him, dragging at his feet, making them so heavy he couldn't lift them . . .

'Of course, when you had Keith killed, I was a bit put out,' Ramona said conversationally, and Damon slumped back down abruptly onto his chair, all strength leaving his knees.

At their table, Frank and Les held their breaths.

'What?' Joe King yelped, a cold, hard fury rising in

his mind, along with a rushing instinct for self-survival.

Ramona forced herself to look across the table, her eyes cool. 'Oh, come now, Daddy. Keith didn't commit suicide. He didn't have it in him. I told him to change his will in my favour, just as a precaution. In case of a *real* accident. Murder didn't cross my mind. I suppose,' she mused, 'he must have found something out that really scared him and made him confront you?'

Joe King's eyes narrowed into slits. Treadstone had, in fact, stumbled onto Jeff Doyle and the back-up plan. And Treadstone had wanted nothing to do with potential mass murder. The fool. The back-up plan had only ever been a last resort in case things went seriously wrong. All Treadstone had had to do was keep his mouth shut . . . But no. He'd threatened to go to the police. Joe began to breathe heavily. Things were getting out of hand. Daughter or not, there were some things he would tell nobody. 'Let's get back to the *Alexandria*, shall we?' he said, his voice grating. 'As soon as she docks in Florida I'll file the takeover plans.'

Ramona, in that instant, knew he was not going to admit to killing Keith, and she felt impotent fury wash over her. Meeting his wary, gloating eyes, she wanted to launch herself across the table and beat the truth out of him. Instead, she forced herself to swallow her rage and summoned her brain back into the forefront. She had to do something!

At their table, Les felt his shoulders slump. Whilst they had enough to send King away for some years, they didn't have the big one. They didn't have murder. Ramona, however, refused to admit defeat. Instead, her brain, her ally throughout her life, was coming swiftly to the rescue. After all, there were more ways than one of skinning a cat. Slowly she leaned back and once more began swinging her glass. 'Well, you can always *file*, of course,' she said, emphasizing the word with a cool smile, 'but without the back-up of all those lovely shares dear Keith left me, you won't succeed.'

In the corner, Damon leaned forward, leaning his elbows on his knees, his eyes feathering closed. Would this nightmare never end? Was she so greedy she'd even defy her father, who was obviously a dangerous psychopath?

Joe King drew in a breath that sounded uncannily like the hissing of a snake. At the table, Frank's muscles tensed, ready to spring. She was playing this very rough. But what guts she had! 'And what, exactly, does that mean?' Joe said, his voice resembling the cracked ice in his drink.

Ramona laughed and waved her left hand in the air. 'See this ring? Damon gave it to me.'

'So?' Joe snarled, and Ramona knew she was right.

'So? Daddy dearest,' she sighed exasperatedly 'why on earth should I help you take over the company, when all I have to do is marry it, and it's all mine? Damon will do anything, *give* me anything I ask.'

In the corner, Damon shuddered as if hit by a hail of bullets. He almost moaned out loud. Then his head snapped up as he heard a chair scrape sharply across the floor. He saw Joe King standing, glowering down at his daughter, his hands clenching and unclenching into fists. He was instantly on his feet. 'You won't marry Alexander,' Joe King hissed, a small trickle of saliva drooling down his chin. His eyes looked wild. 'You *won't*.'

Ramona felt a burst of fear rocket into her, but the smile she sent his way was as cool as cucumber, in direct contrast to the sweat she could feel trickling down her back. Yet she stubbornly refused the impulse to glance across the room, to make sure her protectors were still there. 'Why, Daddy,' she drawled sweetly. 'How on earth are you going to stop me?'

Joe King smiled widely, showing his teeth like a crocodile. 'Don't push me, girl,' he warned softly. 'You and I have a great future together, but you have to understand who's boss. Just remember, I've killed *one* of your fiancés. I can . . . and will . . . kill the other one.'

Ramona let her breath out carefully. 'So you pulled the trigger on Keith yourself?' she said, her voice cracking.

Joe King smiled. 'It was easy,' he said savagely. 'I simply walked up to him, put the gun to his temple and pulled the trigger.'

Ramona let out her breath in a whoosh. Now she'd got the evidence it was time to look after her own skin. 'Well, in that case . . . perhaps I should give Damon the push. He's hardly in your class.' She made no attempt to hide the flattery. The man was a lunatic. Insane.

Joe King laughed. 'Wise choice, my girl. Now, I have

to get these to my lawyer.' He waved the Markham shares her way. 'I'll see you in Florida?'

Ramona nodded. I'll see you in hell first, Daddy dearest, she thought savagely, and watched him go. Damon too, watched Joe King leave and then moved around the tree-trunk on unsteady legs and began to walk towards her. He wanted to see her tears when he told her that this was one man she wasn't going to use and then just throw away. But, just as he reached her table, she did the strangest thing.

She turned and lowered her head to her beach bag. 'I hope you got all that, fellas, because I don't think I can do it all again.'

Damon spun around as he felt two people suddenly materialize right behind him. Ramona looked up, expecting to see Les and Frank, and gasped. 'Damon!' she said blankly, the colour draining from her face.

'Well done, Dr King,' Les Fortnum said, stepping around Damon Alexander, ignoring him completely. 'We've got it all on tape. And with our testimony, and yours, your father is going away for a very long time. Our man will pick up this second stooge of King's today when he approaches Mr Desmond. On behalf of the Metropolitan police, I can't tell you how grateful we are for your co-operation and, may I say, your bravery,' Les ploughed on, too excited and relieved to pause for breath. 'It must have been tough to go through all that. What with the revelations about your fiancé and all.' He reached out and took her hand, pumping it joyfully, but she hardly heard him. Instead her eyes were fixed on

337

Damon, who was staring at her with growing comprehension and a deep relief that made him sway on his feet.

'Ramona,' he said softly, and Les Fortnum at last glanced up.

'Mr Alexander? You heard all that?' he asked hopefully.

Damon nodded.

Ramona gasped, going a ghastly white. 'Then you must have thought . . . ?' Her voice trembled.

Damon nodded.

'Oh Damon!' she whispered, her eyes flooding. All the time, he'd been listening. Hurting . . .

'Great!' Frank Gless shouted. 'We've got another witness to testify!'

Ramona continued to stare mutely at Damon with great, round blue eyes. Then she launched herself into his arms, hugging him as tightly as she could. 'It's all over,' she said, as if she could hardly believe it. 'It's really all over at last.' He felt solid and warm and so wonderfully strong, as his arms encircled her, protecting her, loving her.

Damon nodded. His voice, when he found it, was little more than a whisper. 'I thought . . . Oh, Ramona, I thought it was all true. That you were . . .' He felt a rush of guilt wash over him. How could he have been so stupid? How could he have believed her to be so evil! 'Oh, darling, I'm so sorry. I'll never doubt you again, I swear it.'

Feverishly, she stopped his words with a kiss, a kiss that turned deeper, more fenzied. 'It doesn't matter,' she said. 'Oh my love, it doesn't matter. I love you. Oh Damon, *I love you*!'

He laughed, hugging her close.

It was all over, at last.

Except, of course, that it wasn't.

Not by a long shot.

CHAPTER 27

Gareth Desmond walked into the sparsely populated cocktail lounge and saw them at once. His eyes went to her first – Joe King's daughter. He took a deep breath and smiled, accepted Damon's handshake and, after a slight hesitation, also shook the long, slim white hand that she too proffered.

'Thanks for agreeing to talk to us, Gareth,' Damon said easily. 'I know it can't have been pleasant, yesterday.'

'Make it short, Damon,' Gareth said gruffly. They were bound for the Bahamas, having left Cuba yesterday evening. It had been a day he was hardly likely to forget, and he was glad to be leaving the place far behind him. It had begun with a complete stranger, a steward, approaching him and showing him awful pictures of his daughter. Following that shock came the ultimatum. Sell the *Alexandria* shares to a company owned by Joe King, or face scandal. Immediately after that, a *hostess*, who later showed him impeccable police credentials, had suddenly upped and arrested the black-mailer on the spot, right in front of him. The following hours had been a little confused, and it wasn't until some hours later that two more senior policemen arrived, identifying themselves as from the London Metropolitan force.

They had been very polite, of course, but hardly informative. He still knew very little, except that Joe King was facing extortion and blackmail charges, amongst others, and that it would be in his, Gareth's, best interests to co-operate. After talking it over with his wife, he'd agreed with them. Their daughter, they decided, needed shock tactics to get her off drugs, and this could very well be their last chance. 'So,' he said grimly, 'what's it all been about? The last time you spoke to me about your fiancée . . .' he began, then stopped as Damon gave him a quick, quelling look.

Ramona caught it, and raised an eyebrow in Damon's direction, who grinned down at her. 'My fiancée, Gareth, was working with the police. While King's snake-in-the-grass steward was putting the stranglehold on you yesterday, this brave lady – ' he reached across and took her hand, kissed the back of her knuckles, then turned back to Desmond – 'was sat in a café with Joe King, wired for sound, getting him to confess not only to blackmailing you, but also to committing the murder of a man called Keith Treadstone.' Damon looked down at her, wondering if the mention of his name still caused her pain. Wordlessly, she squeezed his hand.

Gareth, happily married for thirty years, knew love when he saw it and found himself, in spite of his troubles, smiling. 'That was a gutsy thing to do,' he said, and meant it.

Ramona shrugged. 'My father is a vicious, dangerous man.' Her voice dropped. 'That's why we asked to see you. We wondered . . .'

Gareth held up his hand. 'Don't worry. I've already agreed to co-operate with the British and American police.'

Instantly they both relaxed. 'Thank you,' Ramona said simply. Gareth stood up, glad to have things sorted out, but not eager to stay.

'The next few months are going to be rough for him, and his daughter,' Ramona said softly, regret and anger in her voice, as she watched him walk away. He looked older, somehow.

Damon nodded, then grinned as Ralph Ornsgood diffidently walked up to them. 'Ralph. You haven't met my bride-to-be, have you?' he said, with a wide grin. 'Ramona, meet my right arm. Ralph Ornsgood.'

Ramona smiled. She knew all about the Swede, of course.

Ralph, twiddling his thumbs like a demented spider weaving a web, managed to stop long enough to take the hand she offered. Before she could speak he launched into the apology he'd been rehearsing ever since Damon had button-holed him yesterday and told him all about Cuba. 'Dr King. I want to apologize for . . . well, for my suspicions about you,' he began, his voice tripping over itself. 'I have to tell you that I overheard you closing your deal with Dwight Markham, and informed on you to Damon. I never once suspected . . . I mean, I thought . . . well, that you were a gold-digger of the worst kind and now I feel . . . stupid,' he ended abruptly and miserably.

Whilst Damon had been listening to the apology with a growing grin that threatened to turn into laughter, Ramona froze in shock. Of course! Ralph thought that it had been her intention to trap her father all along. And that meant . . . She turned quickly to Damon, her heart dropping to her boots. It meant Damon thought so too.

'Please, can you forgive me?' Ralph asked miserably.

'Oh Ralph, don't be silly. I mean, there's nothing to forgive. Please, please don't worry about it.'

Ralph saw Damon give her a long, loving look, and almost blushed for the man. He was so obviously in love. 'Thank you, Dr King. I, er . . . have to . . . paperwork,' he mumbled, and quickly shuffled away.

Ramona turned to Damon, her face set and determined. 'Let's go to your suite. I have something important to tell you.'

Instantly, Damon recognized the determined tone of voice, but it was the hard, worried look in her eyes that sent fear hurtling through him. Suddenly, he felt dread rise up and choke him. She was going to tell him it was all over. Tell him that it had never, really, *been*. Hadn't she just used their affair to trap her father into admitting about killing Keith Treadstone? It was really Keith she still loved. Keith she had risked her life for. And now that Joe King was about to be arrested, she no longer had any use for him.

'Damon? Are you alright? You've gone quite pale.'

Damon, somehow, managed a wan smile. 'I'm fine.

343

Come on, let's get this over with.' They walked in silence to his master suite and stepped inside, she still wondering how she could explain it so that he would forgive her, he wondering how he would be able to stand their break-up without falling apart. 'Drink?' he asked, and she nodded her head eagerly. A drink would certainly help.

Outside, the sun rose to its zenith. Damon took a gulp from his glass, then handed her hers, and slumped down in an armchair. He spread his legs straight out in front of him and curled his hands over the thick, padded armrests. He was as ready as he was ever going to be. He fixed a blank look on his face and willed it to stay there, come what may. His heart beat so hard it made him feel sick. He took another deep gulp of his drink. Ramona began to pace. She stared into her drink but unlike him, couldn't touch it. Where to begin? 'This is going to be difficult to explain,' she said, and then couldn't help but laugh. Now there was an understatement.

Damon swallowed hard. 'Just . . .' His voice was harsh, and he cleared his throat and tried again. 'Just start at the beginning and don't stop until you've said it all.' And then walk away before I fall apart, he added silently and drained his glass with a grim swallow.

Ramona nodded. 'OK. Looking back I think . . . I never really loved Keith. At least, I did, but not in the way I should have. He was more like a brother, really. We'd known each other for ever, you see. We were . . . comfortable together, more than anything. My mother knew. She . . . Oh hell.' Ramona couldn't look at him.

If she had, she might have seen the look of total surprise on Damon's face. She took a deep breath. 'I think that's why, when Keith died, and apparently by his own hand, I was so . . . out of control. I felt so guilty, and our whole relationship suddenly seemed to have been so pointless. Then I learned about all the shares he bought in your company. When I talked it over with Keith's boss I came to the conclusion that it was probably you who had approached Keith, trying to illicitly raise your stake in the *Alexandria*.'

Damon leaned forward on the chair, his mouth hanging open. A wild happiness was beginning to bubble up within him. She wasn't going to leave him!

'So I came along for the ride. At first, I wasn't sure if it was you,' she said, trying in some small way to give herself a kind of defence. 'And then . . . after you'd proposed to me, my father withdrew from Keith's old firm, taking with it any threat of embezzlement procedures, and then I was sure it was you. Oh, Damon, don't you see?' she turned to him at last, her eyes wide and pleading. 'When I got those shares from Dwight Markham, I *did* want to take the ship away from you. It was only later, after Les Fortnum met me and told me it was really my father that was behind it all, that I agreed to help them. Damon. Why are you grinning like the Cheshire cat?' she finished exasperatedly.

Damon got to his feet slowly and approached her. There was that look in his eyes, and immediately her vagina tightened, her nipples stood to attention and her

345

insides melted. 'Damon?' she said warningly, shaking her head, backing away. 'What's going on?'

Damon smiled. 'I thought you were going to leave me.'

'What? I thought you'd want me to go, once you'd heard me out.'

'Fat chance, woman,' he growled, following her around a large coffee table as she continued backing away. Still she continued to back away across the oriental carpet, but her lips were twitching now. 'You don't care I was out for your blood?' she whispered, her voice impossibly husky.

He shook his head. 'Hell, woman, you can have it if you want it,' he growled, shouting the last word as he lunged for her. She shrieked playfully and turned in full flight, headed, of course, for the big king-sized bed. He caught her in a ferocious rugby tackle that had them both bouncing on the bed in a tangle of limbs and laughter. He turned her over, capturing both her hands in his and anchoring them either side of her head, then looked down deeply into her eyes.

'I love you,' he said softly.

'I love you too,' she agreed.

'Then let's celebrate.'

Her eyebrows arched and her breath caught in a gasp of desire. 'Good idea.'

He smiled, holding her lascivious gaze for a second longer, then leaned across to the telephone and dialled a number. Ramona scowled, her breasts tingling in angry frustration. She wanted his lips on her. His hands on her. His body . . . 'Damon,' she yelled.

'Hello, galley? This is Damon Alexander here, can I speak to the chef, please?' In the heat and mayhem of the galley, Rene de la Tour was quickly summoned away from his daily lunch time hysterics. The executive chef didn't take kindly to his histrionics being interrupted just when his voice was rising to its falsetto best, but when the owner of the ship asked for the chef, he didn't mean the busboy.

'*Oui*. This is Rene,' he announced grandly.

Damon grinned as he heard the imperious tone. 'Ah, Rene. My fiancée and I are having a special celebration,' Damon said, his eyes laughing down into her scowling face. But, in her eyes, he saw the laughter lurking behind the mask. 'So I was wondering if you could prepare us something special? I don't know . . . say . . .' He stopped as she struggled playfully in his arms and he quickly subdued her with a playful squeeze of her rounded derrière. 'Salmon in champagne sauce? And strawberries?'

Rene sighed theatrically, but was immensely flattered. '*Oui*, Monsieur Alexander. For you, Rene will create a masterpiece.'

'Thank you,' Damon said, and hung up. Ramona let her scowl turn into a growl. 'That's what you call celebrating?' she said huffily. Damon lowered his head until his lips were only millimetres from hers. 'No. That's not what I call celebrating. But after we've finished what I *do* call celebrating – ' his voice lowered and his lips twitched – 'we'll both be starving.' And his hand swung down from her wrist and cupped her breast.

She gasped, then smiled. 'Oh. That's alright then,' she said huskily.

Greg could stand it no longer. He didn't care that it was noon, and the ship was full of passengers making their way to the dining rooms who might see him. He didn't care that he could lose his job. All night he had lain staring at the ceiling, thinking. And, like all roads leading to Rome, all his thoughts led to Verity. Now he stood outside her cabin door and knocked purposefully. He didn't look around, he didn't care who might be watching. When she opened the door, he saw her eyes widen, saw the love flood into them before she quickly hid it behind blandness. 'Captain?' she said, her voice cool. 'Shouldn't you be lunching with the passengers?'

Greg smiled. 'As you can see, I'm not. May I come in?'

Verity moved aside, heart thumping. As he passed her, she wanted to reach out and touch his broad back, which she knew would feel warm and smooth and oh-so-good beneath the crisp white shirt he wore. Shakily, she shut the door behind her.

Greg turned and looked at her, seeing the slight pallor beneath her healthy suntan, the blue-black lines under her eyes. He said, simply 'I know, Verity.'

Verity felt the breath shoot out of her, and it took her a few shocked seconds before she could draw another. 'Know?' she queried, but he was already shaking his head. He took off his cap and threw it on the chair, then moved towards her, taking her gently in his arms. 'No more of that,' he said gently. 'John Gardner told me.'

'He had no right . . .'

'Don't,' Greg said, his voice firm, his gaze steady.

'Oh Greg,' she said, tears helplessly flooding her eyes.

With a small moan he pulled her to him, his hands shaking slightly as he cupped her waist and shoulders in his hands. 'It's alright. It is going to be alright,' he whispered, moving his chin back as she raised her head to look up at him.

Grimly determined, she wiped the tears from her eyes and tried to step back, but he wouldn't let her. 'It's not going to be alright, Greg,' she denied, her voice wavering but becoming stronger. 'I know. I'm a doctor. I have months left. At most,' she said, faltering only slightly over the words.

'Then we'll spend them together,' Greg said simply, not letting her eyes get away from him. 'Once we dock in Florida, I'm going to tell Damon that I'm leaving.'

'No,' Verity said sharply. 'This job is all you'll have. After I'm gone.'

He saw at once that she was serious about this, and quickly nodded, not prepared to argue, not prepared to waste one precious second. 'OK, then I'll ask for a leave of absence. A year. I don't care if I get demoted back to another ship. I'll have the rest of my life to work my way back up again. But, Verity,' he said gently, reaching out and placing his palm gently against her cheek, 'don't stop me from doing this. And don't try to pretend. I'm sick of it. I love you,' he said, the words leaving him with relief, the sound of them never more certain in his ears. 'I never imagined I'd ever say that. I never have, not to any of the others . . .'

She made a small sound, deep in her throat. She didn't want to know about any others. It felt as if she'd waited for this moment ever since she'd first boarded this ship. 'I love you too, Greg,' she said. 'But you have to understand what . . . what's likely to happen.'

Greg nodded, understanding her need to be totally honest. 'Alright,' he said softly. Gently he led her to the bed and pulled her down beside him. He made no move to touch her. Instead, he turned her face towards him. 'Tell me,' he said softly. 'But no matter how bad it is, I'm going to stay with you. I love you and want you to marry me. As soon as we get to Florida. Till death us do part. Do you understand, Verity?' he asked gruffly, and she nodded, two silent tears slipping down her cheeks.

'Yes, Greg. I do. And . . . Thank you.' It was such a simple thing to say. But it meant so very, very much.

He nodded, knowing they needed no other words. 'Now,' he said, taking a deep breath. 'Tell me.'

In the kitchens, it was hectic. The early diners had chosen their courses and the chefs were working flat out. In the middle of it all, Rene expertly filleted a small, fresh salmon and gathered together the ingredients for the champagne sauce. Freshly-squeezed lemon juice. Herbs, flour, eggs, milk. 'Champagne,' Rene muttered, bustling briskly to the temperature controlled room and glancing at the first racks of wine. '*Non*,' he shook his head, still muttering to himself. A special occasion called for the very best champagne. He walked deep into the back of the room, until he came to those marked for the final night's masked champagne ball. 'Ahh . . .' he said, and selected a white champagne from the best French vineyard. He didn't see the tiny puncture mark in the cork where a needle had been inserted. With a smile of satisfaction, he carried his prize back to the kitchen. Who knows, after creating the culinary masterpiece for the ship's owner and his beautiful lady, perhaps he'd drink a glass of the champagne for himself. He deserved it. His job was sheer hell. But let anybody try to steal it and he'd take the butcher's meat cleaver to him. As he returned to his table he opened and poured in the champagne. A really fine, fine vintage. Yes, he'd have a glass, when the salmon was cooked. He'd never get the chance again to drink such a fine wine.

'And then . . . then it will all be over,' Verity finished, her voice little more than a whisper. It had been frightening, talking about her own death, but not as frightening as before. Now, Greg's hand was holding hers, strong and tight, and when she looked up, she was staring love right in the face.

'You've taken some more of that drug Gordon Dryer smuggled to you?' he asked, and saw her face freeze.

'You even know about that?'

Greg smiled. 'You can't keep any more secrets from me. It's too much like hard work. And talking about work,' he said, glancing at his watch. 'I still have my daily rounds to do.'

Verity couldn't hide her disappointment. 'Of course.'

'Want to come with me?' Greg asked, smiling as her head shot up, her eyes brightening.

'You mean it? But Greg . . . I'm a passenger. If you take me around the ship, everyone will know . . .'

Greg nodded. 'I know. Darling, that's the whole point. I love you, and I'm so damned proud of you, I'm sure my chest will burst if I don't tell the whole damn world. Come with me,' he begged, then his face creased into an anxious frown. 'If you feel up to it, of course.'

Verity took a deep breath and got to her feet. 'Of course I feel up to it,' she said, her voice determinedly carefree. 'We have plenty of time yet,' she added softly. 'Let's make the most of every second.'

Greg felt a bone-deep sadness at the same instant as he became aware of a soaring love. He got to his feet and held out his hand. 'Come on then. We'll start off with the galley. At this time of day, it's a sight to behold.'

She laughed and followed him, and the moment she stepped foot into the place, she agreed with him. It was so hot, it was like a butterfly house. Steam rose to the air and condensation formed on the walls. The chefs were everywhere, as were waiters and other staff. It was like a madhouse.

'It makes you wonder how the passengers ever get fed, doesn't it?' Greg whispered as one of the pastry chefs glanced up, his face a picture of curiosity. Greg nodded at him, his eyes hard and challenging, and the young man ducked his head.

'Ah, there's Rene,' Greg said, taking her hand and guiding her through the ovens and worktops. 'You'll like him. Well, not *like* actually,' Greg corrected. 'He's

352

fascinating, rather than likeable. Lives on his nerves. Stand by to batten down the hatches when he sees you, a mere passenger and a woman to boot, in his galley . . .' Greg rolled his eyes and Verity giggled. But, as they approached the executive chef, he obviously had other things on his mind. He was staring sadly down at the dish in front of him, shaking his head.

'Incredible,' he muttered, giving it the French pronunciation. 'It eese . . . terrible. Look at that colour . . . Ugh, like dog vomit,' he all but howled the final words, and both Greg and Verity looked down automatically at the dish. It did, indeed, look terrible. The salmon, whilst tender and pick and delicious looking was covered in a sauce that did, indeed, look lumpy and unappetizing, and a strange lime green colour. Greg fervently hoped that no seasick passenger was ever offered that. 'Chef. Trouble?'

Rene looked up, his eyes truly bewildered. 'I don't understand it. The champagne sauce . . . it is . . .' he gestured at it with his hands commically. 'It is . . . disaster.'

And for once, it was.

Verity, who had been about to laugh, suddenly looked at the dish again. 'Champagne sauce?' she said, her voice sharp. 'Tell me, Chef, what goes into it, exactly?' Rene, for once, didn't take exception to being asked for one of his receipes and ran through the list of ingredients.

'Lemon juice you say?' Verity asked, her voice sharp now, and Greg glanced at her, a frown playing with his dark brows.

'*Oui*. See?' Rene held up the squeezed lemon rind. 'I do not understand this. I make this recipe many, many times. Never before do I have this awful . . . greenishness.'

'What's wrong?' Greg asked softly as Verity glanced from the dish to him, frowning.

'This may sound mad, but lemon juice is full of acetic acid. It's natural in the fruit. It reacts very strongly to one particular strain of poisoning. A derivitive of botulism.'

Rene drew in his breath in a hiss, then, mindful of the full room around him, lowered his voice to a whisper. 'You say we have food poisoning in *my* galley?'

Verity shook her head. 'Not natural food poisoning, no. The poison I'm talking about doesn't occur naturally. It's a manufactured derivitive of . . .' She saw their blank faces, and shook her head. 'Never mind. Chef, can you squeeze some lemon juice into different containers, and then add a bit of each of the ingredients of the sauce?'

Rene glanced at the captain, who nodded his head quickly. It took them only a matter of minutes to complete. But it was only as the champagne was added to the lemon juice that they watched the mixture turn slowly green. Greg grabbed the bottle and looked at it. He smelt it, and shook his head. 'Seems fine to me,' he said. 'Chef, you have the cork?'

Rene handed it over. As they watched him examine it minutely, Greg's jaw clenched. 'Where did this come from?' he demanded, his voice icy. Wordlessly, the now pale-faced executive chef led them to the wine bins. At first, Greg saw nothing on any of the bottles. Only when he came to the stockpile of the very best did he find more of the tiny puncture holes. Verity saw them too. He glanced at her, but they never spoke. They both knew something very serious was going on. 'Chef, I don't want you to say a word about this to anyone,' Greg warned grimly, and Rene nodded meekly. 'And I want a cordon put around these bottles. Nobody is to use them, understand?'

'*Oui*, Captain. But the masked ball . . .'

'Pick up some champagne at Nassau.'

Rene opened his mouth to explain that Nassau was hardly the best place to buy fine champagne, then caught the look in Greg's eye and shut it again. He nodded.

'Come on,' Greg said, returning to the galley and picking up the tainted bottle on the way out. He walked so quickly she almost had to run to keep up with him. 'Where are we going?' she asked.

'To John. We need this stuff analyzed.' Greg waved the bottle in his hand and she nodded.

'Good idea. If it's the poison I think it is, it could be very dangerous, used in strong doses.'

If John Gardner was surprised to see them together, he didn't show it. As they walked quickly into his office he sensed instantly something was wrong. It took Greg only moments to explain what they had found, and at the mention of the lime-green reaction with acetic acid, John also named a Botulism-derivitive as most likely. They piled quickly into the lab, Greg standing back, feeling a bit useless as the two doctors quickly set about the tests. First they established the poison, then it's dosage. A half-hour later, John stared down at the written notes in his hand. 'No doubt about it. This would have been enough to give anyone who drank a couple of glasses of it a severe case of diarrhoea and sickness, probably stomach cramps too. And, if someone had been really greedy and guzzled enough of it . . . death.'

The last word hung in the air. The three of them looked at one another and then, inevitably, Verity and John turned to Greg. 'What are you going to do?' she asked him quietly.

Greg smiled grimly. 'Somebody wanted to cause trouble for the ship, that's for sure. But who? And why?'

Verity said softly 'We must tell Damon.'

Greg nodded. They thanked John and left, heading quickly for Damon's suite. John went back to his office a worried man. As he took his seat, the telephone rang, and he lifted the receiver. 'Yes?'

Ramona slipped on Damon's bathrobe and hugged it close around her. It smelled of him. He lay on the bed, naked and sated, watching her. She was about to go across to him, lured by the somnolent desire in his eyes, when there came a solid thumping on the door. Instinctively Damon jerked upright and then reached for his slacks, pulling them on and walking barefoot to the door. Outside stood his captain and Verity Fox. Damon's smile came quickly. 'Verity. I knew you were on board. How come we've kept missing each other?'

Verity smiled. It hadn't been accidental. Joceline had been her main concern, and not wanting to discuss her, she had kept purposefully away from him. Now she smiled. That was all over. Joceline no longer terrified her. 'I still haven't forgotten the time you cut off my pony-tail with the gardener's shears,' she remonstrated with a mock scowl.

Damon laughed. 'I was only twelve. And you *were* being a total pest.' Greg coughed, and suddenly Verity's smile faded. 'Damon, we have something to tell you.'

Damon, sensing the change in the atmosphere, glanced at them sharply, then stepped aside. They walked in, then stopped in a slightly embarrassed silence as they spotted Ramona in the bathrobe, her long hair mussed. Then she grinned unabashedly at them, and Verity grinned back. For a few seconds the two friends looked at each other, woman to woman, in mutual happiness. Ramona's gaze went from Greg, to Verity, and her grin widened even further.

Greg turned discreetly away from her and met Damon's level gaze. He got straight to the point. 'We've discovered some doctored champagne in the ship's galley.' Briefly he told them how they came to discover it, and Verity finished with a technical description of the poison, its easy availability, and its effects.

'It was in the champagne set aside for the ball you say?' It was Ramona who was the first to break the heavy silence that settled after they'd finished explaining.

Greg glanced at her. 'Yes, Dr King. Is that significant?'

Ramona glanced at Damon, then at Verity. 'Verity, how long would those symptoms take to emerge? Twelve hours. More?'

'Slightly more, but not more than a day.'

Ramona nodded. 'So if everyone had drunk it on the final night at sea, then when the ship docked the next afternoon, everybody would be ill by then?'

'And the press in Florida would have had a field day,' Damon finished, catching on.

Greg glanced at Ramona, a look of respect in his eyes. But his voice was bewildered, as he said grimly, 'But who would want to do that?'

Ramona and Damon stared at each other. 'The steward?' Ramona said and Damon nodded. They'd both, in their newfound happiness, forgotten that Jeff Doyle was still on board. Les wanted to pick him up when the ship docked in Florida, after they'd had a chance to learn more about him. Merely being seen talking with Joe King was not a crime, and they had no proof Doyle had done anything wrong. Yet.

Greg bridled. 'If something has been going on, Mr Alexander,' he said, his voice cold and official now, 'don't you think that I, as captain, should have been informed?'

Damon glanced at him sharply, then almost immediately nodded. 'You're right, of course,' he admitted quietly. 'But we didn't keep you in the dark deliberately, Greg,' he said, not taking offence at the captain's tone of voice. Damon glanced questioningly at Ramona, who nodded, giving her silent assent. She walked to the cabinet and poured them a drink as Damon gave a brief history of Joe King and the takeover bid, the blackmail of Gareth Desmond, the presence of King's man on board, the steward, and the murder of Keith Treadstone and Ramona's part in gathering the evidence the police needed.

Verity glanced across at her friend, her eyes wide and admiring but full of sympathy. 'That must have been tough,' she said simply, as Greg's respect for the boss's lady rose even higher.

Ramona smiled and shrugged. 'It wasn't exactly a picnic.'

'Thank God you had Verity with you in the galley,' Damon said, his eyes a little mischievous as he looked from his old childhood friend to his ship's captain. Greg opened his mouth, but before he could say anything, Damon held up his hand. 'I think, unless I'm very much mistaken, congratulations are in order,' he said softly. 'To us.'

All four of them grinned. 'To us.' They drank.

'And the *Alexandria*,' Ramona added softly.

Again they drank. For a while there was a peaceable silence. 'Well, I'm glad that's all sorted out,' Verity said getting to her feet.

Greg glanced at her and easily read her silent plea to leave. 'Yes, we must be going. I have to get back to the bridge,' he muttered, but when he looked at Verity they both knew he was going to no such place.

Ramona and Damon knew it too, and grinned at each other conspiratorially. Damon walked them to the door, shut it behind them, and then turned. 'So what do you think about your captain breaking the cardinal rule and having an affair with a passenger?' Ramona asked, without any worry.

Damon grinned. 'I say he would have been a fool not to snap her up. Next to one other person I know, Verity Fox is the most beautiful and brainy woman around.'

Ramona grinned. Verity and Greg would make a wonderful couple. 'I suppose this means we don't get our salmon in champagne sauce,' she said woefully. 'And I'm so hungry.'

'Shame,' Damon walked towards her. 'I suppose we could order a steak instead. But then, of course, we'd have to work up even more of an appetite for something so . . . meaty and substantial.' He raised a wicked eyebrow.

Ramona sighed. 'I suppose we shall,' she said regretfully. Then, sticking out her foot she tripped him up neatly and caught him as he landed in her lap.

Greg and Verity couldn't hide their chagrin as they saw John Gardner hovering outside her door. Verity groaned. 'Oh no,' she said softly, under her breath. 'Not now, John!'

He looked up as they approached, but before Greg could laughingly tell him to sling his hook they saw the look on his face. Greg felt his throat go bone-dry. 'What is it?'

John glanced around nervously, but his expression lightened 'I think we'd better go inside.'

Verity's hands shook as she fumbled for her key card.

Once inside, John could contain himself no longer.

'I just heard from Gordon. Verity, he's cracked it. The side effects, I mean. It was so simple, we all missed it. It was a matter of blood protein . . .' For a few minutes he let rip with medical jargon that left Greg completely in the dark. Only the growing joy and comprehension on Verity's face as John explained what Gordon had discovered told him that the miracle he had been praying for had been granted him.

'You're going to be alright?' he said, his quiet, choked voice cutting across the two doctors' excited medical talk as cleanly as a scalpel. Verity quickly turned to him, her face a picture of remorse for forgetting him. 'Oh darling, I'm so sorry. *Yes.* Yes, I think I am,' she said, her voice and face almost glowing with happiness.

'If Gordon is right,' John explained happily, 'the drug Verity's been taking is perfectly safe, so long as it's taken together with a simple protein . . .' Suddenly he stopped, and looked at them looking at each other. He stood and quietly excused himself, doubting they heard him, or the closing of the door as he left. Suddenly they were just alone.

'You're going to live,' Greg said, carefully pronunciating each word, just to make absolutely certain he understood.

Verity looked at him, too full, too happy to do anything but nod. It was as if they couldn't believe it. It was all just too much to have hoped for. Then, shakily, she said 'You still want to marry me, Greg? Till death us do part? In, say, about fifty years time?'

Greg began to laugh. And cry. Wordlessly he held

open his arms and then she was in them, and they were kissing and laughing and crying and then kissing again.

'Just try and stop me from marrying you,' Greg said huskily.

'I wouldn't dare,' she whispered. 'Oh Greg. When we get to Nassau let's go to the first church we find.'

'To be married?'

Verity laughed and shook her head. 'Huh-huh. You don't get away with it so easy. My mother will want us to get married in St Paul's. I'm afraid she's very rich, did I tell you?'

Greg groaned. 'Never mind. I'll forgive her.'

Verity laughed. 'She's going to love you – a ship's captain, no less. And how much more romantic can you get, falling in love on a cruise with the captain of the ship?' Then she sobered and he looked down at her, his heart in his eyes. 'I want to go to the first church we see,' she said softly 'just to thank God for giving me *our* life back,' she explained, needing him to understand, and choosing her words carefully.

'Yes,' he agreed, swallowing the painfully happy lump in his throat, his eyes brimming with happiness. 'For giving us *our life* back,' he stressed, echoing her words gratefully.

Then he kissed her.

CHAPTER 28

The Bahamas

The Bahamas, Ramona thought blissfully.

She was standing on one of the mid decks as the ship's huge anchors were being slowly released, holding the *Alexandria* a mile north of Grand Providence Island. The Bahamas she knew, are a coral archipelago, consisting of some seven hundred low-lying islands and over 2,000 quays, pronounced 'keys'. Of all the wonderful places the *Alexandria* had taken them throughout her cruise, Ramona thought, the Bahamas were the most scattered, the most tiny, the most intriguing. Below her, she could see that the tenders bound for New Providence Island, the home of Nassau and the most famous of the Bahamian islands, were being boarded. Although the centre of the islands, New Providence was one of the smallest major islands, with Andros to the west, and the Berry Islands to the north, surrounded by arcs of the Eleutheral to the north-east, and the Exuma to the east and south-east. Most people, though, wanted to see Nassau, and Greg had put down the anchor at the best strategic point to accomodate them.

She waved as she spotted Verity and the captain, who was dressed in 'civvies' of long, cool white slacks and a simple black and orange T-shirt, get in a tender. They held hands as they boarded, and already rumours had begun to fly around the ship that the captain had captured himself a bride on the *Alexandria*'s maiden voyage.

'Ready?' She jumped as the deep voice sounded in her ear just as two strong, warm arms curled around her waist.

'For what?' she asked archly, leaning back into his strong chest, wishing they were not in a public place, so that his hands could wander up over her breasts and his thumb could brush her nipple in a way that instantly drove her crazy.

'For Nassau, of course,' Damon said gruffly, reading her mind and turning his thumbs in ever-tightening circles just over her middle rib.

She sighed. 'Oh, *Nassau*.'

Joe King was waiting for them the moment they stepped off the tender, though neither saw him getting out of a long black American limousine. It was only when he deliberately intersected their path that they became aware of him. Ramona stiffened. Damon drew in a sharp, short breath. Together they stood and waited.

Joe King was smiling. He felt good. He'd been talking to his lawyers all night, and the takeover papers were on their way to the Alexander Line. He'd felt so good, in fact, that instead of flying to Florida, he'd changed his plans at the Cuban airport at the last minute, and flew into Nassau instead. He wanted to see Damon Alexander's face personally, when he told him he'd lost the *Alexandria*. That was why, at that very moment, a puzzled deputy of police and D.A. officials were waiting, in vain, at Miami airport. It was also why, having decided to see it through to the end, Frank and Les had been at the airport and realized his change of plans. It had taken some doing, but a badge of law enforcement was a badge of law enforcement, even in Cuba, and they had managed to get on the same plane as their quarry. Now, drawing up behind the limo, they saw the confrontation coming.

Frank swore. 'Do we have the warrants?'

Les sighed. 'The deputation at Miami has the full go-ahead.'

Frank groaned. 'The last thing we want to do is mess it all up now. We give his lawyers even the slightest rope to play with, just a hint of improper procedure, and we can kiss it all goodbye.'

Les grinned. 'You're learning, kid. But I learned it all long ago.' From his pocket, like a magician removing rabbits from a hat, he withdrew a bundle of long slim papers. 'Duplicates, and perfectly legal,' he said smugly.

Frank grinned. 'Don't take this the wrong way, Les, but I think I love you.'

Les laughed. 'Feel like arresting Joe King?'

'Oh, I think I can force myself,' Frank grinned. The two men stepped out into the hot, Bahamian sun.

Meanwhile, Joe King was still smiling. 'Hello, Ramona. Surprised to see me?'

For an awful instant, Ramona thought that he knew. For a second she half expected him to withdraw a gun and shoot them both, and her hand reached instinctively for Damon's. Then common sense prevailed. 'Hello, Father,' she said carefully, and Damon found himself admiring her cool tone. For himself, he could only watch the man like a hawk.

Joe looked from his daughter's neutral face to Damon, and as he did so, Ramona spotted Les Fortnum and Frank Gless crossing the road a hundred yards away and almost wilted in relief.

'Alexander. I'm Joe King.'

Damon nodded, allowing himself a cool smile. Arrogant bastard! 'I know who and what you are. So do the police.'

For an instant it was as if Joe King didn't hear him, or didn't understand him. For just a moment the smug look of a crocodile about to bite stayed in his eyes. Then, at last, the look flickered. 'What?'

'I was wired for sound,' Ramona said simply. 'In Cuba. It's all over, Mr King.' She refused to call him Father.

Joe recoiled as if he'd been bit. '*What* did you say?'

'You heard her, Mr King,' Les Fortnum said from behind him, neatly stepping away as the man swung around. With perfect timing, Frank moved in from the right and grabbed Joe King's arm. 'Joseph Jason King, you are under arrest,' Les Fortnum said, and never had words sounded sweeter. Briefly he outlined the charges and Joe King's rights, but Frank was already putting on the cuffs.

Ramona looked away. Her eyes settled on a pelican, its ponderous body flying low across the gentle sea.

Joe King said nothing. He glanced once at Ramona's profile, his face tight and deadly. He never even glanced Damon's way.

'Are you alright?' Les asked them. He had to take King to the local jail for the moment. Extradition papers needed to be signed, but that would be no problem. Damon nodded and watched as Joe King was led away. Then he turned to her.

'Are you really alright?' he asked softly. She turned, her eyes hurt but not defeated. She nodded and managed a sightly wan smile. 'I will be,' she said softly, then looked around, her backbone stiffening, her shoulders coming back. 'I will be,' she said more firmly. 'This is the last port of call. I want to see everything. Let's get some snorkelling gear and check out the wrecks around here. It's about time we saw some marine life.' She was determined she was going to enjoy this last, exotic island, come what may.

Damon grinned, instantly catching her mood. 'You're on,' he said. 'And I bet I spot more fish than you do.'

'Big head. Feel like putting your money where your mouth is?' she challenged, her blue eyes sparking like summer lightning.

'Sure,' he said easily. 'Loser gets to give the winner a foot massage.'

She smiled. 'I just fancy a foot massage.'

'Of course, the winner has to quote all the species *he's*

seen,' he said, stressing the masculine, a wickedly triumphant look in his eyes. From the look on his face it was obvious he wasn't going to take 'those greeny things with a yellow tail' as a real answer, and was already looking forward to having his toes rubbed and perhaps, if he was lucky, sucked . . .

'Oh? Such as yellowtail snappers, you mean,' she said blandly, and saw his head swivel her way. 'And angel fish, parrot fish, horse-eyed jacks, silversides, even blacktip reef sharks?' she added, one eyebrow rising into her hairline. Already Joe King was receding further and further from their minds.

'How did you . . . ?' he asked, beginning to laugh.

'And then there're the non-fish to think about,' she mused, as they headed for a charter-and-hire company. 'Sponges, and coral, eagle rays . . .'

'An eagle ray is a fish,' he pounced, but already he was resigning himself to doing the toe-sucking. It was not, all in all, a hard thought to accommodate. 'Dr King, how knowledgeable you are,' he drawled, admitting defeat with reasonable grace. 'Anyone would think you were an Oxford Don . . . *Ouch!*'

In the city, Greg was holding Verity's hand tightly as they strolled along. But although they passed the Bahamas Historical Society, and the pink Government House, Gregory's Arch and the Postern Gate, they never stopped to explore. It was only when their meandering tour brought them to Christ Church Cathedral to the south of Lex House, that they stopped.

'The first church we've seen,' Verity said softly.

Greg nodded. And together they walked into the church.

In the Nassau jail, Joe King watched the two British policemen and two other Bahamian police officers pace around the interrogation room. 'I want to see my lawyer,' Joe said, the first words he had spoken since being hustled off the dock in handcuffs. 'In private.' The policemen looked at one another and shrugged. They had no right to deny him his phone call. For a long moment, in the hot jail cell, Joe stared at the phone. Then he lifted the receiver and dialled.

But he did not dial his lawyers. They'd find out soon enough where he was and why, and he had no intention of making any statement until they got here. But he also knew, deep in his guts, that even they would not be able to get him out of this mess. This time he was going down. But he was not going to go down alone.

The telephone was answered. 'Yes?' The single, cautious word and familiar voice made Joe almost melt with relief. If they had picked up Doyle too, he wasn't sure what he would have done. 'It's me,' he said, giving no names. The phone might be bugged.

In his cabin on the *Alexandria*, Jeff Doyle sat up straighter on the chair, his mind sharpening to diamond-hard clarity.

'I want you to abandon plan Atlanta,' Joe said clearly. 'I now want you to go with plan Andromeda.'

Now that he knew that the *Alexandria* could never be his, he was determined that the beautiful temptress of

369

the sea would not be anybody's. Joe King had just given the order to have her sunk.

In his cabin, Jeff Doyle felt his heart flutter with excitement. It had been a long time since he'd felt that way. 'You said that Andromeda wasn't likely to be used.' Even for Jeff Doyle, the task of sinking an ocean liner was a huge, daunting job. He had to be sure.

Joe felt a wave of rage almost choke him. 'I know that,' he snapped. 'I was . . . wrong.' Never before in his life had Joe King been forced to admit such a thing. 'Go with Andromeda,' he reiterated, his voice deadly.

'That means more money,' Jeff said quickly. 'Danger money.' A sinking ship, full of panicking passengers, was always a dangerous place to be. Jeff knew that the crew and passengers had all been through lifeboat drills over six times. But dry runs were one thing, and the real thing . . . The lifeboats were more than ample to take every man, woman and child aboard the *Alexandria*, but when people panicked, logic hardly mattered.

'Don't worry about that,' Joe gritted. Money was the least of his troubles.

Jeff nodded. 'You know that Andromeda might get . . . fatal.'

Joe King closed his eyes. He saw his daughter, his beautiful, treacherous daughter, drowning in the blue Bahamian ocean, her lover, Damon Alexander, trampling all over her in a panicked effort to reach a lifeboat. It was a sweet, sweet thought. 'Do it,' he said and hung up.

A few minutes later, the police came back. Joe said nothing, but kept glancing at Les Fortnum's watch all through that long afternoon. At eight-thirty, when he knew the ship was about to sail, he cracked his first smile. It sent a chill through all of the men in the room.

On the bridge, Greg gave the order for the anchors to be lifted. It was always his favourite time of any cruise – the sense of anticipation, the promise of new destinations, the thrill of a mighty ship heading on her way. As he gave the orders to engineering to start the mighty twin-screws, he felt the familiar rush. There was no harbour pilot to take the ship out to sea, for they were already at sea. It was just him, the ship, his crew, and the sea. He didn't know that below, opening up a locker that was situated directly under the sonar equipment, there was also Jeff Doyle.

The sun was sinking over the horizon, slow and magnificent, a red globe setting the blue sea ablaze with magenta. The passenger decks were lined, as they always were at this time of night, but especially so this evening. The Bahamas had been the last port of call. Tomorrow there was a full day's sailing, then the final night's masked ball, and then home and back to reality. Nobody really wanted it to end. The *Alexandria*, the floating palace, the glamorous fantasy lady that they had all fallen in love with, could not possibly go home, but must sail the seas forever.

Jeff Doyle, in the dark, murky heat of the locker room, checked his watch, then glanced at the map. He knew the direct route the ship was going to take as it navigated the many low, coral islands. Every ship's captain knew there were reefs that could rip the bottom out of a boat, even one as big as the cruisers that regularly called here, and the highways and byways were clearly marked. With newly-learned skill, Jeff Doyle plotted their course. With relaxed cold-bloodedness, he turned on the small black magnets that slowly, degree by degree, began to change the compasses on the bridge. He had already picked out the graveyard that would receive the *Alexandria*. It was called 'Calico Reef', a particularly large, particularly nasty submerged reef to the west of Grand Bahama Island. It would be fully dark by the time the ship reached it. The magnets would have fooled the compass into thinking they were well out from it. Only the lights from the island would provide some clue, but no captain, no matter how good, would be able to gauge from them that they were off course.

Jeff Doyle hunkered down on his haunches and mentally ran through the route to the nearest lifeboat station. He wasn't worried. He would make it. As for the others . . . It was every man for himself.

Verity tapped on the door a little hesitantly, but she needn't have worried. When Ramona opened the door, she was alone. 'Hello? No Damon?'

Ramona grinned. 'For the moment. Come on in. You ready for dinner?' she added unnecessarily, glancing at the black velvet dress Verity was wearing.

'Uh-huh. Don't worry, I'm not going to play goose-berry. I just wanted to see if everything was alright?'

Ramona poured them a drink. 'Fine. And you will join us for dinner. I insist.' As Verity began to argue good-naturedly, the ship sailed on in the dark night, only a half an hour now from Grand Bahama, and the Calico Reef.

Greg glanced at his watch. Nine o'clock. They'd all be sitting down to dinner. He wanted, actually ached, to be with Verity, sitting in some corner table of the quietest restaurant, tasting Rene the Terrible's wonderful food, laughing into her eyes over the candlelight. But the dangerous waters around the Bahamas demanded his presence on the bridge. Tomorrow, at the masked ball, it would be different. He glanced at the lights coming across the water from Grand Bahama. The moon had risen in a crystal clear night, making the lights appear nearer and brighter than he would have expected. Automatically, he glanced at the compasses, checking first one, then, on impulse, the back-up.

As he moved from left to right across the bridge, he was already beginning to feel a cold shiver climb up his spine. A second later, the reason for his instinctive anxiety became clear. The back-up compass was showing a two degree difference. He frowned, and tapped the glass. Jim Goldsmith glanced up from the navigation panels at the small sound, and frowned. 'Problems, Greg?'

'The back-up compass is reading . . .' He reached for the notepad tethered to the table-top by the captain's chair and wrote down the markings as he spoke. Jim automatically read the compass at his end of the bridge. 'Two degrees out,' Jim confirmed. 'The back-up must be faulty.'

Greg glanced out again at the lights of the island. It could be the glass of the bridge making them appear brighter and larger, so he stepped outside onto the deck, grabbing the binoculars as he went. For a few moments he stood on the deck, the moonlight turning his hair to silver, his eyes straining behind the binoculars. He knew Calico Reef, of course. What ship's captain didn't? He also knew the navigational course like the back of his hand. Everything looked alright and yet . . . He went back to the bridge, and found Jim already leaning over the sonar and the depth gauge attachment. 'Depth?'

Jim read it off crisply, and relaxed. He too, knew the Calico Reef. It could rip them apart like a knife going through butter. But the Calico Reef was set in a very shallow ridge of water. The depth gauge was showing way too much water for them to be two degrees off course. Besides, according to their radar, the Calico Reef was showing up way to their starboard. For a few minutes, Greg and Jim stared at the radar and the long green blip that was the Calico Reef. Then Greg glanced at the island of Grand Bahama again. The Calico Reef was about eighteen minutes sailing ahead. It was long, and jagged and deadly, but they were well away from it. Weren't they?

Greg felt the sweat suddenly pop out on his skin and turn icy. 'I don't like it,' he said softly. He walked once more to the compass. What could cause it. Magnets? But the radar and sonar and depth gauge all showed normal. Surely they couldn't all be wrong? Could that damned steward in Joe King's pay have fiddled with the compass? Maybe. Something as simple as a magnet could still send even the most sophisticated instruments haywire. But the sonar? Radar? Again Greg turned to the instrument panel and all the reassuring technology. It looked alright. So why didn't it *feel* alright? He lifted the telephone, pressing the button for engineering. Like himself, Jock was staying on duty until the Bahamas were far behind. "Jock, Greg. I'm slowing the ship for a while. Cutting power to half . . .' He turned and nodded to Jim, who looked puzzled but immediately did as he was ordered. Instantly the throb of the ships engines lowered in tone.

In the dining room, where Verity, Damon and Ramona were eating shark, it was hardly audible, but in the quiet locker room, Jeff Doyle felt the slight change immediately. He glanced at his watch, then at the map and scowled. Why was the ship slowing? It had no reason to, not if the captain was relying on his instruments, which should be telling him everything was fine. But what if they weren't? What if Joe King's all-purpose gismo had got a few wires crossed? There was nothing else for it. He had to find out.

Jeff dug deep into the locker and withdrew a long, black handgun. For a professional like himself, it had been easy to dismantle it and hide the bits and pieces in his luggage. Now, quickly and expertly he began to screw on the silencer. He would rather have sunk the ship anonymously, but if he had to, he could kill the bridge crew and watch the ship head for its graveyard from the bridge. He moved quickly and purposefully.

On the bridge, Greg reached for the telephone once

more. 'Jock? When was the last time you did a systems check?' he asked, although, as captain, he already knew. Jock nevertheless confirmed it. 'And that included radar, compass and sonar?'

'Naturally,' Jock drawled, from the depths of engineering. Then, more slowly, he asked 'What's goin' on, Greg?' his broad Scottish accent thickening perceptibly.

'Nothing. Yet. Standby.'

Jim watched the captain glance once more into the night. Greg's nervousness was catching. 'You think the sonar's out too?' Jim ventured, hardly able to believe it possible.

Greg was just about to answer when the door opened and a man stepped in. He was dressed in dark denims and a black shirt, but it was not his clothes that riveted his attention. It was the gun in his hand. In that instant, Greg knew that Joe King had had more than one saboteur on board, and his heart sank. Unable to stop himself, he glanced out into the night once more. He was right. They were off course.

'Gentlemen,' Jeff Doyle said.

'The Calico Reef,' Greg whispered, appalled.

Jeff Doyle smiled. 'Yes, Captain. Perhaps you'd care to put the ship back up to normal speed?'

Greg looked at him, his jaw clenching. He never let his gaze waver from the saboteur's dark, calm eyes. The gun he ignored completely. 'I wouldn't care to do that at all,' Greg said clearly.

Jeff smiled. 'I suppose not. But if you don't, I'll shoot you.'

'That won't put the ship back to full speed.'

'No, but you'll be dead, and then your second-in-command over there will do it.'

'Not me,' Jim Goldsmith said stiffly. He was afraid, but he was also determined, and Jeff Doyle recognized heroism when he saw it. He sighed, then glanced at his watch. Twelve minutes to go, at the present speed. He shrugged, glanced once behind him, and then leaned against the bulkhead, the gun level and sure, covering both men. He wasn't in *that* much of a hurry.

Greg knew the ship, the beautiful *Alexandria*, had only minutes to live. And all the passengers were at risk. He had to do *something*. It was no good trying to jump him, that was for sure. He would only get himself killed, and the *Alexandria* would still be sunk. No. He had to try something else. 'So you're Joe King's hired assassin?' he mused, seeing with satisfaction the man start. 'Oh yes, we know all about Joe King. Damon Alexander, the owner of this ship, will know who hired you, even where to start looking for you. If this boat sinks, he will hunt you down and find you.'

Jeff Doyle's eyes narrowed. The captain was right. Joe King, if put under pressure, might talk to save his skin, and Jeff couldn't have that. Damon Alexander was a rich and powerful man. The captain and Damon Alexander would both have to die. 'Who else knows?' he asked softly, but Greg, instantly alert to the danger, said nothing. Jeff lifted the telephone receiver and moved back. 'Call Alexander up here.'

Greg, knowing the man's mind, said softly, 'Go to hell.'

Jeff Doyle swung the gun to Jim Goldsmith. 'Do it now, or he dies.'

Greg glanced across at his friend. He just couldn't let the man be murdered right in front of his eyes without doing something to save him. Besides, Greg was a good judge of men. Damon Alexander, in a situation like this, could only be an asset. Slowly, he lifted the receiver and reached the switchboard. Damon was quickly located, and a maître d' brought the phone over to his table.

Damon thanked him. 'Yes? Damon Alexander.'

'Damon, it's Greg. Look, can you come up to the bridge? We have a . . . minor problem I think you should know about.'

'OK, I'll be right there.' He hung up quickly. 'Greg wants to see me,' he said thoughtfully, and saw Verity's head shoot up from her baked Alaska. He grinned. 'Fancy seeing the bridge, ladies? Of course, tradition-ally it's bad luck . . .'

'Just keep us away,' Ramona laughed, already getting to her feet, Verity eagerly following suit.

It was a wonderful night outside, and as they emerged from the lift and began to climb the steps to the bridge, Verity was in front, anxious to see the look on Greg's face when she walked through the door. Right behind her was Damon. Suddenly, Ramona's heel stuck, and she lost her shoe on the middle of the stairs. She cursed softly, bending down to slip it back on. What happened next, happened very fast.

Doyle was flattened against the bulkhead beside the door and saw the black material of a dress before he saw anything else. He saw the captain's face fall and heard

him say, obviously shocked and dismayed, 'Verity.' He
saw a woman step in, and almost cursed aloud. This job
was rapidly beginning to look very messy. Then he
heard the man's voice, right behind her.

'Hello Greg, what's up?'

The moment Damon stepped through the door, Jeff's
arm shot out and slammed it shut. Verity, who had just
had time to register the look of dismay on Greg's face,
shot around, as did Damon. Both of them found themselves staring down the barrel of a very nasty looking
gun. On the stairs, Ramona heard the door slam shut and
frowned. She walked quickly up the remaining steps and
froze. Although the darkened glass surrounding the
bridge was impenetrable, the door to the bridge had a
small square of normal glass. Through it she saw a man
with a gun. She watched Verity take a step back and Greg
move up behind her, taking her in his arms. She saw
Damon's face tighten. Instantly, without even thinking
about it, she moved back out of sight as the man with the
gun glanced over his shoulder. She prayed he hadn't seen
her.

For a second, her body froze and her mind raced. In
the matter of a mere second she understood most of it.
Her father's accomplice, Jeff Doyle, had turned assassin
too. Damon, Greg, Verity, they were all in danger. And
somehow, she knew, so was the ship. What could she
do? She couldn't rush in, and get them all killed. And
she knew nothing about the bridge and how it worked.
She had to get help. And only one person sprang
instantly to mind. As she ran, she had no idea that
she had only seven minutes left.

Jock recognized the lass the instant she cannoned into the engineering room, wild-eyed and out of breath. She had no difficulty picking out Jock's small, wiry frame and grizzled face as belonging to the chief engineer. 'Damon, the captain, and one of the passengers are being held at gunpoint on the bridge,' she gasped. 'And the ship's in danger, although I don't know how,' she added, forcing back her panic.

For an instant Jock stared at her. But he had heard only good reports of Damon Alexander's bride-to-be from both the doctor and Greg himself and it was not because he doubted her words that he hesitated, but because he was thinking instead of Greg's earlier call. Sonar. Radar. Compass. And he knew where they were. Near Grand Bahama. His face paled. 'The Calico Reef,' he whispered in horror.

The words meant nothing to Ramona. 'We have to do something. Now!' she insisted, nearly shouting. But Jock was already moving. First he went to a cupboard and came back with two rifles, thrusting one at her without a word. To the men he said 'Watch the room,' and was gone. Ramona, after a startled silence, ran after him, clutching the rifle in her hands. She had no idea there had been firearms aboard the *Alexandria*, nor did she know how to use one. But she knew she'd follow Jock to the ends of the earth if it meant giving Damon and the others a chance to live.

As they raced towards the bridge, the words 'Calico Reef' echoed in her head. What was it? But she could guess, even though she was no mariner. It meant the death of the *Alexandria* unless they could stop it.

At the top deck, Jock stopped dead and Ramona almost cannoned into the back of him.

'Directly under the bridge is the men's locker room,' Jock said, who'd been thinking as he'd run. 'Fitted into the ceiling, which is the bridge's floor, there's a trap door.' He was not about to waste time explaining the logistics of its position. Time enough to go over the ship's construction manual later. 'It's hidden in the bridge and you can only see it by the small faint square lines in the carpet. I doubt our friend up there has noticed it. I'm going to open it from the locker room. You have to get him to stand over it.'

They were on the deck, the breeze blowing their hair. Ramona angrily pushed a strand from her eyes. 'Me? But how?'

Jock glanced at his watch. Minutes. They had minutes! 'You have to. Or we're all finished. By the time you get up there I'll be in the locker room. The instant I open the hatch, he has to be standing right over it so that he falls through.'

Ramona didn't know how she was going to do it, but she nodded. 'Alright. A square in the carpet you said?'

Jock nodded. 'Behind the captain's chair. Good luck, lassie,' he said softly, and was gone.

Ramona saw him disappear into the locker room and quickly started up the stairs. Her heart raced. Her palms, cradling the rifle, felt slick with sweat. At the door, she peeped in cautiously. Greg, another officer she hadn't see before, Verity and Damon were all on the far side of the bridge, and they were all staring out to sea.

The reason was simple. Jeff Doyle had just told the others where they were headed and what would happen.

Verity reached for Greg's hand and he squeezed it tight. It just wasn't fair. To be facing death, now, after all that had gone before. It just wasn't *fair*. He felt helpless and sick with rage. He wanted to protect her. He wanted to kill the saboteur. He prayed for the ship. Damon stared at Jeff Doyle, trying to gauge the distance to the gun. He couldn't just let the maniac run the ship over the reef. At the speed she was going the *Alexandria* would be out of the shallow water and back into deep water before she sunk. The loss of life could be enormous. It was unthinkable. He *had* to stop it. Even if he jumped him and got shot, surely the other two would have time to overpower him and steer the ship to safety? He glanced at Greg, and saw that the captain, who had been watching his face closely, had accurately read his mind. Greg's eyes widened in respect and apprehension as their eyes met. He gave an imperceptible nod. They would both do what had to be done . . .

At that instant, the door flew open, slamming against the bulkhead with a loud crash. Jeff Doyle spun around, the gun rising, his finger on the trigger. Had it been anyone else, he would have fired automatically and instantly. But the sight of her, her hair swirling around her head like silver, her eyes blazing like blue fire even across the distance of the bridge, paralyzed him for a vital second. His nemesis!

And in that second he saw the rifle. She was aiming it straight at him. But she had released no safety catch, and she wasn't even even sure if it was loaded, let alone ready to fire. 'Move away,' she said, her voice unnaturally calm. 'To the left.' Jeff Doyle glanced from the rifle to her. Her eyes dazzled him. On her left finger, the Ceylon sapphire of her engagement ring caught a ray from the moon, and diamonds of blue and silver light sparkled into the bridge.

Jeff swallowed hard. Silver! Hadn't he always known? He felt his legs doing as they were bid without being aware of having given them the order to move. Ramona glanced for the first time to the floor, and saw the square. She felt an instant of relief, then an instant of despair, as she saw the carpet begin to sag. Jock was already opening it!

Damon took a step forward, seeing only that she was in mortal danger. Greg's hand shot out and curled around his arm, stopping him, but he reacted with only half of his mind, for his eyes were glued out to sea. In the light of the moon he thought he could see the silver-topped waters that foamed over the reef. The Calico Reef.

He glanced at the useless sonar. They were in mere feet of water now, they must be. How much longer before they were ripped apart?

'Move!' Ramona snapped in desperation, her whiplash voice making all of them jump.

Jeff Doyle felt an instant of mind-numbing, superstitious fear, then a raging anger. He stepped to his left, raising his gun, his eyes like jet, dark and full of death. He was going to kill his nemesis once and for all.

Damon screamed her name.

But then, suddenly, there was no ground under him. Jeff Doyle's face was almost comical as he fell sideways, his gun hand going up wildly as he fought for his balance. There was an evil hiss as the silencer deadened the sound of a bullet the lodged harmlessly in the ceiling. Instinctively, Ramona ducked. Again, Damon screamed her name and launched himself at Doyle. But, suddenly, Jeff Doyle was no longer there.

Jim Goldsmith, after a stunned micro-second, understood what had happened. The trap door had been lifted. But Greg was already moving, not towards the open trap door but to the wheel. '*Jim!*' he yelled, and began the procedure that would turn the ship. Never before had that simple procedure seemed to stretch so long. Jim reacted instantly, going to his aid. As the two men struggled to save the ship, from down below, came the roar of a rifle shot.

'Jock McMannon,' she said numbly, as Damon and Verity stared at her uncomprehendingly. 'The engineer,' she added. She felt curiously numb now. Everything had happened so fast. It now seemed like a second-long nightmare.

A moment later, a grizzled head appeared in the space of the trap door. 'He's dead,' Jock said bluntly, then heaved the rest of himself lithely through the trap door. His eyes bored into Greg's back. Suddenly, all eyes turned to the captain and staff captain, frantically working at the control panels. Outside the window, the white and foaming water covering the reef was plainly visible.

Ramona saw it, so close, and knew there was no way a

ship the size of the *Alexandria* could avoid it in time. But she was wrong. The ship, responding to Greg's hands like a woman being caressed, turned like a graceful white swan on a peaceful river, and the reef slid by on their starboard, still deadly, but no longer a threat to them.

Greg collapsed back into the captain's chair. He was sweating and shaking. For a long while, nobody spoke. Nobody could. Then Greg said hoarsely, 'Jock, there has to be some sort of device below taking out our sonar. Find it, will you?' Jock nodded and started for the hatch. He too felt weak-kneed. He had never had to kill a man before.

Verity walked to the captain's chair and looped her hands around his neck. Wordlessly she kissed the side of his neck, her silent tears of relief hot against their cheeks. Greg's hands covered her own shaking ones. Their fingers tightened in mutual unity.

Ramona glanced down blankly as she felt a tugging on her hands. Damon, unseen by her, had moved across to her and was taking the rifle out of her numb hands. She looked up at him, her pupils dilated in shock, hardly able to believe they were all alright. His face was beautiful. A slight shadow on his chin. A sheen of sweat on his forehead. Deep, wonderful eyes. He had never looked more handsome, she thought. He was alive.

'I thought he was going to kill you,' she said, her voice horrified. 'I was so angry. I just . . . I was so *angry*!' she finished, as if her actions needed justifying.

'I know,' Damon said, beginning to smile. 'You

should have seen the look on your face when you came through that door. It was fierce.'

At the trap door, Jock, half in and half out, glanced across at her. Everybody owed their life to the beautiful blonde lady with as much courage and brains as she had beauty.

'Aye. She's some lassie you have there, Mr Alexander. No doubt about it,' Jock said, his voice so matter-of-fact and ordinary, it was almost bland.

And suddenly everybody was laughing.

In the beautiful, moonlit Caribbean night, the *Alexandria* sailed placidly and majestically on.

EPILOGUE

In the Grand Salon, festooned with ribbons and balloons, Napoleon swung his masked Josephine in time to an authentic eighteenth-century quadraille. By the fountain of champagne a gorilla leaned drunkenly against William Shakespeare. The *Alexandria* sailed on under the midnight moon, as the ship's last Midnight Buffet of the cruise provided the revellers with prime roast beef, venison, smoked salmon, caviar and dressed swan. Josephine curtsied to Napoleon as the dance ended. 'Thank you, kind sir,' Ramona murmured.

'And thank you, *mon cher*,' Damon said in an atrocious French accent, 'for only standing on my toes twice.'

Ramona fought the laughter. 'How very ungallant you are.'

Damon scowled. 'Hussy,' he said, and glanced around as the orchestra began a Strauss waltz. 'Want to go again?'

'What? And flatten your toes completely?'

Slowly they wandered through the ghosts and

witches, the odd walking banana and a huge mouth on legs, and headed towards the deck. Joceline, resplendent as Marie Antoinette, smiled as she came up to them and reached up and kissed her son warmly on the cheek. Over his shoulder, her eyes met those of the woman who would soon be her daughter-in-law and smiled. They both knew they would never talk of Michael again, but now that his ghost had been laid to rest, they both hoped that Joceline would be able to draw close to her son again. Ramona smiled back in perfect understanding. Damon returned his mother's kiss with surprise but gratification. Joceline drew back and told them that they must come to visit her at home soon, to discuss the wedding. She wandered away, happily planning the future, looking forward to holding her grandson or granddaughter in her arms in the not too distant future.

The Grand Salon deck, completely surrounded by glass, gave an all-round view of the moon silvering a dark sea as the ship sailed through the night, like a beautiful ghost. They could hear the mournful, evocative sound of the ship's horn as she hailed a passing cruise liner headed north.

Ramona's dress was of white sprigged muslin, with tiny handprinted sprigs of pink roses decorating the *décolletage* and the looped hem of the full skirt. With her silver hair up and braided with real pink rosebuds, she had taken his breath away when he had called for her. Her black velvet eye-mask kept drawing his attention back again and again to the electric blue eyes gazing out at him.

388

It was a perfect night. Just then, the music died down and everyone turned to the door, where Captain Greg Harding appeared, appropriately enough, in the full dress uniform of a British Naval Captain of the 1750s. The applause was instant and warm, with everyone clapping enthusiastically, save a pantomime horse, that couldn't quite manage it! But Ramona wondered how much warmer that applause would have been if the passengers realized just how much they truly owed the captain. Without Greg's sharp eyes and sheer instinct, he wouldn't have slowed the Alexandria down, giving them those vital minutes, and the ship would now be lying at the bottom of the Caribbean sea, another tragic Titanic, another wreck for the divers to explore. By his side, Verity was dressed as a pixie, her short dark cap of hair gleaming in the light. She'd found some Mr Spock ears from somewhere, and when she grinned at the applause rising around them, she was a picture of charm. Greg looked faintly embarrassed, but took the applause in good part. He started into the room, taking Verity in his arms, and gave the orchestra a very conspicious nod, and instantly they started to play the theme to 'Love Story'. For a while, Ramona and Damon watched them with indulgent smiles, then he too held out his hand. She took it, and they swept enthusiastically into the gay and fantastic mêlée.

'Where do you want to be married?' he murmured into the top of her hair, his nose picking up the pleasing scent of the pale pink rosebud nestling against his cheek.

'Oxford.'

'Oxford? I thought you weren't going back there?'

Ramona smiled against his chest. 'I'm not, professionally. But Oxford is a beautiful city. Besides, my mother will be disappointed otherwise.' She felt him stiffen just slightly, and looked up, a smile in her eyes and on her lips. 'What's the matter? Nervous? Big bad mother-in-law and all that?'

Damon grinned. 'Something like that.'

Ramona laughed. 'Don't worry. As long as you make it clear to her that you're a sex-mad beast, she'll be happy for me.'

Damon blinked. 'What?'

Ramona laughed and laid her head on his shoulder. Verity and Greg swayed past them, eyes closed, hearts full. Ahead of them all lay Florida, and the triumphant end to a magical voyage.

But beyond that, for the captain and his lady, and for Dr Ramona King and Damon Alexander, lay the prospect of happy-ever-after.

THE EXCITING NEW NAME
IN WOMEN'S FICTION!

PLEASE HELP ME TO HELP YOU!

Dear *Scarlet* Reader,

As Editor of *Scarlet* Books I want to make sure that the books I offer you every month are up to the high standards *Scarlet* readers expect. And to do that I need to know a little more about you and your reading likes and dislikes. So please spare a few minutes to fill in the short questionnaire on the following pages and send it to me. I'll send *you* a surprise gift as a thank you!

Looking forward to hearing from you,

Sally Cooper

Editor-in-Chief, *Scarlet*

P.S. Only one offer per household.

QUESTIONNAIRE

Please tick the appropriate boxes to indicate your answers

1 Where did you get this Scarlet title?
Bought in Supermarket ☐
Bought at W H Smith ☐
Bought at book exchange or second-hand shop ☐
Borrowed from a friend ☐
Other _____

2 Did you enjoy reading it?
A lot ☐   A little ☐   Not at all ☐

3 What did you particularly like about this book?
Believable characters ☐   Easy to read ☐
Good value for money ☐   Enjoyable locations ☐
Interesting story ☐   Modern setting ☐
Other _____

4 What did you particularly dislike about this book?
_____

5 Would you buy another Scarlet book?
Yes ☐   No ☐

6 What other kinds of book do you enjoy reading?
Horror ☐   Puzzle books ☐   Historical fiction ☐
General fiction ☐   Crime/Detective ☐   Cookery ☐
Other _____

7 Which magazines do you enjoy most?
Bella ☐   Best ☐   Woman's Weekly ☐
Woman and Home ☐   Hello ☐   Cosmopolitan ☐
Good Housekeeping ☐
Other _____

cont.

And now a little about you –

8 How old are you?
   Under 25 ☐   25–34 ☐   35–44 ☐
   45–54 ☐   55–64 ☐   over 65 ☐

9 What is your marital status?
   Single ☐   Married/living with partner ☐
   Widowed ☐   Separated/divorced ☐

10 What is your current occupation?
   Employed full-time ☐   Employed part-time ☐
   Student ☐   Housewife full-time ☐
   Unemployed ☐   Retired ☐

11 Do you have children? If so, how many and how old are they?
   _____
   _____

12 What is your annual household income?
   under £10,000 ☐   £10–20,000 ☐   £20–30,000 ☐
   £30–40,000 ☐   over £40,000 ☐

Miss/Mrs/Ms _____
Address _____
   _____
   _____
   _____

Thank you for completing this questionnaire. Now tear it out – put
it in an envelope and send it before 31 March 1997, to:

Sally Cooper, Editor-in-Chief

SCARLET
FREEPOST LON 3335
LONDON W8 4BR
Please use block capitals for address.
No stamp is required!   CAFLA/9/96

Scarlet titles coming next month:

SUMMER OF FIRE – Jill Sheldon
When Noah Taylor and Annie Laverty meet again, they are
instantly attracted to each other. Unfortunately, because of
his insecure childhood, Noah doesn't believe in love, while
Annie has trouble coming to terms with her terrifying past.
It takes a 'summer of fire' to finally bring Annie and Noah
together . . . forever.

DEVLIN'S DESIRE – Margaret Callaghan
Devlin Winter might *think* he can stroll back into Holly
Scott's life and take up where he left off – but Holly has
other ideas! No longer the fragile innocent Dev seduced
with his charm and sexual expertise, Holly is a woman to be
reckoned with. Dev, though, won't take 'no' for answer, and
he tells Holly: 'You're mine. You've always been mine and
you'll always *be* mine!'

INTOXICATING LADY – Barbara Stewart
Happy in her work and determined never to fall in love,
Danielle can't understand what Kingsley Hunter wants
from her. One minute, he is trying to entice her into his
bed . . . the next he seems to hate her! 'Revenge is sweet'
they say . . . but Danielle, Kingsley's 'intoxicating lady,' has
to convince him that passionate love is even sweeter.

STARSTRUCK – Lianne Conway
'Even ice-cold with indifference, Fergus Hann's eyes demand attention' and they make Layne Denham realize an
awful truth! To be starstruck as a film fan is fun . . . but to
be starstruck in real life is asking for trouble . . . with a
capital 'T' for Temptation.